Kristin Leedy

I0670102

# The Heart Will Lead You Home

*Published by Leedy Publishing*

The Heart Will Lead You Home is a work of fiction. Names, characters, places, and incidents either are the product of the author's imagination or are used fictitiously. Any resemblance to actual persons, living or dead, events, or locales is entirely coincidental.

ISBN: 978-0-6151-8147-9

"Hello, Lizzie." He spoke to her in a voice that was deeper than she remembered and she felt her heart stop when she heard it. Even though she commanded it not to, it came to a momentary halt before it pounded back to life again. She told herself she didn't care or notice all the ways he'd changed.

"Hello." She pushed the words from her dry, sandy throat and heard it crackle out into the warm, summer air.

"Dance with me." Like an intimate but unwanted caress his words wrapped around her and held. It was too much for her to take and she couldn't handle standing there in the same space as him for another second longer.

"Excuse me, boys, but I believe I have to get going." She pushed her way out of the group and refused to look back when she heard him calling her name. Suddenly anger a million times stronger than she had remembered feeling in the past slammed into her, almost buckling her knees out from under her with its force. She forced herself forward and out into the night air.

There was a partially muffled curse that floated to her, and she judged that she had only seconds before Payton came after her. He caught up with her just outside of the barn and grabbed hold of her arm. "Wait! Liz, would you just wait a damn minute."

"No!" She flung his arm away and made it a few steps farther, but she was no match for his speed, and this time he caught her with both of his hands and held her captive in the strength of them.

He whirled her around to face him, and she could tell by the sparks that flew from his eyes that he meant business. "I suggest you get your butt back in that barn and dance with me. I have some things I want to say to you."

Her face lit with fury. "You know, this may come as some surprise to you, Payton Cartwright, but I don't want to dance, and I sure as hell have nothing to say to you."

"Well," he said at long last, "then that just leaves one other thing on my list that I've been thinking about doing tonight." And with that he pulled her hard against his body, knocking her hat off in the process, and ran his strong, sun darkened hands roughly through her hair then down to hold her body in place. He forced his lips down onto her stubborn ones, and kissed her with a passion that had been banked for many long years.

"Hello, Lizzie." He spoke to her in a voice that was deeper than she remembered and she felt her heart stop when she heard it. Even though she commanded it not to, it came to a momentary halt before it pounded back to life again. She told herself she didn't care or notice all the ways he'd changed.

"Hello." She pushed the words from her dry, sandy throat and heard it crackle out into the warm, summer air.

"Dance with me." Like an intimate but unwanted caress his words wrapped around her and held. It was too much for her to take and she couldn't handle standing there in the same space as him for another second longer.

"Excuse me, boys, but I believe I have to get going." She pushed her way out of the group and refused to look back when she heard him calling her name. Suddenly anger a million times stronger than she had remembered feeling in the past slammed into her, almost buckling her knees out from under her with its force. She forced herself forward and out into the night air.

There was a partially muffled curse that floated to her, and she judged that she had only seconds before Payton came after her. He caught up with her just outside of the barn and grabbed hold of her arm. "Wait! Liz, would you just wait a damn minute."

"No!" She flung his arm away and made it a few steps farther, but she was no match for his speed, and this time he caught her with both of his hands and held her captive in the strength of them.

He whirled her around to face him, and she could tell by the sparks that flew from his eyes that he meant business. "I suggest you get your butt back in that barn and dance with me. I have some things I want to say to you."

Her face lit with fury. "You know, this may come as some surprise to you, Payton Cartwright, but I don't want to dance, and I sure as hell have nothing to say to you."

"Well," he said at long last, "then that just leaves one other thing on my list that I've been thinking about doing tonight." And with that he pulled her hard against his body, knocking her hat off in the process, and ran his strong, sun darkened hands roughly through her hair then down to hold her body in place. He forced his lips down onto her stubborn ones, and kissed her with a passion that had been banked for many long years.

For my husband, Kevin. Thank you for all your love, patience, and guidance. Where would I be without you?


In memory of Lenoree Bennett, my Gran. If I had never had your front porch swing to sit, eat my ice cream cones, and watch the cars drive by I would never know the joys of small town life. I love you.

*Prologue*

Lizzie Benford was getting married in two weeks. What should have been the happiest moment in her life was turning into the biggest nightmare this side of Elm Street. It wasn't that she didn't like weddings. She did. She had officiated over at least twenty six of her Ken and Barbie doll weddings growing up. Not to mention that she had written in her diary at the age of ten the way her dream wedding would proceed. At the moment, her diary wedding and the real one couldn't have been more black and white.

Maybe it was the caterer calling her fives times a day with various culinary questions. Or possibly it was the rental company calling to say that half the chairs they had reserved for the date were now green rather than white thanks to mildew problems in the warehouse. There also happened to be that one other issue she kept trying to nudge to the back of her brain. She repeated to herself like a mantra that the issue was small, and prayed that if she said it enough it really would be true. Somehow she was starting to have serious doubts on that matter.

Every time she mentally rehearsed walking down the aisle all the scenery was picture perfect, the audience was smiling at her as she walked closer to the alter, and she would look at the end of the aisle to her husband to be… and that's when the image came to a screeching halt. At the end of the first pew waiting for her there was always another man standing in the place where Josh, her fiancé, should stand. Someone she had sworn to herself she would forget, but in the eleven years Lizzie had been trying, she never had quite accomplished the goal.

Lizzie felt her stomach pitch and reel and start all over again as she dug into her oversized, imitation Prada purse and dug out the extra large bottle of Pepto Bismol she stashed there. Her stomach had been doing that a lot lately and Lizzie had eventually learned to chalk it up to pre-wedding jitters. Still, though, she wondered if consuming half a bottle a day constituted some sort of a dependence problem.

She chunked the bottle onto the passenger seat of her ancient VW bug where she could reach it again on short notice. At least the view outside the old battle scarred vehicle was nice, she thought in an attempt to console herself, even if it was treacherously bleak inside.

Well, it wasn't really *that* bleak- not if you considered the fact that in two weeks she would be marrying Josh Turner, the most high profile corporate accountant in the south east, and moving off to the high life in

Nashville, Tennessee.  By comparison, Nashville certainly couldn't hold a candle to her hometown, Edenville, with all its small town charm and memories that would stay with her a lifetime.  At least in Nashville, though, she could settle in and open her family medicine practice.

One of the first arguments she and Josh had after their engagement was where they would live.  She had desperately wanted to return to Edenville, but Josh was adamant that they live in Nashville.  She could be a family doctor anywhere, he had explained, but he needed a big city for his career.  Lizzie had reluctantly agreed.

Since high school her life had always been on a straight and focused plan:  Get into a top university with a full scholarship, earn top honors, and be accepted to a top medical school.  Yep, she was a certified geek with a capital G, and had been the teacher's pet to boot.  With the exception that she was to have been married by the age of twenty-four and she was now almost thirty and just now getting her wedding dress fitted, she was right on track.  Granted, there had been a few minor bumps along the way, but still, she had gone straight from high school to college and from there immediately on to medical school.  At least *she* was getting married, which was more than a lot of women could say.

What did it matter in the grand scheme of things if she was about to marry someone who only marginally thrilled her sexually and made her want to scream he was so incessantly nice all the time?  To Lizzie it seemed that a few alterations in her dreams for life were a small price to pay for getting a husband who would provide her a beautiful family and a calm, predictable, steady life.

Lizzie crested one of the larger rolling hills that lead into the small, southern town where she had grown up and watched as the sun started to sink behind the white-washed steeple of the town's only church.

It was Baptist, of course.

For the first time in her life she ignored the posted speed limit sign she had so dutifully followed in the past and made her way through the town.  Of course, town- such as it was- consisted of a short strip of stores at most two blocks long, with a pair of flimsy flashing traffic lights that hovered over the dual pedestrian crosswalks that led from one side of Main Street to the other.

She kissed her hand and blew the kiss out the window when the old VW passed the town's sign, and had to smile to herself when she read it.

Welcome to Edenville
"Our little slice of heaven!"

It hadn't been so many years ago when she would have rolled her eyes and made gagging noises at the sign. But now... well, now, that was a different story. Now it meant she was home. The tension that had been her constant companion over the past few months eased a notch, and Lizzie took a deep breath.

At the other end of town, a white wooden fence flanked the drive leading back to her family's house. As if there was anyone in town who didn't know where everyone else lived, a white wooden sign in front of the fence announced: *Welcome to the Benford's.*

The drive was long, and like most drives in this small country town, unpaved. As if meaning to keep the house a surprise until the last minute, large Cherry trees ran along the fence using their bushy foliage as a screen against the view of the house. But at last, the trees fell away and opened some fifty yards before the house to reveal a rather large, two-story wooden house painted white with green shutters accenting the windows.

A red barn stood off to the side in back of the house, and where the fence line picked back up a small pasture sat in the distance. It was home, Lizzie's home, and her lips turned up in a smile at the thought.

Just for good measure she took another swig of pink liquid as she coasted to a stop and waited for her pitiful vehicle to sputter, moan and finally backfire before shutting down in the grass parking area of her parents' backyard. Ah, the things she had learned to put up with as a starving medical student.

Lizzie pushed her sunglasses up into the wildly curling mass of long black hair and watched through the bug splattered windshield as her spitting image poked her head out the screened porch door and smiled. "Lizzie?"

When Lizzie stepped from the Bug, lifting her arms in a shrug, her sister let out a screech that would have made a blue whale proud and took off running across the porch. "Lizzie!" She let herself go in a flying leap off the edge of the porch and landed on top of Lizzie, sending them sprawling in a mass of dark curly hair and long, lean limbs onto the ground.

"Land sakes, Mary Catherine," Lizzie laughed as she pushed her sister off her, "next time at least give me a little warning before you tackle me."

"Tackle you?" Her younger sister playfully pinched her arm. Although Mary Catherine was only twenty-seven, she still acted like a five year old at heart. "Better not let daddy find out you've gone soft. He's only got two weeks to toughen you back up again."

"Who's gone soft?" Lizzie looked up to find her parents hugging each other on the top step of the porch, watching them as they lay sprawled over the grass.

"Daddy!"

"Come here, girl, and let me get a look at you." He made a big show of cupping her chin, turning her head this way and that before he tilted her head back down and stared long and hard into Lizzie's deep emerald green eyes. "Mm-hmm, mm-hmm. Looks good to me. What d'ya think, Faith?"

Her mother laughed. "Oh, stop it, Ed. Leave my baby alone, she's had a long drive." Lizzie let her mother fuss over her, and then stepped into the warmth of her arms, breathing in that scent of clean linens and fresh cut roses only her mother possessed. "Now come on in, darling and you can help MC set the table while I finish making the gravy for the mashed potatoes. Ed, honey, don't forget to help unload the car,"

The smell of cornbread and chicken frying on the stove that hit her as she entered the house should have been a welcome expectation, but it made Lizzie's stomach flip instead. A fleeting thought of racing back to her car and snatching the Pepto Bismol for support ran through her mind, but she forced it and her flipping stomach into submission.

"Mmm, smells great, Mom. Are you still cooking like this all the time? No wonder Dad's grown a little flabby around the middle.

She stirred the pot of butterbeans. "Your father loves his country cooking. I've tried to cut back, and I even tried a few 'light' meals but Mrs. Ramsey informed me at church a few months back that he's been sneaking down to the cafeteria over in Clarkston to get his weekly helping of fried green tomatoes." Faith tapped the stirring spoon on the edge of the pot and set it on the counter as she turned to Lizzie. "I figure if he's gonna go to all that trouble to eat his food, then it might as well be from a good source and full of my love."

Lizzie giggled. "Good plan, Mama. Way to show him who's boss!" Lizzie stripped off the lightweight rain jacket she'd been wearing when she drove down from Atlanta, and hung it on the coat rack that stood in the corner of the room near the refrigerator, listening to her mother hum as she checked the progress of the chicken.

She loved her mother with everything she had in her just the same way she loved this family. Her mother's singing had always been her calm in the midst of any storm. Even now she could feel another layer of tension easing away as she closed her eyes and listened to Faith's soothing melody.

"Grab a seat and help me butter some bread, Lizzie-bean."

It warmed Lizzie to see that nothing much had changed with her family since the last time she had been home. Her mother was still the trim and petite little brunette, bumbling about the house and working avidly in the garden, while her father was still the wonderful man she always remembered. His hair had silvered a little over the years, and his belly had gained a good layer of flesh, but he still had those adorable dimples when he smiled and his features were attractive. They matched well, her mother and him, and Lizzie was thankful that she had never had to worry a single day in her life about divorce or affairs or any of the other crazy, terrible things so many other children had to worry about with their parents.

When it was time for dinner, Ed Benford took his seat at the head of the family table, rubbed his hands together, and then held them out to join in the ring of hands they always formed when they blessed the food the Lord provided them each meal. It was a tradition in their home that had started the day Ed and Faith joined in marriage, and one that would continue on in their children's families as well. It was more than a simple act in this family; it meant values, it meant tradition, it meant home.

A vast spread of Southern cooking sat square in the center of the large family table perched comfortably in the middle of the large kitchen. Macaroni and cheese, mashed potatoes, butter beans, fried chicken, sliced tomatoes, fried okra, and fried cornbread; all prepared by Faith, were served up onto large white dinner dishes and passed around the table. Before the first platter had been passed, the table had erupted into loud chatter and conversation.

"Lizzie, Mary Catherine and I were in town today," Lizzie rolled her eyes under closed lids. Her mother talked as if town were something other than a two-block strip of buildings no more than a quarter of a mile down the road. "We stopped in Mrs. McIntire's alteration's shop and she said that the dress is ready for the final fitting. Isn't that exciting? I told her you and Mary Catherine would come by first thing tomorrow morning and try it on."

"Oh, that's wonderful! Have the bride's maid dresses been fitted yet?"

"Well, Grace called yesterday and said she wouldn't try the dress on until you got home to assure her the color of the dress wasn't pink. She said she couldn't bear it if you made her wear pink with her flame red hair. I know," she said as she watched her daughter's face, "I tried to tell her just to try it on, but she insisted. I told her you'd pick her up and take her with you to get fitted together."

Back to old stomping ground, again, she could see.

"Pick her up? Mama, I'm not picking her up. The shop isn't even far enough away to drive to, and she lives in the closest house to town. It would take me longer to drive down her driveway than it would for her to walk the fifty steps from her front door to the shop."

"Still, I think it'd be nice if you picked her up."

Lizzie breathed a sigh of relief when her father piped up and stole away her chance to respond. "Well, Doc," Ed Benford interjected. "I want to know when this fiancé of yours is getting in to town." He smiled warmly at his oldest daughter, his round, portly face glowing with adoration. Lizzie had always been determined to make something of her life. He had proudly informed the whole town at the town meeting the day his daughter had been accepted to medical school.

Lizzie swallowed a bite of tomato then said, "Josh told me he had some things to finish up at home, so he's supposed to arrive in town next Monday to help finish up the decorating and last minute details."

"Ah, good. Well tell him to bring his gun and we'll head out to the back property and shoot some skeet while he's here."

"Daddy, he doesn't own a gun, remember?"

Her father stared at her blankly, as if he was trying his best to recall that particularly blasphemous bit of information, before he smiled blandly and said, "Oh, right. Well, that's not a problem, he can just borrow one of mine."

Lizzie set her fork down and gingerly patted him on the shoulder in hopes that it would somehow defray the blow she was about to deliver. "No, no, daddy," She said in a little croak. "He's... afraid of guns."

Her father exploded. "Well what I want to know is what in Sam Hill business does a man have in growing up in the South if he can't even shoot a gun without being a little ninny?" His face began to redden and his nostrils began to flare, and Lizzie was definitely afraid that if he didn't calm down she'd be personally escorting him to the hospital for a heart attack.

"Now, Ed, you need to calm down. The doctor said you had a problem with that pressure of yours. Lizzie, do something about your father. Maybe you can explain to him better than I can. Lord knows, I've tried all I can to make him listen to reason."

Exactly what her mother thought she could do was beyond her. Her sister, she noted, was snickering behind the butter bean laden fork she had strategically placed over her mouth. Lizzie pushed her mostly uneaten plate of food away from her and threw her napkin over the remains so her father wouldn't be tempted to finish it off for her. She quickly racked her brain for something to say that would change the subject.

"So, where's Skipper Junior? I didn't see him when I came in."

"Oh, didn't you hear, Lizzie," MC said from across the table. "Mrs. Hooper opened up a grooming salon just off of Main. Hooper's Puppy Paradise- that's what she's calling it. Anyway, SJ's there getting all fixed up for the big day."

"What!"

"I know," Faith added. "MC and I thought it was outrageous but Ed insisted. He'll be back tomorrow after his full body make-over."

Lizzie closed her eyes, praying this was another nightmare she'd wake up from any minute. "Lord."

"Don't bring Him into this," her father said sternly. "Heaven knows that dog needed some strong deodorizing if he was supposed to be present at the reception."

"But dad…"

Her mother must have sensed the tension because she suddenly changed the subject. "Honey, did I tell you that Granny dropped by earlier today and brought us a pound cake."

Eloise "Granny" Thornton was eighty two and the resident grandmother of everyone in town. Not that she actually was their grandmother, but Lizzie knew she liked to mother everyone and so she became their adopted grandma so to speak. And despite her age, she seemed to hold more energy than half the young kids in town and she insisted on walking everywhere she went. Granny said it kept her body kicking when she forced it to work on a regular basis.

"Granny made a pound cake? Yum, I always did love her

cooking."

"Me, too," chimed in Mary Catherine. "Let's have some for dessert."

And so they did. By the time they were finished, only a quarter of the cake remained and Lizzie didn't even want to think about what her waistline was going to look like as a result. Lizzie couldn't help but stifle a yawn. She was beat from her day on the road, and all that warm country cooking was doing it's best to send her into a grease laden deep sleep.

She smiled over at her mother. "Dinner was great, mama, but I'm beat."

"Well, come on, and I'll walk with you upstairs. I want to show you whatt I did to your room." She smiled and patted her daughter's arm as they walked to the bedroom. "I left all your stuff the same, honey, but I hope you don't mind that I painted the room a few weeks ago." Her mother flipped on the overhead light and yanked the cord to set the ceiling fan into motion. The cord lazily clicked against the glass fixture as the blades whirred to life. "And I added a few new framed prints in your bathroom."

"Thanks, mama. It looks nice." Lizzie glanced around, her fingers itching to touch all the links to her past. She had so little time to capture every last detail of Edenville before she moved away, and suddenly she wanted to be alone to absorb it all. "I hope you don't mind, but I'm tired from driving all day. I'm going to turn in early."

Her mother smiled. "Not at all, sweet pea. Sleep well." She kissed her on the forehead and shut the door on her way out.

Lizzie walked around the bedroom where she had grown up, fingering items from her past as she remembered those days gone by. Ribbons she'd won in school mingled between pictures of her and Mary Catherine and her very best friend, Grace. A trophy she'd earned in a softball tournament sat on the edge of a desk her father made when he was younger. It was painted green and if she looked hard enough, on the upper left corner of the side closest to her bed would have *I hate mama* carved into the wood from when she'd felt particularly cruel after a teenage spat with her parents.

There were several shoe boxes that lined the top shelf of her closet, and she took a few minutes to read a few of the notes she and Grace passed back and forth during history class. She found an old, faded friendship bracelet. And in the very bottom of the last box a picture caught her attention, and she gasped. It wasn't the people in the picture that startled her, but rather the way they looked.

Payton Cartwright held her wrapped in his arms and they stood linked together like they somehow always had been, in front of a waterfall. One of Payton's arms faded off the page because he had been the one taking the picture, and both of them were staring at each other, smiling, because as she remembered it, that was just after the first time they had made love.

In a flash anger more intense than she had experienced in years boiled up. Her fingers trembled, and she forced herself to put the picture back in the box and close the lid. It was in the past, she reminded herself. Besides, she was engaged and would be married in two weeks and it was ridiculous to dwell on the past. And she refused, *refused*, to allow any more images of Payton to ruin her mental rehearsal of the wedding. Mrs. Josh Turner, Mrs. Josh Turner, she repeated to herself.

She was still repeating it to herself with her eyes closed as she brushed her teeth, when her mom tapped on the door to her bedroom. "Honey?" Her mom's dark hair and dark eyes peered around the corner.

Lizzie spat in the sink. "In here."

"I forgot to give this to you earlier, but I thought you might want it. It's just some mail that came here for you." Faith edged farther into the room. "Anyway, I'll leave it on the bed. Night, night, now."

"Thanks, mom. Night."

Lizzie washed and dried her face then flipped the light off in her bathroom and sat on the edge of her bed. Her body was tired and she was looking forward to a long night's sleep, but first she'd open the mail. Three pieces were junk mail that her mother should have just thrown away, but the fourth was a white letter size envelope that made her pause. She could have recognized that writing anywhere. Printed on the center of the envelope in tiny, neat script writing were her name and her parent's address. There was no return address, but that didn't matter. Return addresses weren't necessary when you knew the place by heart.

She already knew that when she opened the letter the name signed at the end would be Payton Cartwright. The only problem was… she had no idea what the rest of the letter would say. Nothing in her head could conjure up a legitimate reason that this man, this man that she hadn't laid eyes on in six years, and hadn't had a decent conversation with in eight would need to contact her. Besides, if he needed to talk to her, couldn't he have just called her on the phone?

How many times in her life had she read notes from him?  Perhaps only a handful that she could remember, but she knew without a seed of doubt in her mind, that it was his letter that she held in her hands.  She supposed she should stop stalling and rip the letter open.  She would have preferred ripping it into a thousand tiny shreds and letting them flutter away in the breeze, but her curiosity won out and wouldn't let her do what her heart wanted.

Instead, she found herself gently pulling the seal apart and staring at the beginning of a note she had never in a million lifetimes imagined would be in her hands two weeks before her wedding day.

*Lizzie,*

*I can't tell you how long I sat here wondering how I should even begin this letter.  Do I say, Dear Lizzie, because in reality that is what you are?  Though I doubt you would even know that considering all that has happened in our past.  I decided on just Lizzie, thinking maybe that way you would at least move beyond the first word of this letter.*

*Somehow when I've thought about writing you this letter, I've never quite known how to start it out.  What do I say to you?  Where do I even begin?*

*I'm sorry for not making what I'm about to say more obvious over these past years, and I'm sorry for ever letting life get between us.  But I can never be sorry for sending this to you.  If I didn't I would always wonder... what if.  I would always wonder if it would have made a difference if I had tried to tell you how I feel.  And so here goes...*

*Some people are just special.  Some people have an effect on you that is more profound than you realize in the time you are with them.  And sometimes it takes losing that person to realize how special they truly are, and how much you would give to get them back.*

*That's the way I feel about you, Liz.  Oh, I knew you were special the first day I met you.  It's true.  And I know you thought I was just some dumb jock that only cared about being popular and chasing girls, but I noticed you, and I knew you were something different.  You have this way of walking into a room and lighting it up by just being in it.  And it amazes me still to this day that I have no choice but to smile every time I think about you.*

*I have thought about you for years.  In truth, I have thought about you every day of my life and wondered if there would ever be a time that I would hold you in my arms again. I can only hope against hope that one day I might be able to.*

*Your wedding was something I didn't have to face until a few weeks ago. When I got the invitation to your wedding at your parent's house, it became all too real. And I realized then that this was my last chance to tell you how I feel and hope that by some miracle it makes a difference in your life. I know it makes a difference in mine.*

*I wanted to call you, or see you. I wanted to hear you laugh again, but I was afraid I had messed things up so badly between us that there was no way to repair the damage. I'm a new man, Lizzie. If you could only see me now, what I wouldn't do to prove my love for you.*

*I love you, Lizzie. I love you more than I ever knew I could love someone, and it breaks my heart to know that I may have ruined any chance of ever having my love returned. But I want what is best for you. I don't know Josh, but I trust that you have chosen a good man to be your husband. My only hope is that Josh can give you everything that you deserve. You are one of a kind, Liz, and I hope he knows that. Still though…I would trade every possession I have if I could just have one more chance to show you how special you are to me.*

> *With all my love,*
> *Payton*

Long before the letter had ended, Lizzie had sunk onto the bed, her body facing the ceiling as she read. When the letter was finished, she let it fall to the floor beside her, and she cried herself to sleep.

*Part One: The Old Life*
*Chapter One*

The day she came home from school and found her entire house packed into a moving truck, Lizzie knew her life was about to change forever. She hadn't even fully stepped off the school bus when she spotted the large truck backed up her driveway, and the moving men hauling furniture up the planks into the back of the vehicle. Her father smiled at her when he stepped through the front door carrying a large cardboard box in his arms.

He actually smiled at her. In all her twelve years of life she had never seen a smile so full of regret.

"Hi, Honey. Have a good day at school?"

Lizzie didn't respond. She dropped her book bag on the green grass of their sloping front yard and stared as the moving men hauled her favorite couch through the doors and up the ramp.

"There's some juice and cookies in the kitchen if you want some. We're probably going to be leaving in a few minutes, though."

She still couldn't believe they were moving. Only last week her father sat them all down in the den one night before bed and explained to her and Mary Catherine that they were moving somewhere new. Her mother sat huddled on one corner of the couch with a blanket pulled around her shoulders and tears streaming down her face. Her father even cried at one point, and she couldn't remember a time, ever, that her father had shed tears.

He leaned forward in their old, faded recliner and laced his fingers together between his knees. "Your mother's been sick. You know that, right?"

Lizzie eyed her mother again. She was rocking herself back and forth gently, and Lizzie wondered if she would ever snap out of this depression she'd been in since she lost the baby. Slowly, she turned her gaze back to her father and nodded.

"Well, the doctor's recommended that we make a new start, and to be honest, I have to agree with him. God knows, I haven't agreed with much else."

Lizzie couldn't quite figure out what he was trying to tell them, but she was losing interest and fast. She scrubbed her striped socks across the carpet wondering if rug burn could be felt through socks.

"Anyway... I've bought this beautiful house for us in this nice little town. And I've just been hired there as the branch manager of the local bank." He stood and smiled, acting like this was the best news ever. "You're gonna love the name of this place. Edenville. Edenville, Alabama. Doesn't that sound great?"

Her mother sniffled, and blew noisily into a tissue. Mary Catherine's jaw about hit the ground. Lizzie's insides were doing a funny little flip-flop routine, but outwardly she yawned and twisted one of her long, curly strands of hair around her finger. Moving from Chicago to some nowhere Alabama town wasn't exactly her idea of a good time.

"Well, anyway. I can see you're not that thrilled about it right now, but you'll get used to the idea. We're leaving next week."

That got Lizzie's attention. "Next week! But the school year's already started. What am I going to tell my friends?"

He beamed a smile at her. "I have it all planned out. This weekend we're going to have a big going away party for you and MC's friends. You can tell them goodbye there. It'll be perfect."

A party sounded nice, but she knew it was just a bribe to keep her happy. Lizzie wasn't falling for his tricks, and she glared at her father.

"Dad, how could you? You're taking me away from here, my home, my friends, my *life,* and for what? So mom can get better? Look at her; she's nothing but a bump on a log anymore, anyway!"

He crossed the room in one pace and grabbed her by the arm. "Apologize, immediately." Lizzie shrank back and after a moment she bit out an insincere apology.

"Look at her." He paused and forced her to look at her mother. "This is exactly my point. She needs help, and if I can't help her when I promised to be the person that would at least try, then who's going to do it?" Her father knelt down so they were eye to eye. "You may not like it, and I'm sorry that you don't, but moving is the best option for her right now. Life can't always be about you. Sometimes it's about other people, too."

Angry tears welled up in her eyes, and she wanted so badly to curl up in his arms like she'd always done in the past, but he was the source of her anger right now and she pulled away from him instead.  Lizzie saw the shock that registered in his eyes, and she felt a quick tug of satisfaction.

"I hate you!"  Heartbroken, she stomped dramatically out of the room.

Now, a week later, she stood on the lawn and watched as the men loaded her bedroom suite.  Ed Benford put down the box he'd been hauling and walked over to her.  "Are you ready to go, sweet pea?"

He reached out to touch her hair but she ducked away.  She still wasn't speaking to him, and she wanted to make certain he knew she was angry with him for making them move.

Her father sighed as she walked away.  "I know you're mad at me sweetie, but you'll thank me one day."  Right, when H-E-double hockey sticks froze over.

Thirty minutes later she sat strapped in the farthest corner in the back seat of her parent's station wagon thinking of all the ways she would repay her father as soon as she got the chance.  She could already imagine her satisfaction at watching him wake with toothpaste smeared all over his face.

No.  That wasn't quite good enough.  She'd have to think this one through a little better.

The sun was beginning to set and as it dipped lower in the sky Lizzie squinted against the bright orange light and tried to think of the ultimate payback for this cruel joke her parents were playing on her.  Just looking at them up there in the front seat made her stomach roll.

Her mother leaned against the passenger window pretending to be asleep, even though everyone in the car knew she wasn't.  Her father hummed along to the radio, bopping his head from side to side, looking like he hadn't had a better day in his whole life.

He would think that, she grumbled inwardly.  She'd bet money that inside her parents were thrilled that they had just ruined their oldest daughters life.  They, of course, had nothing better to do than think up ways to ruin their children's life, after all.

A sideways glance at her sister told her Mary Catherine wasn't enjoying their father's humming anymore than she was.  She sat with her long, dark hair- the exact coloring of hers and her fathers- slumped over her face, staring down at a comic book, plugging both her ears with two tiny little fingers trying to drown out his obvious lack in singing skills. Neither one had inherited his awful voice, thank God.

Lizzie punched the pillow that was nestled up next to the window, trying to make the feathers inside it reposition so she could maybe fall asleep. She didn't know where this Edenville was, but she sure wasn't going to stay awake and think about it any longer.

Couldn't her parents at least have decided to do this before school started for the year? The thought snuck in the back door even though she was trying her hardest not to think. She closed her eyes and tried to envision her best friend Sarah's face with her blond curls and insanely blue eyes. Oh, and she could never forget those huge buck teeth that made her look just a little like a donkey. Lizzie thought about the spend the night party they'd had together, and tried to ignore the ache in her heart.

Her father glanced in the rearview mirror and caught her eyeing him with a vicious glare. "How's it going back there?" he asked as he smiled. She shot him the look she'd seen her mother fix on him when she wanted to prove she was M-A-D and hoped that he'd get the message.

Ed Benford watched his daughter glare at him from the back seat with the same maddening look her mother had perfected long, long ago. He'd give just about anything to see Faith shoot him that look now instead of the blank, emotionless void she had been displaying for the past few weeks. Months, actually, if he let himself be realistic.

The doctors tried to tell him that she wasn't getting better. He'd seen it, of course. Ed kept hoping that if he held out a little longer she might snap out of this... funk... eventually.

Depression. That was the term the doctor's were using. Severe post partum depression. She'd lost the baby three days before the due date, and he had never seen anyone so shaken in his entire life. He'd been shaken, too, but it was nothing compared to Faith's apparent misery.

When she stopped sleeping at all during the night and began to wander around the baby's room singing lullaby's to a nonexistent child, he started to worry. She hardly ate, and her beautiful blue eyes were dull and lusterless. She didn't smile, she never talked, and when he could drag a hug out of her she was nothing but bones underneath pale, lifeless skin.

He found her passed out on the bathroom floor one morning with a bottle of pills in her hand, and that had been the wake up call. He couldn't lose his wife. Not now, not ever. He needed her too much to let her go.

He *loved* her too much to let her go.

He glanced over at her and smiled then focused back on the road. He didn't think she'd notice if he was driving naked with a clown nose and purple hair on his head, but the doctor's told him to keep trying and eventually he'd get through to her.

He pulled into line at a drive through when it came time for dinner, having made the executive decision that at least one of the three women would rebel in some form or fashion if he'd actually stopped to get them dinner. A drive-through was so much easier to deal with when a man had three hostile women in the car. He was beginning to think if he could learn to deal with the emotional roller coaster ride living with three women afforded, he could live through anything.

He took the large paper bags of burgers the over large worker handed him and passed it to the back of the station wagon. A pair of hands took the bag. In silent agreement, the entire vehicle devoured the meal in silence, not even a thank you bestowed on the man who purchased the food.

Ed knew he had no room to pout, but still he felt like it. Here he was, simply *trying* to do what was best for his wife and his family, and yet he got no respect for it. Instead, his family looked like a bunch of lemon-heads all puckered and pouting in their respective corners of the car. He could only take so much more of this abuse, he decided, before he would have to call a family meeting and set the crew in line.

That night at the motel room, Ed watched his daughters lying side by side in the double bed across the room. His beautiful, precious daughters. Even though they were two years apart in age, they could pass themselves off as identical twins, and he felt a spurt of pride knowing they were miniature, female versions of him when he was younger. The same dark, thick mass of curling hair, and green eyes that looked like emeralds under the hot, noon sun.

Ed's smile turned to a frown and he wondered how long Lizzie would stay mad at him. He knew Lizzie felt like she been dealt a rough hand, but he hoped that eventually she'd come to understand that he was doing this to save her mother's life.

Mary Catherine was a little younger and seemed to be handling it okay. He'd see about setting up some time with a counselor in Edenville and make sure the girls worked out any issues they had with the move.

Ed yawned. It had been a long, hard day, and he imagined that the next few days were only going to get harder. As he drifted off to sleep, he wondered again how long Lizzie would hold her grudge against him.

*Chapter Two*

They rounded the bend in the mid-morning sunlight and Lizzie spotted the perky wooden sign that read:

Welcome to Edenville
*"Our little slice of heaven!"*

She heard herself groan and she rolled her eyes. This had to be the lamest town they'd ridden through since they'd started darting through little hole-in-the-wall towns earlier that morning. Then the name on the sign registered in her brain, and she let out a little whimper.

Her parents really hated her. They secretly had been planning a way to ruin her life, and this was most definitely it. They had actually succeeded this time. She checked her watch and then felt her pulse, wondering how much longer it would take until her heart finally ground to a halt.

She watched in disgust as they passed a series of old, Victorian houses with trim little flower beds in the front and cute sidewalks that led out to the street. When they passed the small strip of stores in the center of town, she felt her jaw hit the ground. Where was the shopping mall? Where was the arcade where she and her buddies went to play games and talk about boys? Not that she had any experience- or interest- in those creatures yet.

The thought crossed her mind that maybe her parents didn't want to just outright kill her, but instead wanted to enjoy her slow torturous death from misery in this small, no-life town. She watched in outrage as they passed the school on her sister's side of the car. Dixie Academy was printed in bold, black letters above the two central doors leading into the school. In Chicago, no one would have dreamed of naming a school something like Dixie Academy. Obviously it was just the backwoods charm coming out in this small southern town, she thought hideously with her twelve year old mind.

Her father cried, "Here it is girls! Get ready to see beauty," as they approached the dirt drive that led back to their new house. Lizzie was convinced that anything with a dirt drive connected to it couldn't possibly be beautiful, but decided saying such would probably get her grounded.

She already had enough on her plate to worry about without dealing with something like that.

They bounced down the long dirt drive, lined with cherry trees, and she held her breath until the house came into view. It was hardly what she would call beautiful- just as she'd suspected.

The pasture behind the house was severely overgrown, and the fence that had been white at some point during it existence was peeling and faded while several of the boards had fallen or were in the process. The house seemed to be in similar disrepair. The screen door hung off its hinges and Lizzie could spot the gaping hole in it from her spot in the station wagon.

Paint chipped off the house as well, and two of the green shutters hung crooked from the wall. Her father seemed determined to be optimistic and stated emphatically, "It's just beautiful, right girls?" All the girls, including their mother, mumbled under their breath.

The interior of the house didn't have much to boast about either. It was musty and dusty, and the carpet the previous owners had placed on every square inch of the flooring was so hideous Lizzie was really quite afraid to walk on it. So instead, she wandered outside to investigate potential hiding spots from her awful, awful parents.

There was a small barn on the edge of the dilapidated pasture, and Lizzie edged the rusty door open to peer inside. She let out a muffled scream when a tomcat yowled at her and skittered past her legs. Her heart raced, and she thought she might have accidentally wet her pants from fright. The rest of the day she was quite content hanging out close to the safety of what she refused to consider her new home.

"I hope my team is ready to do a little painting," her father said over breakfast the next morning. The only one who looked happy about it was Skipper the Bichon, but that was most likely because Mary Catherine had been slipping little pieces of her burnt bacon to him under the table since she'd sat down to eat.

"Skipper said he'd do it just as soon as he got through eating MC's breakfast." Lizzie smiled smugly. Her sister simply shot her parents a too innocent smile and said, "What?"

"Well, regardless of who's eating whose breakfast, we've got lots of work to do around this place and I suggest we do it soon so this place will start lookin' like home."

"I've got a better idea. Why don't we just go back home?" Lizzie looked hopeful but knew it wasn't promising when her father shot her idea down with a dismissive glint in his eye.  She looked to her mom for a supportive voice in getting out of chores, but her mother looked too focused on lifelessly stirring the applesauce in front of her.

When no other complaints were voiced, her dad spooned a heap of applesauce in his mouth and said, "All right then it's settled.  The girls and I will go to town and buy the paint while Mama unpacks the kitchen. When we get back, we'll start on the bedrooms."

No one looked pleased except for Ed.  Even Skipper, the traitor, had dodged out through the hole in the screen and was busying himself with exploring a particularly fascinating ant hill.

By six o'clock that evening they had gone through six gallons of paint and had more paint fumes to deal with than their small army could handle.  They ate a simple dinner out on the front porch, too exhausted to prepare more than a ham sandwich and some sliced tomatoes.

Lizzie hated to admit it, but the house did look a little better on the inside since they'd painted the bedrooms and a few other spots in the house.  There was no denying that it would still need a lot of work, but begrudgingly she decided that the house might just turn out as beautiful as her father had predicted.  Now, coming to love the place was another story entirely.  One she was willing to bet wouldn't have a good ending.

The night was calm around them as they finished the meal in silence.  No wind blew, but she could hear a few frogs croaking from some pond in the distance, and the last birds of the day gave off their farewell songs to hold the world until the morning.  It wasn't anything comforting or scary to Lizzie, but she took the sounds in and absorbed them- unsure at the moment if they would mean anything to her in the future or not.

She glanced at her mother who sat next to her on the wooden floor of the porch.  Her mother had been quiet all evening, and Lizzie wondered if she would be any happier here in this new place.  "What do you think of it, Mama?"

Her mother stopped pretending to eat and took a sip of the iced tea by her side.  The circles under her eyes hadn't lessened any, but Lizzie was happy to see that at least they hadn't turned worse.  Lizzie sincerely doubted she could get any skinnier than she was, but she didn't really understand how it was possible for her to lose so much weight since all she did was sleep all day anyway.

Faith pulled the shawl a little tighter around her shoulders and looked over at her daughter. She tried to register the question her daughter just asked, but it took a minute to actually focus in on the answer. Lizzie smiled hesitantly at her.

"What do you think of it, Mama?" Lizzie asked again.

"Its fine, Lizzie. I think I'm going to like it here just fine." Faith looked around the place as if noticing her surroundings for the first time. Already she'd felt her brain click into gear more in this one day than she'd felt it work in weeks. It was like cranking an old engine after years of no use. It felt sluggish and weak, but at the same time it was almost a relief to realize her brain still worked after all.

She noted the holes in the ceiling where someone must have hung a porch swing at some point in the past. She could almost picture it: an old wicker seat with a soft cushion. And ferns. She could imagine ferns sitting in heavy iron urns on either side of the front door. Faith was surprised to feel her face turn up in a small smile, and realized it was the first time in months that that had happened.

She'd wanted to kick Ed in the shins the day he'd come home from work and pulled her out from under the covers she'd been wrapped in all day and told her that they were moving. What right had he had, she'd wanted to know, that allowed him to just up and move their family without asking her first? She could still remember the absolute determination framing his handsome face when he'd told her his decision was final and if she didn't like it he'd just find a way to do it anyway. She hadn't had the energy to argue with him, so she'd merely pulled the covers back over her head and fallen right back asleep.

But now... well, she still wasn't excited about the idea of living in a new place and a new home. But she was starting to see, as much as she didn't want to admit, that maybe Ed had been right. Maybe it would do her body good to be somewhere new. Somewhere that every corner she turned, she didn't think about places where new baby items would have gone. At the moment, it wore her out just thinking about it.

When she realized her daughters were both watching her curiously she gave them a half-hearted smile and crossed her legs in front of her. Her beautiful baby girls. She'd been so preoccupied with her own life lately that she hadn't even tried to focus on theirs.

"So girls," she said, and was startled to hear how rusty her voice had become from disuse. "You start school on Monday. Are you excited?"

She wanted to laugh, she really did, when they both simultaneously shot her a look that could kill, but she barely had the strength to talk, much more laugh.

"Yeah, you girls are going to love the new school." Ed chipped in, munching on the remnants of his wife's uneaten sandwich. "I talked with the principal on the phone the other day, and he said you girls would be happy with it."

MC and Lizzie studied their fingernails with supreme concentration, and scraped bits of white paint off their hands.

"That school we passed just outside of town- Dixie Academy- that's the middle and high school. Lizzie you'll be going there. Did you know it's where the kids from the closest five towns go to school?"

"I had no idea." Her voice was thick with teenage boredom.

"And MC, you'll be going to the elementary at the next town over." She mimicked her sister's response with exact precision. Ed rolled his eyes, and Faith wondered when her daughters had become such drama queens.

*Chapter Three*

Lizzie stuck out her tongue to the image in the mirror and a distinct pout broke out on her face. She looked like a two year old that her mother had dressed, and even Skipper whimpered and put a paw over his eyes. It was never a good sign when the dog disapproved.

Today was her first day at Dixie Academy and she was not going to ruin it by showing up in this getup. At the last minute she whipped off the stupid Sunday dress her mother had begged her to wear and threw on a khaki skirt and a white short sleeve button up shirt. It was still warm enough in Edenville to wear sandals so she put those on, too.

One advantage to living in this stupid old town, she thought as she pulled her long curling hair back into a ponytail, was that it would allow her to wear her warm weather clothes longer than she could have in Chicago. August in Chicago was still warm like it was here, but come September her Fall clothes would be coming out. She wondered how long it would take to cool to Fall weather here in Edenville.

She threw her backpack over her shoulders, and pecked her mother quickly on the cheek as she set out the front door to walk all of the quarter mile down the street to school. She had to report to Principal Whiteside's office first thing, and it made her stomach flip to think about it. In Chicago she'd always tried her hardest to be a good student. The last place in the world she liked to be was sitting in a chair waiting to be called in to the principal's office, because as much as she didn't like to admit it, deep down in her heart she really did want to please her parents.

By the time Principal Whiteside had given her a tour of the school and printed out a list of her classes and their room numbers, she was thirty minutes late to the first class of the day. Her heart beat out wild staccato thuds in her chest as she opened the door to her classroom and stepped inside. She had no idea what to expect, and she sent up a silent prayer that she wouldn't do something stupid to attract more than the usual new kid attention.

But, as she recalled later, her prayer seemed to have fallen on deaf ears.

"Okay class," Mrs. Strickland said as she dropped the chalk into the chalk trey and dusted off her hands. "I want to introduce you to our new student. Lizzie, come here." Lizzie obeyed and went to stand facing the class directly in front of the teacher. "Class, this is Lizzie Benford. She's just moved to Edenville with her family from Chicago. Isn't that great?"

They all stared at the Chicagoan like she was a Martian.

"Well, we won't waste anymore time. Lizzie, you can take that seat back there in the back row next to Billy. Billy, wave your hand so Lizzie will know who I'm talking about. And, welcome to eighth grade, Lizzie." As she walked away Mrs. Strickland gave her a friendly pat, making Lizzie feel for the moment that life just might be okay.

The teacher had already turned back to the chalkboard and was scribbling sentences the students were supposed to edit for grammar as she headed down the center row to the back of the class. She was so busy concentrating on trying not to look like a goofball that she completely missed the outstretched leg- she wasn't sure if it was accidental or not, but she had her suspicions. She heard the class roar with laughter as she fell to the floor, and bit her lip to force herself not to cry right there on the spot.

Somehow she managed to pick herself up, and scramble to the back of the class. Billy gave her an evil smile when she sat down next to him, and she quickly realized she was staring into the face of one of her newest found enemies.

She tried her hardest to concentrate on what Mrs. Strickland said in the front of the class, but it was just so difficult when everyone in class seemed so perfectly content staring at her. At first she thought she was imagining things, but then she realized it was true. Every once in a while she'd catch from the corner of her eye someone look in her direction then snicker.

With a muted whimper, Lizzie slunk lower in her seat. She was having even less of a good start than she'd pictured in the nightmares she'd had all weekend.

Instead of allowing herself to think about how much she wanted to crawl under her desk and hide, she bit the inside of her lower lip and studied the classroom. Mrs. Strickland, it seemed, had a flare for educational decorating, and had plastered almost every square inch of wall space with famous historical people, the founding fathers of the US, quotes from a multitude of writers, and even pictures of each of the students in the class. She had a sinking feeling she'd have one snapped of her before the day was over.

The fourth wall of the room was filled with windows that let in the bright light of the day, and a large radiator that obviously was the main heat source for the classroom in the winter. She noticed that the desks were arranged in straight, even rows and that there were little cubbies underneath the desk where students could put their extra books during class.

Since they were now in the eighth grade, Principal Whiteside explained, they would be switching classes every period like the rest of the Academy. She'd wanted to tell him that she'd been switching classes since fifth grade, but held her tongue so she wouldn't offend the man her first day in the school.

She checked her watch to see the time and groaned as she realized it had only been five minutes since she'd taken her seat. They still had fifteen minutes until time to switch classes. Since everyone else seemed so intent on studying her, she decided she might as well study them right back. She started on the row closest to the door and made her way up and down the rows studying each face and figure, wondering which one of them would turn out to be her friends. She even picked out a few that looked like they might be good candidates for friendship.

She had made it to the last row of students- those closest to the windows- and had just finished studying the perky blonde that sat in front when she noticed the boy sitting behind the blonde. He sat in his chair, not slumped or perfectly straight, but his eyes were intent on the teacher. His hair was a dark brown, full mass that brushed along the edge of his collared t-shirt, and she wondered for an instant what color his eyes might be. His body was long and lean already, though it hadn't yet developed the full muscle to go with it. She studied him for longer than she had intended, noting the way he cocked his head sideways like a puppy when the teacher said something particularly interesting to him.

She wondered again what color his eyes were, and found out that they were a clear, brilliant green- nearly the exact same shade as hers- as he turned to stare straight in her direction. His eyes locked with hers, and for a moment she thought she felt a sizzle spark through the air.

When she heard the class roar with laughter she snapped back to attention, and realized that the boy had been staring at her along with the rest of the class. Her face reddened perceptibly. Mrs. Strickland stood with her hands on her hips, a frown edging out on her lips.

"Now Lizzie, I know it's your first day here at the Academy, but even on your first day you have to pay attention. I asked if there was anything about this sentence you wanted to change."

She read the words "I ain't got nowhere to be right now." silently to herself then tried to redeem her previous mistakes by saying, "Yes, ma'am. I think it should say, 'I don't have anywhere to be right now.'"

"Good. That's wonderful, Lizzie. They must have you practicing grammar in first grade up in Chicago." That's when she realized she'd only compounded the problem of failing miserably to impress her classmates when she heard the muffled giggles and a coughed "Teacher's pet" coming from the direction of Charlie.

By lunchtime she was so tired of trying unsuccessfully to make at least one friend that she took her lunch trey to a vacant table and ate by herself. She could hear people talking about her like she couldn't even hear, so she pretended that she really couldn't. It was awful here, and she hated this stupid school.

It was nothing but a bunch of hicks, anyway. So why did she need to be friends with them? She didn't. It wouldn't be long, she just knew it, until her father realized what a terrible mistake he'd made by bringing them to this place and he'd pack them all up and move them home.

She couldn't wait to see the look on Sarah's face when she popped back in to school and gave her a big hug. They'd laugh so hard at all those stupid hick kids from
Edenville and all the ways they made fun of her.

She pretended like she couldn't feel the carrot slices being tossed at her back. Or the nasty comments about her accent. And she didn't even want to think about what that one boy just said.

The rest of the day she sat in the back of each class and stared at the teacher instead of at the curious faces that watched her. She hated feeling like she was the freak show act in the no name circus passing through town, but that was exactly how she felt. She didn't know how she was ever going to make it in this new school, and it depressed her to realize it.

She couldn't quite figure out how she'd gone from being the girl in her previous school that was neither the big fish nor the low man on the totem pole, but somewhere in the comfortable middle to being the absolute scum on the pond floor at this place. But somehow, in a matter of one day at this school she'd managed to do it.

She wondered if her sister was having any more luck than she.

By the time the school bell rang at the end of the day, Lizzie was beyond ready to get out of there, but she wasn't exactly ready to get back home. Nothing was right in this town, nothing seemed familiar. The kids weren't nice, the house was run down and smelled like an old person, and she wanted to go back to Chicago.

Lizzie was too busy scuffing her feet on the concrete sidewalk as she trudged home from school feeling sorry for herself, and she didn't notice the older woman sitting on the front porch of her house, swaying back and forth in a rocker as she knitted.

"Good afternoon to you," the woman called. Lizzie started at the sound of the voice and turned to find its source. There was an elderly woman sitting on the porch, and Lizzie's tense muscles eased when she saw the woman smiling back at her.

"H-Hi." Lizzie returned. She hadn't even seen anyone sitting on that porch when she'd walked past, but that was most likely because she'd been so focused on her misery. Lizzie focused on the woman for a moment, taking in the soft white hair that framed her wrinkling face and the ball of colorful string that she held in her lap. She looked like a nice woman, and for the first time all day she smiled.

When the woman waved at her, Lizzie waved back and turned to head back to the ugly old house that she hated to call her home.

She fell across her bed crying when she got home from school. Her mother tried to console her, but she just turned her head away and closed her eyes. When her father came home from work she felt the weight of his body as he sat on her mattress. For the first time since she'd come home, she rolled over.

"Why do you hate me so much, daddy?" His face went white with shock.

"What? Sweetie, I don't hate you. Why would you ever think that?"

She started crying, and he reached out a tentative hand to stroke her hair. She could feel the warmth of his hand as he held it over her and paused, trying to decide, she knew, if she would pull away when he tried to touch her. When she felt his hand finally settle on her shoulder she didn't jerk away. Instead she curled up in his lap and wrapped her arms around his neck.

"I hate it here, daddy. I miss home, and I miss all my friends. No one likes me here, and they say I have a funny accent."

"Oh, baby." He gently stroked her hair. "I know it's hard right now, but give it some time. Things will get better... they have to."

Lizzie sniffled and wiped a tear on her father's shirt. "Promise?"

"Promise. Now come on, mama's made dinner for us, and then after I thought we'd play a game or something." She sniffed and eyed him suspiciously.

"What kind of game?"

"Your favorite- any game you want, we'll play."

The smile she wore grew from a reluctant twitch at the edge of her lips into a small toothy grin that had her eyes sparkling again. When he reached out a hand to pull her off the bed, she took it and held on to it all the way to the dinner table.

## *Chapter Four*

The next day at school didn't go well either. In fact, as she thought back on it later she decided it had gone considerably worse than the first, though she wasn't quite sure how that was possible. For the next few weeks she dreaded waking up each morning and heading down the street to school. She knew when she got there she'd just be ridiculed and have the vegetable of the day thrown her direction at lunch.

It was awful being the biggest loser in school.

The only thing she had to look forward to each day was her walks home when she'd stop and talk for a minute to the sweet woman who sat on her porch, knitting in her rocker. Lizzie had discovered that her name was Mrs. Thornton, but the woman had told her to call her Granny because that's what all the kids in town called her.

She liked that. Granny. It was almost like instantly having connections in this small town, having roots to this place like she'd been here her whole life. Only she was still happy that she'd lived in Chicago because at least there the kids were nicer than they were here.

When she'd come home from school the first day and noticed that MC's start in the new town had gone almost as disastrously as hers, she'd hugged her younger sister and they'd cried together. It was horrible what they were going through, but inside Lizzie was almost relieved she had someone to go through it with her.

Her father told them that all the other kids were just jealous of them because they'd lived in a big city and had so many other "life experiences" as he liked to call them. She was pretty sure her father was full of malarkey, but if that's what he had to tell himself to feel better about bringing them all then she wasn't going to stop him.

Each night she and MC lay at the foot of either her or her sister's bed and they'd talk. It was usually about school and how awful they thought it was, but every now and then they'd change it up and talk about something new. That was another thing she looked forward to in her day: hanging out with her kid sister.

The only other thing that had come close to making her day nice was being able to watch from a distance that curious boy in the last row of her first period class. It turned out that he had several other classes with her as well, but his seat in the first class gave her the best opportunity to watch him unnoticed.

She'd learned from listening to the teachers call on him that his name was Payton. And she'd learned from watching how the other kids in school treated him that he was one of the untouchables: one of the most popular kids in school and way out of her stomping grounds. Not that she cared a lick about boys, anyway, but still it would be nice if the boy she'd noticed would at least notice her.

It was funny the things she noticed while she passed the time each day. She'd grown accustomed to people watching- observing the different personalities and groups of friends that made up this school- because, let's face it, she had no friends, and no one would talk to her unless it was to poke fun in her direction. But people watching she could do and she found she could learn a lot that way.

For instance, Lizzie had noticed that even though this Payton was the most popular kid in school he didn't necessarily act like it.

The popular kids were some of the cruelest kids in school, taunting the more lowly kids with their cruel jokes and humor. She'd watched because she knew how much it hurt, and she'd been surprised the first time she really noticed that Payton didn't join in with the others. He never did anything to stop them, but he never joined in their taunting and he didn't laugh when they did.

And she liked the way he actually gave the teachers his attention in class instead of rudely talking and passing notes back and forth like the majority of the popular kids did. He was more aloof than the others, but that didn't matter because everyone in school loved him for who he was and for the bright promise of athletic power he held inside of him.

She'd learned from listening to the boy-crazy girls in school that his father had been a big time quarterback for FSU during his college days, and that it was looking like Payton Cartwright was heading right down the path of his father's footsteps. And if his father was any indicator, he'd be just as gorgeous as the man as well. Lizzie wasn't too impressed by his looks quite yet, at least not like the other girls who kept saying odd things about his butt, but she sure was impressed by his personality.

But it didn't make any real difference she reminded herself. She was a nobody, and from the looks of things, she always would be. She doubted sincerely that Payton had ever even noticed the new girl in school, and she was pretty certain that he never would. The dark cloud that had been lingering over her for weeks seemed to be growing darker by the day.

After school that day, she went to the pasture behind their house that her father had recently taken upon himself to mow. It had become one her favorite spots to sit and finish her homework, or play with Skipper, or just think about things. Today as she lay on the fresh cut grass looking at the clouds above her, she could feel the hot trickle of tears begin to run down her face. Skipper whimpered beside her and tried to lick the tears away but she grabbed him up in a big bear hug and wouldn't let him go.

Nobody cared about her. No one in the school liked her. No one wanted to be her friend and she hated the feeling that she would go through her life without a friend to confide in. She had her family of course, but she wanted more. She wanted at least one someone to talk to each day while she had vegetables pegged at her during lunch.

The cold wall of ice slipped in while she was crying and it left her feeling numb and emotionless. It didn't matter what she did or how she acted, she was Lizzie the biggest loser in school, and nothing would change that. She resigned to the position that all the other kids wanted to put her in.

The only people in the school who did care were her teachers, she thought sadly. They actually smiled at her and encouraged her when she answered questions in class. And it felt so good to actually be smiled at by somebody. It hit her as she lay there, and she decided then and there that if getting attention by at least one being in school meant being the smartest in class, then by God that was what she would do. After all, it wasn't like she could be picked on any more than she already was for trying to be the class genius. What else could she possibly lose if she tried?


Payton Cartwright did indeed have his father's athletic genes. He'd started to show potential when he was five and playing in the little league sports games. And now that he was thirteen and in the eighth grade, his potential had grown even more. Payton's coaches had been so impressed by his abilities that they'd moved him up to the Junior Varsity football team- a team that was reserved normally for ninth and most of the tenth graders, and a few of the worst eleventh grade players as well.

But even though everyone knew, including Payton himself, that his talents were likely to grow even more, his mother had cautioned him frequently about the disadvantages of getting a big head, and the boy had taken it to heart.  He would never forget the day he turned seven and his mother had sat him down on the edge of his bed that afternoon and said, "Now, Payton, you listen and you listen good.  Nobody wants to be around a whiner, and nobody wants to be around somebody who's always bragging.  You've got a beautiful head on your shoulders and a lot of talent in your body.  That means you've got a big responsibility to live up to.  You make sure you use that handsome head and body in just the right way, and you'll always have friends to share in the good times with you."

He felt like he'd just received his induction into manhood and he had walked from that bedroom with a smile from ear to ear.  And ever since, he'd made sure that he did just what his mother had asked of him that day.

Right now, though, he was in the mood to play a little bit of some rough football.  Each day, JV football practice started during eighth period and carried on, usually, until the sun went down.  Payton was thinking about the new plays the coach had put together as he crossed the gym and headed toward the locker room.  He nearly made it to the door when he heard two girls from the PE class that was in session yelling at each other.  He turned to see what was happening.

A ring of girls formed around the two girls taunting each other in the middle, and Payton edged closer to see what the taunting was about.  As he closed in on the group, he realized it was Lou Ann Hendley doing most of the talking while another girl he couldn't clearly see edged around the opposite side on the center ring from Lou Ann, holding her hands up into clenched fists.  He remembered who she was the moment he heard her talk.

It was that new girl.  What was her name again?  He flipped through names in the back of his head until his mind settled on Lizzie.  He hadn't paid much attention to the girl since she'd shown up two weeks into school, but from what he did know he certainly didn't remember her ever looking as fierce as she did right then.

Lizzie's eyes- that Payton could clearly see were a brilliant emerald green all the way from where he stood- shown bright and fierce as they glittered with rage.  Her dark, curling mane of hair which she had obviously pulled back into a ponytail that day, was partially back and mostly tumbling wildly around her shoulders as if someone had intentionally tried to rip it out.  He watched as she clenched her fists even tighter, and didn't even realize it was because Lou Ann was picking at her until he heard Lou Ann say, "What's the matter Lizzie?  Can't deny the truth?"

"It is not!"  Her voice was thick with emotion that Payton suspected might blow out at any moment.

"It's the truth isn't it?  You're mama's so crazy that you had to move here to hide her from everyone."

And Payton felt his eyes nearly bulge from his head as he witnessed Lizzie in the next second land a blow so hard to Lou Ann's right eye that she should have been placed into the heavyweight boxing championships sheerly for her effort.  Only, he had no idea that such a fragile looking little girl could punch that hard.  Or as good as she had, he added, as he watched Lou Ann sink immediately to the ground.

He didn't try to stop the girl, but he watched her as she took off in the direction of the girl's locker room, apparently wasting no time in using the awkward silence that occurred as her exit cue.  He shook his head, still shocked that a girl could hit that hard, and headed off to the locker room as well.

He had already forgotten all about the cat fight when he strutted from the locker room fifteen minutes later and jogged across the gym to catch up with his buddies.

"Hey guys!  Wait up!"  He smiled the smile that already at his thirteen years of age was a lethal weapon in some circles of the female population at the school, a mouth full of barely crooked gleaming white teeth, and waved a lean arm in the direction of his friends.

Colin, Bud, and Hank paused where they were and let Payton catch up.  They exchanged the customary high five slap as he jogged past and took his spot in the lead of the group.  The four guys had been friends since before they ever knew how to walk, as their mama's liked to say, and that was something they planned to keep until their dying day.

Payton had always like his three best-friends, ever since he had known them, and he made it a point to keep them as close to his side as possible.  For some reason, the four of them were different.  They didn't find it quite so fun to laugh at someone else's expense as apparently everyone else in the school did.  And not that he was bragging, but he honestly felt like he and his friends had been taught a few manners by their parents.  Even at his young age, that went a long way in his book.

Payton looked around at his friends and smiled.

"Hey, Payton, did you hear about the fight that broke out in the gym while ago?"  Bud looked at his friend with such amusement on his face, as if he had such a great story to tell.

But that was old news to Payton. "Yeah. I saw it actually."

"Cool!" All three of the others yelled in unison.

"I heard it was Lou Ann and that fat chick from second period" Hank chimed in. Payton rolled his eyes.

"Come on. Lou Ann wouldn't have stood a chance against her."

"Well, you were there. Who was it?" Colin looked as annoyed at waiting for an answer as he always did.

"It was Lou Ann and the new girl."

"New Girl?"

"Yep."

"You're telling us that New Girl stood up to Lou Ann "the banshee" Hendley?"

Payton turned and curved his lips up at the edges. "Yep."

"Whoa." All the others stopped and stared at their ring leader in disbelief.

"Come on, boys. Would I lie to you? New Girl's got a fist on her that I'm betting would land any one of you flat on your back."

"Nuh-uh." Bud denied it. "Not me."

"It's the God's honest truth, boys. And believe me, Lou Ann's gonna have the black eye tomorrow to prove it. Speaking of which, I believe the coach promised to hand out a few black eyes of his own if any of us were late to practice again. Let's move." The leader had just offered his ultimatum, and the rest of the gang spent no time disagreeing.

Lizzie wiped the back of her hand across her eyes in a failed attempt to remove the evidence of her tears. She hadn't meant to hit Lou Ann, really she hadn't. It had all happened so fast; one minute she was standing there in the middle of the crowd, and the next thing she remembered she was running for her life, praying that Lou Ann didn't follow.

And now here she sat in hiding. Hopefully no one would spot her here behind the temporary bleachers set up by the football field. The school had placed them here, close to the end zone on the visitors side of the field about two weeks ago when they realized the overflow of fans wasn't going to thin out. She still couldn't grasp that football was such a big deal here. In Chicago only the NFL had been important, but here in this small Alabama town, high school football was an obsession, and its star players like gods.

Lizzie wished again that no one would spot her sitting there under the bleachers and decide that she looked like a good target for after school bully practice. She didn't think she could handle anymore humiliation just then. She still couldn't believe that she had actually punched Lou Ann, one of the untouchables, and definitely the meanest one in the bunch. She and Billy would make a good couple, she decided, and secretly she wished they would never realize that. The trouble those two could make if they teamed up could be disastrous for everyone, especially her.

A few more hot tears trickled down her cheeks and she wiped them away. Her father was going to murder her when he found out what she had done. If she thought her life was bad now, she really didn't want to see what her life was like when he got hold of her. Ed Benford had never been a violent man in his life, at least not that Lizzie had seen, but he sure could discipline with the best of them, and she hated the thought that he might decide to turn to violence today.

She watched the JV football team as they huddled in the center of the field. So far none of the players had noticed she was there, and she hoped it stayed that way. They were a little too far away to hear what was said, but she noted that all the players circled around the coach and watched him intently. A joint "Break!" went out, and she knew that practice was over.

Good. Only a few more minutes and the field would be all to herself. All the players eagerly grabbed their sweaty gear and headed to the locker room to shower before heading home.

Lizzie scanned the sea of players, wondering how these boys could possibly enjoy such a brutally aggressive and disgustingly macho sport. She supposed that was why guys played instead of girls- they had to prove they were strong enough to survive, whereas girls already knew they were. The ringleader of the sport popped out of the huddle just then, his dark hair matted to his head with sweat, his deep tan a little darker from the heat on his skin. She could envision his green eyes, and a little flutter of excitement rushed through her.

He jogged across the field with such ease that he looked like he had been born to be there, one with the grass and the ball, and the blazing lights. He was home there on that turf. She watched him as he tossed the ball to one of his friends then ran long to catch the pass his friend threw back. Payton laughed, she could hear it echo off the stadium and hit the metal bleachers she sat under. It was a good laugh, she decided, one that made her want to join in with him.

She watched him until he disappeared into the outside door of the locker room and then settled her gaze back on the football field, letting it serve as a backdrop to her unseeing eye, focusing her thoughts inward to the misery that awaited her when she got home. She knew her sister would be looking for her by now, but she didn't want to see her sister. MC would just remind her of how dead she was going to be when her father found out.


Meanwhile, in the locker room, Payton grabbed his football bag and backpack, said goodbye to his buddies, and exited the door to the fading fall sunshine. Some days he liked to go back out to the field after everyone left and practice his passes into the dummy net they had set up. Today he settled for sitting on the curb next to the stairs leading down to the field and enjoying the smells that lingered there. Stale popcorn from last week's game, fresh cut grass, and sweat were the main scents that hit him as he watched the evening begin to settle in over the field.

A subtle movement off to his right near the end zone caught his attention. For a minute he couldn't tell what it was, but then he spotted it. The new girl sat underneath the set of temporary bleachers. She sat with her knees pulled close up to her chest, her legs crossed at the ankles, her arms wrapped around her legs like they were the only things holding them on. She was rocking back and forth, her eyes closed, and if he wasn't mistaken she had tears streaming down her face.

His heart broke. He was only fourteen years old but already tears were his weakness. He hoped to the good Lord above that no one, especially no girls, ever found that out because he could only imagine the ways that information could be used to some wily female's advantage.

She looked so little and vulnerable, and something inside him made him want to go over and give her a hug. He could only imagine her reaction if he did, though. Especially after watching the way she had defended herself today. She'd probably reach out and slug him, and he couldn't afford to be beaten up by a girl no matter if he *was* the most popular boy in school. No boy, no matter how popular or athletic could afford to have that clouding his reputation.

Instead, he stayed where he was and watched her from a distance. She wiped at her tears, seeming to try and fight whatever it was that had upset her. *You're mama's so crazy that you had to move here to hide her from everyone.* Payton wondered if there wasn't some truth behind that statement that was hurting Lizzie more than she would ever let on. He suspected that was part of the reason behind the tears.

Something about her called out to him, begged him to protect her. Something in the way she sat there huddled like a little lost soul needing salvation more than a beggar needed food spoke to the heart his mama had always told him to use for good. He didn't know how to go about rescuing her, but he thought about it as he picked up his backpack and headed for home. He thought about it some more that evening as he tried to focus in on the television set in front of him.

*Chapter Five*

Since about the second week of school Lizzie had begun to focus on her schoolwork with a passion so burning that it made her father wonder if she wasn't using schoolwork to avoid other areas of her life. But tonight he found her so thoroughly wrapped up in her books that he suspected something fishy going on. He stood in the doorway and watched her work math problems in her notebook so hard that the lead of her pencil broke every few minutes.

Something smelled fishy all right, but he decided to let her sweat it out a little bit longer.

He was about to turn and leave when he heard the phone ring and he watched his oldest daughter jump so high in her seat that she nearly cracked her skull against the plaster ceiling.

Were they having tuna for dinner? Because he could smell fish from a mile away.

Ed Benford stepped into the central hallway of the house and lifted the phone from the receiver. He dragged the phone and its cord back to the doorway where he'd been propped and leaned a shoulder against the frame once again.

"Hello?" His daughter worked another math problem.

"Well good evening Principal Whiteside." The lead broke on her pencil.

"Oh, this *isn't* a social call. Well, what seems to be the problem then?" Lizzie's face reddened perceptibly.

"She did *what*?" She sank several inches in her chair.

"Oh, don't worry Principal Whiteside. I'll see that she and I talk about it right away." Lizzie gave up all pretense of studying and turned to face her father.

"Don't worry. She'll see you in your office tomorrow morning." Her eyes went round with shock.

Her father hung up the phone so gently that she knew he was furious. If only he knew, she thought miserably. But how could he ever understand?

He was back standing in her doorway before she even had time to prepare, or even to work up a few good alligator tears in her eyes. It wouldn't matter, though. Not with how angry he obviously was. She could always tell he was mad when his nostrils flared with each powerful breath he took.

"Mind telling me exactly what you did today?"

"I went to school, came home, and now I'm studying?" *Flare.*

"Wrong. Try again."

"I got an A- on a test?"

*Flare. Flare.* "I know you can do better than that, Lizzie."

"I know, and I talked to Mrs. Strickland and she said she'd give me some extra help after school if I need it."

*FLARE.* "Elizabeth Ann Benford." Uh-oh. "I'm going to ask you one more time, and you had better give me a straight answer." She swallowed hard. "What did you do today?"

"I'm sorry, daddy!" A single tear dripped down her face. "I didn't mean to, b-but she kept saying such a-awful things and it... it just happened before I could even think to s-stop it."

"Who was it that you punched, Lizzie?"

She sniffed and tried to make the tears stay away but she felt another one revolt and trickle down. Stupid tears. "Her name is Lou Ann Hendley, and she's one of the most popular girls in school, but I don't know why daddy, 'cause she's also the meanest."

Her father crossed his arms and stared at her blankly. "What did she say to you?"

"Nothing."

"Now, Lizzie. She must have said something for you to hit her. Otherwise you're in big trouble little miss."

She looked hopeful for a minute. "And I'm not if she said something really bad?"

"No, you're still in trouble either way, but I need to know what she said."

"I don't want to say."

"Lizzie."

"It's not that important." *Flare.* Okay, maybe it was that important. "Daddy, promise not to get mad if I tell you?"

She saw something flicker in his eyes and she wondered exactly what he was thinking. "Sure, honey. I promise."

Lizzie waited a minute, then two, before she glanced his direction and sighed. Another tear trickled down. "She said mommy was crazy and that we came here so we could hide her from everyone. She also said that I was already turning out just like her."

*Flare, flare.* She knew he was *really* mad when he clenched his jaw and folded his hands into fists. He crossed the room and opened a fist to hold out his hand to her. "Come here, baby." He caught her up in his arms. "I love you, sweetheart. You did well today. Thanks for trying to protect your mama."

Lizzie let out a muffled sob. "You're not mad at me, daddy?"

"No, sugar, I'm not mad at you. But Mrs. Hendley is a different story, however. She wants full payback for her precious daughter having the first black eye of her life. And two weeks before the Harold County eighth grade beauty pageant at that." She laughed at the way he made it all sound so trivial.

"Then you're not going to ground me for life?"

"Look at me, Lizzie." He waited until she did. "I love you, and your mama loves you, too. We're family and family sticks up for each other, even when the times are hard. *Especially* when the times are hard. You're mama isn't feeling well right now, and she needs someone to stick up for her. I'm proud of how you stood up for your family today. But..." He made sure she was listening. "Let's not make a habit of this punching thing, deal?"

She giggled. "Deal."

"Good. Now tomorrow morning I'm going to go have a word with your principal and get all this straightened out."

"No detention, either?"

"Well... I can't guarantee, but I'll try. Now come on, mama's made mashed potatoes and turkey and dressing. I think she's really starting to like this country living thing."

She'd been trying so hard to figure a way out of her troubles that she'd been too nauseous to eat. But now, her stomach gave a big rumble and she felt like she could eat all her mother had prepared all by herself.

Mary Catherine, the little eaves dropper, had apparently heard every word of their conversation because as Lizzie entered the room, MC gave her a big wink and a thumbs up. They both giggled together for the rest of the meal.

Later that night they sat together on the new wicker swing their mother had painted white and hung on the porch the previous week. Skipper lay between them and snored his little Bichon snores. They licked their cherry-vanilla ice cream cones and let their bare feat rub across the smooth wooden floor that had been lacquered over by their father. The wind that had started to blow cooler in the past few days rustled the leaves on the nearby trees that were starting to turn yellow with fall.

"Did you really punch her right in the eye?" MC asked in awed wonder.

"Yeah. But she was asking for it." She knew she sounded a lot tougher than she had felt at the time, but she would never forget the rush of adrenaline she had felt after that punch. She hoped she never had to feel anything that gut wrenching again.

"I hope she squealed like a little baby."

"I think she did, but I wasn't sticking around to find out." They both giggled at that and licked their cones.

Just before she faded off to sleep that night she remembered a figure standing off in the distance as she'd run away from the fight. She couldn't remember who it was until she sat upright in bed, soaked with a cold sweat, at three o'clock the morning. It had been Payton Cartwright.

Had it really been him standing off to the side of the crowd watching what had happened between her and Lou Ann? Had he heard what Lou Ann- the most popular girl in school, and no doubt one of his good friends- what she had said to her? Had he seen what Lizzie did in return? She was mortified. It was bad enough that she had to be the bottom of the barrel of all the kids in school, but she now had to face the fact that she'd just made absolute enemies with all the popular ones.

What must Payton think of her? Who was she kidding? He probably wasn't thinking anything about her. He was probably too busy consoling Lou Ann about how wicked her attacker had been to think a thing about her.

She wasn't positive but she assumed this was what it felt like to die.

## Chapter Six

"I think I'm too sick to go to school today, mama." Lizzie coughed pitifully into her hand to try and play up her sick routine. Her mother wasn't impressed.

"Oh, no. This is awful, Lizzie. Hold on, I'm gonna go get the thermometer and check your temperature." Lizzie lay in bed and moaned to kick the act into high gear. She thought she heard her mother laugh as she left the bedroom but when she returned she seemed more worried than happy.

"Okay, sweetie. Open up." Her mother gently placed the thermometer in her mouth and ran a slender, soothing hand over Lizzie's wild morning hair. "I'll back in a few minutes to check on you."

Lizzie waited until her mother left the room and quickly took the thermometer from her mouth to hold it up to the light. When she heard footsteps in the hall she quickly put it back and moaned softly.

"Let's check the temp. Open up." Lizzie did as asked.

Her mother made a big show of checking the temperature then made a sorrowful face and said, "Sorry, pumpkin. I might believe a 102 or 103 temperature, but 112 is not going to cut it. Guess you'll have to go to school and face the music, anyway."

Lizzie pouted while her mother kissed her check, then dramatically flung her body out of bed and stomped toward the shower. It was going to be the worst day in recorded history.

She dressed in what she felt was an appropriately fitting all black outfit, but was vetoed as she sat down to breakfast. So, she wrapped a striped shirt around her waist to appease the fashion gods, then pulled her backpack over her shoulders and set out to school.

"Hey, wait up, charger!" She knew it wasn't any of the school kids calling out to her, and it sounded too much like her father to be anyone else. She turned and waited for him, not quite old enough yet to believe that it wasn't cool to walk with your parents to school. Besides, walking with her father was the least of her worries at the moment.

They walked in silence, her thoughts deeply embedded in exactly how horrible detention would be since she'd never had to experience it before, his thoughts occupied on exactly how far he could tell Mrs. Hendley to shove it without being outright rude.

Not far, he presumed.

Lizzie found herself sitting ramrod straight in the chair outside of the principal's office some forty minutes later, twiddling her thumbs and wishing desperately that she couldn't hear the shouting going on behind the closed door. She could distinctly hear her father's voice, which was raised and much more harsh than usual, and another prim female voice that she could only assume was Mrs. Hendley. Every once in a while she'd hear an intervening male voice that had to be Principal Whiteside. No other man could quiet a room full of children, or adults for that matter, like Principal Whiteside.

She'd just heard the first four letter expletive float through the crack under the door, when the main door to the front office pushed open. She felt her cheeks flush then flare with heat when a pair of green eyes scanned the room then came to rest solidly on her. The same little jolt and vibration of electricity ran through her that she'd felt the first day of school, and she barely had time to register the feeling before those eyes ripped away from hers.

What the heck was the matter with her? She couldn't seem to put a finger on the feelings that had started creeping through her recently, but those feelings seemed to run rampant when a particular green eyed boy was in the room.

Boys. Boys were so stupid. She had no idea why God created them, but she knew He must have done it for some good reason because there sure were plenty of them around.

She tried to focus on what was going on behind the principal's door, but her eyes kept flicking over to check out what Payton was doing. She heard a particularly loud expletive float from the office and winced perceptibly. She blushed involuntarily because it had been her father that had been using the bad words that time around. She didn't miss the fact that the secretary stifled a quick laugh and then went about typing again on the typewriter.

Whatever Payton had been doing in the office, he seemed to be finished with his mission. He turned to walk to the door of the office, and she awkwardly followed his movements with her eyes. She liked the way he walked: all confidence, but not cockiness. It fit his personality well, she decided.

She tried to figure out what it was that the boy-crazy girls found so fascinating about boy's butts, and had her head cocked sideways staring when she noticed that he'd stopped walking. Her gaze moved up his still boyish body and stopped when her eyes met his once again. This time she knew her face turned flame red.

Payton's mouth twitched a little at the corners and he watched her for a second more, and then he was gone, through the door, and out of her view.

She had no idea what had just happened.

Lizzie realized that there had been silence in the principal's office for a full two minutes, and she waited on the edge of her seat, like a criminal waits in the parole office to hear the ruling. Her father was the first out of the room, followed by a prissy Mrs. Henderson who looked down her pointed nose at Lizzie with utter disgust. Lou Ann was next, and Lizzie cheered inwardly when she saw the swollen black eye that she had caused. The last one out was Principal Whiteside who looked down at her solemnly and said, "Lizzie, I'd like to see you and your father in my office now."

She wanted to cry, but she felt a little stronger when her father took hold of her shoulder and whispered, "Its gonna be okay, sweetie. We're just going to talk for a few minutes."

Yeah. Talk about the end of her life.


Payton couldn't quite figure it out. There was something about the new girl that piqued his curiosity, yet he couldn't quite put a finger on it. He couldn't begin to explain it, but something, some power totally beyond him, was driving him, forcing him to dig deeper into the question of who exactly was Lizzie Benford. Maybe it was the fact that she was new and he had yet to learn anything about her.

He supposed that could be the answer. More likely, though, was that her innocent look didn't quite fit on the body of a misfit. He barely knew anything about her, but he knew after watching the way she fought yesterday she sure was a tough one to beat down. And yet, if he hadn't seen it with his own eyes, he would have sworn that skinny body, and those curious green eyes were meant for nothing more than studying books all day in a library.

He'd been so curious to know what had been the fate of her well-rumored meeting with the principal that he'd had to make up an excuse to get Mrs. Strickland to let him out of class.

She'd looked sort of cute- well, he'd classify her more as a curiosity- sitting there looking like a scared Halloween cat, dressed in all black with her black, curly hair flowing past her shoulders. He had to admit, he kind of liked her style in clothing. It wasn't the same old stuff that all the other girls chose to wear. No, she did her own thing, and for that he had to give her at least a little respect.

What a pity it was that she hadn't even been given a chance. Why was that, he wondered? He had barely begun considering the reasons when he heard his name being called from down the hall.

"Hey, Payton." He turned and waved as Sam Ellis, a ninth grader, strutted down the hall.

"Hey, Sam. What're you doing out of class?"

"Skipping, like you should be doing." Payton just laughed.

"And have Mrs. Strickland get a shot at punishing me for it? I don't think so." It was Sam's turn to laugh.

"That's cool, man. Hey, did you see Lou Ann yet today?"

"Yep. Saw her on my way in to class this morning. She looked pretty rough. I'll say one thing for the new girl- she's got a solid right hook."

"Looks like it. I hear Lou Ann's planning something big time to pay back the new girl." Payton had never been one to join in the fun, but he'd also never been one to stop it. Somehow, though, he didn't think he liked the sound of that. Lou Ann could be one difficult Queen Bee to recon with when she set her mind up for revenge. Her nickname wasn't "the Banshee" for nothing.

"Listen, I'll catch you later. I've got to get back before old Strick finds out I've been gone too long."

"Yeah. See you in practice." They slapped high five and went their separate ways.

He turned the corner and nearly ran smack into Leena McLain, the hottest girl in the ninth grade.

"Hi, Leena." He tried to make his voice sound confident, but he was sure it sounded like a hormonal eighth grade boys.

"Oh, hi Payton." She sipped slowly from the water fountain, making him drool over her wet lips. "See you later, Payton." She smiled and batted her eyes, then slowly sauntered away, swishing her hips delicately from side to side just for him.

He nearly passed out from the sight. He hadn't had a care in the world about the insignificant opposite sex of women until recently. It seemed to hit him over the summer, when he'd gone swimming at the local pool with Bud, Hank, and Colin. Lou Ann and some of her friends had been swimming nearby and out of nowhere, *wham*, he'd noticed something fascinating filling out the top portion of their swimsuits.

He, of course, chalked it up to some minor summer illness, but the next day, and the next after that he'd grown consistently more fascinated with the large mounds of flesh barely exposed by those strapless bikinis the girl's chose to wear. He decided he wouldn't go to the pool for a week and see if that helped his predicament any.

It didn't.

He'd finally broken down and confessed his terminal illness to his father one night after his mother had gone to bed. He didn't want to depress her with the news of his ailment. He could remember quite vividly how hard his father had tried not to laugh, but had broken down anyway because of the serious, somber look his son was giving him as he broke the news. Payton wasn't laughing. His father had tears in his eyes.

Payton had nearly jumped through the roof with joy when his father explained the real situation to him.

And when he'd arrived at school the first day of eighth grade, he'd look at the girls in a whole new light. One girl in particular was the hottie ninth grader Leena McLain. Man, would he like to get his hands on her.

But thinking about her wasn't doing anything good for keeping his hormones under control, so he switched to thinking about football and all he enjoyed about the game as he made his way back to his seat at the other end of Mrs. Strickland's room.

Since it was Friday and this would be the fifth game of the season, the older boys had promised Payton and his buddies that they could come along to the post-game party at one of the ninth grade boy's barn. If they won, of course. But that didn't concern Payton too much, considering that both the JV and Varsity teams were the number one ranked team in the tri-county area, and had been for the past five years. He didn't for-see his team's reputation going too far down hill- not since they were playing Valley View High, the last ranked team in the area.

As he changed classes he waved at his buddies, and at a few of the eighth grade girls that weren't too shy to talk to boys, but his thoughts remained on the game and the post-game party. Coach had promised him the position of starting quarterback the first half of the JV game, and Payton was beside himself with nervous energy.

"Hey, QB," Colin called from across the flow of teenage traffic moving along the halls.

"What's up, wing man?" Payton flashed his buddy a quick grin and they slapped high five across the crowd.

"Ready for the game tonight?"

"As I'll ever be."

"Good, 'cause you look like you've got ants in your pants. And I don't think I need to remind you that Leena will be there tonight."

"Yeah." They'd already thoroughly discussed the rewards the ninth grade girls handed out to their favorite quarterback stars.

"Well, just remember, win tonight and you'll officially be a god around this place."

"Wait. I thought I already was?" Colin laughed as he walked away, because even though they both knew it was the truth, Payton never took it to heart. Maybe that was why he loved him like a brother even more every day.

## *Chapter Seven*

"Are you going to the game tonight?" Faith peeled apples and sliced them into eighths over the sink, then handed them one by one to her two daughters as an afternoon snack.

"I don't think so."

"What? Why not? You've made excuses for all the other ones; I can't wait to hear the excuse for this one."

"We have a really big test coming up soon and I want to make sure I do really well on it."

Her mother turned and put a slender hand on her hips. Lizzie was happy to see that at least a little flesh had returned to what used to be purely bone. She took a large bite of apple.

"Uh-huh. And what day is the test on?"

"Next Friday."

"You haven't made less than an A- all year. Why don't you take your sister and go to the game tonight?" Faith watched the desperation fill her daughter's eyes, but she refused to back down. She knew how hard it was to make friends in a new town- she'd been dragged around as an Army brat the first eighteen years of her life- but hiding away in a room studying for the rest of her life wasn't going to help.

Lizzie could see that her mother wasn't taking no for an answer, so reluctantly she agreed. Mary Catherine couldn't have looked happier.

They filed in to the stadium with a wild mass of other students later that evening, and Lizzie tried to act like she wasn't impressed. The football team had been one of the worst teams around back in Chicago, and they'd had the budget to prove it. But here, in Edenville, the JV team got to play in the massive stadium where the Varsity team played on Saturday nights. Football was a way of life here in this small town, and it was obvious by the turnout for even the Junior Varsity game.

There were huge concrete stadium stands on either side of the field, and a large press box at the top of the home team's side of the stadium. Massive lights hovered on poles around the track that surrounded the field, and they were already lit and pumping out bright white light onto the field.

Lizzie grabbed on to her sister's hand as they made their way up into the seating, and she purposely selected a seat far away from the other students, and more into the area where all the parents sat to avoid any confrontation.  She knew very well that Lou Ann was looking for her chance to get revenge, and Lizzie certainly didn't want it to happen tonight.  She realized she couldn't avoid it forever, but this one evening she just wanted to sit in peace and enjoy life for a while.

All the prissy cheerleaders with their petite little bodies and long perky hair pulled into ponytails on top of their heads, bounced out onto the field, and loud whoops of encouragement poured out from the fans.  They carried big banners with them, and since Lizzie had never been to a game like this before she wondered what they would do with them.  Soon enough, though, she saw them anchor the banners underneath the goal post and the football team lined up behind.

It took her breath away when the team smashed through and destroyed the banners in a matter of seconds.  But, apparently that was what the cheerleaders had wanted because they ran in front of the team like crazed models on speed, doing somersaults and flips, and more gymnastics than Lizzie could name.

She felt a little spurt of wild jealousy and wondered where that had come from.

The first play of the game was a joke- Dixie Academy pushed through Valley View's line like they were pushing through Jell-O, and the receiver ran the pass all the way to the in-zone.  The crowd erupted into crazed applause.  The cheerleaders did their touchdown cheer, then seven push-ups- which Lizzie couldn't quite understand why they did that.  She also wondered what they did when the score got really high.

By the middle of the fourth quarter she was so into the game that she didn't even realize anymore she was standing up yelling like the rest of the fans, cheering her head off.  She'd even memorized a few of the cheers, and secretly decided to practice one or two when she was behind her closed and locked bedroom door that evening.

She might even be a good cheerleader if she put her mind to it.


Payton, good ole number sixteen, looked up as the offensive team broke from the huddle to see if he could spot Leena in the crowd.  Sure enough, he spotted her standing in the middle of the cool kid section wearing a pretty, light weight sweater that framed her body in such a way that she looked like a naughty little present all wrapped up just for him.  He saw her wave out to the field, but he didn't respond because he was supposed to be focusing on the game, not checking out who was in the stands.

But come on, the game was such a joke. Already Dixie had scored forty-nine points, and they had even let Valley View score a touchdown of their own out of sympathy. Even he could see that the cheerleaders were getting tired of doing push-ups by this point. If they did many more, they wouldn't be very much fun at the post-game party that night. And no winning football man wanted his cheerleaders tired.

Number Sixteen had almost finished scanning the stadium, when an unfamiliar sight caught his attention. Over near the section where all the parents sat he saw the new girl, and what looked to be a slightly smaller version of her. What struck him as interesting was the way she was wildly yelling out to the ballplayers, her hands cupped around her mouth, giving it all she had. He hadn't seen that much energy from her since the day she whooped Lou Ann's butt.

Good for her, he mused as he stepped in the line and prepared to call the hut-hut.

And then everything faded from his mind. He used all the skills that his father had passed on to him by both teaching and genetics, and all the noise faded away. It was just him and the ball, and the receiver who at the moment was taking his sweet time breaking free from Valley View's defense. But then, there he was, and Payton let the ball fly, soaring through the air as if he was really a pro player rather than an eighth grade second string quarterback.

He let the noise fade back in when the receiver crossed the goal line and the buzzer sounded the end of the game.

"Man, you sure did let that last one fly," Colin congratulated him just outside the party with a big slap on the back.

"Yeah. Better hope the Varsity coach wasn't there to see that one," one of the ninth grade boys chimed in. "If he sees any of those, he'll have you up playing Varsity before you even get in the door to ninth grade."

That was pretty much what Payton was hoping.

"Come on, sixteen. Everyone's waiting for the QB to get here so we can start the party." Sure enough, when sixteen walked in, the band, which was really just one of the guy's radios, started up, and the crowd let out a roar for the winning JV team. Payton could only wonder how impressive the party's would be once they were on Varsity.

He had just popped open a can of soda when, as if by magic, the crowd parted and Leena McLain stepped through the mass of people swirling around. She was still wearing that form fitting sweater, and a pair of khaki pants that practically begged him to rip them off. Seeing as how he had never in his life come even remotely close to ripping pants off a girl, he wasn't quite sure how to go about that. But, given the opportunity- and he felt like tonight might just be his golden one- he'd gladly give ripping pants off a go.

He felt the kick of his hormones as they shifted down to center just below his waist, so he settled back against the make-shift table to watch her as she came his way. He tried out the pose that he'd seen the male models make in all the magazines when they leaned back like they were bronzed gods. Apparently it worked, because she smiled at him, tucked a stray strand of hair behind her ear, then licked her soft, pouty lips and batted her eyes at him

He nearly died on the spot.

"Hi, Leena." He took a sip of his drink and pretended he didn't really want to figure out what was underneath that sweater.

"Hi, yourself, QB. That was some hell of a game."

Was her voice just a little too sexy for her own good, or what?

"So, you came, huh? I was too busy playing to notice."

"That's okay. You looked really good out there." An idea of sheer genius struck him and he smiled the smile he'd been practicing in the mirror for just such and occasion. He, apparently, was right on the money because when he said, "You know who else is looking good tonight?" and slipped his arm around her waist, she blushed and smiled that sweet innocent smile that still didn't hide the fact that she really wasn't.

No one noticed, or at least they did a good job of pretending not to, when the couple slipped to back of the barn and shimmied up the ladder leading to the hay loft above.

Lizzie lay in her bed and slammed her eyes shut. It wasn't as if she couldn't hear the radio blaring over in Brian Hauser's barn or anything. A single tear trickled down her cheek, and she wiped it quickly away. She buried her face in Skipper's white fur and let the dog lick away a few more of her unwanted tears. Dogs were always good to have around when your heart was breaking.

Why? Why did she have to be the one kid in school that no one would talk to, and insisted on picking on? If she ever got the chance to move back to Chicago she swore she would never pick on another geeky kid again. She'd even sign a blood oath if that meant she might be released from this misery. It was so bad, she thought miserably, that it was almost as if being associated with her was like signing up to participate in a swim across a toxic waste dump.

Come on, she couldn't be that bad, could she?

She'd just been labeled wrong that was all. She did her own thing, and lived her own way, just like that Payton. But instead of people falling all over her like they did with him, they fled the opposite direction. And she was getting sick of it.

She made up her mind right then, as she wiped away the latest tear that had fallen, that no longer would she worry about what anyone said. She didn't care anymore if people tossed green beans into her backpack, or wrote nasty messages on her locker. She was immune to it and that was final. From this moment forward she would hold her head high and give anyone who tried to tear her down the hell that they deserved.

She flopped a hand over her eyes and tried to fall asleep, but couldn't. So, she plugged her ears with her fingers and thought about all the things she had started to like about living here in Edenville. For one, her parents had almost finished fixing up the house, and she was amazed at what a little paint and some lacquer on the hard wood floors could accomplish. Her mother, thank God, was on the brink of returning to her old happy, loving, healthy self, and Lizzie could hardly wait till she was at one hundred percent. She supposed that a large part of it had been because they moved here, so she felt another lick of resentment toward the town fading away.

What else did she like? Well, she supposed being in the middle of so much nature had its advantages. She liked the way the crickets would lull her to sleep at night with their soft serenade through her open bedroom window- which was much more than she could say for the racket the football team was making over at the Hauser's place. And she would never forget the day she'd walked out to the back pasture and seen a cow- a real, live cow! - standing in the middle. She'd gone running into the house, her eyes wide with surprise and her father had chuckled. It was the neighbor's he explained, and yes, she could touch it if she wanted. It was a little too big and intimidating for her, but watching it had been kind of nice.

There were more things than she had expected, she realized, as she rolled in her bed and tried to drown the bass from the radio bouncing through her bedroom.  Like the fact that she could always count on Grannie to be sitting on her porch every afternoon when she walked home from class.  And that the bells at the top of the church steeple always played short hymns every Sunday morning, as if calling all of Edenville to praise the precious Lord.

The music once again pulled her from her thinking so she rolled out of her simple single bed and snuck across the room, hoping none of the floorboards would creak.  She knelt down in front of the moonlight and tried to see what was happening over at her next-door neighbor's barn, but she couldn't see anything through the distance.

She remembered that her father kept a pair of binoculars stashed in the big oak desk in the hallway, so she crept to the desk and snuck the pair out.  A quick glance over her shoulder told her no one was awake, so she tip-toed back into the room and knelt back at the window.

She had just finished adjusting the binoculars to her vision when she spotted the crowd going into and out of the barn.  Just as she'd suspected- all the football team, the cheerleaders, and who else but the most popular gang in school.  One day, she vowed, one day she too would be one of the lucky ones who got their chance to hang out in a barn with all the coolest people in school.

## *Chapter Eight*

Today was the last day of Lizzie's first year at Dixie Academy and it really stunk. Big time. Here she sat, on her birthday no less, reading a book in detention. Again. If only she could be on time to school every once in a while, she admonished herself. It was only a five minute walk from her house to the school, for crying out loud, but still she couldn't be on time to save her life. Her father had offered a million bribes, and even threatened a time or two to try and get her there on time.

She supposed it was just her way of rebelling.

Lizzie licked her finger and flipped the page of her current favorite sci-fi novel, when the door opened to the vacant classroom the school used to hold detention after school.

Oh, great, she thought with a little disconsolate sigh. Here comes "the gang", as she had not so affectionately termed the popular kids. She had done pretty well the past few months at ignoring their repeated attempts to bug her. Just be strong, she commanded herself as she ducked her head back behind the pages of the book, just missing the last person to enter the room and shut the door quietly behind him.

It took quite a while- much longer than Lizzie thought necessary- for the gang to readjust the desks to their liking and get seated to start their detention time. She felt it quite revolting that the detention teacher barked at her every time she turned a page, yet she didn't say a word as the gang noisily slid the desks from one side of the room to another.

Was there any justice in the world?

Apparently not, because as soon as the gang got settled, Mrs. Fleming left the room to go check on something down the hall. The gang wasted no time in using her absence to their advantage.

She could hear whispering among the clustered desks, but she refused to look up from her book. Be strong, Lizzie, be strong. Then there were giggles, and she itched to see what it was they found so funny. When Billy, the male equivalent of Lou Ann in character and rudeness, burped as loud as he could, Lizzie felt absolutely like begging to spend the rest of her summer scraping gum off the bottom of desks rather than remain in the room with these people.

Finally, since she saw no reason to hold back her scorn, considering everyone in the school hated her anyway, she looked up from the book and gave her most insulted glare in their direction. As it turned out, that was exactly all the prompting they needed.

Billy- later she termed him Billy-bob because it helped her to imagine a more backwoods, redneck kind of guy- burped even louder, and the gang was fit to be tied. The only one in the group, who didn't seem to find it quite as funny as the rest was Payton, even though he was at least smiling. Since, as yet, Lizzie hadn't realized he was in the room; she quickly pulled the book back up in front of her face and pretended she was deeply focused on the novel.

"Hey, New Girl."

She ignored the taunt, but she could feel the little twitch she got in her eye when she was beginning to get mad start kicking in to overdrive.

"I said, Hey, New Girl."

"My name's not New Girl." She said it through clenched teeth still buried behind the book.

"Oh, somebody's a tough girl." *Oh, somebody wants a black eye.* She put the book a fraction lower and glared at Billy over the upper edge.

"Hey, man, I'd watch out if I were you. She's got something funky going on with her eye." Colin wasn't interested in watching his friend get beat by a girl.

"Yeah, Billy," chimed in Lou Ann. "I'd hate for you to be the next on her list of black eye recipients."

"Why? I'd just send in your mama to take care of it," Billy shot back.

"Ouch!" The entire gang cried out in unison. The only one who seemed to be taking part as spectator rather than participant was Payton. He was more focused on playing kissy-face with his girlfriend, Leena, to really worry about the rest of the gang, Lizzie thought with an edge of depression settling over her heart.

Not that it mattered to her in the slightest. Nope. She could care less about boys, particularly the ones who did disgusting things with their mouths like what Payton was currently doing. Yuck- how could anyone enjoy that? But, apparently the two of them found it pretty interesting.

And thank the dear Lord above, about that time the detention teacher came back in, and the gang was quiet the rest of the hour. It was blessed relief when their time was up and she could pretend to finish reading the last part of the chapter, then quietly slip out long after all the rest of the gang had split school for the summer. She'd even heard one last disgusting burp from Billy-*bob* on his way down the hall.

Over the summer, Lizzie had grown accustomed to the laid back lifestyle of the South. She had a strong hunch that the reason people in small towns in the South were so laid back was because it was so blasted hot and humid *all the time*. That was another bit of information she'd just keep to herself.

Her favorite part of each day was pulling a Popsicle out of the freezer and following Skipper down to the cattle pond behind Grannie Thornton's house. The pond was actually owned by Grannie, but anyone that wanted to could use her pond anytime. Everyone called it a cattle pond, but it hadn't really been used to water cattle since Grannie got rid of her last herd five years ago. She complained that they made too much noise for her, but Lizzie suspected it was mainly because they reminded her too much of her late husband, Earl.

Lizzie didn't really have any fond desire for the pond so much, but she liked the old hardwood trees that surrounded it. She'd take a good book with her, and she'd climb up onto one of those strong branches, and read for hours. Yes, these were the times that made her realize she was beginning to like Edenville very much- there weren't many opportunities to sit in old trees by a cattle pond in Chicago.

She loved dangling her legs down from the limb and leaning back against the big, sturdy trunk as she read her favorite novel. She had come to understand that a good book could take her places that she had never seen before, and it certainly helped her to forget about her lack of friends.

It was as she was sitting there, way up in the branches of an oak tree, that she saw the bushes rustle along the edge of the overgrown path that led down to the pond. Skipper hadn't come with her to the pond that day because he'd been too fascinated with the baby goats at the neighbor's farm to notice she'd left without him. Lizzie was curious to see what was rustling in the bushes.

About that time she heard voices, male voices, and she froze where she sat, praying she might go unnoticed. And wasn't it just her luck? Payton and his sidekicks Colin, Bud, and Hank following after him, had come to the pond for a little afternoon swim. Lizzie could feel her blood freezing in her veins.

What would she do if they found her sitting in the trees above them? Would they think she had been spying on them? A million horrors and an equal number of rationalizations flooded through her mind, but nothing seemed to help her absolute misery at the moment. She wished she had her own magic rubbing lamp to get her out of this mess.

She resigned to the fact that there was nothing she could do at this point, but sit still and pray like crazy that the boys never noticed she was there. It might be kind of fun, she heard her brain say, being a fly on the wall so to speak. Lizzie seriously doubted anything about this ordeal would be fun.

Payton had stripped down to his swimming trunks and was into the pond quick as a flash. He swam a few strokes across the pond, and then waited for his friends to join him.

"Come on in, boys! The water's fine."

"Yeah, yeah. We're coming. We're not as skilled at removing our clothes as some people apparently are." A pointed stare was cast in Payton's direction, and he let loose a carefree childish laugh with a grin as wide as the Grand Canyon.

"You guys need to get some action more often."

Lizzie thought she might die.

"By the way, Payton, you promised to fill us in on the details with Leena." Payton ducked under the water and Lizzie could feel her face turning red. She *really* hoped the boys didn't see her now.

"Now, now, boys. A man doesn't kiss and tell."

By this time the other three had joined him in the pond, and they slam dunked his head under the water for that one.

"Come on, Payton, you promised. Apparently she's been spreading the word with the ninth grade girls that our friend here has the moves of a god." Payton liked that one.

"Well, what can I say? Not only am I talented at football, but I'm talented in all of life's athletic endeavors." Oh, please. How pig headed could a guy be? Lizzie had been holding on to the limb where she sat, trying her hardest not to die of mortification, but she felt her arms nearly slip and her body almost slide from the limb with that comment. Her heart was slamming into her ribs. Was she really hearing this conversation? Oh, the boys would really have her head if they found this out.

"At least give us a few pointers then," Colin wailed.

"Yeah." Bud and Hank barked in unison.

Payton studied them as if they were sick. "Okay men," he said after a slight pause. His voice got a little lower. "Gather 'round. Now, what you need to do is ..." Lizzie leaned forward, aching to hear what it was they needed to do, wanting desperately to know for herself, even though she promised herself she really didn't.

"Oh, man! That is so cool!" *What was so cool? What?*

"And you did that to Leena?" She could tell by his affirming nod that he had indeed done *that* to Leena. "And she liked it?"

"Well, she said I had the moves of a god, didn't she?" Lizzie giggled, slapping a hand over her mouth. Had they heard that?

"What was that?" All the boys stopped talking and looked around. Fortunately for her, they never looked up in the trees. "Must not have been anything. Alright, now that that's out of the way, what d'ya say about a game of touch football."

"You're on!" All four boys were out of the water, their sleek, not quite yet developed bodies glistening in the summer sunshine. Lizzie breathed deeply when they had gone and tried to get her heart beat under control.

What was the matter with her? Ever since that first, awful day of school, when she'd locked eyes with Payton, she been having these weird sensations floating around in her body. She hadn't yet put a finger on what was happening inside her, but whatever it was she didn't think she really liked it.

She climbed down from the tree and sat against the base of the trunk. These... feelings. They really kicked into gear whenever Payton was around. Now why was that, she mused. It was probably because he was the only one in the "gang" that hadn't bothered to chastise her in some form or fashion. Sure, that was it, definitely.

It was absolutely not because she thought his green eyes matched hers perfectly. Wouldn't they look good in pictures together? And it certainly wasn't because she thought the way he smiled at all the other girls in the school was just a smidgen too cute.

Wait a second. Her hand flew to her lips as she sucked in a ragged breath. Did she... could she... was it really possible that she.... *No!* She jumped up from her perch and took off running for home. She refused to believe that she had a crush on Payton.

This was awful.

It was just like her, wasn't it, to pick a guy who was *way* out of her ballpark. He probably didn't even know her name, so how did she expect for him to ever return the crush? He wouldn't of course. Sure, he was blatantly nicer than all the rest of his cohorts, but that didn't mean he would humor some silly little crush from the lowest kid in school. She could already see it now… Mr. I'm-already-a-stud-athlete laughing until he was blue in the face when she professed her crush on him.

That would not do at all.

That was it, and final. She'd just have to figure out some way so change her mind. That was easy, wasn't it? Sure it was. First of all, she didn't like boys anyway, so getting rid of a crush on a boy would be a piece of cake. Now all she had to do was figure out how.

Payton slapped the baseball into the glove on his hand, then picked it up and tossed it against the wall of his house. He knew it was probably making his mother mad, but he was bored, and he had nothing else to do. He bounced the ball off the wood siding again, and winced when he heard his mother smacking the window in the kitchen with a spatula to get his attention. He hated that because it always meant he was about five minutes away from a good ear boxing.

He scowled up at the kitchen window and stuck his tongue out at his mother after she turned away from the window. Since tossing his baseball was out of the question for a while, he tossed his glove on the ground, and lay beside it in the grass to catch some sun.

He stared up at the clear blue sky above, and closed his eyes, enjoying the warmth on his skin. Summers were fun, he supposed, because he could be alone for a while and just think about life for a change. He was more of a loner, he'd figured out in the past year. He liked going to parties and spending time with his friends, but he also enjoyed just spending time by himself, not doing anything really important. It gave him time to recharge.

Not that he didn't love being in school. But when he was in school he was constantly being bombarded with stuff to do with his friends. His friends were great, he thought, and for some reason that got him thinking about all the kids in the world who weren't lucky enough to have good friends like his. Or any at all, for that matter.

A pair of green eyes flashed through his mind, and he thought about Lizzie for a minute. He never had figured out why no one would give her a chance. She wasn't completely ugly, he decided as he brought up a picture of her in his memory. But she definitely didn't have all the curves and flares like Leena had, either.

To be honest, he felt sort of sorry for her because of how the entire school treated her. She didn't deserve- no one deserved- to have people call her names all day, or for the girls to pick on her during PE class. And he really hated the wall they threw spit balls at her during the pep rallies. That was just cruel.

He always had had a soft heart for people that were hurting. Maybe to some people that made him vulnerable or wimpy, but in his mind he didn't think so. He felt it made him stronger because he could be compassionate to those in need. There was nothing worse than a jock that treats people bad, his mother used to say. Maybe that was why he felt so strongly about treating everyone nice.

Regardless though, he thought, he certainly hadn't been doing anything to help stop the way his friends had been treating the new girl. He had always hated seeing the look of disgust in her eyes when his friends taunted her. It was just as bad that he let them do it as if he had joined in with them. And he knew that all he had to do was say the words and they would stop forever.

So what was he waiting for, he wondered? He wasn't quite sure.

## *Chapter Nine*

It was time to start school again, already, and Lizzie couldn't believe it was actually time for her to start ninth grade. She'd begged her mother to take her shopping in Clarkston, the "big city"- an actual city with a shopping mall about an hour away from where they lived. So now she stood in front of her mirror inspecting the way her pretty fall skirt swirled around her knees. It was one that she was assured was in the height of fashion. And she had to admit that the blouse she bought to go with it accented the tiny bud of breasts that she kept praying would spring forth at any moment.

Almost all the other girls at school had already matured into their more womanly figures, as her mother liked to call it, but little Lizzie's body had been quiet as a mouse. It was utterly humiliating to know that here she stood on the brink of her first day of ninth grade, and she still had to stuff her bra when the other girls filled theirs out with their own bodies.

She consoled herself with knowing that she had at least three new outfits that she was sure would make all the other girls die from envy. If she couldn't fit in with the rest of the school, at least she could be more fashionable. But fashionable or not, she was still itching to be accepted by at least a few people at Dixie. Today was her new chance. Today was the day that she'd show up for school, and instead of being the brunt of everyone's mockery, maybe today she could just sink into the woodwork, and go unnoticed for a while.

Yes, she was at the point where even going unnoticed was a heck of a lot better than being made fun of all the time. That would mean they would have forgotten about her, and when she was out of mind then she didn't get nearly as many spit balls thrown at her.

Lizzie took her image in one more time in the mirror, smiled at herself to make sure she had the smile she'd been working on all summer just right, then slipped into her backpack and headed out the door.

"Wait a minute, honey," her mother called from down the hall. "Don't forget your lunch, and where is my kiss, baby girl? Are you too old for kisses now?"

"No, mama." Lizzie smiled and gave silent thanks that she finally had her old mom back. She was no longer skin and bones, and her skin had her healthy glow back like Lizzie had always remembered.

"Good luck at school today, sweetie. You're an official high school girl now. I never thought I'd see the day. Well, here's your lunch, now run on to school." Faith watched her as her daughter that was growing up far too fast strolled down the sidewalk. When she reached the end and was about to cross the road Faith called out, "You look beautiful today, honey."

Lizzie didn't turn around, but she heard her mother's call and she smiled. It was just what she needed to hear.

By the end of first period Lizzie looked around and blinked. It seemed, somehow, that her miracle plan had worked. She checked her backpack, then checked it again and found, sure enough, no signs of nasty notes or other foul play in that region. She felt her hair, three times, and felt no sign of spit balls that had whizzed in her direction. And, she mused with a half grin on her face as she strolled to her locker and exchanged a few books; no one had even poked a taunt in her face either.

No one had noticed her.

Lizzie wanted to jump for joy. If this kept up she just might be home free. She just might be able to forget about some of the awful reasons that she hated this school so much. She closed her locker then headed off to second period- Mrs. Fleming's ninth grade math. Math was her least favorite subject, but she promised herself that if she made her way through it and learned the material then she would reward herself by getting her mom to take her on another shopping spree.

All through second period, and third and fourth as well, her plan to go unnoticed succeeded wonderfully. No one even glanced in her direction, and she wondered if it was just some awful first year ritual that everyone had to go through when they were new to this place. When she got in the line for lunch, her brain was busy trying to comprehend the fact that she hadn't been picked on for an entire half day. She wasn't quite sure what to do when no one was. She must be having a lucky streak.

She picked her tray up off the edge of the counter where the cash register was and began to maneuver through the mass of moving bodies and their personal belongings. Her tray blocked her vision from one backpack in particular, and before she knew it she was lying face down with her face nose deep in her bowl of mashed potatoes.

So much for that streak of good luck.

She could hear people laughing and then her nickname started being chanted, first from the cool kid table, but it rapidly spread throughout the room. "Loser Lizzie. Loser Lizzie. Loser Lizzie." Over and over again. Couldn't she just disappear and die?

She was busy trying to collect the English peas that had rolled all over the place, and had finally collected the last one when a hand, a decidedly masculine hand, came into her line of vision. She recoiled from it, afraid that it was someone about to strike out at her or possibly rub some of the mashed potatoes she still had on her face into her hair as well. But the hand stayed outstretched, and she realized it was someone trying to help her up.

Since she was having a hard time trying to get a foothold on the slippery mashed potato floor, she grabbed hold without looking and let the person help her up.

"Than-" The rest came out in a squeak as she looked up for the first time and saw Payton Cartwright attached to the other end of that hand. She stood speechless, and she knew her face had turned a hideous shade of flame red from the roar of laughter that pulsed through the cafeteria again.

Payton took his hand back, and Lizzie realized with horror that she had been holding on to her crush's hand for a solid fifteen seconds. What a shame she couldn't remember what it felt like, she thought later. But at the time all she could remember thinking was that she would never wash that hand again as long as she lived.

He had smiled at her, she did remember that. And that smile had been like a burst of sunshine burning through everything bad that had happened to her minutes before. It was the same smile that he bestowed on other girls in the school, the one that made her eyes roll because he wasn't giving it to her, and because it made the other girls giggle and fall all over him like he was a male model.

And now she knew why they did that. One look at that smile- one which she knew from experience he must have practiced in the mirror at least a few hundred times- and her crush was solidified. How could she help it, really? Oh, she supposed she could, but what was the harm, seeing as he was so far out of her league and she already knew she had no chance whatsoever of winning him.

Instead of listening to that ugly nickname the school had bestowed upon her- Loser Lizzie was so stupid, wasn't it? - She thought about Payton Cartwright the rest of the day. He'd grown taller over the summer, and his hair that was normally a dark shade of brown, had bleached just a little and had cute little highlights all around. His body had grown thicker, and muscle was beginning to fill in where the little boy's body was giving way to a man's. But his eyes, his eyes were still the same brilliant shade of green, a hybrid of emeralds and lush green summer grass. She could look into those eyes all day, she imagined, if only she were given the chance.

Her walk home wasn't nearly as happy as her walk to school had been, but she waved at Grannie and said hello, and forced herself to remember how good she had looked in her outfit that day, regardless of whether she'd had to wear mashed potatoes on it or not.

Even her sister had said so when she joined her at the front steps of Dixie just after school that day. It was Mary Catherine's first day of seventh grade, and also her first day at Dixie. Lizzie was slightly jealous that she seemed to making friends, at least one or two, while Lizzie still didn't have any. But she loved her sister too much to be jealous for too long.

That afternoon Skipper and the two girls took beach towels and walked down the road to Granny's pond. They had to pass several hay fields along the way, and they spotted several of the kids from school standing in the center of one playing a game of baseball. They were too far away to hear much of what they were saying, but every once in a while both girls could hear the other kids laughing, and Lizzie felt her heart tug. She had loved playing baseball with her friends back in Chicago. Of course, there it hadn't been played in a hay field, but in the middle of the street when no cars were coming, but it was still something she missed like crazy.

If she had had more confidence, or at least known the other kids wouldn't laugh her out of the field, she would have considered asking them to play. But instead she took her sister's hand and they made their way through the rickety old fence that blocked the dirt drive down to the pond.

They skipped rocks for while; trying to see which one's rocks would skip the farthest. It made Lizzie feel good that she could at least win at that. When they tired, they took turns pushing the other in the old tire swing that hung at the edge of the water. Lizzie had seen some of the other kids use it to see who could hurl themselves the farthest out into the pond, but she liked it mainly because even though she'd never swung in a tire before, she found it comforting somehow.

They spent the rest of the afternoon catching up on life, filling in each other on their days while they lay on the towels stretched out in a sunny spot close to the pond. The squawk of a hawk caught their attention, and at dinner that night that was all they seemed to remember about their day: the magnificent wing span of the great bird and how elegantly it had dived with its talons out to capture some unsuspecting prey. Their parent's were quite impressed.

She liked thinking back on their visit to the pond that night as she lay in her bed. If she found nothing else while she spent her days in Edenville, at least she had found out there was a lot more to nature than what she had known when she left Chicago. Her father had taken her and Mary Catherine camping at the end of the summer, and they'd spent most of that long weekend hiking through the woods not too far from their home, identifying trees, and watching birds and other wildlife that sauntered into their view. That alone had opened Lizzie's eyes to the world outside of the continuous buzz of the big city, and what life was like in a calmer, quieter, more serene kind of setting.

As the days grew shorter, and time marched on toward Christmas, Lizzie found herself still the brunt of the majority of the jokes at school. But at least now her skin had grown so thick, and her mind so full of comebacks she would probably never use, that she didn't seem to mind the taunting so much.

She had made it her mission that when someone threw a barb at her she would focus on her comeback line instead of how much the comment hurt, and she found her feelings not getting hurt quite so much. She also focused on her wardrobe, and she was pleased with the sense of style she seemed to have developed. It wasn't exactly trendy, at least not like the exact replicas that everybody else wore to copy the gang. No, since she didn't have to worry about whether it made her look cool or not, she could wear whatever felt good to her.

She had just stepped out of first period, when she heard the buzzing going on around her. She tried to ignore the talking, afraid if she looked at any one person in particular that they might single her out for spitball target practice later on in lunch that day. Lizzie kept her head ducked, but her ears on full alert as she made her way to her locker, and was surprised at what she heard.

"Hey Lou Ann," Billy called across to the group of girls huddled near her locker. Lizzie didn't dare look that direction, but she knew Lou Ann must have looked his way because she heard Billy say, "Have you seen the new girl yet? She's almost as red headed as your mama."

Lizzie thought she was the only new girl in school, but since she obviously didn't have hair even remotely close to red she knew he couldn't have been talking about her. Was it true? Was there a new girl in school? Lizzie's mind raced with a million different thoughts, one of which was if she could possibly make friends with her.

She pondered about this new girl all through the next three periods until it was time for lunch. And when she walked in to the cafeteria with her bagged lunch, she saw exactly what she had feared.

The rest of the school was christening the new girl's backpack.

Slate McDermott, the biggest bully in all of Dixie Academy, and possibly all the schools surrounding it, held her backpack well above the short, pudgy, red headed girl's outstretched arms, and laughed as she jumped as high as she could, which unfortunately wasn't very high. A big double bowl full of applesauce was in his other hand, and Lizzie watched in horror as a single tear dripped down the red heads face. Oh, no! She should never have let them see her cry. She was a now goner for sure.

"Stop it! Stop it you big bully!" But Slate just kept right on laughing, his nasty brown, crooked teeth glittering under the fluorescent light, and when he poured the applesauce into her open backpack, Lizzie could have sworn she saw smoke puffing out from the new girl's ears. The red head reared back and slammed her fist into Slate's stomach then snatched her backpack from him as he doubled over howling in pain, and ran like mad to the other side of the lunchroom. Fortunately for her the teachers on duty came in right about then, because Slate didn't have a chance to make his payback in time.

But Lizzie saw the wicked gleam in his eye, and she knew that the red head better be on the lookout, because Slate was well known to hold a grudge, and he got his payback no matter how long it took to get. He was definitely the wrong guy to pick on the first day at a new school.

Lizzie sidled up next to the table where the new girl sat all alone and softly cleared her throat to let the girl know she was there. She hadn't expected the girl to whirl on her so quickly, or for the two fists that came up, ready to land a crushing blow to whoever or whatever was currently bothering her.

"H-Hi," Lizzie said softly, taking a small step back and out of the way of those obviously dangerous fists.

The red heads eyes glittered with a ferocity that Lizzie could only assume came with the practice of being on the low end of the totem pole for a long, long time. The girl slowly perused Lizzie's face, and she watched as the new girl's fists slowly uncurled and went back down by her sides. She never smiled, but the light of fire went out of her eyes, so Lizzie assumed she was fairly safe from harm.

"Hi," she said again, a little more confident this time. "My name is Lizzie. Lizzie Benford. I moved here about a year ago. Just thought I'd let you know you're not alone." Was the girl mute? Why hadn't she said anything? Lizzie felt uncomfortable being the social one in the group for a change, so she kept on talking to try and ease the discomfort she felt. "This is actually my table, but I'd be happy for you to sit here if you want."

The girl sat again, and Lizzie was tired of talking so she let her own backpack fall to the floor then took a seat on the opposite side of the table from the girl. She dug into her brown bag and pulled out the turkey sandwich her mother had packed for lunch.

"You know," she said after a while, "That Slate guy, he's not very friendly, and he holds big time grudges. I'd watch out for him if you ask me."

"No body asked you, and it wouldn't be the first time."

"Excuse me?"

The red head stared at her levelly, obviously not in the mood to put up with any more crap that day. "You heard me. I've had plenty of run-ins with the school bully. You just have to know how to handle 'em is all."

"Oh." How did you handle a bully, she wondered, without running and screaming and trying to hide?

"Just stick with me kid, and you'll be all right." Lizzie shook her head, and tried not to laugh. Was it that obvious? Was it written on her face that she had no friends and she'd been picked on way more times than she could possibly keep track of? Apparently so, because the red head poked out her hand and smiled blandly.

"I'm Grace. Grace Jacobs. Obviously I'm the new kid here. So, what's your story?"

Lizzie told her and when she asked the same, Grace had shrugged her shoulders and replied, "My mama died when I was three, and my daddy just got a job at the mill here in town. Hopefully he can hang on to his job long enough to let me make few friends, and maybe spend more than a few years in one place this time around."

Lizzie didn't miss that her baby blue eyes looked a little sad, or that she talked a lot tougher than Lizzie was willing to bet she felt.  She knew what it was like to have hard times, both in a family and in school. For the first time in months, Lizzie felt her heart give a happy tug.  At last, at last, at last, she had finally found someone to be her friend.

The two had been inseparable ever since.  Between classes they waited for the other, and when times were hard they stood up for one another.  They walked home, along with MC, every afternoon, and every Friday night they spent the night together.  It was almost as common to have three little girls at the dinner table around the Benford place as it was to have two.  But the Benford's welcomed little Grace with open arms.

One afternoon in particular, shortly after they had been let out for Christmas Break, Lizzie and Grace took a stroll down to town to buy a milkshake from the pharmacy store.  Lizzie liked the way the bar stools set up at the low counter in the front of the store would let you swivel back and forth, and Mr. Gilchrist, the old white haired man that ran the Pharmacy, always put a big cherry and lots of whipped cream on top of their milkshakes.  Grace said it was because he had a crush on them, but Lizzie just thought it was because he knew they needed the extra attention.

They were sitting on the stools, facing out the window, having a good time talking about life, when Lizzie stiffened and her gaze fixed out the window on something just on the opposite side of Main Street.  Grace followed her gaze and saw the group of boys leaning back against the wall of the brick front to the hardware store.  Grace recognized them from school, but she'd just passed them off as dumb jocks and hadn't given them a second thought.

"They mean something special to you?"  Grace watched as Lizzie turned a little pink, then looked down, apparently fascinated, by her milkshake.

"No."  But Grace could tell that they did.

"Oh, okay."  She sipped her shake through a straw, having to pause every few sips to get the clumps of ice cream out of the straw.  She'd glance out the window every few minutes just to see what the boys were doing.

"Have you, like, ever had a boyfriend, Grace?"

"No, boys are dumb.  All they do is burp and talk about sports."

"Oh, yeah.  Sure."  Grace smiled when Lizzie wasn't looking.

"Why?  You got a boy in mind for me?"

"No!"

"Well, then, what about for you?" Lizzie turned noticeably red.

"Liz, Liz, Liz. Seeing as I'm your best friend and all, I'm afraid I'm going to have to approve this relationship. And, I'm going to tell you this for your benefit- if you don't learn how to cut that blushing out, you're totally gonna give yourself away."

"I don't blush! And, just for that I'm not gonna tell you."

"Yes you are." But Lizzie clamped her mouth around the straw of her shake and refused to give Grace an answer. Grace figured it out, though, when not more than two minutes later, Lizzie started smacking her hard in the leg and chanting, "Oh my God, oh my God, oh my God!" over and over again under her breath.

"Lizzie, snap out of it. What's the matter with.... Oh." And there, in front of the store, walking across the street directly toward the pharmacy was Mr. Home-Town-Hero himself. Payton Cartwright, in all of his ninth grade glory, jogged across the street, his blue jeans molded ever so slightly to the muscles that were beginning to shape up nicely underneath, and his letter jacket keeping him warm from the almost chilly Southern winter. When he smiled back at the rest of the boys that called something after him, both girls sighed so long and deep, Mr. Gilchrist almost laughed out loud.

They buried themselves in their shakes as Payton walked through the door and tried not to listen as he chatted for a while with Mr. Gilchrist. He didn't stay in the store for longer than five minutes, and neither one of them could think up a decent conversation to have while he was there. On his way out the front door of the store, he paused, and looked back at them, just like he'd known they had been sitting there all along.

"Hi," he said, his voice already deep and smooth from the change in his body. Then he smiled, that deep lazy smile that made his eyes sparkle and that dimple show, and if either girl had thought about responding before, there was no way they could now.

They giggled until the sun went down that night over that one.

Late that night as they lay in Lizzie's bed talking about their dreams for the future, Lizzie turned to Grace and asked, "Who are you going to marry when you grow up?"

"Well, since I already know the answer for you I won't even think of asking you the same." Grace laughed while Lizzie smacked her with her feather pillow, and wished with every ounce of her body that Grace could really see the future.

"Come on, you didn't answer. Who's it going to be?"

"Let me think..." She fluffed her flaming hair out around on the pillow. "I'm going to marry a rock star."

"A rock star? That's kind of weird."

"No it's not. I would say a prince, because they're famous and powerful, but they're also too stuffy and formal and all they get to do all day is sit around in their castle wearing that big old crown and ordering people to go to war and stuff."

"Yeah, that does sound kind of boring."

"But a rock star. He's got a voice that can sing me to sleep at night or tell me how much he loves me in a song. And he's famous and powerful, but he also gets to go have fun and enjoy his fame while he's at it."

"Kind of like having the cake and eating it."

"Exactly what I was thinking."

Lizzie made it all the way past Easter break, but it looked like her luck was out. Slate had been itching for a fight with her for weeks, for some reason that Lizzie didn't quite understand except for that maybe it was because she was one of the school losers. But was that any good reason to pick on her? Lizzie didn't think so.

Regardless, Slate had been stalking her between classes and at the end of sixth period he had her cornered in front of her locker like a deer caught in the headlights. Slate's laugh was decidedly wicked, and she tried her hardest to dodge the doggie breath that he was blowing her direction. It was useless seeing as he had her by her shirtfront and was getting closer by the second.

"Listen Loser Lizzie, someone's gonna pay for that test I flunked and it just so happens that someone is you." Why did she have to pay because he flunked a test? She would have asked but figured that would only make the bully spit red. But on second thought, she remembered what Grace had said, and thought she might try it out, seeing as the foreseeable end to her future lay ahead, anyway.

"Sorry Slate, but I fail to figure how you flunking a test is my fault." Yep, he was spitting red all right.

"What did you say to me?" Lizzie clenched her fists and got ready to punch.

"I said..." But Slate suddenly dropped her and quickly straightened the wrinkles he'd put in her shirt. He backed away quickly and for good measure Lizzie held up her fists in the best fighting pose she could muster and bared her teeth like a rabid dog.

"Look, I got to get to class: we'll pick this up later." Then he quickly walked away.

Wow. She had done it, she had actually stood up to the bully, and he had backed down. See, it wasn't so hard to deal with Slate McDermott after all. Lizzie felt like patting herself on the back, but knew that would look foolish so she turned to finish fishing her books out of the locker before seventh period.

"Lizzie," She turned when she felt a hand on her shoulder and a definite masculine voice call her name. She stared right into those sparkling green eyes and got lost.

"Are you alright?"

"Ah..." Was that really a squeak that had just come from her throat? Had Payton Cartwright really just called her by name?

"I saw Slate picking on you and I tried to stop him before he did anything too bad. He didn't hurt you did he?"

"Ah..." Yep, she was squeaking all right. He looked at her kind of funny, then shrugged his shoulders and turned away. She tried her hardest to call after him, but nothing would come. The best she could manage was just before he rounded the corner to head down the next hall. She croaked out a hoarse, "Thanks!" and watched him turn back to her and give that heart-stealing grin that made her and every other girl at Dixie Academy melt to the floor.

But this time it had been all for her.

She floated on cloud nine the rest of the day and on her way home from school. Grace wanted to slap her to wipe the goofy smile from her face, and the dreamy look out of her eyes, but MC told her to leave Lizzie alone, and find someone else to pick on. Lizzie was oblivious to the whole conversation.

Slate didn't touch her for the rest of the year. The closest he came was one day after lunch when she saw him stalking her way. She ducked behind the book she was reading and prayed he wouldn't notice her. Sure enough, he walked past with only a sneer on his face. She thought about the day that Payton had come to her rescue, and she wondered if he had had any part in her near miss of Slate that day, as well.

Sure enough, a minute later she saw Payton saunter away from the general area, and her suspicions were affirmed.

Why was he doing this, she wondered. It wasn't like anyone had appointed him as her guardian, and no one else in the school seemed to take an interest in her lack of a life. And it wasn't as if he didn't have the rest of the school to entertain with his gorgeous good looks that got better by the year, or his wonderful talent at football that had already landed him a spot on the varsity team.

It baffled her, but she certainly wasn't going to march over to him and ask him to stop protecting her from the school bully. It just puzzled her as to why he would do it. What motive did the most popular boy this side of high school have in watching over her?

Payton slung his backpack down on the floor and stripped off his shirt to change for football practice. Coach had promoted him to the varsity team just after the final game of the season, and he had been ecstatic. He had been practicing with the older boys for several months now, and he felt like it had really been improving his game. If all went well, he'd be able to start a few of the games next year against some of the easier teams in their league.

But he found his mind wandering off to other aspects of life rather than the game at hand. One of which was his current girlfriend, Leena. She was pretty, he had to give her that, but he wasn't really interested in her anymore. They made a good couple though, and everyone knew that the hottest couple in school was Leena and Payton.

It made him sick to think about it. She was a nice girl, he had to give her that, but she was just so damn pushy. He wasn't comfortable making out in odd public places all the time, and it seemed like that was all Leena wanted to do. At first it had given him a thrill, but the last straw had been in front of the Sheriff's office, and that had just grossed him out.

Besides, all she wanted to talk about was her hair or her nails, or one of a million vain things that he assumed all girls must talk about. He'd grown so accustomed to tuning her out, just to preserve his masculinity that he sincerely believed he hadn't listened to a full conversation of theirs in months.

Nothing was pointing to a happy ending in this relationship. But really, when he thought about it, which he was currently doing as he slipped into his pads and flipped a jersey over the top, he couldn't be too upset about the prospect of breaking up with her.

More fame and fortune would come from the break-up than from the relationship, he had to admit. She'd have all the guys drooling after her, and he'd have a million fawning girls after him. How bad could that possibly be?

A pair of green eyes floated through his mind, and his thoughts paused on Lizzie Benford. What was it about that girl, he wondered, that made him want to hold her tight and protect her from anything bad that came her way? No one had appointed him her freaking guardian, but still he found himself finding subtle ways of keeping Slate off her back, or one of a dozen other idiots that were determined to use her as their personal insult board.

Whatever it was, though, he thought with a sigh, he needed to get over it quick. She was sweet, but she wasn't someone he needed to mess around with, end of story. He was a no good football guy that liked to see how far women would go with him, and she... well, she was too sweet. Too innocent. He liked a girl with a little more experience, he told himself, as if he'd ever really gone all the way more than once or twice with the one girl he'd done anything with: Leena.

But that was going to change soon. If, and when, he broke up with her, he was determined to make it in the single world for a while. Not just one girl would tie down his time. Nope. He was going to find out what being an eligible bachelor was like, and only when he was good and ready would he settle for hanging out with one girl again.

He picked up his helmet and headed out the door to the football fields beyond. The smell of fresh cut grass filled his nose, and he smiled when he took a deep breath. The field: his friend, his home. There was no place better to be than standing on the fifty-yard line in center of Dixie Stadium. Hello boys, here comes Payton.

## Chapter Ten

Summertime this year was going to be a blast, Lizzie just knew it, because this summer she had Grace and MC to pal around with, and spending her days down by Granny's pond wouldn't be half bad. Unfortunately, though, Grace's father had different plans for his daughter, and he shipped her off to summer camp three days out of school.

Lizzie was totally bummed. She supposed it still wouldn't be bad to hang out with MC and Skipper, but it wasn't the same without Gracie around. She spent most of her days reading on the front porch swing with Skipper snoring at her feet and MC singing at the top of her lungs to the headphones she wore like a transplant on her ears. It was getting a little obnoxious, even their parent's had to admit, but at least she had a decent voice they said to console Lizzie, and she stomped off pouting to her room.

Three boring weeks into summer she'd pulled a scoop of homemade vanilla ice cream into a cone and grabbed a towel and her current book to head down to the pond. Skipper was busy chasing SnagglePuss, the neighbor's orange and white tabby, and missed her whistle as she headed off down the road.

A group of kids were playing baseball in one of the hay field's again, and she could see from the road that Payton stood on the center mound, a pile of hay serving as the pitcher's mound, and focused his concentration on the batter in front of him. She didn't want to appear like she was spying on them so she watched them as she walked on and could hear them yelling for the base runners to bust a move as she reached the gate to Granny's pond.

It would have been nice to play with them, but not with Payton around, she told herself. She would only make herself look like a complete fool with the way she always got so nervous around him. It would only make her look like she couldn't play ball to save her life. In reality, though, she had been pretty good at baseball. At least she had been when she'd played with all the Chicago kids. Who knew how she would play against all these athletic genes down here in the South.

She left her towel and her flip flops at the base of her favorite tree and shimmied up the bark to her branch. The sun was bright and the day was warm, but it felt good in the shade of the tree's leaves, and she snuggled up against the trunk and set out to enjoy the story of *Huckleberry Finn*.

She was too absorbed in the action of the book to notice the bushes rustling, or the lone teenage boy that strutted that unconscious male walk down to the edge of the pond with a fishing pole in tow. Not until she looked up and saw him standing there, Mr. I'm too gorgeous with my glowing green eyes, with his shirt off and only his bright red swim trunks on, did she notice that she was no longer alone at Granny's pond.

Her heart pounded in her chest, because once again she was in a sticky spot. Lizzie wasn't certain if she should jump from the tree, and attempt, even though she knew her voice most likely wouldn't work, to make some excuse as to why she was and wasn't spying on him. But instead, she tucked her feet up into the branches and prayed he'd leave quickly and without noticing her.

He didn't leave quickly, but instead he stayed for a good three hours. By the time he left, her butt was so numb from sitting on that hard branch and praying he wouldn't notice her that she felt like her legs would fall off from lack of circulation. But she had had fun watching him all the same.

He seemed so at ease in his skin, she noticed. She liked watching him slowly cast the line on the pole out into the water, then watch with those perceptive eyes to see if anything beneath the surface would take his bait. When something did, she got a kick out of watching those muscles that were already clearly defined, bunch and buckle underneath the smooth surface of his tanned skin.

And he liked to whistle, she noted. It wasn't one of those obnoxious whistles that made you cringe when you heard it, but it was one that actually carried a pretty good tune. She closed her eyes for a while and pretended he was serenading her.

She had heard a rumor shortly after school let out for summer that he and Leena had broken up. She didn't know why but she had actually been sad to hear it. Now instead of only having to contend with one other female in his life, she would have to deal with the hoard of girls that would flock after him now that he was available.

It was hard having a crush on the most popular guy in school, she decided as she sat there staring at his beautiful body wishing she could have a guarantee that he wouldn't notice her there in that tree.

The emotions kicking around in her body had recently hit high gear, and she'd found herself wanting to know more and more about how the male body ticked. Now as she sat folded up in the leaves high in the tree, she watched that male form she wanted increasingly to know more than anyone else in the world.

His skin had grown slick with perspiration, and she licked her lips when he set down his pole and dove into the water. He swam back and forth for a while, and then just floated on the top of the water like a turtle sunning himself in the rays of the afternoon sun. When he finally pulled himself from the water and shook himself off like a dog, she had just managed to force herself to read a few more pages of her book. He grabbed his pole and headed back up the path and she breathed a sigh of relief as he headed up the path.

Something must have distracted him though, because he looked back, and looked right at the base of the tree where her towel and sandals lay. She held her breath, ready to die if the moment presented itself, but he never looked up and she felt like fainting when he finally faded off in the distance.

That was a little too close to call.

A week later she had finally convinced herself that sitting on her favorite branch was still okay, after all Payton and his buddies didn't own the pond, and if he thought she was spying on him then that was his tough luck.

But she didn't feel so brave when she spotted him making his way down the path to the pond some forty-five minutes later. He carried that same fishing pole, and wore the red swim trunks that made her mouth salivate at the sight.

He went right about his business of setting up the fish shop, and whistled a happy tune as he did. He made his way slowly around the edge of the pond, stopping here and there to watch and see what the fish did below the surface.

Lizzie had forced herself to read another page in her book, and had finally lost herself in the words on the page when she noticed she didn't hear him whistling anymore. She looked up, startled, because she didn't see him fishing at the pond. Had he left? No, because his pole was lying over there on the ground. Was he swimming? Was he drowning? She hadn't seen him come up for air recently, and she didn't see any air bubbles floating up to the top.

She leaned forward, skimming the surface of the pond, holding her breath, waiting to determine if she needed to race to Payton's rescue. Yeah right. Like Payton needed rescuing from anything.

"Hi." Suddenly a male form filled her vision and she screamed louder than she had in her whole life. The world tipped up on its axis and she felt the wind rush passed her as she tumbled off her favorite branch in the tree.

Something strong and sturdy caught her, but her eyes were closed so tight she couldn't see.

"Easy there, trigger. You could have killed yourself." Lizzie's eyes popped open and she realized it was Payton that had caught her. A moment later she realized it was Payton that had scared her.

She leapt from his arms and brushed herself off, momentarily forgetting that she was the school loser while he was the total opposite. She lit into him like nobody's business. "*I* could have killed myself? *I* could have? At least *I* wasn't the one sneaking up on people, making them fall out of trees." She realized he wasn't offended, but more likely amused because his face was lit up with a grin that made his dimple poke out on his cheek.

That only made her madder, and she stormed up the path with a huff trying to act dignified in the act of doing so. He caught up with her about the time she reached the old rickety gate, and took her by the arm.

"Wait. You forgot your stuff. Besides, I was just having a little fun with you. I wasn't really trying to scare you."

"Having fun with me? Sure, why not? Join the club. People do that at my expense every day, so why not you, too?"

"See, there you go."

"What?"

"Why don't you do this in school? If you did half as good a job at telling people off in school like you just did me then you'd have no problems at all."

Lizzie blinked.

"Now come on, I saw you up in the trees a few days ago, and couldn't help myself. Come back down to the pond, you can fish with me if you want."

Fishing with Payton Cartwright. Right. She must be dreaming. But she followed him back to the pond with him stopping every few feet to ensure she was behind him, and she reluctantly took a seat by the edge of the pond close to where he was fishing.

"Your buddies aren't coming to fish with you?" She wasn't sure she could handle being seen in public with him, especially not around his buddies. People would probably think she'd paid him good money to hang out with her.

"Nope. They're all gone to camp, won't be back for another few weeks." She thought of Grace and how much she missed her. Only a few more weeks and she'd have her buddy back as well.

He fished on in silence, and she read her book by the side of the pond, sighing occasionally at different parts of the novel. She felt splashes of water when he leapt over her head into the pond and merely glanced up in his direction when he began to swim laps in the water.

"Hey, New Girl." She never looked up, she kept right on reading. Just as she suspected, he didn't even know her name.

"Lizzie." She looked up then, only because- shockingly- he'd used her name, and in a tone of voice that strangely made her blood feel sluggish in her veins. When she did she found him kneeling in the shallow water not three feet from her, staring at her face with green eyes glowing brightly in that tanned summer face.

A slow jolt of electricity pulsed through her as he held her gaze for a beat.

He'd wanted to say something else, but instead he said, "Why do you let them pick on you like that?" It took a while for her brain to register and the tongue that felt like minced meat to kick into action.

She sighed then said, "It's not like I ask them to do it."

"Yeah, but I don't get it. What is it about you that they don't like?"

She sniffed. "Trust me, if I knew I'd change it."

He kicked back and floated on top of the water for a while, and she turned back to her book. It was strange; this odd kinship the two of them seemed to be sharing. At the same time, though, it was really nice, and she sighed at the thought. Here she was enjoying a lazy day reading a book and in the company of Payton Cartwright no less. Wait till she told Grace about this!

"You do that a lot." She glanced up from her book to find him watching her while he treaded water.

"What?"

"Sigh. I hear you do it a lot."

Lizzie cocked her head to the side in thought then shrugged her shoulders. "Well, it manages to cover a multitude of emotions." He didn't say anything and she felt the need to elaborate. "For instance, you can sigh in exasperation or frustration." She let out a short huff of a sigh. "Or, it can signal feelings of helplessness." She paused to think of other ways she could use a sigh. "Oh, and you can use it to show satisfaction."

He laughed at her final sigh of contentment. "I guess you're right. Never thought of it that way."

"See how beneficial it is to know a dork that has too much time on her hands?"

He watched her for a minute, his eyes slowly assaulting her, leaving her feeling exposed and vulnerable with precisely the person she didn't want to feel that way around. At last he shook his head and lent her a sympathetic smile. "You're not a dork, Lizzie. You're just misunderstood."

He pulled himself out of the water after a while and flopped down on the grassy hillside beside her. He stared at the blue sky above and closed his eyes, shutting out the brilliant green light Lizzie was getting too accustomed to seeing. When he opened them again he focused in on her and studied her features in the sunlight.

Her hair was longer, almost down to her waist, than when she had first come to the school. She wore it down today, something that she almost never did when they were in classes. His fingers itched, briefly, to run through that silky curling mass, but he knew he shouldn't so he kept his mind off that train of thought. She was wearing cut off blue jean shorts and a yellow halter top, both of which accentuated the long, willowy lines of her body. He absolutely refused to think about what he would like to do that portion of her.

She was so focused on that book she read, he remembered that she was always reading something or other, and he wondered if she did it to take her mind off her life or if she actually enjoyed them. He tried to imagine what she would look like without a book in her hand, and failed to draw up more than a brief image. A book in her hand was like pom-poms to a cheerleader.

"Do you always read?" She glanced up at him, startled that he had shifted so close to hear without her even realizing it.

"Usually."

"Why?"

"Why not? It passes the time." Shock registered on his features.

"Is that what life is to you?  Time to kill?"

What else could it be when you were at the bottom of the heap and not going anywhere.  But she laughed and shrugged it off.  "Isn't that what it is to most people?"

"No."  She realized he was dead serious.

"Oh."  She couldn't think of what else to say.

"Why did your family come here?"  There was blatant curiosity in his tone, but she glanced over at him, unsure what his motive was.  Instead of answering him immediately, she decided to ride the wave of anger she felt.

"Why do you care?  So you can go tell all your friends that my family really does have a freak in it?"

"No."  He held up a hand as if to pledge his oath.  "I swear it."

She sniffed as she skimmed the surface of the lake with her eyes.  "Like you really care, anyway."

"Try me."  She didn't want to, but the way he smiled with that cute dimple popping out on his left cheek, she couldn't help it.

He couldn't possibly really care so she decided she wasn't going to answer, but after a while she marked her spot in the book and put it down beside her.  She sighed deeply, but still he waited patiently.  After another minute she spoke.

"I grew up in Chicago, and believe it or not I did have friends there, and I really liked it.  My mom, Faith, she adores kids and always wanted about five or six to make her happy.  She tried and tried after Mary Catherine, but she never could.  When she finally did we were all so excited we had a big party to celebrate.

"At about seven months she got so nervous that something might not go right.  One night she lay down to go to sleep, but she couldn't feel the baby kick.  She waited until morning then went to the hospital and they told her the baby had died while she slept.  He was wrapped in the cord.

"Anyway, she got so depressed she tried to commit suicide and the doctors told my father the best thing he could do was take her somewhere that wasn't anything like her life now.  Move her and the family away and start over somewhere that she wouldn't remember all the grief.  It took a while, but we're here and she's better."

She hadn't meant to share as much as she had but once she'd started it just kept spilling out.  That was surprising, but what had shocked her most was that Payton's attention had remained riveted on her the entire time, and not once had he yawned or looked bored or tried to stop her. Not even when that one sad little tear had trickled down from the corner of her eye.

"If you tell anyone about this, I swear I'll … I'll …"

"You'll what?"

"I don't know," she whined, "But I'll think of something."

"Then spit on it."

"Huh?"

"Spit on it."

"Spit on what?" She tried to remember Grace's advice and not blush, but that was a lot easier said than done, and it was especially hard when the most popular guy in school was currently laughing at her apparently stupid comment.

"No, spit on it. It's like a pinky promise that I won't tell; only it's more serious."

"Oh." She pretended that she understood completely when really she didn't understand at all.

"Come on you'll like it." But when she watched him spit on his hand and hold it out, waiting for her to do the same, she smiled softly and said, "No thanks. I'll take your word, and a pinky promise."

"What? Are you afraid I've got koodies or something?" She looked shocked.

"No! Koodies are so third grade, anyway."

"Then what's the hold up?" He smiled because he knew he had her cornered, and like the winner he was born be, like the champion blood he had running through his veins, he wasn't one to let the kill go unnoticed.

She couldn't let him see that he'd won, so she spat the smallest amount of spit possible into her hand and quickly held it out to him, clenching her eyes shut, turning her head as if to avoid the whole messy process all together. She waited, but nothing happened. She opened first one eye, then slowly the other, and laughed when she saw him watching her as if she had lost her mind.

"Okay. Here's the deal, if you're going to look like you're about to be force fed cockroaches then it's no good." The second time around she only crinkled her nose and cringed inwardly, but she promised herself when she got home that night she'd wash her hands at least a dozen times. That spit shake thing was for the birds. Her only consolation was that she had actually touched Payton's hand, and this time around she remembered what it felt like.

His hand had been warm and strong with a small ridge of calluses that were beginning to form from a life of rough play and hard work. She liked the way their hands had looked together, his big and broad, while hers was small and pale compared to his. She hoped he hadn't noticed the same quick pulse she always had when he was near, or the odd reaction her body had had to his touch. Whatever it was, though, she was quite curious to figure out if it was going to happen every time he touched her.

She studied him when he lay back into the grass again, oblivious to her curious stare.

"Why are you so nice," she asked him at last, and he slowly opened his eyes and looked over at her, genuinely surprised.

"What are you talking about? I'm not nice." Right and her shirt wasn't yellow. She laughed. "Why are you laughing? I told you I'm not nice."

"Okay."

"Okay? Why don't believe me?"

"Because- and trust me on this one, I've had plenty of time to people watch over the past two years, and you're just about as nice as they come."

"Name one nice thing I've done." His jaw dropped when she rattled off about ten. "Okay, I think we should call that stalking."

It was her turn to drop the jaw. "I... I wasn't stalking you."

"Jeez, ease up, trigger. I didn't say you were I just didn't know you knew that much about me."

"Well, it's kind of hard not to notice the most popular guy in school."

The funny thing was, though, for the most popular boy, it was getting harder and harder not to notice the least popular girl in school as well.

A secret friendship was formed on the banks of the pond that day, and for the rest of the summer Lizzie looked for him when she went down to the pond each afternoon. Sometimes she'd see him, and sometimes she wouldn't, but she had fun thinking about the time she had spent with him even when he wasn't there.

One afternoon as she sat on her branch in that old oak tree, she heard someone come out of the woods and she smiled as she caught a peek of a familiar pair of red swim trunks, but kept her head ducked and focused on the book. She refused to look obviously interested in him, because that would only put her on the same playing field as every other girl in the school.

Her legs dangled from the branch and she had just finally forgotten about the other person at the pond when she felt a swift tug on her foot and her world turned upside down.

"Wh-Whoa!" She screamed as she toppled from the branch, landing squarely in Payton's arms.

"You know, you really should have better balance if you're going to be sitting in those trees all the time. What if I hadn't been here to save you from that fall?"

She glared at him through slitted eyes. "If you hadn't been here I wouldn't have fallen."

"Oh, so you only have bad balance when there are cute boys to catch you." Her lips twitched, but she refused to let him see her smile.

"Some boys sure do have mighty big impressions of themselves, don't they?" And with that he dropped her on her feet, and ran off to dive into the water. Talk about a walking case of hormone confusion. If ever there was a boy to make her blood boil, it was him. And at the same time, he… well, she wouldn't get in to how big her crush on him had grown.

"How old are you anyway, Lizzie?" She took a seat on the edge of the bank and watched his muscles ripple, all sleek with warm pond water, as he glided through the waves he had made.

"I turned fifteen in May. What about you?"

"Fifteen. I'll be sixteen in August."

"Oh." She watched as he ducked under the water, and for the first time all summer her skin itched to crawl in the water with him. She looked away when he surfaced and pretended to study a blue bird that landed on a nearby tree.

"Hot?"

"Hmm?"

"Are you hot?" He watched her from just above the surface of the water where his body treaded water as if he did it for hours every day. His eyes, green like the grass she sat on, watched her like an alligator stalking its prey.  She suddenly felt very self-conscious.

"No.  Well, maybe a little."  She wanted very much to change the subject.  "When does football practice start again?"

"One week.  Why don't you come into the water with me?"

"One week, wow, that's soon.  Are all your friends playing this year too?"

"Some, most are still on JV.  The water feels good, come on in."  She scooted back as he came a little closer.  She laughed nervously and ran her fingers sub-consciously through her hair.

"Can you believe you're a tenth grader and the new starting quarter back for the varsity team?"

"Uh-huh."  His mind was focused now and he no longer heard her weak attempts to out maneuver him.  For some mind-boggling reason he'd been itching to get her into the water with him for days, and yet she always refused.  Well, his teenage hormones wouldn't hold out any longer, and it was today or never that he got her in with him, clothes and all.

With one final stroke he made it close enough to her to reach out and encircle her ankle.  She yelped when he gave a fierce tug and sent her careening out in the water.  She came up sputtering with her dark, waving hair plastered to her face like some monster out of a horror flick.  He laughed hard as he watched her flail around trying to push herself out of the water with her heavy, wet clothes weighing her down.

"Funny.  Very funny, Payton Cartwright!"  And she fumed as she turned away from him and pulled herself onto the shore.

"Oh, come on.  You looked like you were dying out there, I was just trying to cool you off."  And see how insanely cute that body looked when it was wet instead of dry.

"You're nothing but a dumb jock!  I can't believe you did that!"

"Whoa.  There aren't any dumb jocks around here."  She could see she'd made him mad, but she didn't care.  Mr. I have no idea how to *not* flirt with my adorable green eyes deserved to be mad at her, because she sure was mad at him.

"Oh yes there are."

"Fine."  And with that he was out of the water on top of her, and before she knew it she had landed back out in the middle of the pond thanks to Payton's talented arm muscles.

She sputtered again as she surfaced, and he stood on the bank with his arms folded over his chest.  Lizzie couldn't help but notice the definition that had formed over the pec region even in the short three months of that summer. He looked defiant and arrogant standing there on that shore looking down at her. His face held no sign of sympathy or friendliness, and she recognized at once the power he had within him.

She swam to the shore opposite from him and pulled herself out, ringing the dripping pond water from her shirt and shorts. She was out of breath from dragging the wet clothes in the water, so she sank to the ground and rested under the bright summer sun for a while.

"How did you get that name, anyway?" She asked it quietly after she calmed her thoughts, still a little a shaky from the brief edge of power she had seen pulsing out of him.

"What?" She supposed he'd been expecting a fight, because she heard him sigh deeply and run his strong hands through his wet hair. "Payton Cartwright? It's a family name. One of my grandfathers, or maybe a great-grandfather was a senator. Perfect name for a senator. My parent's decided it was the boy that grew into his name instead of the other way around, and felt if they named me after him that I'd grow up to be something great one day."

"Oh." Figured. He certainly looked like was going to be something great one day- he definitely had the stubborn set to his jaw when he wanted something done his way. Not that she'd ever tell him that.

He left shortly after, and she wondered if she'd done something to upset him, but tried not to dwell too much on it. She'd been thinking too much about him lately as it was, and she certainly didn't want him weighing on her mind even more. He had no idea what he'd done by befriending her that summer, and she hoped more than anything that when they started school in the fall he wouldn't treat her like she was still that same piece of dirt that she'd been the past two years.

Grace returned home two weeks before school started, and Lizzie was ecstatic to have her friend back. Her normally brilliant red, short cropped hair that framed a pudgy little face, had grown a little longer until it almost skimmed the top of her shoulders. Little freckles had popped out on her skin from all the sun she received at camp, but none of that mattered to Lizzie, because at last her friend was home.

They spent an entire day trying to convince Faith to take them to Clarkston for a pre-school shopping spree, and finally wore her down just before supper that night. The next morning, the girls were buzzing around

Lizzie's room chattering about all the cool clothes they would buy on their trip that day.

Two hours later they strolled through the mall, having convinced Faith to come back for them at five that afternoon to pick them up. So for now, it was the two of them, and an entire summer to catch up on. Lizzie had been dying to tell Grace about her days by the pond, and she couldn't wait any longer.

She leaned over and whispered it into her ear.

"You spent an entire summer with who?" Grace yelled it so loud Lizzie was positive the entire mall would stop shopping to listen. Lizzie slapped a hand over her friend's mouth and gave her the evil eye.

"Shh. What are you trying to do, tell the whole world?"

"Oh, come on. Like the whole world doesn't already know. You don't spend your days goofing off with the most popular guy in school and expect for everyone not to know."

"Well, I'm pretty sure that's how it was, and I'm pretty sure that's how it's going to stay." The pleading in her eyes was desperate, and Grace finally gave in to her friend.

"All right, well let's hear the details seeing as my summer was way too boring for words."

Three brand new outfits later and the summer details had been shed. Grace stood open mouthed outside the dressing room door, whispering frantically through the slits in the door to her friend on the other side.

"He pulled you into the water!"

"Yes, now keep your voice down," Lizzie hissed.

"Was it like, the coolest thing that has ever happened to you?" Silence on the other side. "Well, was it?"

"I'm sure it's not like meeting your future rock star lover or anything, but yeah, it was." Grace knew it, she just knew it, and she beamed on the opposite side of the door.

"You know what this means, don't you?"

"What?"

"You're going to have to put out for him." The door swung open and Grace found herself being drug inside by surprisingly strong arms.

"What!"

"You heard me. He's a jock, Lizzie, and jocks expect for girls to put out. That's just part of their genetics or something."

"Oh, shut up!  He pulled me into the pond, he didn't ask to marry me, and it's not even like he's going to talk to me when we get back to school.  He was just bummed because his friends were off at camp."  Grace folded her arms and gave Lizzie a look.  "What's that look for?  It's true."

"I don't believe it."

"Well believe it, Carrot, because it's true."

"He's gonna make you put out and—did you just call me Carrot?"

"Yeah."  Lizzie smiled and slid the top she'd been trying on back onto the coat hanger.  "You look like a carrot with that red hair and all those freckles.  It's kind of cute."

Grace didn't look like she thought it was too cute.  "Yeah?  Well, you look like a string bean.  You're so tall and skinny."  Lizzie hugged her friend to cheer her up.

"You can call me Bean if I can call you Carrot."

"Or we could come up with cooler names like…Spike and Killer."  But she laughed when Lizzie turned her nose up at those names.  "All right.  Spike, er, Bean and Kil— Carrot it is."

"Now, swear to me that what you said isn't true," Lizzie said as they walked to the cash register.  She pinched the red head when she simply shrugged her shoulders.

"Ouch.  Okay, if you say that you and Payton are just friends then I think you're safe.  But boys don't pull girls into the water just to be funny, and when you find out what his ulterior motive is, I'm pretty sure there's gonna be some putting out involved."

That made Lizzie's stomach hurt so she refused to talk about that or Payton for the rest of the summer.

## Chapter Eleven

Ed Benford watched his two daughters get ready for the first home football game of the season. In his opinion any make-up was too much make-up, and he was having a really hard time not saying anything about the blush and mascara Lizzie was currently damaging her face with.

Tenth grade. Could his oldest baby actually be in the tenth grade? And little Mary Catherine was in the eighth. His heart felt a little tight, and he wondered if he was having early signs of a heart attack.

Ever since this summer, Lizzie had really taken to watching her appearance, and it sort of disturbed him. He supposed it was only natural for a teenage girl to want to look her best, but it made him feel like he was losing her to life and he wasn't ready for that.

"Okay girls, mama said it's time for dinner." He cleared the slight frog in his throat.

Both girls groaned. "But dad, we're doing our make-up."

"Nope. Make-up doesn't constitute a dinner skip. No anorexics in this household, and I mean it. You've got five minutes to get to that table or we're blessing it without you." It was a definite no-no to arrive at the table after the blessing, so Lizzie and Mary Catherine got their make-up doing butts in gear.

They had fifteen minutes before kick-off by the time they had scarfed down the potato salad, creamed corn, and bar-b-q pork their mom had fixed, so they finished primping and hurried out the door. Lizzie was so excited about the game she could hardly wait.

She, Grace, and Mary Catherine had already planned to make their move closer to the section in the stadium where all the high-school kids sat and she had a nervous pitch to her stomach. She wanted it to go well, and a sliver of hope that it just might crept into her body.

She smiled at Grace as she caught up with them, and they all linked arms as they walked the rest of the way. Yes, this year was definitely turning out better than the last two. A recent memory floated up in her mind.

On her first day back to school, Slate had cornered her at her locker and she'd been ready to give the big bully a piece of her mind, when a blur of a male form shoved him out of the way and stepped in between them. She stared straight into Payton's muscular back and loved the scent of him standing there in front of her as he defended her.

"Stop it, Slate."

"Stop what?" Slate laughed sheepishly. "Oh, me and New Girl weren't doing nothing. I was just asking her about her summer." But he'd dropped his eyes when Payton's gaze remained direct and hard on his face. "Honest, Payton, I wasn't doing nothing."

"Listen, and listen hard, Slate. No one picks on her anymore, and I mean no one. If you've got a problem with her then bring it to me and I'll straighten it out."

Slate had slunk away like a wounded puppy-dog and Lizzie's heart had been pounding in her chest. She would never forget the way those green eyes lit with fury and rage as he'd turned to her. "Don't let him treat you like that, Lizzie. I mean it. You come get me if he…" he paused to lift her chin so she was looking him dead in the eye. Little sparks went off inside her. "If he or anyone tries anything, you let me know. Okay?"

He'd smiled then, and those emerald eyes softened in that tanned gorgeous face.

"Okay," she'd said weakly, and watched as he faded off down the hall.

An instant memory was etched in her mind of that adorable butt as it strutted off with the rest of his body, and she smiled as she finally got it. For once, she finally understood what the boy-crazy girls meant.

The stadium was already almost filled to over flowing, and the roar of the crowd as they talked over the blaring band was like music to Lizzie's ears. It still amazed her that football, especially high school football, could mean so much to a town, but in a way she also loved this little town for all the support they gave their team. Even all of Granny's friends, the town safety patrol, had banded together and reserved a row of the bleachers where they sat at all the home team games.

Lizzie could feel her body beating to the rhythm of the drums in the band, and she smiled to her friends as they took their seats near the back of the section where all the high school kids sat. She cheered with the rest of the school when the varsity cheerleaders ran out from the bottom ramp of the stadium followed by the hulking forms of Dixie Academy's Varsity players.

She spotted number sixteen right away, along with a mass of other girls that screamed their heads off to catch the attention of the now available quarterback. There wasn't a more desirable boy in school.

Lizzie rolled her eyes and thanked the stars that she had more sense than to join in with them.

The team was up against Hillside High for the first game of the season, and it was well known that Hillside had a killer defense. But, Lizzie had heard the rumors flying that the team had been preparing for weeks for this game and they should pull through with no problem.

Unfortunately it looked like the team missed the memo, because they stunk up the field and looked like an even worse team than Valley View by five minutes into the first quarter, and even the cheerleaders looked a little like they could use a pep talk before they went on. The end of the first quarter came, and Dixie's starting quarterback, Blake Holden, had been sacked and in the process seemed to have done some damage to one of his knees. The coach pulled him from the field and sent him to the hospital he was in that much pain.

The crowd went wild when the second string quarterback, Payton Cartwright was called in. It looked, if Lizzie didn't know any better that Payton was going to be the new leading man on the football team. Secretly, it made her happy. No one deserved success like him.

By half time Dixie had kicked into high gear and the fans were cheering their heads off and cheerleaders were doing push-ups all over the place to keep up with the touchdowns the team was making. It was more fun than Lizzie remembered having at a game since, well… last season.

She paused to take in the sights and scents around her. Smiling fans, laughing school kids, peppy cheerleaders. The scent of popcorn and coke, the smell of grass cut that afternoon and now roughened from the force of all those moving bodies. The clash of bodies and pads, the lights that buzzed around the track and sent rays of light down on the field.

For some reason she had loved these games since the first time she had gone, and now it was just another part of her that would always remind her of the good times in this town. Maybe it was this, sitting here in the bleachers screaming her head off with the other fans that made her know that more than any place on Earth, Edenville was her home.

For the first time in her life, she felt that missing link click into place. She closed her eyes and lifted her head up to the darkened evening sky, and felt peace as it washed over her. At last, she thought. At last she had found home.

Payton rubbed his throwing arm and set the ice pack back on it as he slipped his pads off his shoulders. Tonight had been a rough game, but the team had come through, and he had survived his first full game as the starting quarterback of the varsity team. It was a high all its own, this feeling of knowing he controlled the shots, and he controlled the fate of his team.

What a humbling experience, he thought all at once, and for the first time that night he felt exhaustion caving in on him.

A strong hand on his back brought him to attention, and he turned to see the dark brown eyes of his father watching him. "Good job, son. I'm real proud of you."

Payton smiled, the light of the world reflected in his eyes. Here before him, his hero, his idol, his father stood telling him what a good job he'd done. There was nothing sweeter to his ears.

"Thanks dad. I owe it all to you." And he meant every word that he said.

"Listen son, I know you're headed out to the post-game party, but I just wanted to catch you before you left. Have fun tonight, and don't get in to too much trouble."

"Thanks, I'll try." He turned back to throw his muddied jersey into his duffel bag. "Hey, dad? You want to go fishing with me tomorrow?"

He knew the answer by looking in his dad's eyes, but he tried not to be disappointed. "Sorry, kiddo. I've got a business meeting out of town, but I'll be back in a few days, and we'll go then. I'm leaving now, so look after your mother for me, alright?"

"Sure, dad." He wrapped a towel around his waist, and turned back to his locker. "See you when you get back."


The insane flock of female bodies knocked him around when he got to the party, but he smiled and took the red plastic cup that someone handed him. The mass of bodies pressed against him, each trying with all her might to convince him she was the next one to fill his vacant girlfriend position.

For a moment he could imagine on a smaller scale what it must be like to be some famous rock or movie star and have people hanging all over you every time you stepped out the front door. It was fun now, considering it was the first game of the season, but he could imagine that it would get old pretty quick, but at the moment Payton smiled at all the girls huddled around him telling him how great he'd looked in his jersey as he'd thrown the winning touchdown.

You'd have thought with the way all the girls hung on him, that he was a famous quarterback from a major NFL team instead of a tenth grade football player. But it didn't take a genius to realize that in this small southern town, even tenth grade football players could be stars, heroes, and gods. And it was obvious that for Payton this was the case.

Even last week when he'd stopped in the pharmacy to pick up his mom's prescription, a little first grader named Tim had asked him for an autograph. Payton had been floored, and had grinned from ear to ear the whole way home.

Currently, some girl from a neighboring high school was tucking her number into the front pocket of his pants, brushing curiously close to something she had no right to be touching, and Payton jumped back in startled surprised. "Hey, whatcha doin' there, sweetheart?" The girl giggled and sauntered off, making sure he was watching her shapely backside sway back and forth as she went.

"Payton, over here!" He looked around to find Colin, Bud, and Hank waving to him from a safe spot a few yards away in the bed of Hank's pickup truck.

"Hey, Man. Awesome game, QB." Bud smacked him hard on the back and grinned widely as the hero of the hour jump and landed gracefully on the lowered tailgate of the truck.

"Yeah, it was pretty good, wasn't it? We couldn't have done it without our three key offensive linemen, though." Payton laughed when the three puffed out their chests and gave each other congratulatory pats as well.

He skimmed the crowd as the others talked about which cheerleader was the hottest, but didn't find what he was looking for. He wondered why he had even bothered looking, but he had hoped that maybe Lizzie would have decided to pass up a Friday night of studying and come to the post-game party instead.

He knew better than to really expect her there, but some small part of him had hoped, and he couldn't help but feel the briefest tug of regret that she hadn't shown.

What was it about her? He wondered, as his friends discussed strategies for conquering next week's opponent. And why did he even care about a dark haired science geek when he could take his pick from any one of a hundred girls roaming about the party. Just then he pictured her face all wet and pouty after he had thrown her in the pond last summer, and he smiled to himself. He had had more fun with her over the summer than he had realized at the time.

It was almost like the girl he had discovered over the summer was a completely different person than the one he passed in the halls of school every day. The girl at school was quiet, and shy. She kept to herself, didn't talk unless provoked, and she always studied. Not that she wasn't always reading when he saw her over the summer, too.

But the girl he had seen in those hot summer months was energetic and alive. She had a spark to her and he could see a hint of something even more powerful underneath. It was almost as if the real Lizzie was who he had seen when he was alone with her during those days at the pond. The one he had seen just a glimpse of the day Lou Ann taunted her into a fight at school. There was something about her, Payton mused as he let his brain float back to the party. Something that he could see, but no one else could.

How long, he wondered, until she couldn't keep it bottled up anymore?

"Wow, deep thoughts going on in that head of yours?" Colin waved a hand in front of Payton's face, then snapped his fingers to bring him back to attention.

"Huh?"

"You've been, like, staring off into the distance for at least five minutes. Snap out of it or people will start to think that defensive lineman hit you harder than we thought."

"Oh, sorry. I guess I'm just out of it." Payton took a sip of his drink and waved as two tenth grade girls smiled as they passed by.

"So, who's it gonna be?" Payton looked momentarily confused at Hank's question. "Okay, man, you're starting to freak me out. If we aren't talking about football we're talking about girls, right? So, who's the lucky girl gonna be?"

Payton sipped his drink and tried to avoid the conversation, but he couldn't think of a decent way out. "I'm not really interested in anyone right now."

"Not interested? You've got the entire female population of Dixie Academy drooling after you, and you aren't interested? Would you mind sending that out in a memo so maybe the rest of us will have a shot in the dark here with at least a few of them?"

"Boys, boys." Seeing his previous answer wasn't satisfactory, he huddled them closer and decided to lead them off the trail by evasive maneuvering tactics. "I broke up with Leena all of ten seconds ago. Now a man, and I mean a *real* man, has to play his cards well this day in age."

He could see he had them right where he wanted them so he rubbed his hands together, and gave a sly grin. "But let me tell you, you can't just pick the first girl that comes along. Oh, no. You have to wait and watch. A man has to search the masses, choose from his narrowed selection of choice prime female, and go in for the hunt from there."

Satisfied that he had sufficiently thrown them from his tracks, Payton downed the rest of his drink, and then slid from the tailgate. "Take my advice boys. It works every time. Now about searching the masses..."

Payton sauntered quickly off into the night, thankful that a throng of women hadn't pursued him when he left. Before, when he'd been dating Leena, all he could think about was breaking up with her and being free to spend time with as many women as he wanted. Countless women, he had remembered thinking, all his for the taking. And now that he was available he didn't want any of them. Well... that wasn't entirely true. There was one girl that popped into his mind every now and then, but she wasn't his type and he refused to even think about going there.

The stars in the night sky glittered down at him and the moon lit his path as he walked. He liked it out here in the country, with land all around him and no tall buildings to block his view.

He knew some people preferred a big city with all its glitter and glitz, but for him, crickets lulling him to sleep and being able to see the stars at night was what really mattered. Stepping out and smelling clean fresh air with a hint of lush grass was heaven compared to the scent of exhaust and fumes from expensive foreign cars.

He supposed it was because he had always lived here, and that was what he knew, but did it really matter? He honestly believed that he could have lived all over the world in every kind of place imaginable and he would still choose the country and its way of living to anything else out there. He didn't need some great sign of fate to show him what he already knew: this was home, and this was where he would always stay.

He clicked the lock into place as quietly as possible when he slipped in through the front door of his house a few minutes later. His mother had left a light on for him on the entry table, and he flicked it off as he tip-toed past. It was late, he knew, and he hoped that he wouldn't wake his mother when he walked past her room on the way to the kitchen.

His stomach had been a bottomless pit for years, but in the past few months it had seemed to grow even more demanding of food. He pulled some ham, a tomato and mayonnaise from the fridge and quickly pulled two slices of bread off the loaf. He had just added the finishing touches to his sandwich when his mom poked her head around the corner and smiled at him.

"Hey, sweetie. You made it home, I see." Sleep held her lids lower over her eyes than normal, and Payton smiled at her as she came up behind him and wrapped her arms around his shoulders.

"Hey, mom. Want a sandwich?"

"No, thanks. I'm not blessed with my son's sky high metabolism. But I sure would love it if I was." She watched with envy as he devoured the sandwich, then gave in and made another. His body, she noted, had filled out in the past months, giving way to more muscle and leaving him looking more and more like the spitting image of his father every day.

The only thing he had been blessed with from her part of the gene pool was her depthless green eyes, and she was proud that he got to see the world from what she considered her greatest attribute.

"So, the town's all abuzz with the night's victory. I can only assume my darling son had a major hand in this."

"You heard, huh? It's great, isn't it?" He smiled, that lazy smile like his father's that had stolen her breath nearly twenty years before and still did to this day.

Her heart gave a tug with a love only a mother could hold, and watched him as he celebrated his victory with her. She pulled a chair out from the small rounded breakfast table in the center of the bay window of the kitchen, and sat to watch her handsome son as he ate. She smiled as he told her each play by play of the night, and felt pride beyond any she had ever known before.

When he finally stood from the table to go to bed, he gently kissed the top of her head and said softly, "I love you, mom. I hope I find someone as great as you one day."

A single tear slipped down her cheek as he walked from the room, and she quietly turned out the lights in the kitchen and slipped silently into her room.

## *Chapter Twelve*

Lizzie snuck quietly through the fence of the pasture and took a seat fairly close to the gate just in case she needed to get up and run for her life. The day was bright and though still slightly chilled from the winter they had just come out of, the air held a promise of warmth of the new spring that was blooming. Already Lizzie could see the leaves budding out on the trees showing promise of greenery. Just this morning she had spotted the first tulips as their buds started to spring forth.

It had been months since anyone had dared to pick on her, she consoled herself trying to hear reason through the maddening pounding of her heart. No one had even bothered to throw spit balls at her in class, thanks to the lightening fast spread of the threat of the Payton's wrath. There was nothing better than having the most popular boy in school to help get your taunting and teasing immediately put to a cease-fire.

Lizzie pulled her legs up in front of her and wrapped her arms around them, resting her chin on her knees as she watched the group of tenth and eleventh graders playing baseball out in the field. She had been on her way down to the pond, and normally would have walked right past, but the thought of just being able to watch for a little while was too appealing for her to pass up. So here she sat, hoping that being in the same field as some of the most popular kids in Dixie wouldn't jeopardize her chances of not being taunted anymore.

She skimmed the sea of players, and noted Payton wasn't among the group. Lizzie wondered where he was, but was almost thankful that he wasn't there. Quiet murmuring had gone on when she passed in the halls now. People were curious to know exactly why it was that Payton had become her protector. Was there something going on between them?

It was plain as day to her that there was nothing even remotely close going on with the two of them, but that didn't stop the girls as school from eyeing her with jealousy anyway. Besides, just being around that boy made her tongue swell up so much that she couldn't talk in coherent sentences, and her brain switched gears and overheated all together. Yes, it was much better that Payton wasn't around the field today.

She watched in silence for a while as Bud took over Payton's usual position as pitcher. The other team gave it their best shot up at the mound and occasionally hit a ball or two. But the majority struck out against

Bud's "curve ball of fame" as he liked to call it, and left Bud's team bored pretty quickly.

"The score's five to zero, and it's looking like it's only gonna get worse from here," Hank taunted the other team from his spot guarding second base.

"Oh, yeah?  Well if you'd actually make the teams even for once, maybe we'd have a shot at winning," called back Colin who had been shuffled to the losing team this game, and was obviously wounded because of it.

"Well, New Girl's over there.  We'll let you have an extra player if you put her on your team."  Lizzie sat up in shock.  She hadn't realized they'd even seen her, but apparently they had.

"Oh, come on man!  That's not even close to right.  She reads books all the damn time, how is she a fair addition?"  Colin whined but he looked over at New Girl as if to size her up.

"Hey New Girl!"  Hank yelled out to her.  She looked around, sure that they couldn't possibly be calling out to her.

"Don't look around.  I'm calling you!"  Hank jogged a few steps closer, and Bud and Colin followed him.

Lizzie stretched her legs out, and tried to pretend her body wasn't shaking from nerves.  She was ready to jump and run at any moment, if one of those boys tried to pull anything funny on her.

"What?"

"Wanna play some baseball with us?"  Lizzie tried to look severe and size him up at the same time.

"Oh, come on Hank.  Leave her alone.  I bet she hasn't ever even touched a baseball before."  Colin tugged on his sleeve and tried to pull him back to the game.

"No, wait a minute.  Let's just see if she wants to play."

"What do you want me to play for?"  She was itching to play, she could almost feel the bat in her hands, but she wasn't going to let them know that.

"See, she doesn't want to play.  Now let's go finish slaughtering my team," cried Colin as he started to head back to the game.

"Wait," Bud called.  "Let's put a little bet on this."  Colin paused, and Lizzie turned to see what kind of bet they could possibly put on her.  "Five dollars says that New Girl can't hit the ball on the first three swings."

Lizzie could feel her blood start to boil, and her fingers clamped down into a fist.

"Interesting bet, Bud, but how does that help me?"

"Okay, Colin. For every run that New Girl gets, your team gets two points. If she hits it out of the park, your team wins the game." Colin chewed on his lip and thought it over. Odds were, he'd be losing this game, but it was at least worth a shot.

Lizzie studied him, and tried to remember to breathe. When at last he looked her way, he shoved his hands in his pockets and said, "All right, New Girl. You're on my team. Just try to see if you can hit the ball, okay?"

And with that, Colin slunk back over to the game. Bud and Hank grinned from ear to ear and headed back to the game they were sure to win.

"Who's turn to hit next?" one of the girls on Colin's team asked.

"Oh, let's put New Girl in. Might as well get the slaughtering over with."

Lizzie couldn't hear over the roar in her veins, and she was pretty sure she had no feeling in her fingers from fisting her hands so tightly, but she saw herself lift the bat on the batting mound as if she were in a dream. She took a deep breath, tried to settle her nerves, and got in position to smack the ball with all her might.

"Okay, Bud. Just try and throw an easy one this time, alright?" Colin was whining again from the sidelines.

Bud grinned. "Sure thing, Coli-pooh." He sent the ball whizzing past the plate, before Lizzie had time to blink.

"Jesus, Bud. Did you have to be that mean about it? We already know New Girl's practically never seen a baseball before. Give it to her easy alright?"

Oh, Lizzie was starting to get mad. It wasn't like she was *deaf* or anything, and she had *definitely* seen a baseball before. Not like she was going to tell any of them that, though.

"Two more and she's out Colin. Then it's your turn to pitch and you can do it however you like."

"Fine, just remember you said that."

Bud smiled innocently at Lizzie, but this time she wasn't fooled by his look. She kept her eyes focused on the ball, and watched as it flew at her at breakneck speed. She swung in the general vicinity of the ball, knowing full well she was missing by ten miles, and tried not to giggle outwardly. She was just testing out her swing.

She heard Colin groan and the rest of the team gave her a half hearted cheer to pep her up, but she remained focused on the evil twins, Bud and Hank out in the field. When Bud smiled at her this time, just before he wound up for the throw, she smiled back then settled her eyes on the ball and nothing else.

This time it came at her in slow motion, and she followed it every step of the way. She felt her body twist into the swing as the ball crept her way, and she felt herself lunge forward as the bat cracked against the ball.

Every mouth on the field sat agape as she rounded the bases. Colin finally found his voice three bases into her homerun, and cheered his head off for her. Bud and Hank only found her homerun slightly amusing.

Payton stood on the other side of the fence and watched as Lizzie stepped up to the plate. She was the last person in the world he had expected to see on the field that day, and he certainly hadn't been prepared to watch her bat. How had that happened, he wondered, but kept his thoughts to himself and decided to watch what happened.

He winced as the ball whizzed past her on the first pitch and silently sided with Colin. Bud was just trying to be a jerk in his own nice way. He was too good natured and honest to be a real jerk about anything, and besides his mama would have his hide if he was ever caught being the school bully.

Payton focused in on Lizzie during the second pitch, and noted with some amusement that she was way off in her swing. Maybe he'd teach her how to swing and play baseball if he ever caught up with her at the pond next summer. It might be fun to teach her how to play, he thought, then shook his head and tried to get those thoughts from his head.

When the bat cracked the ball and sent it flying on the third pitch, he felt his jaw drop like the rest of the players, and immediately retracted his thoughts on teaching her to play. She didn't need any lessons on playing, and if he didn't know better, from the slight grin spread across her face, it might seem that she had just been playing with them all along.

She was bent over retying her shoes when finally made his way up behind her. He thought it odd that she nearly jumped out of her skin when someone called his name, so he waited until she slowly stood and turned toward him to smile and say, "Some batting arm you've got there, Lizzie.

You've been holding out on us, haven't you?"

She didn't respond, but the twinkle in her eye told him everything, and he wondered what else that girl had been holding out on him.

"Mind if I join your team?"

"*Sure*," Colin said, sarcasm evident in his voice. "Show up now after we've already got a star player." For the rest of the game he kept his eye on her, and really wasn't the least surprised after watching her bat that her out fielding was just as spectacular.

The game ended with Colin's team winning by three points, and Colin gloating about it while Bud and Hank walked off pouting.

"Hey New Girl," Colin called as she was about to slip through the fence and head home. She turned back to see what he wanted, catching a glimpse of Payton from the corner of her eye. God, he's gorgeous, she thought, and tucked that tidbit away to analyze later.

"Yes?"

"We're playing again tomorrow, if you want to come. You can play on my team." Lizzie smiled, and turned away.

She made herself walk until she was well out of eye sight of the field, even though she really felt like skipping. When she knew no one could see her, she ran as fast as her legs could carry her. Finally! Her father would be so proud that she was finally starting to fit in, and she couldn't wait to tell him.


"Are you sure it's okay if I come play with you, Bean," Carrot asked as they walked down the road toward the field where all the baseball games were held.

Lizzie rolled her eyes and gently jabbed her friend with her elbow. "Are you gonna whine like this the whole time?" She waited until Grace gave her a sullen shake of her head.

"Good. Because if you are, you can always walk back home." Lizzie gave her best friend the fiercest stare she could muster up, and watched as Carrot nibbled on her lower lip.

"No, I won't whine. It's just that... never mind."

"Good, because you're gonna have fun I promise. Just remember what I taught you and you'll be fine."

It had been four weeks since she'd started playing ball with the other kids and Lizzie couldn't remember a time when she'd been so happy. Finally things were starting to look up for her, and she was ecstatic. The only problem was that Carrot hadn't been included in the games, and that had made Lizzie sad.

But Lizzie was about to change that. Colin's team had titled her the Home Run Queen after her tenth homerun, and it was pretty much fact that she single handedly could whoop Bud and Hank's team with one arm tied behind her back. Well, as long as Payton wasn't on the other team, that is. She still wasn't sure, but something about that boy was like Kryptonite to Superman, and whatever it was when he was around, it was useless to try and think straight.

But today she was on a mission, and she intended to get her point made. She held Carrot close to her, to prevent her from running off once they got into the field, and the two of them together marched out to where the others were getting ready to play.

"What you got there, New Girl? Bring along the cheerleading squad?" She ignored Bud's half-hearted attempt at teasing, and found Colin before her courage wore out.

"Colin, I'd like a word with you." He was busy trying to teach another girl how to catch pop-flies, even bribing her with money if she'd just catch one, and turned only after Lizzie continued to tap him on the shoulder.

"What, Lizzie?" He eyed the flaming red mop of hair on Lizzie's sidekick with vague curiosity. "What's up?"

"I've brought Grace to play."

"You what?"

"You heard me. Either she plays, or I don't."

"Whoa, ease up cowgirl." Colin looked Grace over from head to toe, and circled her one time for good measure. "I don't know, Lizzie."

"Come on, Colin. You can't afford to lose the Home Run Queen can you?" Having leverage was so great.

"Well..." He scratched his chin and thought, but all he could picture was the rest of his bumbling team that refused to catch pop flies. "Can she catch?"

"I've taught her everything I know."

"Well, put her in the field then, and we'll see how she does, but I'm not promising anything much."

Lizzie was so excited she forgot to be scared, and for the first time ever she stood up on her tip toes and threw her arms around Colin. "Oh, thank you, thank you! You won't regret this."

"Wow," Payton said as he walked up to his friend just then. "You coming up with some moves that I don't know about?" Payton grinned when Colin scowled and walked away, but inside Payton had secretly felt himself wanting to know what that hug had felt like.

He was happy to see that Lizzie was finally starting to make a name for herself around the school. It seemed to him that people were starting to like her, and her image as dork of the school was beginning ever so slowly to wear off. Now, if someone could just convince her to put down her school books every once in a while, she'd just be that much better off.

And it wasn't his imagination, he realized as he watched her in the outfield. She was definitely starting to smile more, and with that smile came a pair of glittering eyes that danced with life. Reluctantly, he had to admit to himself, that when she smiled, her face was more than just cute. Her body hadn't yet caught up with her good looks, he noted as he skimmed his eyes over her body, but when it did... he hated to think of how his already humming body would react when he saw what she looked like as a woman.

Payton played on Bud and Hank's team for the game, and when it came time for Lizzie to bat, he took a deep breath and tried to focus on striking out the opponent, which was no small feat he soon discovered.

She stepped up to the plate, and positioned her body just right so that her tiny little butt barely poked out behind her. He noted with amusement that her tongue licked at the edges of her lips when she was concentrating, and at the moment her tongue was working hard on the right edge. He could see those green eyes all the way from the pitcher's mound, and he was about to throw to her when his eyes locked with hers and held.

For what felt like a full minute, but must have been only a second, his eyes held hers, and tearing them away would have been like ripping the sun from his world. He shook his head, to remove the buzz that had settled there, and forced himself to focus on the pitch.

He let the ball go, and for the first time in his life the ball sailed skyward instead of towards the plate, and everyone on the field stopped in shock.

Bud, the team coach, jogged over to the pitcher's mound and tossed an arm around Payton's shoulder. He huddled in close and whispered to Payton, "You okay there, QB?"

"Yeah I'm fine. It was just a bee buzzing around. It won't happen again."

Bud took a minute to assess his player and seemed to determine him eligible to pitch because he patted him once on the back and took back off the field. Payton got the ball back from the catcher and tried to focus his thoughts on the game. He slammed the ball into his glove a few times for good measure and scuffed his feet as if he were the bull ready to charge and let the ball fly again.

Three pitches later and he ended up walking her.

Bud stepped up to the mound shaking his head, and placed his hands on Payton's shoulders. "What's up man? We need to pull you for a while? You don't look so good."

Payton bent over for a minute to catch his breath then said, "No, I'm okay. Let's play ball."

By the end of the game, Lizzie had hit two home runs, been walked three times, and hadn't struck out once. Payton had struck out everyone but her, and Grace had caught every pop fly in her area. Colin asked her to come back, and said he would pay her to catch pop flies for him the rest of the time she played.

Grace laughed. "You don't have to pay me, Colin." She batted her eyes and flipped her flame of hair. "But you can take me to the barn party next weekend."

Colin smiled sheepishly and turned a light shade of red as she turned to walk away. The other three walked over to him. "So, you got a date, huh? Never dated a red-head before," Hank chimed in. "But I hear they're lots of fun." He chuckled and clapped his friend on the shoulder as he walked off.

Colin waited until the other guys drifted off and caught up with Payton on his way out of the field. "Uh, Payton."

"Yeah, man."

"I've never, uh... had a date before." Payton tried to stifle his laugh, and merely grinned instead.

"Hmmm. And you wanted to know..."

"Yeah, well, uh..." He ran a finger under the rim of his shirt. "I was, uh..."

"Just say it."

"I'd feel better if you were there to... you know, make sure I do it right."

"Uh, man, that's sick. I'm not going to watch you do it."

"No! I mean go on the date, like a double date, and make sure I don't screw it up."

"Fine, but I'm not going to be the third wheel."

"Ask New Girl."

"I can't."

"Why not?" Payton searched his head to try and find a legitimate excuse but nothing, absolutely nothing, came to mind.

"Just because, I can't."

"What? Don't be a baby. Just ask her, and let's go together." Payton thought it over for a minute, and was about to say no again when Colin added, "You know Payton, you're an awesome QB, but wouldn't it be tragic if none of your offensive line was there to defend you in the next game?"

Payton smirked, "You're blackmailing me? Now that's original, Colin."

"You bet your ass I'm blackmailing you. Now quite stalling and help me out already." Payton thought it over. What if he did ask her to go? Would it be so bad to ask Lizzie out? If he was honest with himself for five seconds he'd realize he'd been curious about what it would be like for a while now. At least this way he could pawn it off as a charity cause for his friend and she would never know the difference.

"Okay, this one time. But that's it."

"Thanks, man. I owe you one."

*Chapter Thirteen*

Payton shoved his books in his locker and wondered how the hell he was supposed to go about asking Lizzie to go to the barn party with him. He slammed the locker door and leaned back against it, waving every once in a while to the various groups of girls as they strolled down the hall. His mind was totally preoccupied though, so he got no real kick out of waving at them.

How exactly was he supposed to propose this question to her? He must have been momentarily insane when he'd agreed to ask Lizzie to go to the barn party. There was no way he was asking her to go with him. Besides she'd probably be studying or catching up on all of Shakespeare's works. He couldn't ask her to go with him to this party because if he did the first thing she would assume was that this was a date, and that was the last thing he wanted. He was a free man, able to flirt with whoever he wanted, able to play the market and not feel guilty. Asking Lizzie to go to the barn party with him was like sealing his doom.

It crossed his mind as he made his way down the hall to first period, had she ever even had a date before? He sincerely doubted it.

Yep, he had to face it. This was going to end up being a date unless he did something to make it look like it wasn't. But what? Payton hunkered down in his chair and hoped the teacher wouldn't call his name so maybe he could sort this problem out.

About half way in to the class while everyone else was solving math equations, Payton still mulled the thought over in his brain. Colin expected him to ask Lizzie to go so he could take the red head with him to the party. Only Payton didn't want a date to the party- he wasn't ready to be saddled with some girl again. Nope. He'd had all the fun he wanted with Leena and now he wanted to sow his oats with lots of different girls, not just one. And certainly not just one who looked like a future librarian and who probably had read front to back more text books that he could say he read even ten pages out of.

Maybe he was just in a bad mood that day, or he was catching some kind of bug. Possibly that was the explanation as to why he seemed so hell bent on not asking her to go with him. Something about that girl kept crawling under his skin lately, and it was definitely in a way that didn't please him. He wasn't sure exactly what it was- nothing that he could put a finger on, but whatever it was, he was certain that spending any time in a relatively close vicinity to her wouldn't help the problem go away.

He gnawed the edge of his pencil and scribbled something on his notebook paper to throw the teacher off for a few more minutes. She'd been looking curiously in his direction and he didn't want her calling on him. Now... if only he could solve his date problem as easily as he could find ways to blend into a classroom crowd.

And that's when the idea struck him. He didn't have to go on a date at all. He could mention to Lizzie that a group of people were going together to the party and see if she and the red head wanted to tag along. His idea seemed ingenious, and he smiled to himself.

"Happy that you solved the problem, Mr. Cartwright?" Payton looked up to find the teacher standing over him staring at his almost blank sheet of paper. He grinned sheepishly and tried to think of something cute to say.

Instead he came out with, "Yeah."

"Good. Then why don't you go to the board and show the class how you solved it without using any of your scratch paper."

Man, was he ever in trouble.

By the time first period ended Payton had had to weasel pretty hard to work himself out of Ms. Yorkshire's bad graces. He'd smiled extra hard and even resorted to flexing his muscles (because he knew all the girls liked that) and still she hadn't bought into his routine. In the end he'd settled for an extra hour with her at lunch the next day so he could rework the problems he'd skipped over in class.

He breathed a sigh of relief when the bell rang and he was released. Now all he needed to do was find Lizzie and ask her to come with the gang to the Barn Party. He caught sight of her walking down the hallway a few people in front of him, and just his luck she was alone. For a minute he just there, alone in a mass of swirling people, enjoying the view her walk afforded him. He didn't even realize that exactly what he had been trying to avoid only thirty minutes prior was what was now subconsciously being entertained in his mind.

She looked pretty cute, all dressed in a brown skirt and brown and cream checkered short sleeved sweater. She had her hair pulled back in a long pony tail with a few strands wrapped around the holder to make it look like only her hair held the pony tail in place.

Something inside him felt odd, not like it did when he saw Lena in the hallway before they had dated. No, he knew exactly what that feeling was. That was the raw, primal urge of a man lusting after a woman. This... this was more of something... well, something inside him that wanted her in his arms and his body wrapped around hers to explore her every curve, but at the same time to protect her from any danger that may come her way. It was a feeling that begged him to take what he wanted from her and to give her back all he was in return. It was a feeling that scared him so much that he instantly shut the door on it, afraid to know that a tenth grader could feel something as strong as that, and afraid that if he let it, it might devour him whole.

Shaking his head in disgust at himself for letting the quarterback of Dixie Academy's consciousness get so carried away, he forced himself to focus on the task at hand. Invite the girl to the party, make his goofy friend's day. Right. Got it. Onward march.

And then he snapped back to attention and got lost in her walk all over again, enjoying the way her small bottom swayed unconsciously along with her hips. He liked watching her body like that because he knew it was unintentional. Lizzie wasn't the kind of girl who tried to attract guys by using her looks. He honestly doubted she even knew that she was remotely attractive.

When he skimmed down past her hips and studied her legs, he saw that he liked what there as well. Her thin legs weren't straight sticks, but instead had shapely calves that showed lines of muscle when she walked. He could see the power housed in them, and couldn't help but enjoy them for a minute longer.

Finally he shook himself back into reality and made his way down the hall to where she stood in front of her locker exchanging books for the next class.

"Lizzie." She jumped almost a foot off the ground and he could see that he had startled her. "Sorry, did I scare you?"

"N-No." But she gave him a weak smile and her pupils were about five sizes too big, so he just smiled and continued on.

"Listen, You know about the barn parties that we have around here, don't you?"

She shoved a book in her locker and pulled out a notebook, trying not to stare directly into his gorgeously green eyes or his tanned face. "Yes."

"Well, there's gonna be one this Saturday night."

"Oh? That's interesting." She hoped her voice sounded nonchalant, because inside her blood was rushing and her palms were sweating.

"Yeah, well, anyway, a bunch of the people you play with out in the field are going to be there, and, well, I just wanted to invite you and your friend to come along if you want to."

She turned and faced him, hoping her voice wouldn't crack. Praying she wasn't turning beet red like she felt like she was. "You- you want us to come?"

"Yeah, sure. Colin said you deserved a reward after all the hard work you two put in at the games over at the field."

"Well... if you're sure, then I guess we'd love to come."

Payton smiled, those white teeth sparkling even in the dingy fluorescent lighting of the school hallway. "Great. See you there."

He was walking away and she was staring at his tight butt when she remembered that she forgot to ask him what time. "Hey!" She waited till he turned and smiled at her, his eyes locking with hers for a minute, then asked, "What time?"

"Hmmm?"

"You forgot to tell me the time. You know, for the party."

"Oh! Right! Nine. It starts at eight, but everyone shows up just after nine."

"Thanks." Payton just smiled and turned away.


Lizzie raced frantically around her bedroom and tried on yet another outfit from her closet. Already she had twelve pairs of pants, five skirts, and countless blouses strewn haphazardly across her bed, and her floor looked like a national disaster site ready for clean-up. At least three different bras hung from chairs, the top of her dresser, and one from her ceiling fan where she had flung it in an absolute state of desperation.

What was she going to wear?

This was so unlike her to be paranoid about her clothing. Yes, she was fashion conscious, and yes, she liked to make sure she looked good. But, changing clothes this many times was considered paranoia by her standards.

It was nerves. She knew it. She had had nightmares every night since Monday when Payton had asked her and Grace to come to the barn party. She had never been asked to do anything with anyone in the entire time that she had lived in this town, and for the first time she was. By *the* most popular boy in school no less.

She would positively die if she didn't look perfect tonight.

The door bell rang and Lizzie nearly jumped out of her skin from nerves. A minute later Grace burst through her bedroom door to observe the utter chaos that was Lizzie's room.

"Bean." Grace folded her arms across her chest and observed the insanity. "What are you doing? It's nearly nine now, we've got to go if we're going. And what are you wearing?" Lizzie could tell this wasn't the right outfit by Grace's cocked eyebrows.

"I know. I *know*," Lizzie whined. "I've tried on everything and nothing works. I'm just going to go crawl into my sheets and go to sleep instead."

"Oh, no you're not. If I'm going, you're going. And wild horses couldn't keep me from being there tonight. You do realize if you blow this invitation off it's like kissing any chance of having a life right out the window, don't you?"

"I don't believe that, Gracie."

"Well, it's true."

"Nope. Sorry, hon. I don't buy it."

"Fine, go crawl under your covers and I'll go to the barn party. But when I'm popular and having a blast, don't expect me to pull you out of the trenches."

Lizzie eyed her friend to measure her sincerity. "You wouldn't do that."

"Try me." Only problem was, Lizzie didn't want to. She wanted to go to the party just as badly as Grace.

"Fine," She gave in at last. "Give me five minutes and I'll be ready."

"Deal."

By the time Lizzie was dressed and ready to go, Grace had her family laughing in hysterics as some crazy joke she had learned somewhere along the way. Lizzie stood in the doorway of the den and watched as her parents hugged on the sofa and Mary Catherine sat on the floor near the television laughing at Lizzie's best friend tell a joke. It was good, she realized, so good to finally see her mother laugh again.

For that one laugh alone, Lizzie realized with warmth in her heart, she would have given up Chicago again and again and moved here every time. Every day of heartache she had had to endure was worth it just to see her mother happy again.

She bit back the tears of joy that wanted to come and stepped in to the room. "Well, looks like I sure know how to pick the entertainment, huh?" Her father smiled at his daughter and hugged his wife closer.

"Alright you two." He stood and planted a light kiss on his oldest daughter's cheek. "Have a good time. Try not to get into too much trouble."

"Yeah, whatever dad. You know me, the regular hellion." Her eyes sparkled as she watched her dad. This could quite possibly be the most exciting night of her life. Assuming she made it to the party without losing her nerves… and her dinner… all in Grace's car.

*Chapter Fourteen*

Farmer Murphy's barn was in the middle of a large pasture about ten minutes outside of the city of Edenville. There wasn't another house for miles, just land and woods, and the occasional cow that mooed in the distance. The stars and the moon were the brightest kind of lighting other the headlights off the pickup trucks that circled around the perimeter of the barn.

Grace had turned sixteen at the beginning of the year, and had been the lifeline for the two of them to civilization. It seemed they couldn't remember how they had survived before when one of their parents' had to drive them to the mall every time they wanted to go shopping.

So, as usual, Grace drove them the barn party and pulled to a slow creep as they approached the pasture Payton had told them to come to for the party. They obviously had the right place, Lizzie thought, because there were cars and trucks all over the place. But she had never seen anything like this in all her life.

Lizzie gawked in silence as Grace slowly drove them over the cattle grates at the edge of the pasture and down the bumpy, sandy road that led into the field. She guessed at least sixty vehicles were parked in the field, most of them being trucks. That meant that half of Dixie Academy and probably some kids from nearby schools were there at the party that night.

The red barn that stood in the middle of the pasture was lit up brighter than the Las Vegas strip with all the blazing headlights aimed in its direction. Just outside the barn, Lizzie noted a makeshift stage where a band made up of several Dixie boys was setting up their equipment. She wondered what kind of music they would play, and then remembered that they were at a barn party, so it would most likely be something country. Thankfully she had acquired a taste for the twangy sound of it since she had been in Edenville, otherwise she didn't know how she was going to put up with it all night.

Grace stuck by Lizzie's side as they climbed out of the car, both nervous and edgy, and neither wanted to admit it. But inside they were also excited and eager to see where the night would lead them. They walked together towards the milling mass of bodies before them, each trying to absorb every little detail. Every little ounce of excitement they could cram into their brains they would, and later as they fell asleep at Lizzie's house, they would giggle late into the night about all the things they had seen and done.

There was laughter and shouting everywhere as people greeted other people to the party. Lizzie couldn't help but feel a little envious. Even though Payton had invited them to come, she sincerely doubted anyone would be making them a grand welcome shout out. Grace noticed that people were grabbing drinks out of coolers in the bed of a pickup near the barn, so they headed that way to grab one as well.

Payton, Colin, and Hank stood in a group of guys all laughing about something stupid Bud had done at spring football practice the other day. Bud's face was beet red from the embarrassment, but he smiled and took his jabbing in stride. They had just made the switch from ribbing Bud to now Hank, when something caught Payton's attention.

He glanced over to Hank's truck where all the coolers had landed for the party, and noticed two girls making there way over to grab a drink. He could tell by the fire engine hair that one of the girl's was Grace, so he had to assume the other was Lizzie. But if it was, she looked completely different tonight.

He studied the girl with interest, curious to know who she was. The girl had her back to him now, but her hair was down, in long lazy curls that ended just above the small of her back. From the distance he stood away from her, he could only really see a white shirt and long, long legs that were covered by a short black skirt that stopped about mid-thigh.

Whoever she was, or if she was Lizzie, she certainly didn't dress like Lizzie tonight.

Colin jabbed him in the ribs, bringing him back to the guys, "What's the matter? Never seen a girl before?" Colin smirked at his own joke and Payton gave him a sideways roll of his eye.

"Yes, just I don't think that one." He nodded at the girl in question. "Come on, let's go welcome her to the party."

The two set off toward the coolers, keeping the red head and her friend in view. As they neared Payton could make out more of the girl's features, and was surprised to realize as he came within a few feet of her that it was Lizzie after all. He made his way to the cooler first, grabbed a drink then turned and caught Lizzie staring directly at him. That feeling, that sparking jolt of electricity that was beginning to become a normal but still unnerving occurrence when he was around her, coursed through him as he met her eyes and held them.

"Glad to see you two could make it." He smiled that lazy smile that Lizzie long ago had fallen victim to, and she could feel her skin tingling from her head to her toes.

"I thought we nearly wouldn't," Grace chimed in. "Ms Fashion Model over here had to change clothes at least fifteen- ouch what was that for?" Grace rubbed the rib that had just been elbowed by Lizzie, and giggled nervously when she realized what she had been saying.

"Thanks for inviting us," Lizzie added, her voice a tiny nervous squeak mixed with all the other noises of the night. Her heart was pounding like a run away freight train, and she wouldn't have been surprised if everyone within a ten foot radius could hear it slamming nervously in her chest.

Payton sipped his drink and watched as Colin took over the conversation. Grace was instantly enthralled with him, and laughed until she couldn't breathe at just about everything he said. He was amused with her, intrigued that she found his friend so hysterical, and for a while he just leaned back against the bed of the truck and enjoyed the show the two of them put on.

But as he let the two of them carry on, he couldn't help but watch from the corner of his eye the way Lizzie looked that night. She had actually put on make-up for once making her look a little older. It also made her look alive and the green of her eyes danced in the moonlight, shadowed only by the dark lashes she had made darker with mascara. He wondered briefly what it would feel like to kiss some of that red lipstick off her lips- how she would react if he did that, and then the thought was gone.

He forced it from his mind and refused to let it resurface. He was single, and he liked it that way. For now anyway. Not that a kiss meant anything serious to him. But to her… yes, he couldn't imagine how someone as obviously innocent as her could take a kiss to mean anything else.

To break the thoughts running through his head he stood up to his full height and interrupted the conversation between Grace and Colin. "Well, I'm sure you want to talk with some other people here tonight as well. Why don't Colin and I introduce you to some of our friends. I think it's time you two met some new faces at Dixie for a change."

The foursome managed to push through the ever growing party population, Payton and Colin ignoring the usual stares and hellos others gave them as they sauntered through the crowd.  For Grace and Lizzie, though, being ignored was the standard for them, so to now have people obviously paying attention was a little unnerving to say the least.

They smiled awkwardly and tried not to look nervous as the curious stares followed them wherever they went.  It was only natural for people to stare and wonder.  After all, it wasn't every day that two of the most popular boys in school walked through the biggest party of the year with the two least popular girls in school.  As they pushed through the crowds, whispers starting flying, and before the night was over, the entire school of Dixie would know that Lizzie and Grace were the two new chosen girls.

Of course, Lizzie and Grace wouldn't know that.  Not yet.  How could they?  It would be like waking up and realizing over night you had become a Princess.  But in Edevnille, Payton Cartwright was king, however humble he may be about it.  And when he chose someone to spend his time with, that person became an untouchable as well.

Payton and Colin pushed their way up to a group of about ten guys and girls, all mixed together and laughing about something.  The group looked up and welcomed the boys, and tried to not look so curious as to the two girls they had drug along.

"Hey gang, I want you to meet two of Colin and my new friends," Payton said as he skimmed the group before him.  "This is Grace Jacobs and Lizzie Benford."

A round of hello's coursed from the group.

Colin took over the talking then.  "Of course, you know Bud and Hank."  He waited for the two girls to nod their heads.  He introduced the rest of the guys and then the girls.  "This is Jade and Summer, and over there talking with Bud is Sellars and Lou Ann."

Lizzie remembered Lou Ann alright, but hoped that maybe tonight she could slip through the cracks and not get in a fight with the drama queen.

"Nice to meet you," Lizzie and Grace said simultaneously, both hoping their voices wouldn't show the nervousness they felt.  Something was different in the air that night.  Something was happening though neither could put their finger on it.  But somehow it felt special, so they both made a note in their minds to not forget this moment. They had a feeling it was going to go down in their history books for sure.

Not long after Colin and Payton introduced them to everyone, all the boys disappeared, leaving Grace and Lizzie with the other girls. Lizzie could feel the girls silently measuring her up, so she stood tall, and held her head high, and just in case she needed to punch someone and run for cover, she fisted a hand behind her back to be prepared.

Lou Ann, just at Lizzie feared, was the first to attack. "So, you thought you'd just show up to the party and weasel your way into my group, huh?"

Lizzie and Grace stood quiet, waiting for the other's to attack as well. Lou Ann didn't wait for a response, instead she made her way across the short distance and pushed a finger right in Lizzie's face. "Listen up girlie. I've got news for you. You're nobody, and you always will be. Don't go sticking yourself somewhere that nobody invited you." She paused to take a breathe so she could let loose on Lizzie again when she felt someone push her out of the way and block Lizzie from her view. Lou Ann looked up to find Payton standing over her, his eyes hard and cold, his features set in stone.

"Give it up Lou Ann. I invited her to be here tonight, and she's welcome in this group as long as she wants to be. She's not going to fight you, and all you've ever been is a jerk to everyone. If you're going to be a bully, go find someplace else to do your work. There's not enough room in this group for arrogance like yours."

Lou Ann glared at him, trying to determine if he would do anything to her, wanting desperately to rip her claws down his face, knowing that would only solidify her downward spiral in the school. Instead, she turned her back on the group and slinked off into the night to lick her wounds. She'd be back she promised herself, and there wouldn't be room at the top for both her and Lizzie. She'd bide her time for now, but one day, the day Lizzie least suspected it, she'd be back and she'd get even.

Payton turned to Lizzie and took her by the arms. "Are you okay? She didn't hurt you did she?" He searched her face, and held her shoulders, catching hold of her eyes and holding them in place with his. She shuddered involuntarily, enjoying the thrill of sensations that pulsed through her, but not wanting to cause a scene in front of these new people.

"I'm fine. Thanks, Payton." She smiled weakly, wishing she had

enough courage to kiss him full on the lips for coming to her rescue yet
again, but knowing she wasn't that brave.

"Okay," He said at last, and let her go.  He moved away, back to
where the guys stood talking not far away, and let her get to know the girls
he hoped would take her under their wing.

"Sorry about that," Jade said, "Lou Ann is just a big jerk.  We've
been meaning to do something about that for a while now."  Summer and
Sellars agreed.

"So girls," Summer asked, "Those two invited you to the party?"
She nodded her head in the direction of Payton and Colin.

"Yeah, something like that."

"That's nice.  That Payton always has had a good heart."  Lizzie
was surprised to hear the instant friendliness in Summer's voice and felt
some of her tension slipping away.

"Yeah," Jade added.  "That's why all the girl's like him, you know.
Well, besides the fact that he's completely gorgeous.  But I mean,
seriously, where could you find a nicer guy?"  Summer and Sellars agreed,
and Lizzie and Grace found themselves nodding as well.

"But don't you think Colin's nice, too?"  Grace questioned, a little
afraid that the girl's would mock her for adding her own opinion.

"Oh, yeah.  He's a sweetheart, too."  Jade instantly agreed, as did
the others.

"But you just can't find the whole package like Payton's got."
Inside Lizzie found herself agreeing whole heartedly with Summer's
words, and found herself enjoying the conversation they were having.  It
was different, completely different, than what she had been expecting.
She had been expecting a fight, but it seemed like, after all, they would be
having a good time with these girls.

"So, Lizzie, you're outfit is great.  Where do you get your
clothes?"  Sellars looked at her with interest, obviously waiting for an
answer.  Lizzie was so shocked with the compliment that she stood
dumbfounded for a minute.  She finally realized she had been asked a
question and stared down at her clothes, trying for the life of her to think
up where she had found the outfit.

"Uh… Oh, yeah.  Grace and I found this adorable boutique about
five minutes from the big mall in Clarkston.  I buy a lot of my clothes
there."

"Yeah, I've noticed you have great style," Summer said, shocking Lizzie further. She didn't realize people even noticed she wore clothes to school.

"Thanks."

"You too Grace."

"Really? Me too?"

The other girls giggled and gave her a hug. "Honey, you're just too cute. And by the way, how do you get your hair that bright. It's gorgeous. Do you dye it?"

"Oh, no!" The five of them talked on for hours, letting the time slip past them as they made new friends that night at the barn party. Lizzie didn't even notice the blare of the band in the background or the swirl of the party around her she was so fascinated by the instant acceptance from these girls and the good time they were having together.

She didn't notice the buzz of whispers circling around them as the rest of the world began to realize the shift in power that was taking place in their school, or the fact that Payton watched her throughout the night, proud that she had finally found the place he knew she belonged in. She didn't notice that he watched her with fascination, enchanted by her growing beauty and with curiosity at the woman she was fast becoming.

Payton himself didn't realize that each hour that past he found himself more and more enthralled by her, by her looks, by her spirit and personality. The one thing he did know was that he was happy that he had been able to help her find her new place, the place in the school and with the people she deserved to be with. He could do that for her at least, if nothing else.

Lizzie happened to look down at her watch and noticed that it read half past midnight. Her heart leapt into her throat. She hadn't been out that late ever! She would just bet her father was pacing the halls of the house right now, having an absolute cow that she wasn't home. She was surprised that he hadn't already barreled into the party and drug her home by the hair on her head.

"Uh, Grace," She whispered into her friend's ear. "I hate to break this up, but we're late and my dad is going to kill us."

Grace glanced at her watch and paled considerably. "Oh man, we are in seriously deep doo-doo. Let's go."

"Got to go so soon, girls?" Jade asked as they got up to leave from where they had settled on the bed of Colin's pick up.

"Yeah.  My dad'll kill me if we don't get home soon."

"Oh, okay.  Well, see you girls on Monday?"  Lizzie and Grace stared at each other in disbelief.

"Sure."

"Great.  Sit with us at lunch.  We'll be looking for you."

Lizzie and Grace drove home in utter disbelief.  They just had the most fantastic night of their lives, and not to mention that the most popular girls in school wanted them to sit with them at lunch on Monday.  Life couldn't be better.

It was so good in fact that not even the fact that her father reprimanded them until he was blue in the face made either one of them stop smiling for the rest of the weekend.

## *Chapter Fifteen*

It was the last day of school again, the last day of tenth grade, and she was thrilled that she wasn't having to spend it reading in detention. Nope. Today she was going with Grace, Summer, and Jade to a swimming party over at Sellars's house, and then they were all going on a summer shopping spree that night at the mall in Clarkston. If they were lucky, she might be able to convince her mom to let them see a movie there as well, and then let them spend the night over at Summer's house.

Yep. This summer was going to be awesome. She had grown into a fast friendship with the girls she had met at the barn party, and she had been having so much fun ever since. Even her father found it difficult to find things to complain at her about, he was so happy that she had finally found her place in Edenville.

He was thrilled that she didn't spend every weekend night locked in her bedroom, studying and reading and petting Skipper until his fur fell out. No, now she had so many phone calls that he'd had to give her a time limit on the phone each night, and she was busy almost every night of the week. He was ecstatic about her new life, and knew that moving them here had been the right move after all.

Lizzie swung into the passenger seat of Grace's car and rolled down the window. Summer had hit, and it was blazing hot there in the South. Already the thermometer read eighty-nine degrees, but it felt hotter than that sit sitting on the warm leather of Grace's car seat.

"Come on, poky, hurry up!" Grace, Lizzie and Summer called out to Jade who waved goodbye to her boyfriend and hurried to join them in the car.

"Okay, Okay, I'm here. We can go. Do you all have your swimsuits?" All the girls nodded. "Great, let's see 'em."

They made friendly ribbing cat calls as each girl held up her suit and showed the others. Lizzie held up her tiny two piece flame red suit with white strips and the other girls whistled. "Better hope Payton doesn't see you in that. He'll blow a gasket for sure."

"Shut up!" Lizzie turned red and hid her head behind her t-shirt. "Besides, he doesn't even like me. He totally wants some other chick that lives over in Clarkston."

"Uh-huh. Whatever," Jade joked. "That's not what I see when I catch him staring at you when you walk down the hall."

"That's it, you're walking. Grace, pull over and dump her on her ear." The girls all laughed and continued on down the road, their windows down, the radio blaring some country tune as they headed to the outskirts of town to Sellars's house.

Sellars's family, the Johnstone's, had been crawling in money for centuries. But for some reason they enjoyed living in this little town instead of with the other big money in Clarkston. Their house was on the edge of town, and was massive by Edenville standards. The girls pulled through the brick and iron entry gates and down the paved drive to the back of the two story sprawling stone and stucco house. The house must have sat on at least sixty acres by Lizzie's guesstimate, probably more if she thought about all the woods behind the house.

At the rear of the house was another iron gate that led into a courtyard. That led back to the tennis courts and swimming pool. To say the least, it was the nicest home Lizzie had ever been invited to.

Mrs. Johnstone made the girls virgin daiquiris while they changed into their swimsuits, and Lizzie felt a little nervous when it was finally time to shed her cover-up to enter the pool. She felt awkward because all the other girls had long ago developed into their adult body, and here she sat just beginning her stage of it. Grace had found this suit for her while they were shopping one day and bought it for her as a gift. Lizzie wanted to refuse, but Grace insisted, and now she was stuck wearing it today so Grace wouldn't be offended.

Fortunately, Sellars had assured her no boys would be coming to the pool party. And fortunately, none of the girls made a peep, so Lizzie chalked it up to Grace warning them within an inch of their lives if they said anything about her suit. She finally settled into the shallow end of the pool with the other girls, a daiquiri in hand, while they giggled about life and the latest gossip they had heard at school.

"What are y'all cooking up over there?" All the girls turned to find Lou Ann standing at the edge of the pool.

"What is she doing here?" Jade asked with a hiss. The others looked at Sellars, wondering the same.

"I sort of asked her."

"You did what!" Grace looked shocked.

"Well, I mean, she's been part of the group forever. I just thought…"

"Well, you thought wrong," said Summer, and everyone else agreed.

"It's okay," Lou Ann said. "I understand. I was an ass and I deserve it." Somehow Lizzie got the feeling that she was merely playing up a pity card but she felt almost sorry for her.

"Wait," Lizzie called as Lou Ann turned to leave. "It's okay with me if you stay."

The other girls looked at her like she'd sprouted horns. "Are you sure?" Lou Ann asked with a smile. Lizzie nodded.

There was a tense silence for a minute, but eventually the others asked her to stay and after a while they were back to their gossip.

"All right," Jade said as she turned the music louder on the radio. "Let's decide here and now the hottest boy in school." She turned back to face them, and smiled around the straw where she sipped her daiquiri.

"I know what Grace is going to answer," Summer commented.

"Who?"

"Colin."

"You can't be serious. I'm way over him."

"Really?"

"Yep. Been there, seen all of that. I'm on to new stomping grounds now."

"Wait," Jade gasped. "Does that mean you've..." Grace gave a confirming nod.

"No!" All the girls said in unison. Lizzie was shocked.

"But, when did this happen?" Lizzie asked, innocence filling her eyes. The others weren't nearly as naïve and they giggled at her purity.

"Lizzie, honestly. A week after the barn party, and then again maybe a few weeks ago. But down worry, I washed him off with a good romp with Clint- you know, Clint Hawkins in twelfth grade? Yeah him." All the girls, minus Lizzie who was still shocked and confused, gave approving nods.

"Seriously, Lizzie. You don't have to look like Armageddon just arrived." Grace studied her friend, and realized that as well as she knew her, she had overseen this one aspect of her life. "Wait, you don't mean to tell me that..."

"What? Tell you what?" Summer quizzed.

"Lizzie, tell me you've at least *kissed* a guy before?" Lizzie opened her mouth to speak, but no words would come. All the girls giggled, and gave her a group hug.

"Oh, it's all right, honey. But, why not, if you don't mind me asking?" Jade asked with a sympathetic giggle in her voice.

"Why not what?" All the girls turned to find Payton, followed by a group of guys, as they all sauntered onto the pool deck. Lizzie thought she was just going to die. She noticed that Payton didn't look her direction and she prayed with every ounce of her being that he hadn't heard the conversation the girls were having. It was one thing for the girls to know she'd never kissed anyone, but entirely another story for a guy to know. Especially a guy named Payton.

Lizzie shrugged her shoulders to herself, since all the attention had instantly been riveted to where the guys stood stripping of t-shirts on the opposite side of the pool, and tried to hide her flaming face behind her daiquiri. Why did it matter if she'd never kissed a guy before when her best friend had already been romping, as she apparently liked to call it, with multiple guys? Was that bad? She didn't think so.

So what if she thought of herself as awkward and not impressive to guys. She didn't see many guys knocking down her door to get a shot at her. And besides, she wasn't interested in anyone enough to want to figure out why anyone would even bother with something like romping, or anything more than kissing. Well, minus that one stupid crush on Payton that had hung around for far too long.

She watched as Colin and Bud leapt off the diving board, one right after the other, and both did double flips into the pool. All the other girls laughed like hyenas and applauded until she thought she would gag simply from their overbearing flirtatiousness. She had to admit, with a roll of her eye, that even though she had expressly been promised no guys would show, she was happy to have their company around. This way she didn't have to give away any more horrifying secrets that had already slipped through the cracks that day. And besides, even though she didn't want any of those guys, it was still nice to see their strong bodies all slick with pool water and tanned from the sun.

Lizzie perched her empty daiquiri glass on the edge of the pool and leaned back against the smooth stone edging the water when she felt a sharp tug on her ankles and she immediately sank underneath the water. She was stunned for a minute until she felt a strong body pull her close, then release her before she had time to think.

She came up gasping for breath, her eyes wide with stunned shock, her hair, thankfully, had been swept back as she surfaced so she could see who her attacker had been. She opened her eyes and felt that all too familiar jerk she felt every time she found herself staring into that pair of eyes every bit as green and translucent as her own.

Payton's face was arrow straight for a moment, but he gave himself away with the gradually increasing twitch at the edge of his lips, and then the round of laughter he could no longer contain. She glared at him but tried to make light of the fact that her skin was still tingling from where their bodies had recently touched.

"Ha, ha, Payton. Very funny. Do you always get your kicks picking on smaller people?" He smiled, that little dimple popping out, before he sank beneath the surface of the water and quietly swam away. She wondered what she had said after he swam away that had made him leave her alone. Whatever it was- surprisingly, she realized- it hadn't been her intention.

"Hey, wanna play a game of pool volleyball?" Bud asked it just before he leapt from the board again.

"Yeah." All the guys jumped out of the pool to go fetch the net while the girls found a ball and divided up the teams. Lizzie ended up being on the opposite team from Grace and Payton, and had a sneaking feeling before the match ever started she was going to regret having those two on the same team.

"All right, huddle up team." Payton, who had instantly been deemed team captain, yelled out to his team. They huddled, and Lizzie knew her team was in for disaster.

Somehow she had been elected captain for her team, though she tried to pass it off to one of the guys. Regardless, she knew after the huddle when Grace winked at her and Payton had a grin so wide you could see his teeth sparkling all the way to Texas that she was in for a battle.

Payton looked up from the huddle and tried not to focus in on that incredibly small and revealing two piece Lizzie had strapped to her body. He didn't know where she had found it, but he certainly did know that much more of that and whatever it was that happened to him whenever she was in his vicinity lately would send him over the edge for sure.

He focused in on the plan and sent the team to their places to begin the slaughter match. Payton pushed his way up to the front of the line and just his luck, found himself face to face with the owner of the red and white striped two piece with the maddeningly green eyes.

Lizzie smiled shyly at Payton, her stomach all twisted with nerves and emotions too crazy to name, and she prayed that her team wouldn't be slaughtered too badly.

Payton watched Lizzie smile at him, and he saw the way she cut her eyes down and away. He just knew she was playing with him, trying to flirt in her own way, and it sent his body into overdrive.

The first serve was thrown into the air and everyone watched as the ball bounced back and forth, back and forth. Suddenly, Payton was up in the air slamming the ball to the water below. His team, one point. Her team, zero.

That was fine by her. She wasn't going to give up yet. Her team served and lobbed it over the net. Colin served it back and the ball was going back and forth again. It was Lizzie's shot at the ball and she saw her opening. Up in the air she went, bikini long forgotten as she let her inner instinct drive and she slammed the ball to the water below. His team, one point. Her team, tied.

They went on neck and neck for a while, his team would score, then hers. But in the end, Payton got tired of playing and he and Colin decided they'd had enough fun for the day. They quickly put Lizzie's team out of its misery and happily did their victory dance like a bunch of crazed fools off the diving board.

It was getting later, and the girls needed to get on the road if they still planned to shop before the movie. They had all changed and were climbing in Grace's car when the guys climbed into Payton's truck to head out for a night of their own.

He stopped his truck just beside her window and smiled at the girls, his baseball cap shadowing that beautiful green Lizzie had learned to want so much. Absently she licked her lips, and Payton made sure he looked well away while she did. He was having enough trouble not thinking of her in that red bikini as it was. He turned his attention back to the girls, his smile firmly in place, his strong arm draped over the black metallic paint of his truck.

"Thanks for the fun, girls." All the girls giggled.

"Hey Lizzie?" He said her name slow and easy, like a cool summer spring, and it made her skin tingle just hearing the way he said it.

She looked at him more closely and found him studying her intently. "Am I going to see you at the pond again this summer?"

She smiled at him, remembering all the fun times they had had the last summer. "Maybe. If you're lucky." And with that Grace pulled away and left the guys spitting in her dust.

Payton stared after her while all the other guys laughed and gave high fives in the back.

*Chapter Sixteen*

It had been almost three months since school let out, and nearly that long since she had seen Payton. He had to go away for the summer, he had explained to her the one day she saw him at the pond. His grandparents that lived in Texas were getting older, and he needed to spend the summer on their ranch getting things back into shape before the fall harvest hit.

She knew he had been back for a few weeks now, but it was time for football training for the Varsity team to start, and she knew he was busy with that. Still, it bothered her that not seeing him for this long had upset her. She had no ties to him, but still somehow she felt some odd sort of connection between them.

She had met some guy while she and the girls were in Clarkston one night at the bowling alley, and that at least had kept her mind off of him a little. She kind of thought he was cute- nothing in comparison to Payton, but then again, in her mind, not many guys could ever stand a chance next to him. Still, this guy had his good qualities, and he acted like a gentleman. So, Lizzie had given him her phone number and he had called a few times over the past few weeks.

Lizzie lay on her porch swing, Skipper underneath snoring to his hearts content, while she read a chapter from the latest romance novel she had chosen to read. She had long since finished her summer reading, and had written the reports as well. Now it was time for her to read whatever it was she wanted, and this was what she chose.

The book was set in the 1700's and the heroine was swimming, supposedly unaware that anyone watched, while the hero secretly snuck to where he knew she was and watched her as she swam. He ended up sneaking into the water with her, and they had made love there in the shallow water close to the bank.

Lizzie sighed and put the book aside. Wouldn't it be nice to find a love like that, she thought? Her mind involuntarily moved back to the last day she had seen Payton, and she drifted off to sleep dreaming about that afternoon.

He'd looked gorgeous, she remembered that. His trunks this summer were navy blue and they accented the tan he'd already acquired in the short time he'd been out for summer. His muscles had filled out on his body, that she remembered all too well from the day she had been with him at Sellars' pool.

But that afternoon he'd snuck up behind her where she lay reading by the edge of the pond, and he'd taken her book from her and held it high over his head.

"Give that back, Payton Cartwright. Right now!" He laughed and danced out of her way.

"Or what? You don't look like you could hurt a fly, Liz, but I know better than that from watching you punch Lou Ann."

"That's right, I can punch. Do you want to find out how hard?"

"Is that a threat?" His smile had been wicked and taunting, and she couldn't help but laugh at his obvious tease.

"Come on, you've rescued me too many times for me to hurt you now. Just give the book back and we'll call it even." He'd thought about it for moment, and then smiled again.

"Tell you what. You spend two hours with me at the pond this afternoon doing whatever I ask, and then we'll call it even." She thought about that for a moment herself, then smiled her own impish smile.

"Deal. Now give me back my book." She could tell by the wicked light in his eye he had something up his sleeve, but she wasn't quite sure what.

"Umm… Nope sorry." He made a dash and hid her book back in a thicket of briars where she couldn't reach it. "In two hours you'll have your book back, but not a minute sooner."

It hadn't mattered. Not really. Not even a bagful of snakes would have driven her from that afternoon at the pond, but she pretended to pout anyway just to throw him off. She didn't know how much longer she could go on pretending that she didn't have feelings for him when inside she was dying to know what it felt like just to be in his arms.

She had expected him to immediately tell her what to do, but instead he sat down on her towel and patted the other edge for her to sit next to him. Tentatively, she sat next to him, their legs brushing barely against each other. He smiled at her, his green eyes crinkling behind dark lashes, his white teeth sparkling out from deeply tanned skin.

Every time he smiled at her like that she felt like the whole world had just been handed to her on a silver platter. She would give every piece of fashionable clothing she had to Goodwill if only he would smile at her, and only her, like that for the rest of her life.

He was the first boy she had ever liked, and she couldn't imagine ever finding someone that would, or could, take the place of this crush. She smiled back at him, a little shyly, then turned to study a turtle as it bobbed along the surface of the pond.

They talked for a while about simple things before they circled back to summer vacation.

"What are you doing this summer?" He asked her as they watched a bird dive bomb the water and try to pluck a fish from the pond.

"I'm going to be here, reading, like usual. What about you?"

"What, no big plans with all your new girlfriends?" Lizzie smiled. They both knew it was because of him that she had these new friends.

"Well, I'm sure we'll think of something to do. Maybe a little time at the pool or going to the movies."

"Shoot," he smiled at her and winked once before he looked back at the pond. "I'll bet before I get back to Edenville at the end of the summer you and all your girlfriends will have picked up a throng of admirers over in Clarkston."

She blushed and laughed, almost wishing it would be true that some guy would have a crush on her. And then it hit her. Payton had said when he got back to Edenville.

"Wait," She turned to study him, her eyes growing a little wider. "You're not leaving Edenville for the summer, are you?"

"Yep."

"Well where are you going?"

His grin was wide and playful. "Why? You gonna miss me?"

"Yes." She blurted it out without thinking, and as quickly as it was out she wished it back in. Her face reddened perceptibly. "Well, that is…" She scrambled to think up something to cover her misguided words. "I'm going to miss your athletic abilities around here this summer. Who else is gonna whoop my butt in field baseball, or teach me how to fish?"

"That is true."

"Seriously, though, where are you going?"

"Texas. My grandparents live on a ranch out there and they need someone to help them over the summer. My dad thought it would be a good idea if I went and chipped in around the place."

"That's nice of you to go."

Payton shrugged his shoulders and plucked some grass from the ground to play with. "Yeah, well, it's the least I can do to give back something to them for all they've done for me."

Lizzie didn't know what that meant, or if she should pry, but she was curious. "What do you mean?"

"Oh, nothing really. It's just... I think its neat how hard my mom's parent's worked. They had nothing and scraped together everything they could to raise money to buy that ranch. They worked hard all their life to finally get their daughter married to a Senator's son. Besides, they've set up my college fund so I won't ever have to worry about paying for college. They just do neat stuff like that, and I thought it was time I said thank you."

Wow. Lizzie was impressed. She hadn't ever heard one of her classmates say something like that before, and she never would have expected it out of the most popular boy in school. But here he sat, playing with pieces of grass next to her on a towel, telling her how much he needed to say thanks to his family. That was amazing, to say the least.

"Payton." He turned to look at her. It was the first time in his life he ever noticed her say his name. "You really impress me. Not many guys would think to say thank you for something like that."

He sat on the shoreline beside her, her body warm next to his. Her face was so sincere as she turned it up to him, oblivious to the affect her words had on him. In all his life, he'd had people tell him how great he was, how perfect his throwing arm, his smile, his athletic body, his green eyes were. He'd had girls from two towns away promise him the world just because of his status as a football hero. But never in his life had a girl actually taken the time to look at his character and admire him for that.

His smile was easy, and his eyes caught hers and held. He wasn't sure what she was thinking but he had a hunch it wasn't about the kiss he wanted to give her. And suddenly he couldn't wait another minute to taste her. He leaned in and softly touched his lips to hers. Briefly, the barest meeting of lips and then he pulled away. Her eyes were wide, and her lips still held their puckered shape. Payton chuckled.

That was all Lizzie could take. She had no idea what just happened. One minute she was talking about their summer plans and the next she was fawning all over him, doling out compliments like it was her job, and oh God, she was mortified! He'd obviously just kissed her to shut her up. God, she could be such an idiot sometimes. She had to get up, move away from him for a few minutes. He was too close and she was drowning being near to him. His big body, already well above six feet and filling out everyday with gorgeous, athletic muscle was sending her changing body over the edge. And just realizing how put together he was on the inside made her crush on him that much more severe.

Not to mention that the feel of his lips on hers were seared permanently into every fiber of her being for the rest of her life.

She whipped off her t-shirt and shorts, stripping down to the sensible one piece underneath and dove into the chilly pond water to cool off. She could almost hear the blood rushing through her veins, calling her, begging her to satisfy her craving for him. Only problem was, he would think she was insane, and she had no idea how to even begin going about satisfying the desire she felt for him.

She sliced through the water, and surfaced again on the opposite side of the pond just in time to hear a splash and turn to see Payton's form gliding underneath the rippling water. He shook his head like a dog when he came up, but of course, his hair fell back perfectly against his head, leaving her even more curious than before how to fill this craving for him.

He laughed. "So why didn't you wear that suit you wore at Sellars' house?" Lizzie blushed. She had hoped he would forget about that awful suit.

"That thing? Are you kidding me? Grace picked that out and I only wore it to make her feel like I didn't hate it."

"Do you?"

"What?"

"Hate it?"

She giggled. "Uh...*yeah.*"

"Oh, come on, I think she's got great taste. Especially in swimsuits." He ducked underneath the water and surfaced again a little closer to her. His eyes were intent on her when he came up. He glided just beneath the surface, his eyes and nose the only things protruding, and he didn't even make a ripple as he inched forward, closer and closer to her.

Lizzie felt suddenly nervous, like prey that senses the predator nearby, but she didn't know if she should run or stay. She knew he would never hurt her- he had come to her rescue too many times for him to start playing rough now.  But something in the air told her to run, get out of the way, this boy had danger in his eyes, and they were focused on her.

"Lizzie?"  He watched her, inching forward all the while until he stopped less than a foot from her.  She didn't take her eyes from him.  She didn't dare- she didn't know what he might do.

"Hmm?"

"Have you ever been skinny dipping?"  He nearly laughed when he saw her face crinkle in disgust.

"No!"

"Oh, come on, it's not that bad.  Honest.  It's like... well, the most freeing experience you can have."  He paused to think.  "Well, almost.  You should try it sometime."

"You think so, huh?"

"I certainly do."

"When?  When should I experience this... this freeing thing?"

"Right now would suit me just fine."  She laughed.  Right, like she was that dumb.  He might not try to hurt her, but she wasn't going to let him make a fool out of her.  She snuck a look at her watch and noticed their two hours were up by fifteen minutes.

She held her arm up and smiled impishly, "Oops.  Saved by the bell."

"That's a shame, Liz."  She smiled.  He'd just recently started calling her that, and she thought it was kind of cute.  "You're really missing out on something great."

"I'm sure I am, Payton.  But maybe I'll just try it out by myself first and then I'll go co-ed.  How 'bout I let you know when you get back from Texas."  She pulled herself up on the opposite bank and let some of the water drip off her.  "By the way, when do you get back?"

He'd told her he wouldn't get back until time to leave for summer football training over at a junior college in Clarkston.  Her heart had felt heavy, and she knew it was simply because she was sad he was leaving.  She'd grown accustomed to their summer meetings at the pond.

But maybe it was better he was leaving, she told herself as she walked back slowly to her house.  This way she could get rid of her stupid crush if he wasn't around for her to see him all the time.  It was obvious that she was holding out for something that would never come.  If she held on forever, wishing the boy who didn't even think about her along the same lines she thought about him would make a move, she'd probably be waiting forever.

And who knew, maybe by the time he came back, she would have found some new guy to crush on, and she wouldn't even remember Payton Cartwright's name. She knew that was wishing on big dreams, but it was worth a shot at least.


Payton finished hauling another bail of hay up to the top of his grandparent's barn and paused for a minute to catch his breath. His body ached, and he was exhausted, but he was happy for the exercise and a chance to work his muscles doing something that was not only good for his body, but also gave him a chance to repay his family for everything that had been given to him in his life.

He lay on a bail for a minute, letting the slight breeze flush over him as it whipped up from the breezeway and into the loft. He thought of home, of what his parent's must be doing right then, and of all his friends that he missed like crazy. A pair of green eyes and long dark hair floated through his mind, and he wondered what Lizzie was doing. It seemed so odd that he always thought of her at the strangest time, but somehow whenever he did it made him smile to think of her.

What was it about her that always kept her stuck in his mind, he wondered. And then he thought back on the last few times he'd seen her. She was beginning to change. Not in personality. He didn't think it possible for a girl to remain so unaffected by instant popularity as she had, but he was happy to see that her rise to fame hadn't damaged her loveable attitude. And he'd long ago discovered that not only could she outmatch him any day in a genius contest, she could also hold her own on the sport's field, and when she put her mind to it, she could have him busting a gut laughing at some crazy thought she had rolling around in her brain. She was like the coolest person he'd ever met, and well, lately… something else had come to his attention.

It was, well… her body. He'd begun to notice it in the spring, the way her clothes fit her more snugly and in all the right places as well. He hadn't wanted to notice, but simply by him just being a guy, he had picked up on it.

Then there was the day at Sellars's pool party. Man, he'd thought his hormones would make him die right there on the spot. He'd expected Lizzie to be there, but not in what she had on. For some reason he had been picturing her in her usual conservative attire- some bathing suit that covered every inch of skin, and when he arrived and seen quite the opposite he thought his eyes would pop out of his head.

All he had dreamed about for days was that red and white striped bikini and the small amount of skin it covered. Even now he could picture the small breasts that had started to appear. In the back of his mind he wondered what they looked like now.

God, he had to get her out of his mind. It was driving him insane. If he kept thinking about her like this, he was going to have to go out and find some cheap substitute to take her place so he could get his hormones back in check.

Payton stood and climbed back out of the hay loft. He had at least three truck loads more of hay to unload and then the horses had to be fed before dinner. He hoped it would be enough to sap his energy so when he fell into bed that night it would be a black oblivion instead of filled with dreams of Lizzie.

## *Chapter Seventeen*

Payton broke up the huddle where his offensive line was grouped on the opposing team's thirty yard line, and tried his hardest not to look over at the crowd in the stadium. It was the first game of the season, and he had been crowned the official starting quarterback for the next two years.

That was all well and good, but it wasn't going to get him many pats on the back if he didn't win this game. It was the first game of the season, and just their bad luck, the game was played on the other team's turf. They were nearing the end of the third quarter and his team was down by ten points. Dixie could make that up, easily, if he could just concentrate long enough to throw a decent pass to someone who didn't happen to be surrounded by the other team or end up throwing it to the other team itself.

But that wasn't an easy feat when his ability to tone out the crowd seemed to be failing him miserably tonight. It also wasn't easy when every time he glimpsed over at the fans he caught sight of Lizzie with all her girlfriends.

Focus, he must force himself to focus. He managed to concentrate just long enough to throw the twenty five yard pass to a wide receiver that managed to leap into the end zone before the opposing team's defense pulled him down. Good. Now they were only down by four, soon to be three points if they made this field goal.

He headed off the field and let his defense take control for a while and tried to give his body and mind a break. But he found himself staring across the field, through the defenses pitiful maneuvering, and back into the stands to where Lizzie sat with her sister and their friends.

If he had thought before he left for the summer that she was growing into her looks, he wasn't quite sure what to think of her now. Now... well, let's just say now he had a hard time concentrating whenever those long, long legs, and lush firm breasts came into his mind. Somehow over the summer what was before an attractive teenage girl had now morphed into a stunning, woman that had curves in all the right places and silky smoothness everywhere else.

Payton shifted on the bench, trying to dislodge the thoughts in his mind that were making him rather painful behind his jock strap. He forced himself to study the guys on defense so he could give them pointers in practice on Monday. But whether he wanted to or not, his eyes kept skimming their way back up to the bleachers to the dark, curly hair and big bright smile of Lizzie.

He cursed violently to himself when the defense fell apart and let the other team's player slip through. He crossed into the end zone and slam dunked the ball between his legs, and Payton could hear their crowd behind him going wild. Great, another touchdown to recover before the end of the game, and as it was, there was only ten seconds left in the third. He still had the fourth quarter to catch up, but he knew the odds were stacking up against him, and he could feel the pressure settle on his shoulders like buzzards just waiting for some wounded piece of wildlife to die.

He knew that *he* was that wounded piece of wildlife.

Payton grabbed up his helmet, tried to shrug some of the pressure off of him, and headed out into the field to turn what he feared might be their first loss of the season into a win.

"All right boys, listen up, and listen good. Coach is spitting fire right now and we all know that. Let's get out there and swing this game back into our territory. Jim, I want you to fade back when the ball comes off the line. We're going to fake to the right, and Clint I want you open to catch for the touchdown. We all know we're down to the wire, let's make every step and second count. Got it?"

"Got it!" Payton was glad to hear his team at least sounded optimistic.

"Good, now on three... one, two, three- break!"

Lizzie's stomach was a bundle of nerves as she watched the game beside her sister. No matter what the offense did, Dixie's defense stunk it up every time they hit the field, and Lizzie was worried that Payton's offense couldn't hold the team together very much longer. Whatever the reason, this certainly didn't look like the Dixie football team she remembered from last season.

She cheered with the rest of the fans, trying to get the players back into their momentum, keeping her fingers crossed that they wouldn't lose this first game of the season. Someone bumped into her and down the row she heard a small fight break out, but she was too wrapped up in the game to really care about anything beyond the field.

It was the offenses turn out on the field, and there was only forty-five seconds left in the game. They had managed to eek out a touchdown early in the fourth, but had missed the field goal. Dixie was still down by a solid four points, and needed to make a touchdown to win the game. This was their last chance at winning the opening game of the season.

Lizzie could feel her pulse hammering and her body tensing with nerves. The team crouched, waiting for the ball to snap, and then as if in slow motion, they were off, pushing their way through the defense. From the stands, she could see the player moving down the field, open now for the pass. It was going to be close, as the most enormous player on the field was quickly closing the distance to Payton, intent on taking him out. At the last second, Payton threw the ball, his body perfectly positioned to hurl the ball down the field milliseconds before the defensive lineman took him down.

The crowd stilled, Lizzie's heart skipped a few beats, and then... wham! The ball slammed against the receiver, and he high tailed it the last ten yards into the end-zone. The stadium went wild, the cheerleaders were doing flips all over the place, and Lizzie's heart finally settled back into a semi-normal rhythm again.

The post-game party was going to be a blast.

Payton stood underneath the shower water in the locker room for a solid fifteen minutes, letting the cool water ease his aching muscles and tired brain. He didn't know exactly how it was that they had pulled out a win in those last few seconds, but he knew he was happy about it.

He would have been more excited about a solid smashing of the other team, but a win was a win and it all added up in the play books. One thing was for sure, though, coach was going to work the dog stew out of them in practice on Monday, he was sure of that. But for now it was the weekend and there was the post game party to get to.

Payton wrapped one of the locker room towels around his waist as he shut the water off, and let the water drip from his upper body and head of hair. He quickly stashed his football pads in his mesh football bag to take out to his truck with him, and threw on the change of clothes he'd brought for the rest of the night.

He was just about the last one left in the locker room, but he called out his good byes as he left and headed out into the warm evening air. The stars had finally peeked out from behind a thunderhead that had been threatening to break open throughout the game. Luckily it had held together, and it looked like it was going to turn into a nice night after all.

Perfect, he thought as he climbed into the truck and started the engine. It was turning into the perfect evening for him, and he was ready to be at the party, catching up with his buddies, and maybe even with Lizzie as well.

He let his mind think about her on the short drive out to the party. About the ways she had changed over the summer, and also about the ways she hadn't. No matter what came her way, he noticed, whether it be popularity, or a sudden stunning body, she still had that same sweet personality. Not that she was a pushover. He thought about the way her eyes could light with fire when he'd pushed her too far, and he knew that she could definitely hold her own when pushed enough. Hell, he'd watched her hold her own for years as the school dork and she hadn't done half bad for herself then.

There was something different about her. Something that attracted him to her no matter what the time or the place. She could be a thousand miles away from him, or more, like she was this summer, and he still thought about her. Couldn't get her out of his mind for more than a few hours at a time. She'd somehow even worked her way into his dreams at night. The only place he hadn't managed to find her was in his arms, but he hoped to remedy that sometime soon.

There were cars and trucks everywhere when he pulled into the dirt drive that led back to the party. Apparently the close call win had boosted the party ratings, and people were ready to let lose after their nerves had been on end all night. He knew he sure was ready.

He managed to slip behind the crowd unnoticed and wove his way up to Colin, Bud, and Hank before too many party-goers flocked to his side. He caught the wide grins of his three best-friends as they heard the shrill high-pitched cheers of a group of girls running up to Payton. They all made smoochy-faces at him behind the girls' backs and then rolled their eyes. But Payton was kind and introduced the girls to his friends too, and for a while the girls were content to stand around and chat with them as well. That is, until they realized the star of the hour had slipped away from the group and had disappeared into the night.

Payton grabbed a drink from one of the coolers and wove his way through the crowd, pausing occasionally to say hello to a friend. He saw Grace's flame hair illuminated by the lights of one of the sets of KC lights on a pickup truck and headed her way, knowing where Grace was, Lizzie wasn't far away.  He felt an odd sense of disappointment when he noted she wasn't with Grace, though.

"Hey, Grace."  Grace turned to face him, and smiled.

"Well, hey, stranger.  How was Texas?"

"She told you I went to Texas, huh?"  Grace giggled and flipped her long red hair behind her shoulder.

"Of course, sugar.  We tell each other everything, if you know what I mean."  She paused to wink, and yes, Payton was pretty sure he knew what she meant.

"Well then, since you know everything about her, can you tell me where she's gone off to?"

"Tell you where who's gone off to?"  That sweet, silky voice he would have known anywhere came from behind him, and he turned with a smile on his face.

"Hey… you."  He held his smile in check, but barely.  Beside the girl who had taken up residence in every one of his thoughts, was Brett Faulkner, the punter for Valley View's football team.  He would have been fine if he hadn't noticed they were holding hands and standing pretty close together.  Instead, he felt his stomach churn and the first big punch of loss that he had felt in a long time hit him square in the gut.

"Hey, Payton!"  Lizzie broke the connection between her and Brett and ran to give him a hug.  It was quick, over before he knew it had started, but still it took him back.

"So, who's your friend, Liz?"

"Oh," she paused to giggle.  "Sorry, I've lost my manners.  Payton Cartwright, meet Brett Faulkner.  Brett this is Payton.  Brett and I met at the beginning of the summer.  He goes to Valley View."  She noted that they didn't shake hands, and they half grunted a hello, but she put that behind her and moved on with the conversation.

"You played great tonight, by the way."  She smiled at him, a quick flash of her teeth that went straight through him.

"Thanks.  We barely pulled that out in the end."

"How was Texas?"  She watched him with eyes he could have sworn grew greener over the summer.  Suddenly he felt cramped and suffocated.  He didn't want to be standing there talking to her, watching her body do things to him that made him want to groan, while she snuggled up next to this guy she was obviously dating.

"It was fine. Sorry, I forgot I have somewhere I need to be." And with that he walked away from the group.

Lizzie could recognize that male form from a mile away. She spotted him as she and Brett where walking through the crowd, working their way back to Grace, and she felt her palms begin to sweat just thinking about being close to him. She hadn't seen him since he left for the summer, except for tonight as she watched him from the stands. She enjoyed watching him out on the field, but she had to admit, seeing him out from underneath all those pads, was another sight altogether.

She could hear him talking to Grace, that deep, rich voice that she heard in her dreams, as she edged closer to them, and suddenly she wished Brett, as nice as he may be, wasn't standing beside her. She wished she hadn't invited him to the post-game party after all. But he was attractive and so far a gentleman, and after she had convinced herself that waiting, hopelessly, for Payton to show her the time of day would be like waiting for her to win the lottery, she had agreed to be Brett's girlfriend.

She held on to Brett's hand tighter as she closed the final gap to Payton, and watched his face as he turned and saw her holding Brett's hand. Was that shock on his face? She felt the first tug of satisfaction edge through her. She had somehow, miraculously, made Payton jealous? It couldn't be.

But suddenly he was ending their conversation and walking away. She forced herself not to turn and watch him leave, even though she loved watching the way he carried himself when he walked. Instead, she looked up at Brett and then smiled at Grace, and waved as the other girls in their group came over to join them.

"Was that Payton I just saw?" Jade asked as she joined the group. She craned her neck to focus in on the form fading into the distance.

"Yep."

"Where's he off to?"

"I don't know," Grace commented. "He said something about needing to be somewhere."

Lizzie couldn't help but stifle a laugh at Jade's obvious disappointment. She was almost glad she had Brett here with her tonight. Too many girls were jockeying for Payton's attention these days, it seemed. Good thing she didn't have to be one of them.

"Well, girls, we're off. I was just coming back to say goodnight."

"Goodnight?" Grace looked genuinely shocked. "But you're going to miss all the toasts and stuff later on."

"Sorry, Brett's taking me home…" She left it at that, hoping at least Grace would catch her meaning.

Grace winked and gave her a hug. "Alright, doll. Have a good time. Call me tomorrow, 'kay?"

"Sure thing."


Payton trudged through the field behind the party, too mad to do anything but stomp around in a cow pasture, hoping he didn't step in too many cow patties before his temper cooled. Brett Faulkner. Ugh. He could feel the bile rise up in his throat and he spat on the ground to try and push the taste away.

Why had she picked Brett Faulkner of all guys? Payton had met up with him plenty of times on the football field and knew enough about the guy to know he was up to no good. He had a reputation as being fast and pushy with the ladies, and something told him that Lizzie hadn't gotten to know that side of Brett quite yet.

Something inside of him refused to believe that if Lizzie knew that side of him she would stick around. For that, at least, he was grateful.

He wanted so badly, too badly, to tell her, to try and warn her what this Brett guy was like. But deep inside he had a feeling that Lizzie would just shrug him off if he said anything. God, what was this incessant need inside of him to constantly protect her from everything? He wished he knew, and he wished he knew how to stop it.

Why should it matter to him, in the least, he felt like screaming to the stars. But deep inside it did matter, and no matter how angry he was at her or the situation of the moment, there was nothing he could do to help.

For now, though, there was nothing he could do but stand back and watch, he thought angrily as he paced back and forth among the cows. That was the part that bothered him most of all. He knew what a creep Brett could be, and yet he had no power to make Lizzie the wiser. All he could do was step out of her way, and keep watch on her from the distance. When she fell, and he knew that sooner or later she would, he would be standing by to pick her up from the fall.

*Chapter Eighteen*

Payton's tongue stuck out from between his lips as he scrunched his face in concentration. His hard muscles bunched and rippled, and he even cursed a little, but nothing seemed to make that last damn piece of tape go onto the package he had insisted on wrapping himself.

There. He had finished. He held the small square box wrapped in green and red Christmas paper back to survey. It wasn't completely horrible, he told himself, and slapped a big, red, sticky-bottomed bow on top of the paper. Besides, it's what's inside that counts, he thought as he snatched his keys from the desk in his room and headed out to his truck.

He had seen it the other day when he was walking through the mall looking for Christmas gifts for his family. He hadn't planned to buy Lizzie anything, especially since she still had that loser boyfriend Brett hanging around, but he'd seen it and known it was perfect for her. It was a simple, small, silver, choker chain, but he could picture her wearing it, and he had no choice but to purchase it for her.

He could picture her wearing it with that crimson red silk dress she had worn to the homecoming dance earlier in the year, and he punched the gas harder on his engine to flood the thought from his mind. He had watched her from a distance that evening, as he danced with Jade, his date for the night, and wished he could hold Lizzie in his arms.

Instead, he'd had to watch Brett hold her close and whisper things into her ear that made her giggle and blush. Ugh, he had wanted to walk over to them and rip her from his arms and haul her off somewhere that sleezeballs like Mr. Valley View couldn't find her. But he hadn't. He'd held his tongue, and amazingly, his temper, and the night had gone on as planned. If anything, Payton realized as he drove the last few blocks to her house, watching her dating Brett had only made him realize even more how much he really wished she were dating him.

He pulled up outside her house and quietly slipped the box on top of a card he had signed inside the mailbox. He didn't want to disturb her. After all, he didn't really have any decent excuse to leave her a Christmas present other than just because he wanted to. He would be too embarrassed to give it to her in person.

As he drove away, he wondered what her face would look like when she opened the gift. He could just about picture the way her eyes would light up, and that goofy grin that would spread across her face like it did when something really amused her. Well, regardless, he hoped she liked it even half as much as he thought she would.

"Did you hear something," Grace asked, looking up from the last of Lizzie's toe nails she had been painting.

"Hmm…Maybe. Sounded like a truck engine. Why, you expecting your rock star to come surprise you with a big, sloppy kiss on Christmas Eve?" Lizzie giggled and dodged the magazine Grace managed to hurl in her direction.

"Maybe. That could have been all I asked for from Santa for Christmas, you know."

Lizzie rolled her eyes. "That's really lame, Carrot. Really lame. Now seriously, did you hear something or not?"

"I don't know…"

"Lizzie?" Both girls turned as her mother opened her bedroom door. "Lizzie, honey, this present came for you. It was in the mailbox when I went out to check it a few minutes ago."

"Thanks, mom" She took the gift and the card and waited for her mom to close the door again before she studied them. There was a massive red bow stuck on top of a small box, hand wrapped in not the greatest of precision, in Christmas paper. The bow had to have been about two times too large for the box and gave the present a comical appearance. On the outside of the card was her first name only, printed in tiny, neat script writing, and underlined once with black ink.

She tore into the card, with Grace hanging over shoulder. "Is it from Brett? Is it?"

Lizzie shrugged her off. "I don't know. Back off a minute and I'll tell you."

The card was simple, a black and white picture of snow falling and settling on the rolling pastures of farm land. A lone barn stood in the distance, along with an old farm house with smoke pouring from the chimney. It was blank on the inside except for the same tiny, neat script writing.

*Merry Christmas. Thought of you when I saw this, and wanted you to have it.*

*-Payton.*

Her eyes nearly popped from her head when she saw who had signed the card, and her heart instantly began to race. What was in the little box, she wondered, as she put the card down and began to rip into the paper surrounding the box. From some vague place in her periphery she heard Grace gasp when she read the card, and then together they sat in shock when she pulled the silver choker from its holder in the box.

She put in on immediately and went to the mirror to study it around her neck. It fit perfectly, and was simple, yet the most elegant piece of jewelry she had ever received as a gift. She didn't know what to say. She had nothing to say, but she caught Grace's look in the mirror, and it told her that her best friend understood every thought, every nuance, without her ever having to say a word. She was thankful she didn't have to put her emotions into words just then.

Spring had arrived at last. The time of year when all things are new, the birds are singing, the flowers start blooming, and life is all filled with newness and happiness. Only problem was, Lizzie didn't feel the least bit excited about the season on this particular afternoon. In fact, she felt particularly awful, and had left her house hoping that a walk through the park might clear her head and ease her thoughts.

Lizzie plopped down onto the park bench, wishing she had a tissue in her pocket. She couldn't believe the horrible luck she was having today. First, failing her first test, *ever*, and now being dumped by her first boyfriend. She could feel the tears building up and she tried to fight them even though she knew it was useless. She just hoped no one she knew happened to be walking through the park when they finally decided to come streaming down.

Quickly glancing around and realizing there was nothing to use to mop up her tears when they came, she leaned back against the back of the bench and let her mind go free. Boys. They were so stupid. She hadn't even really liked Brett, and yet here she sat blubbering over him like some love-struck idiot.

It wasn't that. Of that she was sure. No, she was most definitely not love struck by him. She had seen enough of his lack in manners to realize his original show as a gentleman was just that: a show. But it was what he had said that made her heart break. Not for him, but for her.

At first Brett had been patient with her. He told her he would wait forever if she needed to, that he wouldn't push into anything more physical than what she felt comfortable doing. But when weeks and then months had gone by with little more than kisses and the very occasional exploration into other areas, he had begun to get pushy, and rude.

Her suspicion of him being a genuine ass was officially confirmed when he'd called to break up. What kind of inconsiderate jerk *called* to break up? But then, he'd also had the nerve to laugh and say he'd found someone else who knew how to use her body for more than just a way to freeze men out.

Was she really cold and unlovable? She didn't think so. What was the matter with wanting to hold out until the right person came along? Lizzie could feel the tears building, and this time she didn't try to stop them. She could feel her defenses breaking down, and with it the tears began to fall, at first slow and sad, then harder and angrier.

Payton had been standing on the other side of a thick old oak tree for several minutes now, watching Lizzie from a distance. He had been making the cut through from the school to Hank's house when he'd noticed a girl sitting on the park bench and she made his hormones do a double take. At first glance it was the pink spring sweater set and the blue jeans that attracted his attention, but then he'd realized it was Lizzie that he was checking out, and his heart as well had clicked into overdrive.

He was about to head her way to talk when he noticed that her face looked troubled, and he wasn't sure if she would want any company or not. But now that he was watching huge tears fall from her eyes, and her body shake with those desperate attempts to rid herself of emotion, he felt like running over and pulling her into his arms.

He set his jaw, determined to find out who had hurt her and pummel them into the ground. He just couldn't figure out why that no good boyfriend of hers hadn't been around to do it instead of him. He was going to figure that out as well.

He stopped a few feet from her and took a deep breath to settle himself. "Lizzie?"

She jumped from her seat and quickly wiped the tears falling from her eyes. She tried to smile, but he could see her lower lip trembling and knew she was hurting really bad.

"Sit down, Liz. Tell me what happened." She did as he commanded, and as soon as he sat beside her she threw her arms around him, nearly knocking the wind from his unprepared body.

His eyes widened in shock at the sudden embrace, and slowly, uncertainly placed his arms around her, lightly stroking her hair. He didn't really care at that moment if she had ten boyfriends and they were all watching them. In his mind, something was wrong, and he was there to help her.

After a few minutes of calmly whispering to her he held her back a little so he could look into her eyes. The tears had stopped, he was thankful for that, but he could still see the turmoil in her eyes and the pain that was eating at her heart. Something strong and tight clenched around his own.

"Tell me what it is, Liz." His voice was soft and reassuring and he could feel her body start to relax the slightest little bit.

"It's nothing really. Just something stupid that hurt my feelings."

"It's not 'nothing', Lizzie. And I want to know what happened." He kept his eyes focused on her face, and he hoped that she didn't sense the anger he felt welling up inside watching her obvious pain. He willed himself to calm down, all the while watching her intently. After a moment she relented.

"Well, you know that guy, Brett, I've been seeing?" Just the mention of the guy made red flash into his eyes.

"Did he hurt you? I swear, I'll..."

"No! It's nothing like that. At least... well, at least he didn't hurt me physically."

He placed his forefinger beneath her chin and raised her face up so he could look into her eyes. The tears that had stopped were starting again, and gently with his thumb, he smoothed away a lone tear that fell across her cheek.

"I can go kill him for you if that will make you feel better." He forced himself to smile as if it were a joke. But the anger inside thinking about what that asshole could possibly have done to her made him think of violent solutions to her problem. Lizzie managed a weak laugh, but it wasn't heartfelt he could tell.

"No. That's alright. Thanks anyway, though."

"Well, at least tell me what he said. I'd like to know."

Lizzie nibbled her lower lip and considered if Payton really did want to know her troubles. But, it seemed like he'd been her protector in everything else in this town, so far, so why not this as well?

"Really?" She asked, a huge question mark almost visibly looming above her head.

"Really."

She sniffed quietly and took a deep breath to calm herself. Payton watched her quietly, his big green eyes intent on her face, and for a moment she felt special. If only she weren't cold, and unlovable, she heard her mind say, and she wished that at least once, this one time, she could truly be special to him. But if she wasn't he was doing a pretty good job of showing her that she was.

She went on to tell him about Brett's phone call and all that he had said. She could tell Payton was unhappy because of the way his jaw clenched and released, clenched and released, just like her daddy's did, but he didn't say a word until she was finished. He waited a full minute after she stopped talking to respond.

"So let me get this straight. You let some jack-ass from Valley View convince you that you're cold and unlovable because you wouldn't give him the physical action he wanted?"

"Well, I-"

He took her by the arm and hauled her up close to his body. "Listen to me, Lizzie. No one has the right to make you feel anything you don't want to feel. You're not cold or unlovable, and I really want to beat his face in for suggesting that to you." He leaned back a little so he could look at her face. "You don't honestly believe the trash that idiot told you is the truth, do you?"

She didn't respond, and there was no doubt that he could read every emotion on her face. She believed every line that Brett had fed her, and Payton knew it. She could see the anger all over his face, could feel it pulsing in waves from his body. He watched her for a minute and she felt him calm after a while.

He stroked her shoulder and pushed a small strand of hair behind her ear. "I'm not full of great words, Liz, but I do know this: You couldn't be cold and unlovable even if you were shipped to the North Pole for the rest of your life. Trust me, Liz, it just isn't part of your nature. I can't explain it to you, but somehow I just know." He smiled at her.

"Come on, I know what will help this out." He stood and hauled her up with him.

"What's that?" Lizzie asked shakily.

"We're going by Grace's house to pick her up then we're headed to the Pharmacy to grab a milkshake." Lizzie sniffled, and smiled for the first time all day.

*Chapter Nineteen*

Payton checked himself in the mirror one last time, brushed his fingers through his dark hair and grabbed his keys off his dresser. He couldn't believe how fast the school year had gone, and now it was already time for the spring barn party again. He loved going to the barn party every year: all the excitement in the air, people going wild because it was getting closer to the end of the year.

Only this one and one more before they graduated, and Payton could hardly believe then it would be time for college. But tonight he didn't want to the think about the future. Tonight was special, and he wanted to think about only each second as they came his way.

"Night, mom!" He yelled as he scurried down the stairs and out the door. "Don't wait up," He managed to shout out before the door closed behind him.

Julie Cartwright walked to the cut glass front door and watched her son, all grown up at last, as he climbed into his truck and pulled away, red brake lights shining in the distance. She remembered her husband, Rick, surprising Payton with that truck not more than a few months ago. It had been a special gift, from father to son, when Payton had led Dixie's football team to the state Championships and they had won. Rick had been so ecstatic about the win that he'd surprised Payton with it the next week.

God, how she loved those two men in her life. Not a day went by that she didn't thank her lucky stars for them. And here she stood watching one of them growing up in front of her eyes, off to pick up the newest girl in what she feared was quite a growing collection.

That was another thing Payton had inherited from his father. Along with those devastating good looks came the thrill of the chase. She could remember her girlfriends telling her long ago that she should watch herself with Rick. He liked to claim girls and then leave them as quick as they came. She had laughed so hard when they'd told her, then cried herself to sleep that night out of fear that she would lose him.

But Rick had stayed by her side, and the day he'd asked her to marry him, she said yes, and they'd married that afternoon. She had been afraid that if she let him out of her sight, he'd go home and think things over and then change his mind. Yet, twenty years later, here she stood, in his home, still sharing his bed, and they had built so many good memories together.

Julie smiled as she watched the tail lights of Payton's truck fade away then turned to head back to the kitchen to finish up the evening meal's dishes.

Payton pulled the big black truck to a stop in front of Lizzie's front door and took a deep breath before he opened his door and climbed out. It was the first time he had ever shown up at her house with the intention of picking her and her alone, up to go somewhere. Sure, he'd been there plenty of times just to drop by and say hello, or to pick up Lizzie and MC and Grace to go somewhere together. But he had never been here when it was specifically to see her.

Payton thought back on the day last week when he'd finally gotten up the nerve to ask her to go with him to the barn party. It was funny because most people had Payton figured as a guy with nerves of steel. Never flinched when a big linebacker came his way, never had trouble asking girls out on dates. But beneath it all, he had feelings and a case of nerves that flared up on him occasionally, just like it had that day.

He'd watched her as she got her food from the lunch line and made it over to the table where she and he and all their friends ate for lunch every day. That darned piece of ham sandwich had gotten lodged in his dry throat as he watched her silky legs and hips sway back and forth as she came closer his way. He'd nearly coughed up a lung, but managed to get himself under control with a swig of water, and only looked mildly handicapped in the process.

She'd smiled at him, and asked, "Are you okay?"

He'd waited until he caught his breath and added, "Yeah, but I'd be better if you let me take you to the barn party next Friday night." He would never forget the shock that had registered on her face.

Later, she'd found him at his locker. "Payton?"

"Yeah?" He got that same electric jolt he always did when he turned and held her gaze.

"Do you mean... uh... when you asked me earlier... did you mean, well, you and me. Alone?"

He smiled at her, and watched her face begin to turn red in a blush. "That was the general idea. Of course, if you don't want to we can always-"

"No! I mean… no, that's fine. I just wanted to make sure that's what you meant." She'd smiled, bigger than he could remember her smiling in a long, long time and had walked away humming. He'd never forget that exact moment, that exact thrill for as long as he lived.

Her father answered the door, his usual grin plastered to his face, and shook Payton's hand like he always had. Only tonight, Payton felt like he had the scrutiny of a thousand fathers watching him. It was the first time in his life he had been nervous around one of his friend's fathers. Maybe because it was the first time in his life that he actually cared what they thought.

Just then Lizzie walked around the corner from where she'd been sitting in the den with her sister. He could feel his pulse spike and he forced his brain not to even think about how great she looked. She wore a pair of blue jeans that somehow molded just perfectly to her legs along with a black, sleeveless scoop neck top that just barely showed a hint of that luscious cleavage beneath. Her black felt cowboy hat and black cowboy boots made him smile, and he gave her a quick wink before he turned back to her father.

"Thanks for letting Lizzie come with me tonight, Mr. Benford." He gave her father his best gentleman smile, hoping her dad didn't give them too hard a time.

"Don't mention it, Payton. You two have a good time tonight."

"Okay, dad, we will." Lizzie reached up on her tip-toes and planted a kiss on her father's cheek. "See you later." She waved as they walked out the door to his truck.

"Oh, by the way," Payton turned and looked back as her father called. "Try not to have her home too late."

Payton grinned, "Yes, sir."

He waited until they were almost at the party to tell her how incredible she looked, and he noticed for the first time how cute she was when she blushed. It was a little odd, this feeling he had, now that he had her alone in the truck with him. It felt good, but not like the way it did when it was just the two of them down by Granny's pond.

She was uncomfortable; he could tell by the way she kept fidgeting with the hat in her hands. He could understand why. He was the first guy she had let get close to her since she and Brett had broken up, and she was still nervous that somehow all men were as mean as him. He had other plans, though, and if he had anything to say about it, before the night was over, she'd forget everything she had ever known about men until him.

He turned off the engine when they reached the party, but he grabbed hold of her hand before she could make her way out of the truck. He studied her there in the moonlight, thinking how glad he was that he was right here, sitting in this truck with her, more than any other place on earth right now.

"Liz." He could see her watching him with those brilliant green eyes. "Don't be nervous, okay?"

She smiled but didn't say anything.

"I'm the same Payton I always have been. I've always kept you safe before, haven't I?" She nodded, keeping her gaze fixed on him. "Then trust me to do the same tonight."

"I trust you, Payton. I always have."

That one statement alone had his nerves tingling and groin tightening, but he reigned himself in enough to open the door for her to lead her towards the party. They both pulled a drink from the cooler, and found the rest of the gang, dancing like crazed fools on the makeshift dance floor in front of the band.

Bales of hay had been set up around the dance area so people could sit and watch, but Payton pulled her out onto the grassy floor as soon as the band struck up the next tune, and he pulled her in close to his body. Grace and Colin, Jade and Bud, moved closer to them on the dance floor and smiled in their direction.

"Having fun?" Grace whispered to her friend. Lizzie smiled, a half dazed dream like look on her face at the moment. "Hope you know that half the county is talking about the big date tonight. You know, you and Payton- the big date," she added when Lizzie looked confused.

Lizzie smiled and leaned her head against Payton's shoulder and half closed her eyes, enjoying the slow rhythm of the song and the way she fit so perfectly next to his body. She could have cared less if the entire world was talking about them right now. Let them talk. Not even wild horses could have pulled her out of his arms just then.

The song was over before she knew it, and she felt Payton pulling her back a few inches, but only far enough so he could look down into her eyes. He was so close to her, his lips close enough that she could feel his warm breath on her skin, his green eyes close enough that she felt like she was swimming in them.

"Having fun, yet?" He asked with a smile that tugged at the edges of his lips.

"Yes," She managed to get out, even though the whole time she found herself mesmerized, staring helplessly into his eyes. When he broke their gaze and she realized he was staring intently at her lips, she felt her body shudder. She wanted him to kiss her so badly her body ached with just the thought of it. Instead, though, he took her hand and pulled her off the dance area to a more secluded spot to the side.

"Grab your drink, Liz, and let's go find some place to sit down."

"All right." She followed him as he led her by the hand to the back of his pickup truck. Summer and Sellars, Hank, Bud and several other people were already there, enjoying the night air, and laughing about something stupid Bud had done in history class the other day.

"Hey!" They all called out as Payton and Lizzie hopped onto the truck bed and joined the group. "Have a nice dance? You two were dancing awfully close," Hank called out and laughed when Payton playfully punched him in the ribs.

"As I recall, you were getting pretty close and personal yourself with Sarah a little while ago." They all laughed as Payton called Hank out. Hank's scowl only made the group laugh harder.

They talked a while about nothing in particular, just talked about life and the interesting things that made it up. Yet Lizzie couldn't remember a conversation in her life that was more fun to partake in. She couldn't have said exactly why if asked. It just was. Maybe it was the group of people that had come to mean so much in her life. Or perhaps it was the swirl and buzz of music and people all around them in that hayfield.

Mainly though, she thought it had something to do with Payton sitting next to her, closer than she could ever recall him sitting to her before, with his hand linked in hers just like it was something they did everyday. And she couldn't help but notice that every few minutes he'd turn her way and smile, bright teeth flashing, his adorable dimple popping out. A smile meant only for her.

Lizzie couldn't tell how long the group had been sitting on Payton's truck talking, but eventually everyone except for him and her had wandered off somewhere else in the party, leaving just the two of them sitting there on the bed of his truck. He shifted next to her, settling down until he was fully laid back, and she watched him as he turned his eyes up toward the night sky. In turn, Lizzie shifted her focus to the sky and wondered exactly what it was he was looking for.

"Do you ever sit outside at night and look at the stars?" He asked eventually, breaking the calm silence that had settled between them.

"Sometimes. I look at them a lot more than I used to back in Chicago, that's for sure. The sky is a lot clearer here, not as much smog to cover over their brightness."

He glanced at her lying beside him then flicked his gaze back up to the stars. "Do you miss it?"

"I used to. When we first moved here I used to plot ways to run away and hitch-hike back. I figured I could live at my best friend's house. But…I don't know, somehow this place grew on me after a while. I started to see the things that made Edenville special." She turned to look at him. "The people… the lifestyle, just everything about how this town works- I love it all."

Payton had lost himself in her voice as she spoke, and when she turned her focus so those lazy green eyes settled on him, he couldn't help but imagine exactly how magnificent her lips would feel under his.

He hadn't planned it. The last thing he had pictured himself doing that night was kissing her there at the party. Yet something drew him to her, and he found himself leaning in, closing the small gap that existed between them.

Payton could hear her short, indrawn gasp of air just before his lips touched hers. Later he would think back on the look of shock he had seen in her eyes. At the time, though, all he could think about was how perfect everything felt at that exact moment.

Lizzie's emerald eyes never left his face as she watched him lean in, closer and closer to her body. He wasn't more than inch away when she realized, with a gasp, that he was about to kiss her. She shouldn't have been shocked, but she was. The last thing in the world she had imagined the two of them doing that night was lying in the bed of his truck kissing.

But there they were. Payton lying next to her propped up on one of his arms, leaning over her, his breath warm and intoxicating against her body. And then, before she had time to think further, his lips were touching hers. It was just a quick caress. A playful nip, really.

A short meeting of his lips to hers before he drew back to look deep into her eyes.

They were still wide with shock, but he could see she wasn't afraid, and that made his heart trip into double time. When his lips touched hers again, Lizzie could feel the world fall out from underneath her. Payton shifted so one of his hands cradled her head, and his lips settled over hers just as if they had been created for that sole purpose.

They were softer than she had expected them to be, and she couldn't help but whimper a little, sheerly from the things his lips were setting off inside her body. It was like she was waking up from a lifetime of black and white, finally seeing color all around her. Never in her life had she experienced anything like this, and never did she ever want this feeling to stop.

His kiss had turned more urgent, deeper almost, than what it had started out to be. Still, though, Lizzie didn't find herself afraid. Instead, she felt her body giving in to the kiss, letting Payton take from her, and do to her anything his heart desired. Stopping him would have been like taking all the breath from her body. He softly nipped her lips with his teeth, and she absently opened her mouth to object when she felt his whole mouth take over the process of kissing her. Suddenly it was no longer just lips connecting with lips. Now it was lips, teeth, and tongue, all mingling with hers, making her desperate, driving her crazy.

She had never, ever been kissed this way before, never thought that she would want to be, and still she felt like a kiss any other way, with any other man would just be wrong. Wrong. Her whole body was in flames, and instead of lying back, waiting for Payton to continue kissing her, she felt her body, as if in a dream, take over the active role of kissing. Suddenly she was kissing him, teeth, and tongue, and lips. She was going crazy with desire, and it wasn't until she heard him groan that she pulled away, eyes wide in shock.

"Are you okay?" She watched him, afraid that she had done something wrong, still dazed from the intense intoxication she had felt from the kiss. Payton sat up and scrubbed his hands through his hair, then turned back to her and smiled.

"I'm more than okay, Lizzie. Aren't you?" She smiled then, a small, unsure giggle bubbling up in her throat.

"Yeah. I'm pretty sure that I'm more than okay, too."

Payton lay back down where he had been and pulled her up next to him, cradling her in his arms. She could feel his heart beating wildly against his chest, and even though she tried, she couldn't conceal the grin that radiated up from the center of her being.

Payton had kissed her. She wanted to scream it at the top of her lungs. Run wildly through the party telling everyone she passed. It was the most amazing thing she had ever, *ever*, felt in her life.

He was looking up into the night sky, and she thought that maybe he'd fallen asleep when he asked her, "What do you want to do with your life?"

No one had ever asked her that before, certainly no one her age, so she thought about it for a minute. "Well, I'm pretty good at science and I like watching all those medical shows on TV. Maybe I'll be a doctor." She paused, a little thrill going down her spine. She was having such an adult conversation, and she couldn't believe it was with Payton. "What about you?"

He shrugged. "I don't know. All I ever think about is football. Hopefully I'll go pro, but if that doesn't work out..." he trailed off.

"You could coach. You know, at some college or something."

"Yeah, but...I don't know. I've always pictured myself here in Edenville. I like it here."

She smiled. "Me, too. At first this was the worst place I could ever imagine living and raising a family, but I could picture it now."

"But you couldn't be a doctor in Edenville. The closest clinic is in Clarkston."

She thought about that for a while as she studied the sky and listened to his heart beat strong and steady beneath her ear. "Well, if I opened my own place here in Edenville, I bet people would use it." Inside her she could feel the excitement start to build as this new idea began to swirl into formation. She sat up, her eyes bright with excitement and crossed her legs, Indian style, facing him. "That would be really neat. Like a family practice. Everybody in Edenville and the farmers that live beyond the city lines could come in and use it."

Thoughts were clicking in her head, and she smiled at the image in her mind. Payton reached out and touched her, bringing her suddenly back to reality. "Oh, sorry." She giggled. "I'm getting carried away."

His smile was bright in the moonlight and she felt goose bumps prickle down her arms. "No, it's alright. I've never seen you get so excited about something in your life." He leaned in and gently brushed her lips with his thumb. He paused, his face turning somber. "Can I tell you something?"

"Sure."

"The girls I'm used to being with… they always want to talk about me. They don't ever tell me what it is that they like."

Lizzie's face registered shock. "Oh, I'm sorry. I didn't mean to get so carried away about myself, I just-" She paused when she heard him stifle a laugh. "What?"

"No, I'm not upset about it. I'm glad. I can't tell you how nice it is to hear about something other than football for a change." He looked thoughtful. "Now, don't go getting me wrong, football is the single most important subject on the face of the Earth," he smiled, "but I like to be well-rounded in my conversations."

Lizzie laughed. "Oh, right, of course." She caught her breath when she saw him move toward her again. The intensity in his eyes took her breath away, and she sighed when his lips touched hers again. She couldn't remember ever wanting to do this with another person so badly, but with him, she couldn't think of another thing she'd rather be doing.

When Payton sat up a few minutes later and helped her out of the bed of the truck, Lizzie was surprised that it was already time for her to be home. They had just enough time to make their way back to the party and bid their goodbyes before her curfew.

As he walked her to her front door, he took her hand in his and squeezed it tight. She looked over at him and found him watching her with those big green eyes of his.

"I didn't scare you tonight, did I, Liz?" His look was so sincere, she felt almost like laughing, but she realized just how serious he was.

"No, Payton. You didn't scare me. I told you earlier I've always trusted you, remember?"

"Yeah, I remember." He stopped at the front door, and waited for her to lock the door behind her on her way in. He almost said something else but caught himself before he did. Instead, he held up a hand and waved goodnight before he turned and walked back to his truck in the dark.

*Chapter Twenty*

The school year had ended almost a month ago and Lizzie could hardly believe it was already time to think about her senior year of high school and then college. She still had one more year to go at Dixie, though, and she planned to make the most of it.

Currently, she sat in her simply cut yellow bikini on top of an old towel on the cool grass surrounding the pond, and dipped her toes into the warm water as she skimmed a few more pages from a college brochure that had come in the mail earlier that day. She wasn't positive that the University of Georgia was where she wanted to go, but almost all her friends had already decided that was their top choice, so maybe it should be hers too.

"The University of Georgia, huh?" A deep voice sounded over her shoulder, reading the top of the pamphlet. She turned and smiled as Payton sauntered up and sat next to her on the towel. "Going to be like the rest of us and head to Dawg country?"

"Maybe. What's it to you?" She smiled at the spark that it set in his eye.

"I'll tell you what it is to me." And with that he up-ended her over his shoulder so he could carry her to the edge of the water and unceremoniously drop her into the pond.

Lizzie came up sputtering, her hair a wet mop stuck to her head, her eyes lit with fire. "Hey! Pick on someone your own size. Or at least get in here with me so I can properly attempt to drown you." Payton laughed as he slid his shirt over his head and tossed it onto the towel.

Lizzie couldn't help but sigh at the gorgeous sight his body displayed. All those tanned muscles, and hard ridges that begged for her to touch and taste. She hadn't yet grown brave enough to try and kiss any part of him other than his lips, but seeing him now without his shirt, and in those red swim trunks that made his body even more gorgeous, she was having a hard time resisting the thought of what she'd like to do to him.

"Hey, New Girl. See something you like?" She tore her eyes away from his chest and up to his eyes to find him smiling ear to ear, a big smug smile of male sureness spread across his face.

"In your dreams, chump." She took off swimming to the other side of the pond, but was beaten there by two powerful arms and swift kicking legs. She touched the other bank only to find Payton there, leaning against the bank, his hair all wet and tousled like he was her reward waiting for her to take.

"How do you know what I dream about?" She could see the twinkle of mischief in his eyes, and refused to take the bait. "Must be that you spend so much time there, you know exactly what I think about too."

"What are you saying Payton? That I'm the woman of your dreams?" She was merely egging him on, so she didn't expect his honest response, or the swift hand that reached out and took hold of her own before she turned away from him.

"Yeah, Lizzie. That's what I'm saying." She noticed that all his smugness was gone now, leaving only a trace of insecurity edging his face. It was the first time she'd ever seen Payton Cartwright insecure, and she wasn't sure if she should be flattered or afraid of the sight.

"Lizzie…" He paused to make sure he had her attention. "Will you let me touch you?" She wasn't quite sure what he meant by that, but by the way he watched her and the darkness those depthless green eyes were, she presumed it meant more than just the way he was touching her hand right then. Slowly, she nodded her assent and felt the water sway around her as he moved closer to her.

He was close enough now that she could feel his breath on her wet skin, and it gave her chill bumps remembering how good the handful of other times he had been this close to her had felt. His hands were warm and sure as he skimmed them up her arms and through her long, wet hair. He bent his head to kiss her, and when he did, she felt her body flood with warmth so bright and good she was sure she was in heaven. She lost herself in his caress of her lips, and found new sensations washing over her as he moved his hands from her face down and across the hard, pointed tips of her nipples. Little brilliant explosions went off in her body, and she was swamped with even greater warmth than she felt when he kissed her lips.

Now his hands were gently massaging the small of her back, his strong, athletic fingers were like magic wherever they touched. He pulled back from his kiss to watch her for a moment, but Lizzie didn't notice. Her eyes were closed, her body relaxed, and fully compliant to anything he had in store for her just then.

"God," He whispered, almost reverently. "You're so beautiful like that." Lizzie opened her eyes, still dazed from the kiss, and smiled a lazy smile at him.

"Like what?"

"Like this. Your body all relaxed in my arms, your green eyes looking at me like I'm the greatest person on earth." He paused to stroke his strong hand across the rapid pulse in her throat. "I swear, when you look at me like that, I could conquer whole football teams by myself alone- that's how you make me feel."

Lizzie smiled. It was the sweetest thing she'd ever heard him say. Heck, it was the sweetest thing she'd ever heard anyone say, and it made her want to melt into a pile of mush on the pond floor.

Three nights later she lay in her bed, staring up at the ceiling, listening to the crickets serenade her through her bedroom window. She was trying to sleep, and had been for a solid hour, but she just kept thinking about what Payton had said at the pond, and it was driving her crazy with desire.

Lizzie rolled in her bed, trying to find another cool spot on her mattress, and a more conducive position for sleep. Thank the Lord it was summer and they didn't have school the next day, she thought as she peeked at the glowing red numbers from her alarm clock.

She plopped her head back down on the pillow and let out a deep sigh, rolling again, and flopped her arm over her eyes in exaggerated desperation. It was then that she heard the soft tink-tink of something hitting her bedroom window. She lay still in her bed, listening for the sound again. A moment later she heard it again, this time a little harder, but still pretty soft. It sounded almost like a little pebble hitting the glass.

She crept to the window and looked out into the night, half relieved she didn't find some crazy night bug or bat beating itself silly against the window pane. When she looked down, her heart skipped a beat, because there below her stood Payton, smiling up at her like Prince Charming. She held up a finger, telling him to wait, while she quickly threw on a pair of blue jeans and an old t-shirt over her bra.

She crept down the stairs, wincing when one of the stairs creaked, and waited a long, breathless minute to make sure she hadn't woken her parents. Fortunately she hadn't.

"What are you doing here," She asked breathlessly, when she

finally managed to unlock the porch door and slide out into the cool night air.

"I came to kidnap you," He replied, smiling down at her just before he bent down and quickly brushed her lips with his. She felt her heart flutter and her body's instinctive reaction.

"Kidnap me? You can't kidnap me. It's the middle of the night!"

"That's the point. Kidnappings during the day aren't nearly as adventurous."

He had a point there.

"You also don't see many willing abductees who just saunter out their back door and agree to go with their kidnapper either." She crossed her arms and gave him her victory smirk, but he quickly managed to wipe that off her face.

He winked at her, and brushed another kiss across her lips, then smiled deep into her eyes. "I didn't want to have to do this, Liz, but I'll gladly hog tie you if I have to." He watched her jaw drop as he pulled a ball of rope from his back pocket, and reached out to grab her wrists to tie them together.

"No, no!" She whispered quickly, as she took a step back. "I believe you... I guess I don't have a choice then?" Payton smiled. He knew he had won.

"Guess not. Follow me."

They walked in silence until she could tell they weren't in hearing distance from the house. "Where are you taking me?" She demanded to know.

"Nope, sorry. Kidnappers don't reveal their hideouts. You'll have to wait and see."

"That's not fair," she said in a pout.

He smiled at her over his shoulder, pausing so she could catch up to him. "Didn't your daddy ever teach you that life's not fair?" Lizzie tried to give him the best narrow slitted glare she could muster, but inside she was too excited and anxious about where they were going to really give it a good go.

The night air was warmer than she had expected it to be, but what had she really thought it would feel like in the middle of a heat wave, in the South, in mid-July? She thought she recognized the back entrance to Granny's pond, and paused when they got closer to the gate.

"Are you taking me down to Granny's pond?"

He reached out for her hand and took hold of it. "Is there a problem with that?"

"No, not really. Only…"

"Only what?"

"Only, I've never been down there at night. It's going to be really scary, isn't it?" She saw the gleam in Payton's eye, and the smile that turned up the edges of his lips. He bent and brushed a kiss along her lips then smiled into her eyes so big and broad that she forgot anything about scary things that go bump at the pond.

"I promise, if I have anything to say about it, your first night visit to the pond will be anything but scary. Okay?"

"Okay."

"Okay then, let's go." He started off again, pulling her along with him. She liked the way her hand felt in his, and the way he led them forward, so secure in himself, in his body like he always was. It crossed Lizzie's mind to wonder if he was ever uncomfortable or scared, but she sincerely doubted that God had installed those two particular features inside this solid form of a man.

He bent down and grabbed something from behind a bush as they came into view of the pond. Lizzie wondered what it was but soon felt him drop her hand, and watched him spread what was obviously a blanket out onto the ground for them to sit on.

"Sit with me."

"What are we doing out here, Payton?"

She shivered when he shifted closer and looked down at her, his eyes intent on her. "Don't you know?"

He chuckled softly when her eyes rounded in shock. "We're going to watch shooting stars, Liz. There's a meteor shower occurring over the next few days, and this time of night is supposed to be the best time to see them. Why, did you have something else in mind?"

She blushed when he called her on her obvious train of thought, thankful that it was mostly hidden by the darkness around them.

Payton pulled her down onto the blanket and tucked her into the crook of his arm. Every once in a while he'd point to a star when it shot across the sky, and once she closed her eyes and made a wish.

They talked for awhile about nothing that really mattered before he turned to her and asked, "Do you believe in soul mates, Liz?" She'd shifted her attention from the stars to study him, her eyes wide and rounded with surprise. "I do," he answered to the silent question in her eyes, and pulled her slender body closer to his own.

"You do?" She watched as he nodded. "I guess... well, yes, I suppose it's possible. Why?"

"Just wondering." He pushed himself up then with a huff, leaving her lying there on the blanket, and propped his arms on the knees of his bent legs. Lizzie lay on the blanket and folded her hands behind her head. The shocky feeling in her body was still pulsing through her, and she felt like she had suddenly lost about half of her hearing. Had Payton just told her that he believed they were soul mates? It couldn't be possible. Payton was a hero, an idol, an untouchable, and she was... well, she was just someone who was lucky enough to have been chosen to keep him company for a while.

Let's get real here, she thought. She knew the guy had some strange thing about coming to her rescue, and she loved that he decided to spend time with her these days. But she was a science loving dork, the teacher's pet, and a nobody that Payton single handedly had rescued from the lunchroom floor. So, as far as a long term forever sort of commitment went she had long ago figured the odds on that one.

She couldn't even remember what she had said in response to his question. Did she believe in soul mates? Of course she believed in them. That first day at Dixie when she'd felt the air sizzle between them from across a school room she knew for sure there were soul mates. The mere thought that he even knew what a soul mate was sent tingling sensations all through her body.

Lizzie looked over at Payton, studied his back in the moonlight, and enjoyed the way his muscles rippled underneath his shirt. She slowly reached out, her fingers shaking with nervousness, and she outlined the mass of muscle on his lower back. She had never voluntarily touched him before. Always she had waited until he made the first move and even after that she was hesitant to touch him except to copy the exact move he had just made on her.

Tonight, though, she was going to take a chance, her nervousness dulled by Payton's shocking question. She was so afraid that he would pull away from her, but somewhere inside she knew it was now or never to prove to herself that she had the guts to be with this man. She'd wanted this moment for years, and now was her chance to act.

She touched him again, this time with a little more courage. When he shifted to face her she pulled her hand back and dropped it swiftly to her side.

He looked down at her, giving her a reassuring smile. "You don't have to stop, Lizzie." He took her hand, massaging it lightly as he lifted it, and led her hand to the muscles rippling over his belly. "I like it when you touch me."

"You do?"

He nodded, watching her, and his lids fluttered almost imperceptibly as her fingers began to move softly across his t-shirt.

"Here, let me help you with that." He reached up over his head and pulled the t-shirt up and off of his body, leaving him naked from the waist up. "Now, make yourself at home."

She itched to touch him, to feel his warm skin underneath her fingers. Lizzie stretched out a tentative hand then paused. "Payton, I don't want to hurt you."

He laughed softly. "Sweetheart, you're not hurting me. Trust me." He put a hand over hers and moved them together over his body, exploring first the strong muscles of his belly and moving up to examine his chest. "Does this make you nervous?" He asked at last, watching the way she nibbled on her lower lip.

She tore her eyes slowly away from his body and shifted them up to meet his. She nodded her head, and smiled.

"Lizzie," he lay down on the blanket beside her and pulled her up into his arms. "Have I ever done anything to hurt you?"

"No."

"Didn't I promise you before we came down here that nothing scary would happen to you?" She nodded.

"Okay, then." He leaned up on an elbow so he could stroke her hair and look into her wide, soulful eyes. "If I promise to let you know if you hurt me, will you keep touching me like you were?"

She waited a beat, nibbled on her lip some more then smiled up at him. "You promise to tell me?"

"Promise."

"You like it when I touch you here?" She reached out and slowly stroked her hand across his chest.

"Yes, I do."

"And here?" She flicked her eyes from the spot on his belly to his eyes and watched them flutter closed for a second before he opened them to look at her.

"I already told you I liked that spot."

She shifted her hand just a fraction lower and stopped. She nibbled on her lower lip. "What about here?"

His groan made her giggle. "I'll take that as a yes."

Her courage was building and she wanted to touch him more, but something else itched inside her. She leaned forward hesitantly, watching him in case he decided she crossed the line from good to gross. His warm smile encouraged her so she bent in and replaced her hand with her lips.

His skin felt so soft and silky, but with an edge of hardness and danger mixed in. She could feel all those tightly wound muscles underneath as they held his body still, but at the same time she could feel a slight tremor and it excited her knowing that she was the one causing them.. She smelled a hint of soap and aftershave as she trailed back up from his stomach to his chest and neck. He let out a whimper as she shifted from one perfectly rounded nipple and up to dabble at the hollow of his neck.

She giggled. "Are you sure you're not hurting?"

"Oh, I'm hurting alright, but not in a bad way."

She knew that he was aroused. She'd read enough romance books to know that guys responded like that when a girl kissed him, but she had never experienced it herself. At least, not until now. Now she could actually feel the evidence of his excitement and it made her heart pound with a mix of arousal and nerves. She'd never done this before. Ever. Did Payton know? And what did he expect from her now.

She felt his hands clasp onto her shoulders and pull her back from her loving assault on his skin. She glanced up at him, the smile on her lips fading when she saw the seriousness that crept into his eyes.

"I'm hurting you, aren't I? I'll stop- I'm, I'm so sorry." She moved to get up but he pushed her back down onto the blanket.

"Lizzie, stop." He lifted her chin and forced her to look at him. "You're not hurting me, I promise, so stop worrying that you are. Look, if you must know, I've been dreaming about this moment for weeks now." He smiled when her jaw dropped.

"You have?"

"Mmm-Hmm. So stop worrying and have some fun." She regarded him warily.

"But...." He lifted her chin again.

"What's wrong, Liz?"

She had to tell him, she knew she did, but she didn't want to do it. She didn't want to go through the embarrassment of revealing that she was a virgin, with never even more than a kiss. How could she explain to him that she had been saving herself for the one person that meant more to her than anyone else in the world? He would think she was crazy, wouldn't he? Here she sat in front of Payton, the guy she had come to admire so much, and she was going to disappoint him by revealing that she wasn't experienced enough to know what he might like. But on the other hand, he'd been around her enough to know that she was skittish even to kiss him, so it didn't take much imagination to figure out how nervous she would be with everything else between a man and a woman.

"Liz, it's okay." He leaned in and brushed a kiss across her lips, lingering a little at the edges where he knew she liked to be kissed the most. "Whatever it is, it's fine."

Those wide doe eyes shifted from his down the naked top half of his body. She ducked her head so it rested on his chest where she couldn't see his eyes. Taking a deep breath she dove in. "I've never done this before, Payton. I mean, not just the sex part," her face flamed, "well, that is... if you were headed in that direction... but, you know, all of it."

That was it. She'd said it. She could feel him stiffen and she felt red heat sliding up her neck and across her face. He didn't respond, and after a moment she gathered the courage to look up at him.

"Oh, God. You're in shock. I knew that I shouldn't have told you this!"

He blinked. He blinked again. Then he laughed. He laughed so hard Lizzie wondered what he found so funny.

"Liz, trust me. I'm not in shock, and I'm glad that you told me." He grew serious. "You didn't think I'd be mad, did you?"

"The thought had crossed my mind."

He pulled her close and kissed the top of her head. "Sweetheart, I'm not mad at you. There's nothing to be mad about. In fact, I had a pretty good suspicion that you haven't done this kind of thing before." He took a deep breath. "Look, I don't want to pressure you," he paused with a wince. "Sorry, I realize that's probably something Brett would have said." He shifted so they were face to face. She could feel his warm breath on her skin. "Seriously, I'm not here to push you into anything.

I'll stop right now if you want and we can just watch the meteor shower. I really did bring you out here to watch it, but I'm more than happy to do this, too."

He stopped. She wondered what was going through his mind. He looked totatlly comfortable in his skin all the time, but there was a small part of her that wondered if he was just a fraction as flustered as she was right then.

He had just opened his mouth to speak when she interjected. "Okay."

"Huh?"

"Will you stop if I ask you to?"

"Yes, but I want you to know I'm happy to stop right now if you're nervous."

"Oh, I'm definitely nervous, but I want to. You're... you're not like Brett. He said he didn't want to push me, but he was so greedy and I could see it in his eyes that he didn't care. He- he didn't understand that I'd never... well, and that I was saving…"she hid her face again, "saving myself for someone more special than him."

Payton stiffened. "Let's not talk about him anymore. In fact, let's not talk anymore period," he paused to kiss her lips, "I promise to stop if you tell me to."

In a move that completely surprised him, she held out her hand. "Then it's a deal?" He smiled and took her hand.

"Deal." They shook on the deal and Payton used their contact to pull her into his arms, lowering her onto the blanket. He smiled at her, kissing her lips, teasing the flesh there until she let out a little whimper and wound her arms around his neck.

Since his shirt was already off he began to work on hers. "I don't imagine you'll be needing this," he said, pulling it up and over her head, leaving the little pink sports bra as the only other obstacle keeping him from those lovely, pale, silky mounds beneath.

"I won't?"

He shook his head, and she let out a little laugh.

"In that case, I don't think you'll be needing these." She slid her hands down the heated skin of his torso and began to unbutton his jeans. He shifted. She paused.

"Just giving you easier access." His wink set her back at ease. Then he set in to caressing the tender skin below her ear with the tip of his tongue and his excessively sexy lips, and Lizzie forgot anything about being nervous or wanting to tell Payton to stop. Saying stop was the absolute last word on her mind. Yes, yes, *yes* would have been the more appropriate words that sprung to her thoughts.

Then, with an amazing little trick of the tongue and his hands, he was sending little thrills of sensation down her spine and through her body, and she was almost begging him to strip her faster so she could be skin to tingling skin, enjoying the feel of something she had never wanted to experience so desperately in all her life. She felt him remove the last layer of her clothing then watched in awed amazement as he shucked the last of his.

Suddenly they were both naked. Lizzie had always imagined that when she found herself in this particular position with a man she would be edgy and insecure, possibly even a little hysterically nervous. But as Payton leaned back over her and set himself to laving attention to all the parts of her body that had been aching only minutes before, she realized she was far, far from nervous. Instead she found herself wrapped in a warm, hazy cocoon of ecstasy in which nothing could penetrate except for good feelings.

She had expected for there to be awkwardness between them, but in its place stood a comfortable connection that she could easily imagine they were destined to experience. *Do you believe in soul mates, Lizzie? I do.* She looked past the shoulder she was currently suckling and up at the stars above. She didn't see any shooting stars pass by, that would have been a little too cliché, but she did wonder if there wasn't something a little more magical and mystical going on right then than could be explained.

Payton looked down into the sea of green crashing around in her eyes and wondered if she felt half as stunned by this experience as he did at the moment. He was no stranger to this sort of intimate experience- you couldn't be the home town hero and expect to come out a virgin- but he had never felt anything this intense before. He traced the outline of a dark, puckered peak then ran his finger down to the valley between her breasts, studying the goose-bumps that followed in his wake. He took his time suckling the other tip and felt his breath come faster as he heard Lizzie release a frenzied moan and wiggle beneath him. She was incredible, and he doubted very seriously she even knew that she was. How a girl could be so absolutely inexperienced and yet so sensuously delectable all at once he would never understand.

With his lips, he traced the little line of peach fuzz down the center of her belly until he reached the tan line where her bikini would have begun. He stopped, moved a little, and picked up again just on the inside of her thighs, trailing down to her knees. He started on her other knee and made his way, slowly, ever so slowly back up again, smiling at the way she whispered his name and gripped his shoulders, begging him to find her spot for release. Still, he took his time.

He skipped over the sensitive area once again and began to trace a line along her shoulder bones with his finger. Every once in a while he would nibble here or there, leaving delicate little marks where he'd claimed that particular portion of her body. Reverently, he stroked her body with his fingers and repeated the process with his lips. He teased her by trailing down to the hot, slick skin between her legs and dabbling there with an achingly slow and soft touch. She thought she would die if he didn't touch her there again, but he paid no heed and moved on to play elsewhere. When at last he was satisfied with his work, he bent his head and kissed her again full on the lips.

"Do you think you can let me love you now?" He asked in a deep, husky voice. She searched his eyes for some sign of sarcasm, but there was none.

"Only if you'll let me love you, too." He smiled that adorable little dimpled smile and she knew that if she hadn't lost herself to him before she definitely had just then.

He came up over her and settled himself on top letting her adjust to his weight a little at a time. He kissed her again then kissed her some more and finally she felt him push her legs apart and slide into the silky wet heat that she had been dying for him to find. He moved into her slowly, watching her intently for any signs of discomfort, and then began to love her so tenderly, so compassionately that a little tear slipped from her eyes. He kissed the salty wetness away and moved inside her again watching the way her eyes dropped to half mast with the drug of their loving.

She called his name, ran kisses up his hard chest and begged him for release. He stroked her again and again, heard her crying his name, then found one of her hands and linked it with his. When he searched her eyes his silent question found the answer he wanted just as he felt her bunch then explode beneath him with a last gush of breath. His body tensed before he felt the world crumble and he tumbled headlong into oblivion.

*Chapter Twenty-one*

Lizzie and Grace stood in the magazine aisle of Gilchrist's Pharmacy and debated the pros and cons of several selections.

"Do you think the guys will like Seventeen or YM more?" Lizzie's gaze flicked from one magazine to the other then up to see which one Grace would choose. Grace regarded her with skepticism and turned to choose a different color of nail polish.

"I'm going to guess neither. Playboy maybe, but I doubt you're up for buying that, so I suggest we just forego the magazines and get some water balloons instead." She put down the bottle of Passion Pink and picked up Vampire Red in its place.

"Water balloons? I'm pretty sure that's not going to go over well with Sellars. She'd flip a lid if she got her hair wet before she went to bed."

Grace grunted. "It's a camp out. There are no rules on camp outs except to expect the unexpected. Plus, if we don't tell anyone we've got them then we can use them on the boys once they've fallen asleep."

"I don't know, somehow I see that backfiring on us." Lizzie gave the balloons a quick once over and threw them in the basket anyway.

Mr. Gilchrist gave them a curious look as he rang up their purchases, but bagged their stuff without a word. He smiled as they left the store, and shook his head with a smile remembering the good old days.

"So, you told your parents you're staying at my house right?" Grace plopped a jolly-rancher in her mouth and slung one of the pharmacy bags around her wrist.

"Yep, and I'm so dead if they figure out we're actually out camping instead."

"Don't worry. My dad knows we're going- I told him that the girls were going out for our last hoorah before school starts up."

"Hmm. That's a good idea. I'll tell my mom that, too. That way she won't get so freaked out."

The duo worked on their plans a little more as they walked back to Lizzie's house from town, and giggled excitedly as Lizzie threw the rest of her stuff in a duffel bag and slung it over her shoulder. They ran into her mom on the way out and explained that the girls were going camping. Her mom merely planted a solid kiss on her cheeks and told them to have fun.

Lizzie thought she'd just gotten away with murder, and that set them to giggling again as they set off to Grace's house to pick up her car for the trip out to the camping sight.

Most of the gang was already there when they arrived. It was a spot not far from Farmer Murphy's land that was owned by an old miser named Mr. Weatherby. He passed away earlier in the summer and left the land to his only son who lived in California. They guessed he probably wouldn't be showing up for a surprise visit that night, so they assumed this would be the safest spot of any.

Payton, Colin, Hank, and Bud were playing touch football next to the stack of firewood they had gathered while Sellars and Jade tried to assemble the tent they brought to share. Summer, fortunately for Lizzie, was even more dysfunctionally late than Lizzie tended to be, and she still hadn't arrived yet.

"Hey, you made it after all," Hank called out just before Colin took him to the ground. "Hey! I thought this was supposed to be touch football," he complained.

"It is touch football. I touched you when I tackled you, didn't I?"

Hank eyed him crossly, rubbed the sore spot on his butt, and scrambled back up from the ground with Bud's help.

"Good news boys," Jade called from the other side of the campsite. "You guys get to show us you're manly ways of setting up a tent." She smiled her most charming smile, but the boys gave her half a glance, laughed her off and kept playing. All expect Payton who jogged over to where Lizzie and Grace were unloading supplies from the car. He snagged Lizzie around the waist, pulling her back against him and spinning her in fast circles, around and around. When he stopped he bent over her and gave her an upside down kiss. Lizzie noted with surprise that he didn't even seem phased that the other guys made loud kissy noises from the make shift football field.

"Okay, we've got hot dogs, hot cocoa, chocolate, marshmallows, and graham crackers- pretty much your basic camping necessities. Who brought the coat hangers," Grace asked as she chucked the food supplies out onto the ground.

"Coat hangers?" Colin questioned as he strolled up to the car. "Who do you think we are, civilized society? You're supposed to use sticks to roast marshmallows, dimwit." He flicked her playfully on the head and Grace gave him a narrow-slitted glare before turning back to the vehicle.

From across the campsite Bud yelled, "Hey, I have a great idea. After it gets dark we can all strip naked and go streaking!"

"Good one, Bud," one of the other guys retorted, "I'm sure all of Mr. Weatherby's cows will get a kick out of that." The rest of the group laughed.

Just then Summer pulled up in her car and the gang cheered. "Yea, she decided to come to the campout after all." She rolled her eyes and got out of the car.

"Ha, ha. Very funny. You guys know I'm never on time. Cut me some slack. What're you gonna do, give me detention?"

"No, but I might send you to the tent for time out," Hank said as he sauntered over and bent her over with a kiss. The rest of the group made kissy noises like they had for Payton and Lizzie.

The girls spent the afternoon painting each other's toe nails Vampire Red and cheering for the boys as they played touch football and arm wrestled. Towards sunset they built a campfire and the guys took on the macho role of roasting the hotdogs while the girls set out paper plates on the blanket Jade brought for the picnic area. After the dogs had been severely blackened and everyone griped about it for a good minute, they chowed down on the food and laughed at the stupid stunt Bud had pulled to try and get some vulnerable ninth grade girl to go out with him. Before the sun set completely behind the trees, the guys pulled up a few decaying tree stumps for them to sit on around the campfire, and gathered up a few more logs to throw on the fire, while the girls tried as best they could to clean up the mess they had made with dinner.

Sometime after the sun went down and the stars had begun to glow in the night sky, Payton came and found Lizzie enjoying the warmth from the fire next to Grace on one of the old logs. He straddled the log, shifting her off of it and into the V his body made, wrapping her up in his warmth.

"Are you cold?" he asked, looking down into her upturned face, noting the way her thin body had begun to shake from the chill in the air.

"Hmm, I think I'll be okay now."

"Good. Stick close then because I think Colin's about to start his ghost story melodrama."

"What's that? Did I hear my name and ghost stories?"

Everyone in the group groaned.

"Ah, come on.  You know I tell the best stories.  I've even got a new one I saved up to tell just for this trip.  You see, about a hundred years ago Mr. Weatherby's father lived out here on this farmland.  Now, you think Mr. Weatherby was a crotchety old man, you should have met his father-"

"And you have," snickered Bud from across the campfire.  Colin eyed him then shook his head.

"I'm *trying* to add a little enthusiasm to the story, Bud.  Now, as I was saying, Mr. Weatherby's father lived out here.  Well, that man..."

Lizzie snuggled back in the warmth of Payton's body, tuning out Colin's words but letting the deep timbre of it wash over her along with the cozy heat from the fire.  She could hear night crickets calling to each other, and somewhere in the night an owl let out a hoot.  Her head bobbed back and forth with the rise and fall of Payton's strong chest, and she smiled when she felt him begin to gently stroke his hand up her sides where he was holding on to her.

His thumb gently grazed the edge of one of her breasts and she felt her body tingle in its wake.  A little shiver of delight coursed through her.  She thought at first Payton had inadvertently brushed her that way so when she felt him stroke her body again she giggled quietly and felt her body tingle again.  With each successive stroke she felt her body grow warmer until she was almost squirming under his torture.  She knew, though, that Payton felt the same because she could feel his body hard and long against her back.

By the time Colin finished his ghost story Lizzie's body was so enflamed with desire she could barely control herself long enough to make up a decent excuse and head for the tent she and Payton would share that night.  Not long after she heard Payton mumble something and head her way.  She could hear his heavy footsteps as he crunched among the dead leaves on the ground and she felt her body growing tense with her excitement.

In the weeks since they'd first made love Lizzie had grown by leaps in bounds in her confidence at making love.  Payton had been so generous in his patience and thoughtfulness at teaching her how to make love that she could hardly remember the scared, tentative girl she'd been then.  *"Making love is an art, Liz.  And being able to do it takes practice."*  Practice they had done, and Lizzie was more than ready by the time Payton climbed through the entrance to the tent and zipped it shut behind him.

"Man, I'm tired. I think I'm going to hit the hay and get some shut eye." He yawned deeply as he turned toward her, but the twinkle in his eye gave him away.

"Me, too," Lizzie said with a yawn of her own. She snuggled down deeper in the pair of sleeping bags that they'd zipped together to share, enjoying the feel of the slick material against her naked flesh. She couldn't wait to see Payton's face when he found out.

He made a big deal out of digging around in his bag for a few minutes just so he could watch her squirm in anticipation, before finally stripping off his jeans and t-shirt leaving him naked except for his boxers. He flicked off his flashlight and dove under the covers. A second later she heard a sharp hiss of indrawn breath. She smiled at him in the dark, as he turned to face her so they were both lying on their sides.

There was a full moon out that weekend, and a generous portion of light filtered through the blue and red material of the tent so that she could see him watching her. The brilliant white of his teeth flashed and she felt his hand touch the soft skin of her hips. It lingered there for a minute before he slowly stroked up until he brushed the outer edge of a breast. Lizzie felt her nipple pucker, and she moved a little to give him easier access to her body.

"Well, I suppose it's safe to say that I'm not too tired anymore."

Lizzie giggled. "Oh, I'm sorry. Did I wake you up?"

He took her hand and pushed it down so she cupped him outside of his boxers. "What do you think?"

Her eyes rounded, but she wasn't shocked. Instead she reveled that she was the cause of such a wondrous thing. "I suppose I did."

He put his arm around her possessively and slid her so she was lying on top of him. "What do you propose we do about it?" He nipped her lips and pulled back so he could watch her face expectantly.

Lizzie's smile was full of seduction. "I think I have an idea." She put her knees of either side of him and sat back. "And it doesn't involve these," she said as she slid his boxers off him.

Then Lizzie set off in a tour of his body. She explored every last inch of him and when he couldn't take anymore he pulled her up so she was face to face with him. "Your turn," he said, rolling with her until she was underneath him and he had pinned her arms above her head.

His lips claimed hers and ran a trail from her lips down her neck by way of a winding path past her earlobes and in the hollow between her clavicles until they found the valley between her breasts. Tenderly he kissed the skin there then licked a trail up the gentle slopes to their peaks. He blew a cool breeze over them and watched as they puckered into tight little pen tips. Then he suckled them until they had warmed and he could repeat the process over again.

He could hear Lizzie whimpering, trying not to make too much noise so the others wouldn't hear them. His hand stroked down her body and found her more than ready. She arched against him, silently pleading with him to give them both what they wanted. He came up over her, putting his weight on her as her whispered in her ear.

Little prickles of hot, thrilling heat stabbed at her when he whispered, "Put it where you want it, sweetheart." She looked up in his eyes, and after taking a deep breath she moved him so he was ready to claim her.

She thrust against him and felt his hard body push inside. His mouth covered hers just in time to capture the moan she released. She sighed with long awaited contentment as he withdrew and pushed inside once more. She could feel his weight, heavy and wonderful, on top of her, and she felt so safe there, fully protected underneath this wonderful, powerful man.

His body began to shake with the need to release himself, but he looked down into her eyes with all the patience in the world. "That's right, baby. Yeah, just like that," he whispered as she moved against him, her breasts pushing hard against his chest. "God, you are so beautiful like this." His voice was almost reverent.

She could feel her body coiling, getting ready to burst, and she forced herself to open her eyes and stare long and hard into his instead of closing them to enjoy the moment. The green of his eyes linked with the green of hers and she felt herself falling deeper and deeper into his spell. Her world filled with green, her senses consumed with the furnace inside her that was begging to explode, and she gripped him hard, her hands holding his arms, her legs wrapping around his hips.

"Fly, baby. Fly," she heard from somewhere in the back of her mind, and then she knew nothing except that a man named Payton Cartwright who kissed like a god and made love even better had just set her free yet another time. She felt his body tighten, all his muscles going rigid and in the next beat he was flying with her.

"Tell me you believe in soul mates now, Lizzie," he said sometime later when they'd finally gained conscious thought.

"Oh, yes.  I believe I do."

She could die right then, in his arms, and be a very, very happy woman.

## Chapter Twenty-two

Payton sat on the hard wooden bench in the locker room listening to the deafening roar of the crowd as the cheerleaders flipped and tumbled and pumped up the fans for the second half of the game. Sweat dripped from his hair, blood trickled down his arms, and despair pumped through his veins. He had one hell of a job to do to pull his team out of the trenches these next two quarters.

It was the last game before the State Championship game, and the favored team for the playoffs had somehow found itself down three points to the opposing team. Payton snuffed out the sound of the band playing and focused in on the eerily quiet voice of the coach. He knew the coach was furious by his reddened face and bulging neck veins, but he'd lost his voice in the first quarter he'd been screaming so loudly at his players.

"You no good players better get out there and... I want to see that ball move...If you don't get your hands out and ready to...And I had better see some fancy footwork or I will personally...."

Payton hung his head and tried to think of what plays he could run to save the team from considerable disappointment, but his mental list of plays came up blank. Nothing registered except his father's voice still echoing in his head. *Sorry, bucko, but I've got to be out of town this weekend. I'm leaving right after work Friday afternoon and I won't be back until Monday night late. But don't worry, I'll be thinking of you the whole time.* Almost as an afterthought he added, *"You'll take care of your mama, won't you, son? That's my boy."*

Payton rubbed the spot on his shoulder where his father had chucked him, and tried to forget how disappointed he was that his father wasn't there. He snapped back to reality just as the coach let out one more curse just for good measure, finished his rampage and sent the players back out onto the field. Payton took one more deep breath, grabbed his helmet, and followed the team.

Lizzie watched from the stands, screaming along with the rest of the stadium, as the team moved back out onto the field. She spotted number sixteen, *her* number sixteen, and prayed that he could lead them to victory after all. He had his helmet on so she couldn't read his face, but she guessed he was probably tense and ready to get the show on the road.

He had been edgy about this game all week, and she was more than a little afraid that the pressure from the town was making him crack.

The first few plays of the third quarter went smoothly, and Dixie steadily worked its way down the field to the Clinton Ram's fifteen yard line. The ball snapped, the crowd erupted as Payton sent out a perfect pass just barely fitting between two hulking Rams players. At the last second the ball was intercepted by a Ram defensive lineman, and he ran it all the way in for a touchdown.

The announcer came over the speaker. "Well, folks, it's not looking good for Dixie. Can Number Sixteen pull out a few recovery plays? We'll have to wait and see." Even the cheerleaders looked doubtful at this point, Lizzie secretly suspected they enjoyed doing all those crazy push-ups.

In the end it didn't matter how much the cheerleaders chanted, the crowd cheered, or how often the announcer questioned the players' abilities. It didn't even matter how hard Payton struggled to get his ball through to the end-zone. Dixie Academy lost the game 27 to 7, and Payton felt the world land squarely on top of his shoulders. He wanted to bury his head in his locker and never dig it back out.

Lizzie was sitting on the hood of his truck waiting for him when he walked up the ramp from the locker room to the parking lot. He let out a muffled curse and shoved his duffle bag farther onto his shoulder. The last person he wanted to see right now was Lizzie. She'd only try to say something sweet, and give him a hug, and try to make things all better when they really weren't. Nothing could make this night better right then, not even the most special person in the world.

He tried not to look directly at her as he approached the truck so he wouldn't encourage any more conversation than was necessary. Obviously she wasn't taking the hint because she hopped off the hood in that ridiculously wonderful Lizzie way that made him hate her even more right then. Didn't she have any sense to know when someone wanted company and when they didn't?

"Hey, you." Lizzie tucked her hands in her blue jean jacket. "How're you doing?"

He hated the sympathy in her eyes almost as much as he hated it in her voice.

"Fine." He opened the door to his truck and threw the duffel bag across to the other side, hopping in before she could wrap her arms around him. The last thing he wanted was for her to touch him. He had too much pent up inside of him right now, and he couldn't be sure that he wouldn't take it out on her if she made contact.

"It's going to be okay, Payton. No one's angry with you." *He* was angry with him, and besides he knew she was just being nice so he grunted in protest.

"Well, Grace and I are headed over to the post-game party. You're coming aren't you?"

"No, I don't think so." He shoved his fingers through his still wet hair and drummed his fingers on the door impatiently. "Look, I've got to get home and check on my mom. I'll catch you later, alright?"

She eyed him warily, trying not to get her feelings hurt that he so obviously didn't want to be with her tonight. She knew him too well, and could see he was hurting from their loss and just needed time to lick his wounds, but deep inside she couldn't help but wonder if maybe he was upset at her for some reason as well. She thought she might know why.

She took a deep breath and tried to calm her racing nerves. The night before, while they were making love she had been so moved that she couldn't hold back what she felt for him any longer. She had looked deep into his eyes, a tear trailing down her cheek and explained that she had loved him for years. Something in his eyes glittered, and she would never forget the way he had so tenderly wiped the tear from her cheek. She thought that the way he had smiled into her eyes and kissed the tip of her nose after she told him meant that he felt the same, or at least he felt something pretty strong for her as well. But now she wasn't so sure.

"Well, call me tomorrow, okay?"

"Fine."

He wanted to kick himself for it, but something mean had taken residence in his heart that evening so when Lizzie leaned in through the window to give him a kiss he turned his head and let her brush his cheek instead of his lips. He roared the engine to life and peeled out of the parking lot like the hormonal teenage boy he was. He tried not to care that he saw Lizzie from his rearview mirror standing there staring after him with what looked close to tears swimming in her eyes.

He took a detour through the countryside on his way home from the game. The cool night air felt good whipping through the windows and over his hot skin. He hoped that the long drive and cool air might calm his nerves, but he couldn't get the game and all the stupid plays he'd made out of his head, or the fact that his father hadn't been there because he'd had to be out of town on work. His father had always been there for him, cheering him on at all his games. Only this year his dad had seemed so preoccupied with work.

It was that stupid promotion he had been given, Vice President of Marketing Management. Big freaking deal. Just because he had some big title in front of his name and a new salary along with it didn't mean he had to shut out the people in his life who were supposed to be the most important, did it? Payton punched the gas a little harder and watched the needle climb a little higher on the speedometer.

His father wasn't the only person bothering him. Lizzie was doing her fair share of annoying him as well. He knew he was more angry about the game than he was frustrated with her, but there was something about her that was grating on him. Why did she have to go and tell him something so stupid, anyway?

*I love you, Payton. Oh, God, I've loved you for years.*

It was one thing for him to ignore all those damn looks she shot him. The ones where her eyes were practically swimming with love for him. God, those looks were downright impossible to ignore. But it was entirely another for her to profess her love to him.

Yeah, sure, he'd made some stupid comments about them being soul mates or something, but he hadn't directly admitted that they, Payton and Lizzie, were soul mates for Christ sake, and besides, it had been in the heat of lovemaking. What did she expect him to do with her proclamation of love?

"Dammit!" Payton smacked the steering wheel with his hand and shook his head in frustration.

If he'd been honest with himself he knew he would have to admit that somewhere deep inside of him he had loved her almost as long as she had loved him. He cared too much, and that was what scared him most of all. He was the freaking home town hero, worshipped by all, young and old. He had more women hanging around ready to thrill him than any other person he knew. He wasn't the kind of guy that was supposed to find himself falling for science loving cute dweebs like Lizzie. He was supposed to go on to college, find gorgeous big-breasted trophy type women and have them fall in love with him. He could kick himself for what he felt was happening.

He was eighteen. She was seventeen. Too young. They were too young to have found each other. They had years before they should have met somewhere and realized they were the ones for each other. And yet, it had happened now. It scared the hell out of him.

How was he supposed to keep himself from doing something really stupid one night at a post-game party in college while Lizzie wasn't there? He could picture it now, she'd be off studying in the library on a Saturday night and he'd be drunk at a party screwing some blonde bimbo because he was the quarterback and she was a groupie.

It was almost too much for him to think about. But at the same time, something fought against this feeling. Some demon inside him whispered that he was being robbed of all the fun he was supposed to have. He shouldn't have to worry about being faithful now. He was too young, he had too much ahead of him, and inside his anger burned brighter.

He gave himself a hard time about the game, and Lizzie, and his father's absence all the way to the drive of his house, but he still didn't feel any better as he put the truck into park and got out. He rounded the curve of the house and headed up the sidewalk. When he saw his mother sitting on the porch steps he stopped short.

"Mom?" He ran the rest of the way and crouched down in front of her. She had tears streaming down her face, but she just sat there staring straight out into the darkness. Chills ran down his spine.

"Mom," he repeated. "What's the matter?"

She shook her head softly. "I- I didn't mean to... I-I came home e-early from the g-game. I just c-couldn't ta-take anymore." She flicked her eyes to him. "I'm sorry about the game Payton." He hugged her fiercely. Was she upset because she thought he'd be mad that she left early?

"Mom, I don't care that you left early. Who wouldn't after a game like that?" He leaned back, thinking that would make her smile, but she started shaking and crying even harder so he knew that wasn't what was wrong. He waited.

"I-I came in. I thought I heard a noise... but then it was gone. I went back to the bedroom to change...." She broke off, her body shaking so hard now he hugged her again to calm her down. "I didn't m-mean to see...."

"See what, mom?" She didn't answer and he knew she wouldn't. As if he was on autopilot he felt himself rise and move through the house. He heard a noise from the back of the house toward his parent's room. The hallway was dark but he knew the layout by heart. He pushed his parent's door open without a sound, and watched as his day turned from bad to worse. There in his parent's bed, his father, who was supposed to be away on business, lay underneath a blond bombshell of a woman who was riding him like her life depended on it.

Payton bent over, threw up right there on the threshold, turned and walked away. He could hear his father calling him but he kept on walking. His father chased him down the driveway as he drove away, but Payton never looked back.


He was there, lying on the banks of Granny's pond when she found him. He didn't know how she found him, only that she had and that he needed her more right then than he needed anyone in the world. She didn't say anything. She must have known something was wrong because she just watched him with that guarded expression she gave him when she was waiting for him to show her what he needed. Lizzie sat beside him and wrapped the blanket she brought with her around both of their shoulders.

He felt numb. Worse, he felt like the white fuzz that existed on empty television channels. Little pricks of icy, throbbing pain stabbed him over and over again everywhere on his body. He couldn't make the feeling go away, and he was afraid that as much as he wanted her to, Lizzie wouldn't be able to dispel the feeling either.

He stared unseeing up at the cloudy night sky, wishing that he could see the stars so he could distract his mind by pointing out constellations to Lizzie. She lay back on the ground next to him and pushed her way into the crook of his arm. He felt sick, but at the same time he wanted her close to him, so he pulled her into his body and gently kissed the top of her head.

"Want to talk about it?" She asked after a few minutes of silence.

"No." He looked up at the night sky again.

"Payton...I don't know what's happened, but I can tell something is wrong. Don't you want to tell me?" She watched the pain rip through his eyes and wash over his face, but all he did was clench his jaw muscles and hug her tighter. "Please?"

He faced her then with a fierceness replacing the pain. "No, Lizzie!" She looked at him, her jaw trembling a little from the fear she felt right then, but she took a deep breath and lay back down on the ground. She could hear him swearing under his breath and then he rolled to lean up on one elbow so he could look down at her.

He brushed the back of one knuckle down the soft skin of her face and gently kissed her lips. "Look, I'm sorry, Lizzie. Really. I'm still just a little bummed about losing that game."

"Oh, Payton." She threw her arms around his waist and hugged him fiercely. He didn't want it, would have done anything to stop the feeling right then, but still he felt his body stiffen with desire. He held up a hand tentatively over her shoulder, tried to convince his body what his brain already knew- that going ahead with his desire was a really bad idea at that moment- then let his hand settle over her warm skin and pushed her softly back down to the ground.

His eyes were dark and turbulent with the troubles that raged in his mind mixed with the craving he had to sate himself in her body. It was a primal lust that he felt surging through his veins, and the smile he gave her should have been a clanging warning bell in her ears.

Lizzie could tell something wasn't right, wasn't the way it should have been, wasn't the way it had been when they'd made love in the past, but she looped her arms around his neck and readied herself for their kiss, trusting that this man, the man that had always protected her in the past would never think of hurting her now.

His lips settled over hers a little harder than they had in the past, with an urgency and hunger that Lizzie had never experienced before. Oh, she had felt the raging need pulsing through this man before, but nothing as desperate and urgent as it was right then. The lips that had always been soft and warm before felt a little cold and stiff, but she loved him deeply so she overlooked the change and focused on the exhilaration of being in her lover's arms.

He shifted and ran his mouth down her neck and over the material covering her breasts, hearing a little gasp of exhilaration pass through her lips. Swiftly he jerked her shirt up, almost ripping the fabric, and gripped her tender skin harshly. He felt the peaks of her nipples harden and he smiled down at her with a wicked sort of gleam in his eyes just before he ripped the silky cloth that covered her breasts. He laughed, a low savage sort of growl, as she yelped then caught herself and offered herself up to him.

"Yes, oh yes," he whispered. "Give yourself to me." He stroked his hand down her flat belly, and tried to shake loose the demons that had overcome him. He knew that this was not what she deserved, not what he needed to do to her, but something gripped his heart and mind and he couldn't shake it off. He stroked his hand down her again and heard her let out a whimper of desperate need. He smiled, a wicked feral smile, and ripped the buttons of her pants out of their holes. Swiftly, before she gave her assent, he stroked down underneath her panty line and found her ready for him.

Payton ripped her pants off of her and gave her body a once over, approving her long fluid legs and strong body. Then, he rapidly unzipped his pants and spread her legs. In one blatant, masculine thrust he pushed inside of her, heard her release a moan of pleasure as he pulled almost completely out then slammed into her again.

Never had he used, or rather misused, her body in this fashion before, and never had he seen her eyes glitter like they were just then. He couldn't tell if she liked the way he was loving her or if she were merely holding on for the ride. Either way, as much as he wanted to, he really didn't care. All he could picture right then, as much as he wanted to focus on her and all the ways he loved her, he could only picture his father and that wicked hoar of a woman riding him.

He rolled her over so that she was on top of him and pushed her up into a sitting position. Never before had they done this- she had always preferred to be on bottom with his weight heavy on top of her. Now, though, he didn't give her a choice, and he held her up when she would have protested and tried to shift him back to the top. He pushed himself hard into her and thrust his hips into hers. His hands came up to grip her waist and drive her down onto him with a heavy thrust watching her heavy breasts bounce with each successive move. He heard her groan, a deep guttural sound that made him even harder than he already was. He pushed her hard, looking at her face, wishing he could memorize every glorious line as she gave in to the moment and closed her eyes, looping her hands up into her hair so her breasts lifted and puckered even tighter in the cooling night air.

Then that wicked woman's figure popped back in his head, and he rammed her down onto him even harder, making her whimper with either raging desire or pain. Payton was too far gone now to care. Too wrapped up in his own misery to even think about what he was doing to her. He was lost to the torture in his brain, and as much as he loved her and desperately needed her, he suddenly realized he was lost to her.

There, sitting on the banks of Granny's pond with Lizzie bouncing on top of him, a tragic thought came to him. How many times had he been called his father's little shadow? All he could picture from that moment on was what he would do to her if he stayed with her, if she stayed with him, and they went on with their lives together. One day their son would come home from a game, and find her crying on the front steps with him riding some bimbo in their bedroom. One day, he, just like his father, would break his love's heart, and rip their family to shreds. Payton pushed it from his mind. He refused to let himself think about it. Just because his father couldn't keep himself on a leash, didn't mean he'd turn out the same way.

He focused back in on her beautiful body and wanted to cry at the sight of her sliding up and down him, her body glistening from the sweat they had worked up. He slid his hands up her body and over the generous peaks, feeling their firm weight in his hands, for what he knew would be the last time. He could tell she was about to slide over the peak so he leaned up, flicking his tongue over a pebbled nipple, hearing her release a moan into the night air. She convulsed and crumpled on top of him, and as much as he hated himself for it, he felt his traitorous body stiffen and he too slid over the edge into glorious oblivion.

## Chapter Twenty-Three

"Lizzie, are you listening to me?"

Lizzie snapped back to attention and let her eyes focus on Grace across the lunch table. She forced herself to smile. "Sorry, I was up late last night. You were saying?"

"Yeah, so, I was at the mall in Clarkston and I found this purse that is to *die* for…" Grace's voice faded into oblivion again as Lizzie focused over her friend's shoulder to the lunch line. She wanted to scream.

Lou Ann was standing next to Payton in line and not only was she laughing hysterically at whatever he was saying, but she was doing it in a way that her not so little breasts just happened to brush against his arm. Lizzie wished that she had laser beam eye power right then.

And now Lou Ann was lightly punching him on the arm. Payton must have missed flirting 101 classes because it looked to her that he hadn't even picked up that Lou Ann was hitting on him big time. And unfortunately for Lizzie, she'd been doing that more and more lately.

Lizzie frowned down into her lunch sack, and tried unsuccessfully to focus on Grace' story. Instead she kept seeing all the different times she'd seen Lou Ann hitting on her man the past few weeks. It wasn't anything obvious, or it hadn't been at first, but now Lizzie was beginning to wonder exactly what was going on.

She'd worked up the nerve to say something to Payton about it a week ago, but he'd brushed it off. Still, something didn't feel right to her. She should trust him, she knew she should. After all, if he was dumb enough to fall for a girl like Lou Ann then hell, she guessed Lou Ann deserved him. But still…

"Lizzie, are you feeling alright?"

Lizzie's head snapped up. Payton was sitting beside Grace and they were staring at her quizzically. She started to smile, but then she noticed Lou Ann hovering next to Payton. She thought she might lose her lunch.

"I think I might be getting sick. I think I'm going to go home and get some sleep."

Payton looked concerned. "Do you want me to walk you home?"

Lizzie mustered a smile. "No. No, I'll make it just fine."

She grabbed her stuff and started to leave. "I'll call you later, Bean," Grace called after her. She turned to respond and saw Lou Ann slip her hand over Payton's shoulder. Lizzie gripped her backpack tighter and hurried from the lunchroom.

She walked right past Granny on her way home without even noticing she was there. Lizzie was lost in thought. About a month ago her father sat her down after dinner one night and told her the news about Payton's father. She could still feel the shock that had hit her. Why hadn't Payton told her?

She'd been with him that night, could still remember how harsh he'd been when they'd made love, and she supposed now she understood his reasoning. But still, she couldn't imagine them being as close as they were and him not feeling the need to tell her about his parents.

And there was more. She constantly told him she loved him, and yet he'd never returned the phrase. Before, she could see the emotions in his eyes even if he never said them to her, but now she wasn't even sure she could see that. She wasn't sure what she could see anymore.

Lizzie dropped her backpack on the chair in her room and pulled out an old t-shirt and blue jeans. It was a nice day, the winter weather they'd had for the past few months was now turning to spring, and she thought a walk to the pond might help her feelings. She tied the laces to her shoes and pulled her hair into a ponytail. She left her mom a note on her bed and slipped out the back door and headed for the pond.

She decided to push thoughts of Payton from her mind and forced herself to look at the green buds that were starting to push their way out onto the trees around her as she walked. As she neared the pond she thought she heard voices, muffled, but voices all the same. She paused, but she didn't hear anything else so she continued.

It was as she was about to push her way through the thick pile of bushes that had grown up around the perimeter of the pond that she heard the voices again. Familiar voices. Voices that made her heart stand still. And then she saw them.

Lou Ann and Payton at the edge of the pond standing there skipping rocks. That was something that Lizzie and he had done forever and it made her heart hurt. But then she felt it break as she watched Lou Ann turn and lean in to him, and slowly plant a kiss on his lips. She noticed immediately that he didn't react. He stood there for a moment, letting her kiss him, as if trying to decide what to do. And then in the next instant he was kissing her, all hot and heavy, and Lizzie knew all too well what those lips must be doing to Lou Ann right about then.

Lizzie stood there and watched. She felt disgusted by the scene and disgusted with herself for watching, but she couldn't have moved if she tried. She watched as he took her shirt off and just as quickly her bra. His hands claimed their prize and she heard a muffled moan as his fingers pinched and pulled and then his lips suckled on Lou Ann's body. The image burned into Lizzie's memory.

When Payton's hand slid down her body and she heard another woman cry out his name Lizzie's stunned stance ended. She turned and began to move away, but she must have made some unearthly guttural, mourning sound because she heard Payton say, "Oh, God! Lizzie!"

She heard him coming after her, but Lou Ann stopped him. "Just wait, Payton. She'll calm down. Don't go after her now. Give her some time."

"No! Lou Ann, let go of me."

There was crashing in the bushes behind her, and then a firm hand grabbed her. Payton pulled her to a stop and turned her to him, pressing her face against the solid strength of his chest. His heart was pounding against his body, not from running, Lizzie thought with anger, but from the excitement of touching Lou Ann's body.

She pushed away from him and Payton let her go. Lizzie squeezed her hands into fists, digging her nails into the soft flesh of her palms. She forced herself to focus on the pain in her hands and the anger burning her lungs so she wouldn't cry. She refused to cry in front of him. Not now. Not ever again.

"W-what… what are you doing with her!" She hated herself for stammering. It only made her look stupid and childish. It fueled her anger.

"Lizzie, it's not…"

"Oh, don't *even* tell me it's not what it looks like." She noticed Lou Ann had come up behind Payton. She was standing about ten feet away from them, and a smug smile perched on her lips. Lizzie turned her anger on her.

"What are you grinning at?"

"You. Thought you were so smart making your way up in the ranks, using your boyfriend to put me in my place. Well, paybacks a bitch ain't it?"

Lizzie saw red. She went after Lou Ann determined to stop at nothing short of blood, but she felt Payton pull her away. "That's enough, Lou Ann! I think you've done enough damage. Go home."

Lou Ann snorted in disgust. "Like you own me or something. Whatever, I'm out of here."

Payton waited until she'd moved out of sight and turned back to Lizzie. "Liz, I swear, I never meant for that to happen."

She wasn't buying it. "Right. Well, meant to or not, it did. I thought there was something… forget it, it just sounds stupid saying it now." She folded her arms across her, using her limbs as a shield to keep the hurt from digging its way deeper into her. "I can't believe you did this." She flung her arms out in frustration. "Lou Ann? What could you possibly see in Lou Ann?"

A muscle worked in Payton's jaw. "I didn't mean… it just… Jesus, Liz, it just happened."

"Great, so every time you're at a fraternity party in college, I'm going to have to worry about it *just happening* again?"

That same muscle twitched. Lizzie edged closer to him. "No."

"How can you stand here and say that so seriously? What proof can you give me?" She was pushing him and the anger coming out felt good. She edged closer still, and nudged him with her finger. "What proof!"

Payton snapped, pushing her hand away. "None! You're right, I'll probably screw every girl I meet and laugh at you while I do it. Is that what you wanted to hear?" When she took a step away, he grabbed her and pulled her closer. "Well, Liz, is it?"

"No!"

"Well, now that I'm started, why stop now? You know, maybe you're right, maybe it didn't just happen." His eyes were dark with anger, and Lizzie winced at the grip he had on her hand. "Maybe I was sick to death of hearing you say 'I love you, Payton', all the time and I just wanted… out. Maybe I'm just like my dad- can't make a commitment to one woman and keep my pants on around others." He released her and she shrunk away, covering her ears, desperate to not hear anymore damning words.

"Don't!" Her lips were chattering. "Don't say something you can't take back, Payton."

"Like what? That I was just using you?" He shoved his hands into his pockets. "That you were just something fun to occupy my time until I could find bigger and better fish to fry."

She turned away. "No. No I don't believe this."

He grunted and turned her back around. "Well believe it. Maybe I could see that hopelessly devoted, infatuated puppy dog stare from a mile away, and I cashed in on it. There, are you happy?" He pulled her up close and forced her to look him in the eye. "It was fun while it lasted sweetheart, but the game's getting old and I'm ready to move on."

She looked up at him, trying to read him, praying he wasn't telling the truth, but all she could see were a pair of green eyes full of anger and hatred. A tear slipped down from her eyes. "Why are you doing this? Who are you?"

Payton's laugh was low and cruel. "It's me, baby. Don't you recognize me?"

"No." She turned to leave, anxious to get away from him so she couldn't hear anything more damning that what he'd said already. It was suddenly all too clear to her. She'd been a pawn, a cheap joke, used and discarded. Payton hadn't been anymore interested in loving Lizzie than Brett had. Instead she'd just been a fun diversion for him. She should have known to never trust a jock but she'd been stupid enough to go and fall in love with one. She was nothing but a nerd with a crush on some dumb jock.

Always had been, always would be.

Lizzie could hear all those *I love you's* she'd given to him being thrown back in her face and she wanted to crawl under a rock and die.

Payton called after her, and in the darkest recesses of her mind she thought she detected the smallest fraction of agony. "Good, just walk away! That's what I wanted anyway. It's over, Lizzie. You make me sick!" She heard something crash in the bushes, but she didn't turn around. She couldn't care less what it was.

The rest of their senior year went by relatively quickly, much to Payton's surprise. He knew in his gut that he was a world class heel, and wished to all the heavens above he could find a way to apologize to Lizzie. As it was she wasn't speaking to him, and he knew that if she never did again he'd deserve every second of her abuse.

It made him sick thinking about all the words he'd used to hurt her. Stupid words. Words that he could never take back. At the time he'd been so angry and he felt so humiliated for getting caught with Lou Ann that he'd just retaliated out of self preservation. Lizzie hadn't deserved even a second of his abuse, but there was nothing he could do now.

He didn't see Lizzie at all anymore, except on occasion when he would catch sight of her walking down the hallways at school with her friends. During those times he would find himself following her with his gaze, hoping that he could catch a glimpse of her beautiful eyes or a little hint of the smile he had loved for so long.

He never did, though.

It was as if that moment had left her, and him, too, both hollow shells of who they originally were, and in their place walked half-dead people. He heard through Colin and Jade and the rest of their friends that she hardly ever smiled like she used to. Oh, she smiled, they told him, but it wasn't the sincere, warm one he loved so much, but rather a façade that she'd put up to throw people off the trail of her pain. Still, he had hope that on down the line she would forget him and her pain and return to normal.

"Why did you do it?" They would ask him. "What did you do to break her heart?"

Apparently she hadn't felt the itch to destroy him in quite the fashion that he had devastated her. He was certain that Grace had to know what had happened, but she wasn't going to say a word, he soon discovered, and even more surprising was that Lou Ann hadn't told anyone either. So it was left for him to bare the memory alone, to kill him slowly, in a brutal, agonizing torture.

He was too proud, he also discovered, to let their friends in on the secret. Payton didn't want to tell them that he, the crowned king of Dixie, the son of an adulterer might as well be one himself. Whether he wanted to admit it or not, now he was forced to acknowledge that he'd probably just thrown away the best thing that would ever happen to him.

Payton's scandal hadn't even hit the gossip channels, and somehow the pain that he and his mother were enduring hadn't hung in there for too long, though he would never understand exactly how that miracle had occurred. Probably because Lou Ann's mother was the head gossip queen and her daughter had convinced her not to talk.

Payton thought about his father. His father had merely laughed in his mother's face and left town with his mistress that very same night, and even now, months later he hadn't offered a single word of regret, nor a single dime of support.

Payton looked down at the graduation program in his hand and wished the ceremony would go a little faster so he could get out of this town. He, along with almost three-fourths of the rest of their class were headed to the University of Georgia in the fall. He itched, physically itched, with the need to be free of all the terrors that haunted him daily in this place. At least there he could lose himself in the buzz of some thirty thousand plus college students that didn't know a thing about him except that he was there to play ball.

He glanced up a few rows ahead of him to where Lizzie was sitting, her pretty dark hair down and loose about her shoulders with that silly cap and tassel strategically in place. Then he glanced over his shoulder and out into the crowd to where his mother sat. He noted with a dull ache in his chest that his father still hadn't shown, and the space beside his wonderful mother still sat empty, leaving her utterly alone in a sea of people.

His life, he knew, would never again be the same. How could it be, he wondered, that one person could have such a hold on your life that losing them was like losing your soul.

*Part II:  The New Life*
*Chapter Twenty-Four*

Grace gripped the leather on the steering wheel and took a deep breath.  Man, she hated being the go-between.  Here she was, two weeks before her best friends wedding,  sitting in front of Lizzie's house trying to decide if she really wanted to put herself in the middle of what was certain to be an utter disaster, but she couldn't think of a good way out.

Of course, there was the obvious… just stay out of it.  But, heck, that wasn't any fun.  Plus, she could still hear Payton's pitiful voice on the other end of the phone.  *Grace, please, I'm begging you to help me.  Talk to her for me.  She'll listen to you.*  She'd tried to explain that she really didn't think Lizzie would even listen to *her* on this issue, but Payton could be very convincing when he wanted to be.  She eyed her brand spanking new purse on the passenger seat and smiled.

Grace's stomach flipped and she nibbled her lower lip in confusion.  She hated what Payton had done to Lizzie.  No one deserved to be treated that way.  But on the other hand, she'd seen the way they were with each other, how perfect they had been together.  If Payton truly had grown up, and if he truly did love her the way Grace suspected he did, then didn't he deserve a chance to prove it to Lizzie?

And the only way he was going to get that chance was if someone, someone such as herself, could put them together and let him talk to her.  Heaven knew Lizzie wasn't going to be seeking him out on her own.  She'd wear garlic around her neck and carry wooden stakes twenty-four hours a day if she thought that would keep Payton away from her forever.

Grace sighed.  It looked like she didn't have much choice.  She pushed her way from the car and steeled herself, preparing for the battle of wits that was about to begin.  If Lizzie even suspected foul play going on, Payton wouldn't have a snowball's chance in hell at winning her.

Lizzie spotted her through the window and held up a hand.  She was on the phone, most likely with Josh, and she wanted her to wait on the porch.  Grace took a seat on the big, white swing and watched as several cars slowly made their way past the house.  That was a way of life here in Edenville.  She couldn't even count anymore the number of times they'd sat on this porch watching cars and talking about boys as they were growing up.  Of course now the cars went faster, and the radios were louder, but it was still the same and it comforted Grace.

Just then Lizzie came out. Grace watched as her best friend, still as tall and slender as the day they'd met, stomped across the front porch to where she sat.

"Wow, what's got your panties all in a wad?"

Lizzie fixed her emerald eyes on her and huffed. "It's Josh. He wants me to cut my hair for the wedding, and die it blonde." She paused and pulled a strand of the dark, curling hair away from her face. "Can you see me as a blonde?"

Grace made a face. "No. Why does he care anyway?"

"He says … how can I put this delicately…. my face doesn't look quite as radiant when it's long. Oh, and his mother prefers blondes over brunettes." She huffed again. "I've never had short hair in my life, and dear God don't get me started on how much I could care less what color hair his mother prefers."

"Amen." Grace leaned forward. "What'd you tell Josh?"

Grace noted the tension that crept through Lizzie. "I told him I'd think about it."

"You'd *think* about it! Are you crazy, you should have told him to stick it!"

Lizzie rubbed her forehead. "Yeah, well, Josh is pretty adamant about his likes and dislikes. You have to break it to him gently if you plan to do something differently."

Grace shook her head. "Has he always been like this?"

"Pretty much."

Grace couldn't understand what her friend saw in Josh. Something about the guy gave Grace the creeps. She shrugged and decided to switch topics. It wasn't any of her business, just as she reminded herself that it wasn't any of her business if Payton got a chance to explain himself to Lizzie. Man, how did she always get herself into these messes?

Grace moved over and patted the seat next to her, but Lizzie didn't even notice. "So, how're you doing? You know, after the letter and all."

There was a groan, and a hand held up as if to block the thought. "Oh, don't even get me *started* on that."

"Why not?" If looks could kill, she'd be dead. "Err, I mean… what the hell was he thinking?" It was laced with sarcasm, but Lizzie was apparently too worked up to notice.

"Exactly, Carrot! Those were my thoughts exactly!" She bounced to emphasize her frustration.

"Okay, Liz. I don't mean to be rude, but it's a love letter. It's not like the guy just told you he'd run over Skipper Jr."

Lizzie's gasp of horror nearly made her laugh. "The creep wouldn't dare do something like that. I'd rip his no good head off."

"I'm sure you would, Bean, I'm sure you would. Now sit down here and tell me how you see this letter as the end of the world."

"You're kidding me right?"

"He told you he loved you. What's the big deal? I think it's kind of sweet if you ask me."

"Well," Lizzie paused to sniff dramatically, "nobody asked you, and the *big deal* is that he did it two weeks before my wedding!"

"And?"

"And it's to *another* man!"

"I think you need a drink." Just once, Grace thought as she poured both of them a glass of wine, she'd like to be the woman two men wanted at one time. She couldn't remember ever having one guy, not even her father, who really loved her. It must be nice to have so many men fighting over you.

She tried to change the subject when she returned with the wine, but Lizzie wouldn't let her. "Don't try to change the subject on me, Gracie, I see that look in your eye."

"What?"

"This is such a rotten thing he did, and I can't believe you aren't as furious about this as I am." Probably because she'd always thought Payton and her were the best thing since friend chicken, and had always hoped this day would come.

"Honestly, Bean, if you're that mad about it then go tell him off, and stop pacing in front of me like an old wet hen."

Big mistake, she could see, as Lizzie turned on her with a feral gleam in her eye. "I'm not talking to the Cretan, and if he thinks this is going to bring me falling to my knees in front of him he's wrong. Wrong!"

Ah, Grace's brain finally grasped hold of the true meaning of the situation. A little bright light clicked on in her head, and she understood, finally, what the big deal was. Lizzie was torn. Torn between marrying the man she had said yes to, and finally, *hopefully*, getting the man she and every other soul in town knew was meant for her.  So there was hope for Payton after all.  She smiled.

"Then just forget about it."  She reached out and took her friends hand.  "Look, Lizzie, if it bothers you that much then just throw the stupid thing away.  You don't ever have to see Payton again if that's what you want."

But that was just the problem, Grace could see from the look in her eyes that she really, really did want to see him again.  This letter had thrown her so far off her axis she didn't know which side was up right now.  She couldn't decide whether the old Payton, the one with the cheating heart and nasty attitude, or the new Payton with the sweet words and charm was the Payton she wanted to remember.

Grace suspected that more than anything Lizzie wanted her friend to knock her over the head with a horseshoe and tell her to grow up and go figure it out, but that wasn't Grace's job.  Her job was to get Lizzie somewhere that Payton could do the convincing, and now Grace knew that's just what she intended to do.

Lizzie caught her friend's eye.  "What he did to me was terrible."

"You're right.  It was terrible."  Her smile was rueful.  "He doesn't deserve the hot boiled peanut hulls you discard in the trash.  But he wrote that letter and whether you want it or not, you got it.  So deal with it."

Lizzie gave in with a sigh.  "You're right, Carrot, you always are. I'm just tired I guess."  She plopped down next to her friend on the swing. "Now, tell me why it is that you're sitting on my mama's swing."

"There's gonna be a barn party tonight."  She checked her watch. "In about two hours, actually.  I came over to tell you to get ready."

"I don't know.  We've still got tons to do for the wedding and I just don't think it's a good idea for me to go."

Grace quietly studied her friend with an amused smirk on her face before she rolled her eyes and laughed.        "Give it up, Bean.  Your daddy has had the blue prints mapped out for that thing since a week after you told him you were engaged.  I'll bet he won't even let you touch a thing to help him set it all up."

Lizzie rolled her eyes at Grace.  "You know, you always think you know everything don't you?"

Grace chucked her lightly on the shoulder.  "No, you just can't admit that I'm right!  Come on, you haven't seen half of these people in years.  You have to come."

Grace knew she had her, but she let her friend think it over for a few minutes anyway. "Fine," she conceded. "I'll be ready in two hours, but not a minute sooner, got it?"

"That's my girl. I knew you had it in you." Grace gave her friend a fierce hug, and when she pulled away she thought that Lizzie might have started to suspect something because she was watching her with an odd look.

"Just promise me one thing," Lizzie said.

"What's that?"

"Make sure that Payton doesn't come anywhere near that barn party."

Seeing as how Grace had made a promise of exactly the opposite, she simply said, "I'll do my best." Whatever that meant.


Lizzie checked herself from every conceivable angle in the long mirror attached to her closet door- an old habit that would forever stick with her, she supposed. For September, the weather was still exceptionally warm so she'd pulled out some of her summer clothes to wear to the party. When she was absolutely positive that her butt didn't look too big in her new jeans, and that the black halter top she'd paired with it didn't make her breasts look too small, she smiled at herself, making sure one last time that she hadn't lost her famous smile.

She spritzed herself with perfume, threw an old cowboy hat on top of her long, wavy hair, and slid into her favorite pair of well-worn boots. She was ready she supposed, even though butterflies had been flitting around in her stomach all afternoon.

It had been so long since she'd seen some of the people she expected to be there tonight. For some, she hadn't seen them since the day they had walked across the stage together at high school graduation. But the one person she was most worried would show up, even though she'd told Grace to make sure he didn't, was Payton Cartwright. The last thing she wanted was to see him again tonight and drag up old memories she wanted nothing more than to forget about.

Already in the past few hours she'd remembered more about their past than she ever wanted to think about again. She felt her face flush as her brain flitted over the memory of the first time they had made love. No matter how hard she tried, it was something that she would never be able to forget.

Grace blared the horn of her car, and Lizzie's nerves shot straight through the ceiling. Why had she agreed to go tonight? Grace laid on the horn again, and Faith called from the den, "Lizzie, you better get out there now before Gracie causes another noise violation. Sheriff Smith's already had to give her two warnings this month!"

If there was one truth Lizzie couldn't deny about her friend it was that subtlety had never been her strong point. She was redheaded, and blunt, and had more enthusiasm than a stadium full of professional cheerleaders. Lizzie grabbed her purse, though she doubted she would have any use for it in a field full of round bales and coolers full of beer.

"Have fun at the party, hon."

"Thanks, mama. Don't wait up," She called out of habit as she raced out the back door to stop the next honk.

They said little on the five minute drive to Farmer Murphy's barn, and Lizzie could feel her nerves pulling tighter and tighter, like violin strings ready to break as they rounded the bend and the barn came into sight.

The field in front of the barn was nearly full when they pulled in; massive pick-up trucks with wheels almost as big as her car made a big U around the main entrance of the barn, their beds facing inward. This was the beer station, and before they even pulled up Lizzie could already imagine the number of coolers filling the back of each truck. They could already hear the music blaring from the sound system someone had brought, and Lizzie felt her heart thud right along with the bass of the song.

She skimmed the crowd and the sea of vehicles scattered around the field, and breathed a sigh of relief when she didn't see Payton. She told herself to be happy that he hadn't shown, that it didn't really matter how he might have changed in the years since she had seen him. She reminded herself, very sternly, that she was furious with him for all he had done. But her heart was already buying in to the letter he had written, and she found it harder to cast blame on him than she had in the past.

Lizzie made her way to one of the coolers and snagged a beer before she went inside. It was like her courage life-line and she hated herself for being so nervous, but before long she felt herself swept up in the beat of the music and laughter that surrounded her, and she smiled when she saw Colin and Bud head her direction.

"Hello, boys! Haven't seen your smilin' faces in quite some time!"

They grinned and simultaneously wrapped her in a mountain of a bear hug. "Well, if it isn't New Girl, come home to get herself hitched. Thought we'd never see the day."

"Maybe you won't. Who said I was inviting you?" They feigned offense and she laughed. An ease settled over her and she lost herself in their conversation, so she didn't notice when Payton came through the double doors of the barn and stopped to talk to a group of people.

Somewhere during her conversation she looked up and found herself watching a pair of green eyes on top of a long, tall, heart-achingly familiar body headed right her way. She tried to free herself from the conversation and move out of the direct line of his vision, but Colin and Hank, forever Payton's loyal companions, apparently knew this was going to happen and they effectively stalled her.

"So, Lizzie, when's it official? When do you become the Doc?" She heard Colin asking her questions, but her mind had gone blank.

She tried, unsuccessfully, to evade the arm Colin wrapped around her waist. "Uh... Next month. It's a big summer in the Benford family."

"Seems to be," Hank added, stepping up to her other side.

And with the last step she watched Payton take in their direction, all the world seemed to still around her. All the noises faded, all the happy partying around her ceased, and she was left all alone, it felt, in a vast open space with only one man in front of her with eyes as clear and green as a meadow on a summer day.

"Hello, Lizzie." He spoke to her in a voice that was deeper than she remembered and she felt her heart stop when she heard it. Even though she commanded it not to, it came to a momentary halt before it pounded back to life again. She forced herself not to look at him more than as a passing glance. She told herself she didn't care or notice all the ways he'd changed.

"Hello." She pushed the words from her dry, sandy throat and heard it crackle out into the warm, summer air.

"Dance with me." Like an intimate but unwanted caress his words wrapped around her and held. This time her eyes narrowed and she forced herself out from beneath Colin's arm. It was too much for her to take, and she couldn't handle standing there in the same space as him for another second longer.

"Excuse me, boys, but I believe I have to get going." She pushed her way out of the group and refused to look back when she heard him calling her name. Suddenly anger a million times stronger than she had remembered feeling in the past slammed into her, almost buckling her knees out from under her with its force. She forced herself forward and out into the night air.

There was a partially muffled curse that floated to her, and she judged that she had only seconds before Payton came after her. He caught up with her just outside of the barn and grabbed hold of her arm. "Wait! Liz, would you just wait a damn minute."

"No!" She flung his arm away and made it a few steps farther, but she was no match for his speed, and this time he caught her with both of his hands and held her captive in the strength of them.

He whirled her around to face him, and she could tell by the sparks that flew from his eyes that he meant business. "I suggest you get your butt back in that barn and dance with me. I have some things I want to say to you."

Her face lit with fury. "You know, this may come as some surprise to you, Payton Cartwright, but I don't want to dance, and I sure as hell have nothing to say to you."

She watched the muscles in his jaw clench and relax, clench and relax, and knew there was a war going on inside him. For all the time they'd been apart she could still tell when he was deciding whether to hold back or let all his cards fly.

"Well," he said at long last, "then that just leaves one other thing on my list that I've been thinking about doing tonight." And with that he pulled her hard against his body, knocking her hat off in the process, and ran his strong, sun darkened hands roughly through her hair then down to hold her body in place. He forced his lips down onto her stubborn ones, and kissed her with a passion that had been banked for many long years.

She tried to fight him, but he just held on even tighter, and after a while she gave in to the struggle. He gentled his kiss only a fraction, but still she refused to kiss him in return. Those lips, stubborn as the girl they belonged to, kept clamped tight as clam shells, and refused to permit any sense of enjoyment.

But Payton refused to give in, and eventually, like with everything else in his life, he won. He nipped her lip and she opened her mouth to bite back when his whole mouth took over the job of kissing her. Lips and teeth and tongue took over, and before she knew what was happening, she had her arms wrapped around him, and her lips returning his caresses without another thought in the world except for how damn good this man could kiss.

When he pulled away, he kept his gaze on her, and he smiled with satisfaction at the look on her face. Her breath came hard and fast, and her lips felt swollen. And as quickly as the feeling had come, it left again. Fast as lighting she swung at him, landing a flat handed smack across his cheek. "Don't you ever pull a trick like that again, Payton. Got it?"

He clapped a hand over the tender spot on his face, and his eyes narrowed at her. After a minute he spoke, "I know, I completely deserved that, Lizzie. It's just that seeing you…" His words trailed off, and his eyes softened again. His hands ran down her arms, and he took her hand in his. "Don't talk if you don't want to, but please, dance with me."

She was too shaken from his kiss and her reaction to think, so she followed him to a quiet spot just out of the lights of the barn, where they could still hear the music, and let him pull her in close to his body and begin a dance as old as time.

It took her a full minute to come back to her senses, but when she did she realized she was standing in the shadows of the barn, folded in the soft caress of Payton's arms, with at least ten people curiously watching them as they slowly turned in circles on their imaginary dance floor. She tried to muster up the energy to be furious with him, but she was too tired to fight him right now. Instead she let her head fall against his strong shoulder and her body relaxed against his.

She didn't know what to say when the song ended and he leaned back a little to watch the play of emotions flicker across her face. She had so much to say, yet so much she shouldn't. She wanted to say everything at one time, and yet she wished she didn't have to say anything at all.

Lizzie walked away from where they stood and hitched herself onto the bed of a pickup truck towards the back of the field. Payton followed close behind, and stopped at the side of the truck, propping his arms over the rim of the bed, watching her every move.

She studied the stars for a while, enjoying the peace they offered, and wondered exactly where it was this conversation was about to go. She hadn't planned on seeing him tonight, though she should have known that somehow she would. She suspected that at the heart of it, Grace was somehow to blame. So now she was left to talk through things that she had no idea how to talk through or what exactly it was that she wanted to say.

Payton watched as Lizzie studied the stars and wished like hell he could see inside her head and just once know her thoughts. There had been a time that she would tell him anything, and in reality *had* told him everything. But that time had long ago come and gone, and now he was left wishing that somehow he could change her mind and let her see exactly what he felt.

She looked so beautiful sitting there with her long dark hair gently blowing in the night breeze. He wanted to reach out and touch that hair, feel its silky softness. He wanted to do a million things to her that he hadn't been able to get out of his mind for years, but he knew now wasn't the time. Now, he was hanging by a thread.

He watched her as she studied the stars and felt a tug of longing so deep it made him want to groan when she finally shifted her eyes and studied him in the moonlight. Her look was intense, but none of the emotions that he used to see flicking across the surface were evident tonight, and he wondered how it was she had learned to hide her feelings so well.

He couldn't take it any longer. Standing here with her, watching that veiled look on her face, he knew he had no choice. He had to tell her the truth.

"Liz... I need to tell you something." She focused her eyes on him, and waited. "Do you remember what I said to you before we broke up? I said all those cruel and terrible things to you. You remember, right?"

He could tell by her cocked head and narrow slit gaze that she remembered all right. He took a deep breath and let it out in a sigh.

"Well... I didn't... I mean, I never... I was just being a stupid kid."

He shrugged his shoulders and turned away. Looking at her was too unbearable so he studied the night sky as he recounted the story. "I was scared, Liz. A few months before then I'd come home just after a game to check on my mom because I thought my dad was out of town on business." He rubbed the bridge of his nose with his thumb and forefinger. "Apparently he forgot something at home and came back to get it... except he brought his girlfriend with him, and for some ungodly reason they thought that having a quickie in my parents bed before they headed back out would be a good idea."

He took a deep breath and forced himself to unclench his fists. "I watched my dad in that bed with that woman, wishing that I could kill him and her for how he had just ruined my parent's marriage, but I walked out before I could do anything. God, Lizzie, I wanted to die that night."

He turned to her, searching her eyes in the darkness for some sign of understanding, or shock, or anything that he could hang on to for support. She kept her eyes thickly veiled so he sent up a silent prayer and continued on.

"Walking in on my dad... let's just say that didn't do anything to bolster my confidence. Jesus, if anyone understands this, you would. Everything about my life was compared to my dad's. I was supposed to be a walking mini-me of him, and then I see him...." He paused, running a hand through his hair. "I loved you, Lizzie. It scared me blind to know that I did. I had never felt that way about anyone... and I never have since." He paused to look at her, noting, finally, the shock that registered on her face. He took a steadying breath and continued.

"What was I supposed to do? All I could think was that I was going to turn out just like the low life scum my dad was, and end up breaking the heart of the person I cared about most." He chuckled, although it felt more like a painful sob ripping through him. "And then what d'ya know, a few short months later, I end up proving myself right." There was more to say and he forced the words past the lump that was building in his throat.

"I had all these... feelings... inside me. Hell, and then you kept telling me how much you loved me and needed me and I just... started feeling suffocated because I was already going crazy trying to deal with everything else in my life."

He turned away from Lizzie, giving her a minute to register what he'd said. It had always killed him to think that he'd broken her heart. He could never forget the pain in her eyes when he'd said all those things to her. How many times had he woken at night in a cold sweat remembering the pain in those eyes?

"Nothing, nothing that I ever say to you will excuse what I did with Lou Ann, but for what it's worth I'm sorry."

He heard her sniffle, and turned to see her wipe a tear from her eye. Payton ran a hand through his hair and wished he hadn't been such a fool. He could only hope that telling her the truth now might save his life in the end. There was nothing to do now, but wait, and hope.

At last she spoke. "What am I supposed to say to you?" She said, leaving him feeling like he'd just been punched in the gut.

He blinked. "Whatever you want. Whatever you feel."

"Whatever I feel?" She stared off into the distance then flicked her eyes back to him. "What am I supposed to feel? You rip my heart out when I profess my love, and drop me like yesterday's news." She flung her arms out in protest. "Then now, all these years later...two weeks before I get married, you show up and tell me you were *scared* and that you never stopped loving me." Her eyes glittered with rage. "Well, you could have fooled me- you *did* fool me. I never knew you loved me in the first place. So how the hell am I supposed to feel?"

"I had to tell you. I would have hated myself forever if I hadn't."

"Then I'll tell you how I feel, Payton. I feel angry, and used. I feel like you're making me make a decision that's going to break someone's heart no matter which way I turn. And I hate that. I didn't put myself in that role, but *you* did. And now you've left it up to *me* to decide."

He didn't want to take heart, but he couldn't help it. The simple fact that a decision was even part of her vocabulary was good news to him. It meant that she was torn, and even though it meant more waiting, it also meant he wasn't out of the game yet.

He edged his way around the side of the truck and stopped when his leg brushed against the side of hers. He felt her tense and silently cursed himself for pushing her. But he wasn't ready to lose her. Not yet.

"I know this wasn't something you would have wished upon yourself, but it's out there now and I can't take it back. It would be a lie if I did." He reached out and slowly brushed his finger across the silky skin of her face. Her eyes flicked to him, and held with his. "Liz, I do love you. I always have. It's just taken me a while to grow up and figure it all out."

When a tear slipped from her eye he gently brushed it away with his thumb, and tucked a stray strand of her hair behind her ear. He hated doing this but he had to know.

He edged his way up closer to her, keeping his eyes locked with hers. He was an inch from her face and could feel her breath hitch and release. "Liz, if you tell me no, I'll step away and leave you alone, I swear. But we had something too special to throw away for good just because I was a stupid kid once upon a time."

He waited but she didn't respond, so he slowly leaned in and kissed her sweet lips. He couldn't suppress the groan inside of him, and let it out as he ran his lips over hers again and again.

Lizzie couldn't figure out what the heck had come over her. It was like she was on some sort of drug and she couldn't stop herself from kissing Payton. She hated it, but she loved it all at once. It was wrong on so many levels, and yet her body kept saying that it was right. She finally pulled herself together and forced herself to back away from him. His eyes had grown dark like a turbulent sea, but she held her ground and forced herself to stay strong.

"Payton, this is wrong. I loved you once, I honestly did. But I'm getting married and... it's not to you." She shrugged. "My fiancé will be here next week and there's just no time left to try and change things even if you could. I'm sorry. I wish I could tell you this would all end happily for both of us, but I just don't see how."

She stood and walked away before she could change her mind, before she could run to him and tell him that she couldn't stand breaking his heart. But she knew it was weak for her to do that, and she had learned a long time ago that being strong was the only way to be.

## *Chapter Twenty-five*

Payton smacked his head against the pillow and tried to fall asleep, but the red light on his alarm clock just kept ticking away the minutes and with every one he was no closer to visiting the sandman. *Do you believe in soul mates, Liz? I do.* Payton groaned and pulled the pillow over his head. He gave up around three and decided to call it a morning, a very early morning at that.

He stretched as he stumbled from the bed, trying to work out some of the kinks that his fitful few hours of sleep had so generously given to him, and slid into an old pair of jeans, long ago faded and worn down to mold perfectly to his body. Still hot from tossing and turning, he left his shirt off and staggered down the stairs of the old farmhouse in search of some strong coffee.

Payton waited for the coffee maker to noisily grind into action then pushed his way through the screened back door and out onto the porch. Crickets and various other night dwelling creatures went about their business, calling out to each other, and Payton let the sounds sooth him as he watched the night sky. There was only a half moon tonight, but it was bright enough to illuminate the fields of hay behind his house.

His house. Payton could remember looking at this house when he was still in middle school, and thinking it would be neat to live in one day. When his mother had called to say the previous owner had passed away and it was for sale, he'd bought it without even walking through it, and hadn't regretted the decision for a minute.

Of course, it had taken a considerable amount of time and money to bring the old place back up to sturdy living conditions, but that hadn't bothered Payton. It was his now, and to him the time and effort he had put into it would only leave his mark on it better than any other way he could think of.

The only thing missing now was a woman to fill the hole in his heart and the lonely, empty spot in his bed. And maybe down the road a few years a kid or two to swing on that tire swing he could just imagine being slung up from a low branch on the old Pecan tree on the side of the house. The problem with that vision, though, was that the one woman he wanted, the only woman he'd ever really wanted to fill that position didn't have very much concern for his dreams at the moment.

She was too busy trying to get herself hitched to the wrong man.

What did he have to do to convince her to change her mind? He'd already tried pouring his heart out to her and that hadn't seemed to even make her blink twice. Payton certainly wasn't accustomed to begging and pleading, and as far as he was concerned, he'd come as close to that avenue as he dared to wander. Short of kidnapping and brainwashing the girl, he didn't know what other options he had. He supposed waiting her out was his best choice. But since when did Payton Cartwright wait for anything?

Only, this time he really didn't see any other alternative.

"Okay, so you like that dress, but do you think I should wear that one to the bridesmaid's luncheon and wear this one to the rehearsal dinner?" Lizzie held a long, silky dress up over her bra and panties as she faced the mirror. "Or maybe I should wear this one." She tossed a dress on her bed and grabbed another one to hold in front of her.

Grace sat cross legged on the bed and cocked her head to one side. Both eyebrows met in concentration. "Yeah, I don't think either one of those. What else do you have?"

Lizzie groaned in disgust and threw her hands up. "Slave driver." She headed to her closet and was still grumbling as she disappeared inside. She popped out a moment later with a short, yellow dress that was strapless on one shoulder. "Okay, this is my last resort. Otherwise we'll have to go shopping in Clarkston and I don't know--" She stopped when she heard a tap on her bedroom door.

Seconds later the door popped open. "Honey, you'll never guess what the cat drug in." Her mother dashed into the room and took the dress from her hands. "Oh, well I didn't realize you weren't--"

"Hello, sweetheart." Lizzie looked from her mom to the doorway. She blushed.

"Josh! Wow, I was expecting you for... well, days." She smiled, but it didn't feel sincere. She was too shocked. He'd never surprised her like this before. "What are doing here?" She tried to grab the dress back from her mother to cover over her underwear but her mother absentmindedly took it with her as she crossed to the door.

"I'll just let you two catch up."

Josh stepped into the room and nodded to her mother as she ducked back out, and turned his attention back on Lizzie as it clicked closed. "Well aren't you glad to see me?" He smiled.

Lizzie giggled self-consciously and fidgeted with her hair, unsure what to do standing nearly naked in front of her fiancé with her best friend sitting in the room. "Uh, yeah. I just… I mean, I'm," She giggled again. "I'm practically naked here! Can you give me a minute?"

He seemed to notice for the first time. "Oh! Right. Sure, I'll be outside catching up with your mother. Take your time." He nodded to Grace on his way out. Grace lifted an eyebrow.

"That was strange."

Lizzie quickly threw on a pair of blue jeans and an old t-shirt. "What?"

Grace shook her head. "Nothing." She couldn't help herself. "Is he gay?

Lizzie turned in shock. "What!"

"Yeah, forget I said that." She stood from the bed. "I guess we'll finish deciding on the dresses later, huh?"

"Sure thing." She pulled her hair back and quickly crossed to the door. "Come on let's go find Josh and my mom. I don't like to leave them alone together too long. Somehow she feels the need to share every last embarrassing childhood story with Josh." She rolled her eyes. "I'm pretty sure my emotional stability can't handle that sort of abuse right now."

Grace laughed. "Well, I suppose that'll really limit the conversations you two'll be having with your mother on your trips back home."

Lizzie landed her an evil glare. "I'm serious." She heard a muffled, "So am I," before she rounded the corner and found Josh seated at the kitchen table. Her mother was hovering around him.

"Here, Sugar, have some more pound cake. I'm going to fix a nice ham and some butter beans, oh, and some macaroni and cheese for dinner. What else would you like with it?"

"Oh, there you two are!" Lizzie swooped in and planted a big kiss on Josh's lips. "Mom, you're so sweet, but Josh and I already had plans to eat out with Grace and some friends at that new café in town. What's the name of it, Grace?"

Grace looked confused and Lizzie shot her a pleading look. "Oh, right. I forgot."        "Sally Mae's Café," her mother supplied.

Grace snapped her fingers. "Yes, Sally Mae's Café." She didn't miss that Josh looked oh so thrilled by the name. He'd grown up in Atlanta and didn't understand all the oddities of small town life.

"That's great, Hon," he said. "What time are the reservations for?"

"Oh, you don't need reservations at Sally Mae's." Her mother filled a pitcher with water and proceeded to add several scoops of lemonade mix.

Lizzie checked her watch. "Why don't we go now? It's nearly six. We'll beat the dinner crowd."

Josh nearly wheezed he laughed so hard. "Dinner crowd. That's funny. What constitutes a crowd around here? A herd of cows?" He chuckled at his own joke.

"Take the car honey, it'll be dark when you head back. You know, Edenville's not like it used to be. A lot of riff-raff getting into trouble around here lately."

Lizzie rolled her eyes. She had to get out of here and quick. She grabbed the car keys to head off anymore banter between her mother and Josh and practically drug her fiancé out the door with Grace hot on their heels.

Normally Lizzie refused to drive the car to town, considering it was all of a quarter mile from their house, but Josh would prefer to chop an arm off rather than work up a sweat so she knew convincing him to walk in the midst of the late summer heat was hopeless. How he managed to stay fit and trim without ever working up a sweat was beyond her.

They parked in one of the spots on Main Street just outside the café and chose a booth inside close to the air conditioner. Grace sat across from the two of them and smiled at Josh. In typical Grace fashion, she set in asking him questions that had him reeling off answers until the waitress came to take their orders.

Lizzie took a minute to study him. She hadn't seen him in almost three weeks and she found herself trying not to compare him to any other men she might have lodged somewhere in her brain. His hair was sandy brown, and he kept it cut short and trim. He had chocolate brown eyes that were warm and friendly. His body was good- not too tall or too short and just enough muscle to prove he could hold his own if the need arose. He wasn't any super hero, or major football star for that matter, but he was warm and solid and that was what mattered.

She was so busy studying him that she was startled when Josh said,

"Lizzie? The waitress asked what you want to order."

"Oh!" She hadn't even thought about what she should order. She glanced down and back up. Then back down, nibbling on her lower lip in concentration.

"Here, let me do it for you." He took the menu from her hand and gave it to the waitress. "She'll have the house salad with Italian dressing, but make sure you don't include any croutons or cheese- she's on a low carb diet. And she'll have the catfish, but can you grill it rather than fry it?" He made sure the waitress wrote down 'grilled' and then smiled over at Lizzie.

Grace frowned. "Since when are you on a low carb diet, Bean?"

He playfully nudged her elbow and looked over at Grace. "Lizzie's so beautiful, don't you think? She's been trying to watch her weight up until the wedding and honeymoon, haven't you , Hon?"

Lizzie giggled nervously. "You know me, liable to gain fifteen pounds just looking at a pecan pie."

Grace's frown said it all. "Bean, you know you got your nickname for a reason, right? You're tall and skinny like a *bean pole*, remember? And since when did this 'diet' start?"

"I've been on it for a while. Josh and I have actually." She smiled into his brown eyes and looked back at her friend. "Funny, huh? I'm the doctor but he's more of a nutrition freak than I am. Don't worry, though, those baked potatoes that I could never live without before are only a distant memory now." Her smile was wistful. "I hardly ever dream about them. Anymore."

Josh laughed like he thought her comment hysterical, while Grace merely chuckled.

The rest of the meal they spent catching up on wedding plans and chatting about Josh's work. Since Grace worked at the bank in town she was curious to quiz Josh on his knowledge of stocks and bonds. He was an accountant at a major firm in Nashville, but he was also a Certified Financial Planner and Grace was interested in hearing his thoughts on some plans they were making at the bank.

Asking Josh anything about work pretty much guaranteed that no one else would get a word in edge wise for the duration of the conversation so Lizzie plastered a smile on her face and nibbled a piece of lettuce from her salad. It would have tasted much better if had been smothered in, say, blue cheese dressing, but she supposed it was healthier for her this way.

"Hon, you ready?" She looked up to find Josh standing with a hand out to help her out of the booth. "I've paid the bill already." He looked at her oddly. "Are you feeling alright?"

She nodded. "Uh-huh. I must be a little tired. I should prob'ly get more sleep."

He agreed. "Yes, I noticed the dark circles under your eyes. Why don't you use that eye gel I gave you? It'll help you look a lot better." He patted her shoulder and led her out of the restaurant by the small of her back.

Payton had had enough fun for one day, and was ready for a cold beer. It was only Monday and he'd already had more than enough trouble for the week. He had been excited when he'd taken the coaching position at Dixie Academy, but that was before he realized exactly how much the people in the community would want to poke their nose into his business. If it wasn't one of the boy's fathers telling him his son needed more playing time, it was some farmer telling him exactly what sort of fertilizer was best for putting a better coat of green on the turf. And now today, he'd spent the better part of the afternoon convincing the women's portion of the PTA that re-sodding the football field actually was a necessary budget line item, which sent him nearly through the roof with annoyance.

He'd come home from the meeting about ready to spit nails, and only after twenty minutes of pounding on his sandbag had his anger cooled enough to think straight. Now what he needed, he thought as he threw on jeans and an old, comfy shirt, was a cold beer and something other than his TV to keep his mind occupied.

He grabbed his keys off his dresser and flipped the lights off as he exited through the screened front door. It slapped closed behind him, reminding him that he needed to fix the stopper so it wouldn't make quite so much noise. He climbed into the driver's seat and took a deep whiff of the leather and new truck smell that still saturated the truck's interior. He'd had his new truck, a big black diesel he used to haul hay and trailers around his farm, for nearly three months, and he loved it. Almost as much as he loved Lizzie, he thought with an ache.

He'd bought it for himself as a reward for his team winning the state championship two years in a row, and he could remember at the time he bought it thinking how great it would be if Lizzie was sitting next to him in the truck. Payton ground his jaw and set his eyes on the road ahead of him. That dream had shattered about ten years earlier when he'd broken her heart. Dumb fool that he was.

The parking lot at Moe's Pub was about as full as it normally was which wasn't saying much. Moe Henry had opened up this tiny little hole in the wall bar about five years back, and somehow he'd managed to keep the joint going. It was the only bar within fifty miles of town, and typically did pretty well on the weekends and when the college kids came home for the summer, but other than that, it was business as usual.

Payton never understood why Moe named the place Moe's Pub. It sounded a little too Irish to be sitting in small town USA, and Payton knew for a fact that Moe didn't have an ounce of Irish blood running through those veins. Moe always shrugged and smiled that old smile whenever he was asked about the name. Seemed to suit him okay, so who was Payton to object?

Payton tipped his baseball cap to Moe and Sally, the waitress behind the bar, as he entered, and let his eyes adjust to the dim lighting around him. It was a typical small town bar- old wooden tables set up, a few booths set up in one corner, and a make shift dance floor in case anyone got really crazy, or drunk, and wanted to dance. An old juke box that Payton swore was on its very last life stood in the corner, currently playing some sappy Dolly Parton song about painted on blue jeans. Payton thought he actually might like to see what painted on blue jeans looked like.

Bobby Stanley sat in his usual corner booth, his hat slung low so as not to attract company, and a few other stragglers played a game of pool off in the side room. Other than that, the bar was empty, but it was still early and it would liven up at least a little more before the night was over.

"Evenin' Coach," Moe said as he slid a cold frosty glassed mug of beer down the bar.

"Evenin' Moe. What's new around here?" Nothing, Payton suspected, but still he waited and let Moe have his turn.

"Oh, you know. The usual. Did hear some good gossip in town earlier, though."

"Oh, yeah? What's that?" He took a swig of beer and let the cool liquid wash down his throat.

"Heard Miss Lizzie's fiancé showed up in town today looking to buy her some big expensive piece of jewelry. Called it a wedding day present. Seems she's gonna get herself hitched after all." Payton would have laughed at the odd way Moe pronounced fiancé- with an emphasis on the I, instead of the E at the end- had his heart not been turning slowly into a burning heap of pitiful mush. Payton looked ahead, trying not to show his upset.

"Seems that way, Moe. Seems that way."

"You gonna go see her get married off?"

"No, I don't think so. I hear some of the other schools are practicing that day- I think I'll be out scouting their plays." That at least switched Moe off of painful subjects and on to more level playing ground for a while. Besides, just thinking about her man made him want to vomit. He hadn't met the guy yet, but the image of a greasy, slick haired version of a used car salesman with big buck teeth always seemed to spring into his mind.

He'd downed about three beers and watched the small crowd that had gathered since he'd arrived as they milled about the bar. He felt a strong hand clasp his shoulder. A sandy haired guy in his early thirties shot him a friendly grin.

"Mind if I sit down next to you?" The guy asked as he straddled a bar stool.

"Sure thing. Make yourself at home." Payton turned back to his beer and the TV set above the bar.

"What're ya having?" His brown eyes were direct but kind as he watched Payton. Obviously the guy had never been to Moe's before.

"Guinness. It's the only beer Moe keeps on tap."

"I'll have what he's having, and get him another as well," he said to Moe, and smiled at Payton again. Payton had to wonder for a moment if the guy was hitting on him. If he wasn't gay, the guy sure was friendly. A little too friendly, Payton thought, and tried his best to focus back in on the baseball game on TV.

"I'm Josh." He stuck his hand out. Payton hesitated for a second, trying to remember where he'd heard that name before. He seemed familiar somehow, but he couldn't figure it out. He shrugged.

"Payton." He turned back to his beer and the game.

"This Moe, he a friend of yours?" Payton sighed. Obviously he wasn't going to get to watch the game in peace. He sipped his beer.

"More of a beer buddy.  He runs the bar and I like to come here to watch the games on TV."

Josh noticed the TV for the first time, it seemed, and he quieted down as he watched the pitcher strike out two batters.  "What d'ya think the odds are for the Braves to make it to the playoffs this year?"

Payton, never one to shy away from a subject he liked, warmed to the conversation.  "Anything's possible I guess, but I wouldn't bet the ranch on 'em."

"Yeah, but I think they've got some quality new players they've traded for.  I think they could get there."

Payton frowned.  "Maybe, but I think the Red Sox are a better bet."

Moe, who didn't have much else to do at the moment, and always one to discuss sports, sidled over to chat.  "The Cardinals.  Now that's one helluva team to watch, boys."

Payton shook his head firmly and grinned.  "You don't ever give up, d'ya old timer?  Those boys are so far out of World Series range it's pathetic."

Josh laughed.  "Seriously.  Talk about a long shot.  That's like trying to get a hole in one on a par 5.  There's no way."

Payton laughed and elbowed Josh in agreement.  Moe shook his head and grumbled.  The other two ribbed him some more until he moved on to other, safer, topics.

"So, Coach, how's the season ahead looking?"  He dried a few glasses as they talked.

"Oh yeah, you're a coach?  What for?"  Josh watched him curiously, a friendly smile on his face.

"Football.  I'm the head coach over at Dixie."  He turned to answer Moe.  "Well, we're 1 and 1 right now, and there's a lot of younger guys on the team so I think the boys'll have a hard time against the better ranked teams, but they should fair pretty well over all."

"Coach Cartwright.  Payton Cartwright," Josh said with recognition in his voice, and Payton automatically smiled.  Must be one of the boy's relatives, or a fan.  He had a few of those.  Maybe that's why he seemed to know him.

"That's me."  He stuck out his hand.

"Well, I thought I'd be meeting you, just not here.  I'm Josh Turner, Lizzie Benford's fiancé."  He smiled and grabbed Payton's hand, pumping it up and down vigorously.  Payton could feel his blood pounding through him and he forced himself to keep his grip loose so he wouldn't crush the guy's hand.

Josh seemed oblivious to the sudden chance in Payton's demeanor and kept right on chatting. Moe smirked at Payton and he felt like reaching over the bar and punching him.

"Well I hear you have quite a reputation around these parts as the football legend," he heard Josh saying as he tuned back in. "Can't go anywhere in this town and not hear your name being buzzed around." Payton managed a smile.

"I grew up here. Was the starting quarterback. Football's a big deal around here."

Josh chuckled. "So I understand. Lizzie keeps me informed."

Payton winced. What was this, a friendly chat between Lizzie's fiancé and her ex? He felt like he'd just been broadsided by a transfer truck. He thought he'd been having a decent sports conversation with a fellow sports junkie, but really he'd been getting all buddy-buddy with *Josh Turner*.

"So you think the team has a shot at the playoffs this year?"

Payton ground his jaw and forced a sip of beer. Oh, this was going to be good. Even Moe thought so. Payton could tell by the way he settled back on a lone bar stool behind the counter that he was obviously set to eavesdrop while he nonchalantly dried glass beer mugs.

Fine. If Mr. Slick wanted a little chat, he'd give him one, Payton thought as he tightened his grip around the cool glass of the bottle before taking a swig.

"The playoffs?" Payton took another long swig, taking his time, enjoying the fact that even seated on a bar stool he still stood a good two inches over Lizzie's fiancé, and he could, without a doubt, outmuscle the guy any day of the week. "Oh, I feel pretty confident they'll make it there just fine. Then it'll turn out like always. Long and brutal, but my boys'll win it in the end."

"Pretty confident about that, are you?" Pretty boy Josh held his long neck bottle up for a quick drink. Payton didn't like the way he smirked. Not one bit. But he did enjoy the nerves he obviously touched off in Josh when he thunked his bottle on top of the bar and gave him a long, steady, measuring look.

"Yeah, I'm pretty confident. Now, don't go mistaking that for cockiness- I find that sort of thing just down right stupid. But confidence, now that's smart." He grabbed his truck keys off the bar and headed for the door. He wanted to punch something and he had to get outside quick before that something turned into Josh's face.

"Night Moe," he called from the door before heading out into the night.

"Night Coach, see you soon."

"Jeez, what got into him?" Josh asked, oblivious. He finished off his first drink of the night. Moe took his time moving his old body off the bar stool and hobbled over to drop another bottle in front of the out-of-towner. Moe gave Josh a leveling look before he leaned against the counter top, wincing ever so slightly in the process.

"The thing about that man is... he don't like losing, 'specially when it comes to somethin' he's passionate about." He caught Josh's eye and held it before pushing off and bumbling back into the kitchen. Josh didn't quite understand what he had hit on that Payton was so passionate about- other than football that is- but he was beginning to get the feeling that Edenville's head football coach wasn't particularly excited that he was in town.

*Chapter Twenty-six*

"Let's go, pokey." Mary Catherine leaned against the door and studied her sister with a smile. "I'm dieing to see how beautiful I'm gonna look in my bridesmaid dress."

"I'm comin'." Lizzie stuck out her tongue in friendly camaraderie. "Keep your shirt on." She blew on her nails as she twisted the top back on a bottle of nail polish and shuffled her feet into a pair of sandals.

For once she agreed to drive to town instead of walking, and she let MC drive since her nails were still wet. Lizzie rolled down her window and propped her feet up on the dashboard.

"Okay, so what're everybody's bets on the color of the dress this time?"

MC laughed. The first shipment of dresses, including the wedding gown, had arrived a month ago with them all being a vibrant fire engine red- not at all close to the color she had ordered. "Well, mine's for green, Grace's is for red again, and Granny's bridge club has a fifty cent bet on black."

"Fifty cents? Wow, that's gettin' on up there for them."

"I told her to throw another fifteen in there for me, but she said it was against their religion to take outsider bet money."

Lizzie laughed and let the wind blow her hair. The air was certainly cooler than it had been, but it was still determinedly hot for September.

"So, are you ready for the big day," Mary Catherine asked Lizzie with a playful nudge of her elbow.

At the thought Lizzie's heart thundered in her chest and she felt the familiar shortness of breath. She smiled, though, and tilted her sunglasses down a fraction so her sister could see the mischief in her eyes. "Are you kidding?" Lizzie fidgeted with her glasses, pushing them up through her hair and back down on her nose again. "I've been waiting for this day for as long as I can remember."

One of MC's eyebrows rose. "The day, yes. But, the man?"

A scowl broke out on Lizzie's delicate features. "Of course."

"If you're having second thoughts, Liz, you really should put it off a few months." Mary Catherine glanced over at her with a worried expression. "You know, Daddy would rather you be happy and sure, than make you go through with it just because everything is already arranged."

Lizzie frowned in concentration and thought about where her life was headed. Today was Thursday, which meant that in little more than a week she would be getting married. What should have been the happiest moment in her life was turning into a major three ring circus. It wasn't that she didn't like weddings. She loved them. *A Wedding Story* was her favorite TV show ever. But her dreams of how all the planning and all the details leading up to the big day would proceed just weren't turning out like she had envisioned.

Lizzie shot her sister a reassuring smile. "Don't worry about me, MC, I'm just a little stressed. It's only the wedding jitters. You'll have it someday, too." Mary Catherine looked skeptical but she shrugged and kept on driving.

A bright flash of flame red bobbed in the distance, and Lizzie smiled, thankful for a change of topic. How like her best friend to be waiting, hip poking out in impatience in front of Mrs. McIntire's store a full five minutes early. Whereas Grace had been early everywhere she went since the first day of her life, Lizzie couldn't be on time to save her life. Perhaps that was one of the reasons that the two had been inseparable since the first day they met.

Well, that and the fact that they'd had only each other to survive in the earlier days of their friendship.

"Well, if it isn't Grace Jacobs! Fancy meeting you here on this fine morning," called Lizzie as she hung her head out the window as they pulled to a stop in front of Mrs. McIntire's shop.

"Yeah, yeah. You know, Lizzie Benford, if it wouldn't kill me to see you strung up by your toenails, I might just have to end your life for being so dang late all the time."

"It's one of the perks of being a doctor. We have special classes on how to hold everyone up at least five extra minutes."

"Funny. Ha ha. I've got a mind to believe that, you know."

Grace linked arms with MC and smiled. "Now, let's go see what god awful color your sister has chosen for us to wear in this wedding. I swear, though, if it's pink, you'll see me hanging from my daddy's pecan tree at sundown."

Lizzie rolled her eyes. "Oh, shut up, Grace. It's not pink. Would I really do that to you? You know I hate pink." Lizzie rolled her eyes. "What, do you think we're in Steel Magnolias or something? Pepto

Bismol pink is certainly not my idea of a good time." She opened the door to the shop and walked inside. "Besides, I think you'll be pleasantly surprised at what I've picked for you."

"Well, I'm not believing it 'till I see it," Grace mumbled as she followed her friend in to the shop.

"Mrs. McIntire," Lizzie called toward the back of the store. "Yoo-hoo! It's me, Lizzie." They heard a mumble from the back then rolls of fabric hitting the floor before they finally saw Mrs. McIntire stumble from the back, adjusting her skirt, blouse and hair.

"Ah, Mr. McIntire was visiting wasn't he?" The girls giggled when the middle-aged woman blushed a deep crimson and smiled.

"Well, Lizzie Benford. You come right in here and let's try this wedding gown on. And this time, I swear its Ivory white, just like you've been dreaming about."

"Actually, the red one's kind of growing on me. Maybe I should wear that one instead."

Mrs. McIntire looked a little upset. "Well, dear… I suppose you could but, well…"

MC, Grace, and Lizzie laughed. "I'm just messing with you, Mrs. McIntire. But your face was priceless."

Mrs. McIntire looked relieved, but recovered nicely with a twinkle in her eye. "Oh, okay, if you're sure. Now, come on and let's get you all fixed up." She guided Lizzie by the shoulders to the back of the shop. "I swear you and your bridesmaids are going to be the talk of the town for years after this wedding." Lizzie had the distinct feeling she was right, and wasn't quite sure if that was a good thing or a bad.

"Now, what do you think?" Her dress hung on a manikin in the center of the panel of mirrors, and Lizzie felt little pricks of excitement tingle up her arms. This was the dress she'd always imagined wearing on her wedding day.

"Oh, my. It's gorgeous," said Grace.

"Can I wear it when it's my turn," asked MC.

Lizzie laughed. "Let's just get through my turn and then we'll worry about yours."

Fifteen minutes later, Lizzie stood in the center of a massive dressing room staring at her reflection that bounced back from at least five different angles. Her sister and best friend stood beside her, wearing mint green sleeveless dresses.

"Well, it's better than pink," Grace remarked as she smoothed the silky material and admired the way it flattered her figure.

"And it makes both of us look like goddesses, don't you think, Lizzie?"

"And you wonder why I picked them. Honestly, girls, from the look on your faces you'd think I didn't have a lick of fashion sense in my head." Lizzie watched her friends from the mirror as she pulled her hair into a bun while Mrs. McIntire put the veil on top. "I may be a doctor, but I do know a little bit beyond the best color scrubs to wear to make you're butt look the slimmest."

"Amen," Mrs. McIntire added through her teeth, which were clamped around alterations pins. The other girls giggled.

"Okay, so now will the two of you stop harassing me about the dresses? I swear weddings can be such a big production." Mrs. McIntire removed the veil and Lizzie let her hair drop back down around her shoulders. "If you want my advice- elope. Just elope and then tell everyone. It saves about five million headaches, and a few years off your life."

"That's easy for you to say, Lizzie." Grace gave her arms a dramatic flare. "You're getting your fairy tale. A wedding in the front yard of your house, honeymoon in the Southern Caribbean for two weeks, and then off to the big time with your hubby in tow."

Lizzie rolled her eyes, and stepped off the box where she'd been standing while Mrs. McIntire pinned the dress for the fitting. "If you like it so much, why don't you do it?"

"Gladly. Just find me my famous rock star and I'm there."

Lizzie pulled the gown over her head and handed it over the dressing room door. "You're still stuck on that rock star kick? I thought you gave that up in tenth grade."

"Not on your life."

"I think its sweet, Liz," Mary Catherine added as she took one last measuring glance in the mirror and turned away to get dressed. "A girl has to have her dreams."

"I'm not dreaming, MC. I'm serious. There's some amazingly gorgeous man out there who just happens to have the most heart melting voice on record and who's waiting for me."

"Uh-huh. Well, as long as you promise to let me visit you in your mansion, I'll let you marry your rock star." Lizzie slung her purse over her shoulder and winked at her friend. "Now come on, we've got to get home. The caterer's coming this afternoon and I've got things to get done before he does. But we're meeting up at Moe's for girl's night aren't we?"

"Wouldn't miss it for the world, Bean."

"Good, see ya there." Lizzie smiled back at Mrs. McIntire. "See you at church this Sunday, Mrs. M."

"Okay, sweetie. Tell your parents hello." She said it as if she didn't bump in to them in the grocery store aisles every other day.

"Alright. Tell Mr. McIntire hello, too." She didn't miss the slight blush that bloomed on the other woman's cheeks, or the giggle that Grace and MC stifled as they walked out the door.


On Friday night, almost a week before Lizzie's wedding, the old high school gang gathered at Moe's Pub. They'd come to an uneasy agreement that although Josh was Payton's competition for Lizzie's affection he was after all her fiancé and therefore they should treat him like part of the group. The guys invited him along when they'd decided on having a pool tournament after the football game while Lizzie and the other ladies were off having a girl's night of their own.

Payton sat in one of the booths at the back of the bar and was just working his way through the frothy foam of his Guinness when Grace, Lizzie, and the rest of the girls came through the door. Apparently they'd decided to start their evening off at Moe's, and one look at Lizzie's choice of clothes had him choking on his beer as Bud smacked him hard on the back.

He wouldn't have made such a scene but Lizzie's outfit was something he'd never seen her wear and it was driving him crazy. He noticed with grim dissatisfaction that he wasn't the only one in the bar that was howling at the sight of her.

She'd paired a short black mini-skirt with a pair of cowboy boots and a red scoop neck halter top that dipped to a perfect V between her breasts and ended somewhere close to her bellybutton. There wasn't anything other than maybe a small piece of tape that was keeping that shirt from showing every man in that bar every square inch of her chest. A puddle formed in his mouth and he swallowed hard.

A scowl broke out on his face.

Josh rubbed his hands together like a king before his spoils, excused himself from the table, and sauntered over to the girls, placing a possessive arm around Lizzie. Payton could see his eyes as he checked Lizzie over from head to toe, and he wanted to strangle him even though he didn't have any right.

"Come on, man," Colin said, breaking through his gut wrenching session of jealousy. "I've got fifty dollars says I'm gonna whoop your ass by the end of this round of pool."

"*Please*," said Payton with a wicked sneer. "I could beat a long bearded biker dude with studs on his leather collar with one arm tied behind my back. I don't think you're gonna be much competition." He followed Colin to the pool tables, but he couldn't help but watch as Josh gave Lizzie a slow French kiss.

He ground his teeth together.

"Hey lover boy, quit playing tonsil hockey and haul your sorry ass over here." Josh had a broad grin on his face as he sauntered over to the pool table and whispered to the other guys, "Now, tell me you guys don't wish you could have a piece of my woman."

*His woman.* What were they, cavemen? He could feel steam pouring from his ears. Josh was laughing hysterically as he nudged Payton in the ribs, and then he added, "Too bad she doesn't have a killer double D rack to fill out that top."

Payton clenched his fists. "Yeah, too bad."

They played in teams, and he wondered how he was the lucky one to be stuck on Josh's team while Colin and Bud played together on the other team. Josh broke and Payton followed. He was setting up his next play and glanced up in time to watch Lizzie take some cowboy's hat and place it on her head with a wink and a smile, and nearly sent the tip of his pool cue right through the fine felt pad on the top of the pool table. He ground his jaw and forced himself to focus in on the table. He took his time, lined up the balls, and narrowly missed sending them flying into a side hole when he heard her laughing hysterically at the same cowboy whose hat she'd just taken.

Payton looked murderous.

"What's the matter there, QB? Couldn't find your game hat at home?" Colin grinned at him as he took his turn at the table not realizing what was sending Payton's game straight to the crapper.

"Must be my shoulders acting up again. Ever since you left me open on that pass back in tenth grade, I have periodic joint problems."

Bud laughed. "Is that what you're calling it?" His glance toward Lizzie and back to Payton was meaningful. "I'll be sure to remember that." He stepped up when Colin missed sending his ball home and took a go.

He merely chuckled when Josh took his turn at ribbing him, and said, "well, chuckles, I haven't seen you hit one home yet."

Payton decided that since he was going to be stuck with the guy all night, he might be better served to get Josh drunk. Perhaps then it'd be a bit more bearable when he knew that the guy would be suffering from a major hangover in the morning.

"Come on, Josh. Since I obviously can't play worth crap tonight, the least I can do is buy the lucky man a round of shots." He grabbed Josh by the shoulders and hauled him to the bar. "A round of whisky for me and my friend here, Moe."

"Comin' right up."

"So," said Josh, "What're the chances of winning this tournament."

Payton scanned the room and saw Grace and Lizzie take a shot of tequila on the other side of the room as they headed back out to the dance floor. "About as likely as getting those two girls out of here sober once they've started sipping tequila."

Josh grinned. "Yeah, but it sure is fun to take advantage of 'em when they have."

The whiskey came at the perfect time and Payton downed a round and ordered another. "Sure, sure. It's always fun to take advantage of drunk women." He sipped his next shooter. "I especially like it when you're right in the middle of making out and they have to run to the bathroom."

"Ugh, man, that's just gross."

Payton shrugged. "You know, the man of honor prob'ly needs another round or two. Moe, two for Josh, and I'll have a beer." He pushed the glass across to Josh and watched as he downed them in a single sip. "So, what'd you get her for her wedding present?"

Josh grinned. "Funny you should ask. She'd been eyeing this big solitaire diamond necklace back home, so I bought it for her." He took another shot and ordered a beer. "Well, actually it's really an identical cubic zirconium," he said in a stage whisper. "Had to use to rest of my money to get a few buddies of mine out of the hock."

He died laughing as if this were hysterical. "I'd have liked to have bought her a nice trip to the plastic surgeon to have her boobs done, and maybe an inch or two off the waist, but I guess I'll wait a year or two. They like to be pampered and told their real pretty and perfect that first year."

"Yeah, it's a shame to have to wait two whole years to show 'em their imperfections."

Josh was a little slow thanks to all the alcohol he'd imbibed and he laughed. "Damn straight." He looked across the room and found Lizzie dancing with another guy and he laughed. "Damn, I guess all the guys are getting a turn with her. Might as well go get my turn." He stumbled off his bar stool and Payton watched as he broke in and started twirling Lizzie around the room.

Payton tipped the straw cowboy hat on his head a little lower and thought about what Josh said as he watched Lizzie. Bigger boobs and a smaller waist. She was already tall and thin. Those long, awkward legs that had looked like too large legs on an adolescent puppy dog when she'd been growing up were nice and shapely now and didn't stop until they just about reached her chin.

And even though she and Pam Anderson couldn't compete over bra sizes, she sure wasn't flat chested. Payton couldn't remember a time ever in his life that he'd wished she'd been bigger in one spot or smaller in another. She was just right exactly like she was.

And there was no way he'd give her some damn CZ diamond. But that was another one of Josh's character flaws all together that he didn't have the patience to think about tonight.

He waited a few more minutes at the bar and ordered another shot of whiskey for all the guys. He took one with him and had Sally take the rest over to the pool tables.

He tapped Josh on the shoulder as they came around the dance floor. "I believe the man of the night deserves this." He thrust the glass into Josh's hand and tipped his hat at Lizzie. "May I have this dance?"

She narrowed her eyes at him. "You aren't trying to get him drunk are you?"

Payton was all innocence. "I wouldn't dream of doing something like that."

"Why don't I believe you?"

He put her hands around his neck and guided her onto the floor with his hands on her hips- her perfect hips. "Beats the heck out of me. You're dancing off step, Lizzie, pick it up."

She scowled. "I am not."

"Here, move more like this." He used his hands to move her hips in time to the music.

"Billy Joe told me earlier I was doing just fine."

"Billy Joe is a terrible dancer. He only passed ballroom dance class in seventh grade because Mrs. Huckelby had a crush on him."

Lizzie crinkled her nose. "You're a terrible liar."

"At least I'm not a terrible dancer." He twirled her when the end of the song came on and gave her a little dip just in case she'd forgotten how good a dancer he was. As he looked up he saw at least five guys on the other side of the bar trying to look down the slit in her top to her cleavage, he suddenly remembered exactly how little material her top contained, and exactly how much of her breasts he could see even when she wasn't in such a compromising position.

He jerked her up, sending a lethal glare across the bar and jerked her by the arm out the back door of the bar.

"Ouch," she yelled as she jerked her arm away from him once they were on the landing of the back steps. "What was that for?" She rubbed her arm where he'd grabbed her.

"That was for this," said Payton as he pointed at the long slit that traveled nearly down to her belly button. "Since when do you wear shirts that cost more than they cover?"

"Ease up, Gramps. I didn't see anybody in there complaining."

"Well that's just because you were giving them a free show of what they were going to pay to see later on tonight anyway."

She gasped. "Are you calling me a stripper?"

He folded his arms across his chest. "You might as well be with that get up."

She pointed a finger in his chest. "Listen here, buddy. That is uncalled for and I demand an apology right now."

He leaned down, settling his most menacing face on her. "You're not getting one."

"You know, Payton, you gave up the right to care about what I wear a long time ago. The only one who has the right to say that to me now is Josh."

Yeah, but he probably thought she looked good in that get up. Better yet, he probably thought she should've worn something more provocative. He sighed and forced himself to talk in a calmer tone. "Do you actually like what you're wearing?"

She was pouting. "Yes."

"I'm not denying that you look incredible in it, but... does Josh want you to wear that stuff out in public?"

"He says it looks good."

He could think of a few other things he said, too. "Well, if I were him the only place I'd let you wear that is to my bedroom. I don't see how he lets you keep that on for more than five minutes without ripping it off you."

She nibbled on one of her nails, a habit he noticed she'd picked up sometime since they'd lost touch with each other. "He says it makes me look sexier this way."

And she wasn't sexy enough when her shirt wasn't cut down to her toes? "You know, I get the feeling he has a few screwed up ideas about what sexy looks like."

"He thinks it makes my boobs look bigger."

Payton smiled. "Well, I'll give him that one..." He paused and a frown crossed his features. "That shouldn't matter, though."

"I've been thinking about having a breast enhancement procedure. They're supposed to be safe now and... well, what do you think?" She looked up at him so innocently, like she really wanted his opinion, and he wanted so badly to wrap himself around her and tell her that she didn't have to change herself to be better for Josh. If he didn't love her like she was, then nothing she did was ever going to make it better. An image of his father popped into his mind.

He shot her a lopsided grin, willing himself to make it a joke so she wouldn't see that he felt her pain. "Hmmm..." he paused to scratch his chin with his thumb. "If you want my opinion I might need to take a closer look. Here, turn to the side for me so I can get better lighting." Her mouth was gaping open so he did it for her. "Okay, now I'm just going to feel you up for a second."

She laughed and batted him away. "Payton Cartwright, don't you dare!"

His look was stern. "Now, I was just trying to do the neighborly thing here. This is a serious decision that requires lots of hands on attention."

Lizzie laughed again. Just then the door opened and Grace came stumbling out. "Hey! I thought I might find me some lovebirds out here." Half the daiquiri she carried sloshed out onto the concrete. "Oh, you two aren't the lovebirds." In a stage whisper she added, "Don't tell yourself I said this, but you should be." She gave them a group hug. "I love you guys!"

Payton smiled. "How many of those have you had tonight, Miz Grazie?"

"Oh, these old thangs? Maybe three or four." She gave Payton a big sloppy kiss and a bright smile. "Sorry to break up the party, but the girls are leavin'. We've got places to go and people to do." She took Lizzie by the arm. "Come on, Bean. See ya, Payton."

He waved as Grace dragged Lizzie across the back parking lot. "See ya."

One thing was for certain. If Grace didn't talk some sense into that girl then he was going to have to do it himself. No one deserved what she was about to walk into on her wedding day. But he had a feeling when he told her what he had to say things weren't going to go over very pretty.

## *Chapter Twenty-seven*

Payton's head felt like a freight train had run over it at least a dozen times during the night. He rolled over in his bed with a groan and felt along his night stand, not daring to open his eyes, in hopes that a bottle of aspirin would miraculously appear. When none materialized he flopped back in bed and lay there for a minute trying to clear his mind.

He was still wearing what he'd been wearing to Moe's the night before, and gradually his memory came back to him. He groaned and rubbed his hand over his face. What he could remember hadn't been pretty, he knew that much. He thought getting Josh drunk might be the easy way to make it through the night with him, but the drunker he'd been the more trash came out of his mouth, and ultimately the more Payton had grown to despise him.

Eventually, he'd decided getting himself drunk or killing Josh were his only two options left, and apparently he'd taken the first. That had come right about the time that Josh had informed Payton that he thought Lizzie would look great with big porn star breasts and proceeded to list several of his friend's wives that had had their boobs done up like a porn stars. Payton realized that obviously the guy had some sick fascination with big breasts and pornography and he'd known that either Josh wasn't going to make it through the night or he had to get drunk enough to ignore his trash talk. Obviously this sleaze-bag either had some big time power over Lizzie to keep her in the relationship, or he had Siegfried and Roy beat hands down as a master of disguise. Either way, Payton was most definitely not impressed.

Payton pushed himself from bed and stumbled down the stairs in search of a strong pot of coffee. He dug through his cabinets in search of aspirin and grabbed a bottle of beer to drink while he waited on the slowest coffee machine on earth to spit out his coffee.

He blindly poured a cup and leaned against the counter waiting for the caffeine to hit him before he tried to think further. He knew one thing was certain: he wasn't waiting another day to talk to Lizzie. Beyond that or how to go about doing it, he didn't have a clue.

Payton paused. Something was different and he wasn't certain what, but the morning light sure was bright for, he paused to check his watch, six o'clock in the morning. He shrugged, still too hung over to give it much thought. He grabbed his mug to head out to the porch and enjoy the crisp morning air, but stopped short as he glanced out the kitchen window.

"What the..." Payton dropped his coffee mug on the counter and pushed his long frame to the door. "Oh, those two are going to get it for sure."

He pushed his way out the door and stood in the middle of his front yard, trying to register how two drunk girls could possibly string up that much toilet paper in one front yard. They must have been at it for hours. Funny that he hadn't noticed it the night before. Then again, there could have been a whole slew of naked women in his house last night and he wouldn't have noticed them either.

He checked his watch again, and a smile edged up the corners of his lips. It seemed it was time for a little wake up call. He dashed back into the house to grab a few necessary items. Well, dashed in the sense that a turtle on tranquilizers might dash.


Lizzie rolled over in bed and smacked her alarm clock. She fell back in bed and threw the pillow over head. A minute later she smacked the alarm clock again.

"Beep, beep, beep, beep..."

Damn it, why wouldn't that stupid thing quit blaring in her ear?

She finally reached down and unplugged the noisy thing from the wall and put her head under her pillow again.

"Beep, beep, beep, beep..."

"What the *hell* is going on?" She sat straight up in bed and looked at the clock. Yep, it was definitely unplugged. She cocked her head and rubbed her hands over her face to try and wake herself. Maybe she was dreaming she heard the alarm going off.

Then she heard a muffled laugh. A deep muffled laugh that she had most certainly heard before. She heard the beeping coming from her closet. Lizzie picked up the closest object she could find: her favorite teddy bear, and held it up, ready to throw at the person hiding behind that door.

She flung the door open and hurled the teddy bear inside only to hear him laughing again.

"Good morning, sunshine," Payton said as he exited the closet.

"Don't you sunshine me." She turned away from him and stalked

off to the bathroom.  He followed her and leaned his long frame against
the edge of the door.

"Hey, I thought it only fair to return the favor.  Seems you two had
a good time on girl's night last night."

Lizzie opened the door a crack and continued to brush her teeth.  "I
have no idea what you're talking about," she hissed through toothpaste
and toothbrush.  "And aren't you supposed to be in bed with a major
hangover right now?"

"Oh, I don't know.  I couldn't pass up this opportunity to see what
sexy sleepwear you wear these days."  He looked her over from head to
toe.  "If I'd known how sexy cotton pants and a tank top could look I'd
have come over even earlier."

"If I'd known I was going to have company this morning I would
have been a little more selective in my choice."  Payton was imagining a
nice silk teddy when she blurted out, "A nice flannel gown that brushes
my ankles with buttons up to my neck."

He leaned against the door to the bathroom and folded his arms
across his chest.  "Now, don't go knocking those flannel gowns.  My
grand mom had eight children and she wore those every night of her life.
Some men just find women irresistible no matter what they wear.  Kind of
like you."

"Whatever, Payton."  She shut the door and talked through it while
she changed clothes.  "What brings you here this early anyway?  And how
did you get past my dad?  There's no way he'd let you up here."

"Wow, you're crankier than I remember you being in the
mornings.  Need a little caffeine before you're nice, don't you?"  She
opened the door back up as she slipped a pair of cotton socks on her feet.
"And to answer your question, you'd be surprised Lizzie.  You haven't
been here in a while, remember?  Seems that Edenville's former football
hero and most winning football coach can get away with more than you
think."

"And you're here because?"

"Because I found a nice wrapper from a twenty-four pack of
Quilted Northern double roll toilet paper in my trash can and apparently
twenty –four of those rolls just happened to land in my Oak and Pecan
trees.  I thought maybe you'd like to help me track down the culprits.  I'm
thinking one has dark hair and the other has flame red.  What's your
guess?"

Lizzie tucked her shirt into her jeans and began to pull her hair into a ponytail, then into a baseball cap.

"Haven't the foggiest clue what you're talking about." But she smiled as she walked out her bedroom door and down the stairs and straight to the refrigerator. "Care for something to drink? Whiskey perhaps?" She giggled as his face turned a little green.

"No, thanks. I'll take a coke if you've got it. Then we've got to go."

"Go? Go where?"

"Uh-uh. Where's the fun in telling you?"

"Right. Well, unfortunately the wedding is a week away now, and I don't think my father would appreciate me skipping out on my fair share of the work."

Payton popped the top on the can of soda and grinned at Lizzie's back. "Oh, I don't think he'll mind too much. Will you Mr. Benford?"

"Nope."

Lizzie spun from the counter where she'd been pouring a bowl of Cheerios to find her dad grinning at her. "Sorry, sweetie. A deal's a deal." He winked at her daughter and left the room.

"But, daddy…" She let out an exasperated sigh when she realized he wasn't listening. She frowned at Payton and tossed her bowl on the kitchen table, slumped down into a chair, and shoveled a spoonful of cereal into her mouth.

"Why is my daddy being so cooperative with you?" She eyed him curiously. "He knows that you're an evil four letter word around this place."

Payton propped a booted foot on his knee and crossed his arms behind his head. "You're dad and I had a nice little chat this morning and he and I see eye to eye on certain things. He's a most agreeable man when you get on his good side."

Lizzie grunted. "If I find out your mom's pecan pie had anything to do with you and his good side getting together, and I didn't get any, there's gonna be hell to pay."

He laughed and stood. "Let me know when you're ready. I'll be in my truck sleeping off the hangover."

"Oh, I'll let you know. Don't you worry." She gave him her best fake smile, and pretended she didn't feel her heart spin into overtime when he winked at her just before letting the screen door slam behind him. She also pretended she didn't find his butt way too adorably sexy in the pair of jeans that hugged his body.

Then the screen door slapped closed and her mind snapped with it. Something wasn't right about this situation. Didn't her dad realize she was getting *married* in a week to a guy named Josh? And speaking of Josh, what was he going to say when he realized Payton had somehow finagled a way for her to get out of wedding duties so she could go off someplace with Payton? What, was she living in the twilight zone? Did no one understand the situation she was currently living in?

Apparently not, because just then her mother came buzzing through the kitchen, poured herself a cup of coffee and kissed her daughter on the head. She breezed back out humming, and said nonchalantly, "Have fun with Payton today." What the *hell* was going on around here?

Payton. They were talking about Payton Cartwright for crying out loud. Granted, no one but Grace knew that Payton had written her the love letter of a lifetime, but still. Her parents knew all that had happened in their past. How could they possibly think it was okay for she and him to be anywhere in the same vicinity of each other? Something just wasn't right about this.

It put her in a bad mood just thinking about it, so she focused on her Cheerios instead.

She took her time eating her cereal and then sipped her cup of coffee like she had no place else to go. Like she wasn't the least bit curious as to where exactly Mr. A-Deal's-a-Deal was taking her. Finally, when she felt satisfied that she'd wasted enough of his morning, Lizzie pulled on her tennis shoes and headed out the kitchen door to Payton's truck.

She slammed the door extra hard when she climbed in just to watch him jolt awake with a wince.

"Oops, sorry," she said, and smiled an innocent little smile.

Payton merely glanced at her. "Did you get enough breakfast? I could always drop you off at IHOP and come back later when you've had a full serving there as well."

"Ha, ha very funny. Just thought you might need a little extra time to sleep off those twenty shots of whiskey you had." She clicked her seatbelt into position. "How many did you really have anyway?"

"More than I've had in a long time that's for sure." He started the truck and pulled out of her drive.

"New truck?" She sniffed the air and closed her eyes, enjoying the new car scent.

"Yep. Bought it a few months ago. Do you like it?"

"Sure." She paused and thought for a moment then added, "It fits you."

"Gee, thanks."

"Your welcome." Lizzie rolled down the window and let the cool morning air brush against her bare arms. It felt good to be out in the country air, and surprisingly, it felt good to be with Payton. It felt right somehow, and she knew that was exactly what she didn't need to be thinking considering the wedding was in a week.

"Are you going to tell me now where we're going?"

He laughed. "You don't know?"

"Nope." She waved her arm out the window like a bird in flight and leaned her head back against the seat, closing her eyes and enjoying the ride.

"Well, for starters we're going to wake that red headed devil from her alcohol induced sleep, and after that we're headed to my house to do a little clean up detail."

"What?"

"You heard me."

"I thought I told you I didn't have a clue who the guilty party is."

"Sure. Fine. But unfortunately the rollers left their mark on the project and it just so happens to be the same one that you two left at my parent's house quite a few times in high school."

"You're kidding." Lizzie managed to come out with a look of shock and disgust. "Some of your football flunkies must've figured out our mark and stole it. They're probably just playing games on the coach." The look he shot her told Lizzie he wasn't buying that crap of a story for a minute. "Yeah well, then again maybe it was just too much fun to resist." She smiled as she turned her attention back out the window.

"That's exactly what I thought you'd say." Payton pulled into Grace's drive and turned off the truck. "Now, are you going to wake the rest of the rolling party or do I need to do the honors?"

Lizzie smiled. "Oh, no, by all means be my guest." Lizzie had learned long ago not to wake that she-devil before at least noon unless she wanted to lose a body part in the process. "I'll wait right here for you guys."

Payton knew better than that. "Oh, you will?" He waited for her to nod then slowly unfolded himself from the driver's seat. Lizzie got a little nervous when he rounded the front of the truck and pulled open her door as well. She wanted to cry when he grabbed her arm and pulled her out. "Sorry, sweetheart. I've seen what that mop of red hair does to Grace before she's awake. You're going in as my bodyguard."

They marched to the door, Lizzie being propelled by Payton's strong body. "Surely a big strong man like yourself doesn't need a little girl like me to protect you. What are you, chicken?"

"Are you kidding? Of course I am when it comes to her." And with that he pushed her through Grace's front door and up the stairs to the wicked witch's evil lair.

Lizzie tip-toed across the hard wood floor and eased up next to Grace lying in the Queen bed. She gently cleared her throat and said a silent prayer that she wouldn't die a brutal death, then she looked over at Payton waiting outside the open bedroom door and gave him an evil glare. He merely smiled that adorable smile and winked at her before disappearing behind the door again.

He left her stranded, alone, with the crazy monster snoring lightly beside her. Great. She was a goner for sure. She cleared her throat again, this time a little harder and thought about crossing herself, but figured that was somehow sacrilegious seeing as she was Baptist instead of Catholic.

Here goes. She reached down and gently shook Grace. Grace merely rolled in the bed and snuggled deeper in the covers.

She shook her again. "Uh, Grace. Good morning, sweetie."

Nothing.

This time a little louder. "Gracie, it's time to wake up."

A slight stir and a mumble. Lizzie whimpered to herself.

Finally she worked up the courage to just go for it. "GRACE! WAKE UP!"

Oh, Lord. That definitely did it. Grace was out of that bed, yelling every obscenity that came to mind and doing her best to kill what she apparently thought was an intruder standing in her bedroom.

"Grace! Grace! Jeez, ease up, Carrot. It's just me. Remember? Your best friend?" Finally Grace came to her senses and at least eased up on the trying to kill Lizzie part.

"Lizzie. What in the hell are you doing in my bedroom at seven thirty in the morning? Don't you remember how late we were out last night?"

"Yeah, I remember."

Grace flung herself back on the bed and ran her hands through her flame red mop. Then she giggled. Amazing. How did the woman go from spitting mad to laughing in a matter of seconds? "What do you think Payton did when he woke up from that hangover and saw his front yard?"

Lizzie didn't laugh. Well, not that loud at any rate. "Why don't you ask him?"

"Huh?" Grace sat up. Then she winced when she saw Payton poke his head around the corner.

"Yep. You guessed it. Time for clean up detail, pal." Payton shot her a broad, white toothed grin to which Grace groaned and crawled back under the covers.

"That's nice. You guys go ahead without me. I'll be over in a while to check the progress."

"Oh, no you don't. If I have to, you have to. Now get up." Lizzie flipped off Grace's covers and headed to the closet to pick out clothes for her friend. She knew Grace too well. If she didn't help her get moving they'd be there for hours trying to prod her out of the bed. "Now, put on these and brush your teeth. We'll meet you in the truck in ten minutes."

"Sure thing." Grace yawned and flipped the covers back. "I'll be there."

Fifteen minutes later Grace sleepily plugged out her front door, letting the storm door slap closed behind her. A tall silver mug of coffee rested in her hand as if it were a life line keeping her from falling dead asleep on her feet. Lizzie didn't doubt that that could potentially happen.

Grace finally made it to the truck and stood outside the door she had ruthlessly thrown open waiting for Lizzie to move over to the middle seat.

When Lizzie didn't take the nonverbal hint, she added, "Over, Bean. I'm not crawling over you."

Lizzie had claimed her seat on the passenger side of Payton's truck closest to the window, fearing that if she somehow got stuck in the middle next to his warm, masculine body she would be thrown into a tail spin of emotions she just might not recover from. Grace paid no attention to Lizzie's wide eyed signals she tried to throw at her friend. Instead she said, "Lizzie, I'm really *not* in the mood to interpret your lame-brained eye rolls this morning.  Just move over already."

And with that Lizzie begrudgingly moved to the center seat. Stupid, stupid, stupid.  She felt like smacking herself in the head.  Why didn't she just get out of the truck so Grace could sit in the center seat she wondered to herself as Payton pulled out of the dirt drive and onto the road headed out to his house.

No one spoke during the drive.  Even though it was only about a two minute drive out to the patch of land his house sat on, it seemed too much effort on any of their parts to fill that two minute void.  Grace was still too asleep to care, Payton felt like death warmed over, and Lizzie was too preoccupied with not drowning in the scent of a man that had haunted her life for so many years now.  Just keep thinking about Josh she reminded herself.  So she occupied her thoughts with wedding information for the rest of the drive to his place.

The slamming of the driver's door brought Lizzie back into reality.

"Huh?  What?"  She said, shaking her head to bring her out of the daze she was in.

"I said let's get going, honey."  Payton leaned in through the open window of his door and gave her a quizzical stare, one eyebrow cocked higher than the other.  "Are you feeling okay today?  You've either spent the morning being the biggest smart ass this side of the Mississippi, or you've been in Zombie land."

"Sorry."

"That's alright."  He opened the door again and held out his hand to help her out.  She hesitated and then let him pull her out of the truck. "You just had one too many tequila shots.  I understand."

"No," She stated emphatically.  "Unlike some people, I know when to quit drinking.  I've just got a lot on my brain."

"Good.  Hopefully one item in that brain of yours is how you plan to get *that* toilet paper," he paused and pointed at a mess of white in the top of a tall Oak tree, "out of *that* tree."  And with that he left her and Grace in his front yard while he headed off into his house.

Lizzie rolled her eyes at his backside then flipped her gaze back to the white front yard.  The job had been rather fun last night, in the dark, half drunk, laughing her ass off at the thought of what Payton's face would look like when he saw his yard.  But now, in the daylight, stone cold sober, she didn't find the sight or the job quite so funny. She imagined that the trees had grown at least three feet during the night just to spite her.

Well, if the man of the house found himself too good to help in the project at least she had Grace here to help her. And with that they set to work undoing the mess they had created.

Almost thirty minutes into their cleanup campaign she watched as Payton easily strolled out the door and onto his front porch. He must have just finished a work out because he was wearing a pair of navy gym shorts and his bare chest was covered in a sheen of sweat that only served to enhance the muscles that rippled and bunched across his body. The muscles that she could remember so well from her youth had only become better with time, and she wondered before she could stop herself what they would feel like underneath her hands.

Man, he looked good she thought before she could catch herself. She quickly tried to think of Josh but the image wouldn't come. Lizzie forced herself not to drool. She swallowed hard and thought that it was next to impossible to look better than he had in high school, and yet, somehow, he managed to do it. His body had matured and the broad expanse of muscle across his chest that had been drool worthy in high school was now exquisitely polished and perfected. The rest of his body had grown right along with him, she had noticed, and she couldn't help but admire the set of his face now that it too had matured and wizened as well.

Every time she had seen him since their tragic break up in high school she had either been spitting mad and ready to choke him, or she'd been too drunk to care that he was there. But now... she knew that was a different story.

Now she certainly wasn't drunk. And she'd finally realized that she wasn't all that mad anymore, either. Damn it. She still wanted to be angry with him. She wanted that really, *really* badly, but staying angry with him didn't seem to be a possibility anymore. Certainly there were things she still hadn't completely forgiven him for, but at least now she could stand the sight of him without seeing red.

How was it that this man could break her heart so completely and yet she was still fool enough to forgive him? That thought alone had her blood boiling all over again. She was a fool to think that he could ever really love her. He had just written that letter to throw her off, to fool her into calling off the wedding. Just so he could go and break her heart again.

It was so obvious that a man like him was used to women falling all over him all the time. He probably couldn't handle that a woman who used to stop breathing when he walked into a room was moving on and getting married.

But then she looked back over at the porch and found him watching her with a look so powerful that it stole her breath. She didn't want to know what he was thinking just then, she honestly didn't, but she could see the depths of his green eyes clear across the yard as if he was standing right in front of her, and she could read the message written there. She could see clear as day that he was imagining what it would be like to make love to her- what it would feel like to run his hands over her naked body. And it wasn't just raw, instinctual, animal sex that he envisioned, but pure, honest, heart and soul love making.

Heat coursed through Lizzie's body from her head to the tips of her pinky toe.

Payton sipped a tall glass of lemonade and smiled a slow, sensual smile at Lizzie before she had the chance to look away, sending her yet one step closer to that ledge she so desperately was trying to avoid.

*Do you believe in soul mates, Liz? I do.*

"Doing an excellent job girls," he called. "Don't mind me. I'm just going to go lay over there in that hammock. Pull a little sheriff patrol for the misfits on my property."

Both of the girls rolled her eyes at him. "Thanks Payton," they called. "By the way," Lizzie added, "my daddy's gonna kill you when he finds out this is what you convinced him to let me out of wedding duty for."

Payton laughed as he finished settling into the hammock and pulled his baseball cap down low onto his head to block out the sunlight from his eyes. "Nope. Somehow I just don't imagine he'll really kill me for this. I imagine he might kill *you*, though, when he hears what you did to my prize winning Pecan trees."

"And let all the money he spent on this wedding go to waste? Heck no!"

"Mmm-hmm. We'll just see about that when I take you home later. Did I mention that my digital camera is just itching to send out a few hundred copies of this occasion to all your family and friends?"

"Fine by me." She flashed him a devilish grin that he obviously couldn't see through his shielded and closed eyes, but she felt better for it anyway.

Payton closed his eyes against the sunlight and let the sounds of the light wind blowing the leaves in the trees and the sounds of Grace and Lizzie talking with birds chirping in the background lull him to sleep. The sun felt good against his skin, warming him while the breeze helped to cool him just enough. He focused in on Lizzie's sweet voice- the cadence of her speech soothing him.

He dreamed about her. He could see her in his dreams looking the way she did now, all grown up and just as beautiful as the day he'd met her. Only in his dreams he could see her laughing, her eyes all lit up and dancing like they used to do when he'd known her back then. She was smiling and happy, and when she focused her gaze on him he could see the love shining from her eyes straight into his heart.

He smiled in his half asleep state, his eyes still closed to the world around him. It was amazing that even in his dreams he could smell her. That sweet smell that was all her own and that could intoxicate him faster than any whiskey ever could. Funny, she smelled so close to him. He could almost imagine that if he reached out his arms she'd be close enough to touch. Close enough to wrap her in his arms and haul her down into the hammock to take a nap with him.

Close enough that when his world turned upside down and he felt himself flying through the air then thudding clumsily onto the ground he immediately knew who the guilty party was. And the fact that he heard her giggling hysterically right beside him clued him pretty fast as well.

"Lizzie!" He turned his head to see her tennis shoes level with his eyes in the grass. Aw, hell. Now he was going to do something he might regret, he could already feel it growing in his bones.

She bent over at the waist and her upside down smile and sparkling eyes shot fire through him. "Thought the prison warden might want a little wake up call to know we're all done here, sir." She smiled that smug little smile that had him wanting to slap a kiss over her lips just to make it go away.

He settled instead for returning the favor in like kind. His hand shot out from his side and circled her ankle. He could see that she had just begun to register what he planned to do when he gave a sharp pull and sent her flying to the ground, but in the last second he rolled to catch her so she wouldn't really hurt herself. He continued the roll so he ended up on top of her, effectively pinning her to the ground.

Her eyes went wide, and he could feel her breasts push against him as she struggled to pull in air to her startled lungs. Instinctively his body responded, and he felt himself go hard. She knew it, too. He could see the realization in her eyes, and the blush that followed. He smiled down at her.

"Thought I might return the favor. You didn't get hurt when you fell, did you now, sweetheart?"

She narrowed her eyes at him until they were nothing more than cat like slits. "No, *honey*, I didn't. Now, if you don't mind, I think it's time you took me home." But instead of pushing against him and trying to free herself, she just lay there lost in his eyes.

Somewhere in the distance they heard a conspicuous clearing of a throat. "Speaking of home, I've got to run. I've gotta take Snickers to the vet for her annual feline check-up. Uh, guys? Did you hear what I said?" Grace cocked a hip out to the side and raised her eyebrows. It took a minute, but eventually Lizzie and Payton realized she was there and they tore their focus from each other. Simultaneously they turned their head to where she was leaning against a Pecan tree.

"Hi, remember me?" She smiled. "Look, I totally forgot. Payton, I really need to get to her there today and they close in thirty minutes. Mind if I take your truck and head on to town? It'd really save me a bunch of time from walking back home."

Lizzie pushed herself out from under Payton and brushed the grass from her hair. "Don't worry about it Grace. I need to get home, too. I'm sure my dad is about to kill me for being gone this long. Payton, can you drop her off in town on your way to drop me off?"

Oddly enough, Lizzie thought, Payton's eyes went round with shock at the same time Grace said, "No! Uh, I mean… you know what? I really need to get to town *right now*. I don't have time for you to drop Lizzie off, Payton. Can't I please borrow your truck?"

"Sure," Payton quickly replied. "Just make sure you don't wreck it, alright?"

And with a quick thanks Grace jumped into Payton's truck and sped off down the gravel drive like a NASCAR driver on speed.

"Jeez. What was that about?" Lizzie stood up from the ground and uselessly tried to brush the green grass stains off the legs of her jeans. "She certainly streaked out of here, don't you think?"

"Ah, well, that's Grace for you. A little whacked in the head if you ask me."

"You would think that. Look, it's getting late and I really need to get home. Thanks for the wedding diversion and all, but I've got to head home now."

"Wait!" Payton cringed inwardly. He sounded a little desperate, didn't he? "I mean... wait a second, okay? I need to run inside and grab a shirt. It'll only take a minute and then I'll drive you home."

"But, you just lent Grace your truck, remember?"

"Sure I do. But I have another truck in the garage. It's old and beat to hell and back, but it runs."

"Oh, well. Okay." She plopped down into the hammock and propped one tennis shoe on top of the other one, settling in to wait until Payton came back to take her home.

He returned a few minutes later wearing a pair of jeans and a burgundy t-shirt with an ad for Corona on the back. He crossed the yard to the hammock and held out his hand to her. "Come on. There's someplace I want to take you."

"Take me? But I really need to get back home."

"I'll take you there, too, but there's someplace I want to go with you first."

She eyed him curiously. Did she dare go anywhere with him? She knew that it probably wasn't a good idea. It was probably a really *bad* idea, in fact, but she heard herself give in, and she held out her hand for him to help her up.

"Great. Hang on a second and I'll back the truck out of the garage." He'd no sooner helped her up when he disappeared back into the house and she heard the electric garage door opener begin to pull the heavy door up. The ugliest, most beat up truck in the world came rattling out of the garage, leaving her to stare in disbelief at its exterior.

"I told you it was ugly and beat to hell. Get in, and let's go." Payton yelled out to her through the open window then bent over the passenger side to open the door for her from the inside.

"Where are you taking me," she asked as they drove out of the gravel drive.

"You'll see."

"This isn't another wise-ass move to get me to do something for you that you're too lazy to do, is it?"

Payton's lips twitched at the corners. "I'm not lazy, and no, it's not."

"Good, because one good deed a day is all I can stand."

"You know, the thought occurs to me that you sure do like to get under my skin. Do you do it on purpose, or is this just an annoying habit you've picked up since high school?"

It was her turn to smile. "I don't know what you're talking about."

"Uh-huh. That's what I thought."

They drove in silence for a while. They had come back into to town and just reached her side of town when Payton pulled the old truck into a dirt drive that Lizzie recognized. It was the drive to Granny's pond.

"What are you up to Payton?"

He stopped the truck and turned off the ignition. "I'm not up to anything. Just... trust me, okay?" He thought she might refuse and demand he take her home. He found himself holding his breath until he heard her say okay.

"Good. Now, go on down to the pond. You remember the way, right? Okay, well go on and I'll meet you there in a minute." He waited until she was out of sight and then he leaned his head back against the old, worn leather of the seat and took a deep breath. He was crazy. He knew it. What he was doing could only be described as lunacy, but here he was.

He took a deep breath and got out of the truck. Before he set off after Lizzie he grabbed the picnic basket that he'd stowed in the bed of the pickup truck before he'd pulled out of the garage. He sent up a silent prayer for luck and headed down the path leading down to the edge of the pond.

## Chapter Twenty-eight

Lizzie had been staring out across the pond watching a turtle lazily crawl onto a stump to sun bathe when she heard the bushes rustle behind her. She turned as Payton cursed a bush that almost tripped him and then headed out into the clearing surrounding the pond. There was a basket in his hand, she noticed, that looked oddly like a picnic basket.

Lizzie got a sinking feeling in the pit of her stomach.

"What exactly are you up to, Payton?"

He pretended that he didn't hear her and set the basket on the ground. He started to hum softly to himself as he spread a big blanket out on the ground for them to sit on.

"At the risk of sounding like a broken record I'm going to repeat myself. What exactly are you up to, Payton?"

He continued to ignore her until he had meticulously straightened each and every corner of the blanket and then plopped down on one edge and patted a spot on the blanket beside him. He obviously wanted her to sit next to him, but Lizzie crossed her arms and cocked out a hip, raising her eyebrows at him like he was insane.

"Oh, come on, Liz. Give a guy a break, okay?"

"Not until you tell me what you're doing."

Payton wanted to jump up and force her down on the blanket beside him, but he settled for cursing violently under his breath and releasing a deep sigh. "What does it look like I'm doing? I'm *trying* to have a picnic lunch with you."

"Why?"

He slapped his hand to his face and ran it through his hair leaving it tousled. "Jesus, Liz, don't you ever get tired of asking questions? Fine." He flipped open this lid of the basket and fished inside until he found what he was looking for. "Happy Anniversary, for crying out loud. There, are you happy now?" He whipped out a single white cupcake covered in chocolate icing and topped with a single candle.

"Anniversary?"

"Yeah. Anniversary of the first day I ever met you."

Lizzie's eyes went wide, and he saw the corners of her mouth begin to turn up in a grin before she quickly squashed the smile. One hand that had been wrapped around her waste inched itself up toward her mouth to cover her gaping jaw.

"Y-you remember that day?" She looked at him in disbelief.

"Of course I remember that day. You were wearing a khaki skirt and white top with your hair pulled back and those big green eyes that looked like you were going to cry when everyone caught you staring at me." He smiled. "I never knew a face could get as red as yours did, but I thought it was sweet."

Lizzie's legs weren't going to hold out anymore so she sank to the closest edge of the blanket. "You certainly didn't give anything away. I thought you didn't even know I existed."

Payton smiled. "Well, you got me there. I knew you existed but it just took a while before I let anybody know about it."

"But you remember that day! Why on earth? I wasn't even friends with you then. Hell, I didn't have *any* friends then."

Payton looked away to start pulling things from the basket, figuring since he had her distracted for a minute he'd get everything out in hopes that then she wouldn't refuse to enjoy the lunch he'd brought. "I remember another day too. The day you punched Lou Ann in the face. Remember that?"

"Oh, God, kill me now."

"I was so impressed that you could use a right hook that well. And then I saw you crying under the stadium."

"I thought my dad was going to kill me for getting in a fight."

He nodded. "I wanted to give you a big hug, you looked so sad, but I figured you were better off not knowing that I saw you."

Lizzie looked at all the food he had pulled from the basket and relaxed enough to let a smile form on her lips. "So, you want to have lunch with me to celebrate me getting caught embarrassing myself in front of you a million times?"

He laughed. "Surprise." He smiled over at her with that broad, lazy smile that used to melt her heart. He wondered what it was doing to her heart right now.

"No funny business, right?"

"I'm on my best behavior, I promise." He did one of those scout's honor hand signals.

Lizzie considered the pros and cons of this situation for a minute, added up that the cons way outnumbered the pros, and then decided she didn't really care. For once in her life she didn't really care. "Okay. Let's eat."

Payton smiled again. "Good. I was hoping you would say that." He glanced at the food then scratched his head and shot her a sheepish grin. "I hope you're in the mood for peanut butter and jelly. It's all I had in the house."

Lizzie laughed. "What, you mean you were too busy playing the big bad warden role to go out and get a real meal?" She picked up one of the sandwiches and took a bite. "Mmm, I always did like PB&J's. Now I just need something to wash it down."

"Ah, I have just the thing." Payton reached into the cooler he'd brought and whipped out two Bud Lights, handing her one.

"Wow, I'm impressed. This is shaping up to be a pretty good lunch."

Payton took a bite of sandwich and talked around his food. "Yeah? Well, if you like this, you're gonna love dessert."

Lizzie laughed. She realized she'd been doing that more today than she had in a long time. "Hmm, wonder what it is. If you say Oreo's and milk I think I'll be in heaven."

Payton took another bite and smiled. "Guess you'll have to wait and see." He ate in silence for a minute then asked, "Do you still want to open your own clinic one day?"

She thought for a minute. "I suppose so, but Nashville's already so congested with doctor's offices. I'd be better off working for someone and then just buying them out one day."

"What about Edenville? You don't want to live here anymore?"

"Yes, but now's there two of us to think about, and I can work anywhere. Josh needs Nashville to support his career."

Payton's jaw ticked. "He's an investment banker. Why does he have to live in Nashville for that?"

Lizzie stopped eating. "What are you getting at, Payton?"

"You give up a lot for him."

"So? It's called a relationship, that's what's supposed to happen."

"Yeah, but what does he give up for you?"

"You don't need to be poking your nose in my business." A warning note sounded in her voice.

"Just answer the question."

She gave up all pretense of eating and dropped the sandwich on her plate. "A lot. He buys me stuff all the time and he spends his time over at my apartment because his mother doesn't really like me and she thinks women look cheap when they sleep at men's houses."

"His mother?" Payton groaned. "How old is this guy? He still bases his life around his mother's thoughts?"

"Let's just leave her out of this, alright?"

"Fine." He looked murderous. "But just because he buys you stuff and sleeps at your place does *not* mean he gives up a lot for you. You're giving up the place you used to love, Liz. And what about your family?"

She threw up her arms. "What about them?"

"You're moving to Nashville, so you can live with Josh and his wacko mom, and leaving your family here. Don't you want to be with them?"

"Yes, but I also want to be with Josh and sometimes you can't have everything you want. I get the cake, but I don't get to eat it, so to speak."

"What flavor?"

She cocked her head. "*What*?"

"Just answer me!"

"Chocolate."

"Aha! That's what you think." She looked at him like he'd gone insane. Maybe he had, but he had to finish his thought. "Look, in a week, you're walking down the aisle to a chocolate covered cake, but when you cut into it you're going to find out its caramel instead." He scrubbed a hand across his face. "I've tried, Liz, I have. I wanted to be nice to him, regardless of the fact that he's marrying the girl that I wish could be mine. But he's not right for you."

Lizzie jaw clenched and her fingers curled into fists. "Be careful what you say about him."

"I know you don't want to hear this, but I want you to hear it now before it's too late. You think he loves you, Liz, but he loves the *idea* of you, not *you*. Grace and I have talked..."

"Whoa. You've been talking about me behind my back?"

He ignored her and kept on talking. He knew he was in trouble but he had to finish. "He's constantly doing little things to undermine your confidence like ordering for you and telling you to watch your diet. He wants you to change your hair color for crying out loud! And last night he told me that he wants you to have a boob job so you'll look more like a porn star."

Her look was blank.

"Jesus! You're not a porn star, for God's sake!" He punched his arm in the air. "You're a beautiful woman with a perfect body who shouldn't have to change her body just to please her husband. If he doesn't love you now, he's not ever no matter what you do."

She stood and turned away from him. "I want you to take me home. Now."

"Sure, fine." He was furious with her, just as much as he was furious with himself for getting so carried away. But she was just so stubborn at times, and why wouldn't she listen to him? She was just right the way she was, and no one deserved to be treated like she was. He gathered up their food and drove her home in silence. Before she yanked her arm away from him and slammed his truck door in his face, he calmly said, "You know, Liz, for such a smart girl, you sure can be dumb sometimes."

.

Ed leaned against the wall and watched as Lizzie pedaled fast and furiously on the old stationary bike they had stashed in the back bedroom of their house. She mumbled occasionally and he thought he caught a *sure can be dumb sometimes* before she looked up and spotted him standing there. She shot him a look.

"Did that rat come here and talk to you about me and him?"

"By rat, I assume you mean Payton, and he came here to tell me you and Grace used quite a bit of toilet paper on his yard." He smiled. "If we happened to have a heart to heart while he was here then that's none of your business."

Lizzie pedaled faster. "Yeah? Well did he also mention that he was planning to take me on a picnic and tell me what a terrible guy I picked for a husband?"

The smile faded from his face. "No, he didn't."

She mopped her face with the towel wrapped around her neck. "Well he did."

So that was what this was all about. Faith had warned him that Lizzie was a tad touchy this afternoon, and he chalked it up to wedding stress, but this was more than that. He shrugged. "Listen, sweet pea, if he told you that he doesn't like him then he must have some reason."

She grunted. "What is it with you people? I mean, I knew that head coaches got special treatment in this town, but brain washing privileges, too?  Come on!"

He dismissed her comment with a chuckle, but he felt his heartbeat pick up.  He'd spent a fortune on this wedding and he could picture it all going right down the toilet.  But, he had to remind himself that if that's what it took to see his baby happy then it was worth it.

He frowned.  "Are you having second thoughts?  Is that what this is about?"

"No, daddy."

His sigh of relief was audible, but he pressed her again just to be certain.  "Are you happy with Josh, Lizzie?"

She looked up at him with shocked eyes.  "Yes!  We're beyond happy together!  We're deliriously happy... we've never been... we're...."  She stopped pedaling and looked down at the ground.

"Lizzie?"  He took a cautious step forward when he saw her body shaking.  Not until he heard the sobs did he know she was crying.  "Oh, baby.  Come here."  He pulled his precious daughter off the bike and into his arms.  He would do anything to see her never cry again.  Didn't she know it broke his heart to see her upset?

"What is it, sweet pea?  What's wrong?  Did he hurt you?"

She sniffled.  He wiped a tear off her face.  "No, daddy.  Nothing like that.  It's just... I guess I'm tired from all the things leading up to the wedding, but I'm just... I don't know if I'm ready for this."

He rubbed her shoulder and kissed her forehead.  "Of course you don't know.  It's a big commitment, and the way we've always said it around here- it's forever.  If that's not scary, I don't know what is."

"Did you ever get worried about you and mom?"

He chuckled.  "Heavens, yes.  I was so excited when she said she'd marry me, and then I thought I'd crawl out of my skin the last week before we got married I was so uptight."

Lizzie breathed a little lighter.  "Okay, good.  Here I was thinking I was the only one to ever feel this way.  I was scared for a minute there."

Ed hugged his daughter tightly.  "No, Lizzie.  And don't forget, you're not alone.  Your mom and I will always talk with you if you need us.  Just get some rest.  These last few days are going to fly by and then you'll be off on your honeymoon, and you and Josh will laugh over how silly this whole thing was."

She smiled.  "You're right.  I know, you're completely right."

He felt good about his peace making skills as he left her and made his way out to the garden to check the status of the pansies and the fountain they were installing for the reception. If there was one thing he could do, it was console an upset female. Thank God for Ed Benford, he laughed to himself. Thousands upon thousands of dollars, and at least three major credit cards were at risk of certain demise if he hadn't been around to resolve that crisis.

What he didn't know was that despite his talk, Lizzie was still as uptight as ever, and not at all certain that Josh Turner was the man she was willing to have spend eternity by her side… especially if he expected her to have blond hair and massive, perfectly positioned breasts all the while.

*Chapter Twenty-nine*

By Wednesday, three days and counting until the big day, Lizzie wasn't sleeping and she was so nervous that all she would eat was a bagel and two rolls of Tums a day. Grace tried to show concern but all she'd received for her effort was a tongue lashing and a dissertation on the problems with weddings today.

Lizzie had taken Grace's head off about five times too many for her to endure anymore of this abuse, so she brushed her hair out and dabbed some lip gloss on her lips and grabbed her purse as she headed out the door.

Josh had moved into the Motel 6 with his mother when she'd arrived in town on Tuesday. Grace prayed she'd be out shopping at some pricey boutique store in Clarkston when she got there. One perk to living in a small town was that she knew all the hotel staff, had gone to high school with probably three fourths of them, and in Grace's case, slept with more than a few.

It just so happened that she'd had an extended relationship with the concierge who informed her that Mrs. Turner was out checking over the last minute details for the rehearsal dinner and Josh was alone in his hotel room, number 216. Grace's lip turned up in a wicked Grinch Who Stole Christmas type smile.


Three days later Payton studied himself in the mirror; black suit, white shirt, silver tie. Outwardly he was ready, from his neatly combed hair down to his shined and polished shoes. But inwardly…. He sighed.

As much as he hadn't wanted to attend Lizzie's wedding, somehow he found himself thinking about it, and when the time had come he had showered and dressed. So here he stood staring back at his reflection in the mirror.

He still had thirty minutes to go until he needed to leave for the church, but he felt edgy and even the intense workout he had done that morning didn't seem to be helping his nerves. Instead of pacing the old hardwood floors of his house he picked up his house keys and locked the front door behind him as he left. He might be a little sweaty from walking the two miles to the church in the heat, but he figured no one would be looking at him anyway, so what did it really matter?

Memories that he had never quite forgotten came back to him as he walked: making love by the lake and then again in his truck bed; Lizzie laughing at him when he'd spilled a milkshake down his shirt by accident; bonfires out at Murphy's farm with all the gang, and Lizzie tucked up in his arms hiding her face from the scary stories Colin or Hank would tell. There were so many memories to think over that he almost walked past the front steps of the church.

It struck him as odd that Lizzie's father hadn't thought to at least line the railings leading up to the white double front doors with greenery, or that the church bells weren't ringing, but he made his way up the stairs and through the doors anyway. What really struck him, though, was when he walked into the sanctuary and not a single person was in sight.

Had something happened? And why wasn't he informed if it had? Payton sat in the last pew of the church until fifteen minutes past seven, but no one from the wedding party ever showed. A few people Payton didn't recognize came in, took one look at the empty church and left shrugging their shoulders at him.

By seven-thirty he decided that either the wedding wasn't taking place or he was wrong about the date. He knew from all the times he had stared at that invitation in disbelief that the date wasn't wrong, but he was too hopeful that Lizzie had changed her mind to put much stock in it. Somehow his luck never seemed to hold when it came to her.

He waited another thirty minutes just to be sure, and then he picked up the tie he had chucked during his wait and started the long walk home. Surprisingly the night was cooling down and a nice breeze was blowing the lush green leaves in the trees. Payton decided on a detour through the town park on his walk home, and pushed open the old iron gate that lead into the park.

Why hadn't Lizzie shown for her wedding? The thought troubled him. Was he responsible for her decision or had something happened to Josh to change his mind? He tried to suppress it, but he felt the first few licks of hope beginning to gnaw at his stomach. He made his way along the pebbled concrete pathway edging the small river that wound through the park. He wanted to walk to her house and find out straight from her what had happened, but he figured that wasn't probably the best course of action today. Instead he continued his journey through the park.

He had just reached the bend in the path when he spotted her sitting on a bench tucked back among a cluster of Tulip-poplars and Magnolias. She was wearing old faded blue jeans with the beginnings of a hole at the knees, and the same soft pale pink plaid flannel shirt she had worn camping with the gang in high school. On top of her head she wore the soft tulle material of her veil that perched there with the help of a pearl encrusted headband.

Payton ducked behind the thick trunk of an old Pecan tree and watched her for a few minutes. Lizzie's eyes were closed, and her bottom lip was drawn into her mouth at the corner where she could chew on it. He remembered her doing that at times in high school when she was trying to work through a difficult problem. She heaved a heavy sigh and shook her head to some imaginary question rambling around in her head.

Lizzie didn't hear him coming so she jolted when he sank onto the space on the bench beside her. She flicked her eyes over him, looking sad and irritated all in one cute, half flannel half tulle covered bundle.

"What are you doing here?" she asked as she turned her head away to watch two squirrels chase each other across the park.

"I was walking home from the church."

"Didn't anyone call you?"

"Apparently not." He paused and ran a hand through his hair. "Want to talk about it?"

She shook her head as she started to nibble her lower lip again. He could tell she was uncomfortable with him being there, but he didn't care. She was hurting and he wanted to help.

"Care to explain this?" He lifted the soft, sheer material that floated around her shoulders.

"Actually, I'd rather not."

Payton pulled the hand that had been touching the veil back down into his lap. He searched his brain for something to say besides what ate at his thoughts, but came up empty.

"It's a nice night for a walk. Care to take one with me?"

She didn't respond.

"What about if I promise not to ask you the obvious questions that are lurking in my mind?"

She blinked up at him, killing him with the vulnerability he saw there.

"Promise?"

"Promise."

She made a show of studying her nails, which Payton noticed had been painted clear with little half moons of white at the tips. "Okay, I guess."

He held out his broad hand to help her up then tucked it gently underneath his arm like a gentleman caller from long, long ago. The crickets that lay hidden in the tall grass serenaded them as they strolled along the pebbled path. The sun, bright orange and warm on their skin was settling in the distance casting long shadows through the trees.

Payton chuckled to himself.

"What? Are you laughing at me?" Lizzie regarded him insecurely.

"No, I'm not laughing at you. I'm laughing at that stupid old dog you used to have."

Lizzie turned her lip out in a pout. "Skipper wasn't stupid. He had a brilliant brain."

"I have my doubts about that, but I will give him kudos for his personality disorders."

"Disorders? You can hardly call tracking a trail a personality disorder."

Payton stopped short and regarded her quizzically. Lizzie couldn't help but give a little smile at the face he made at her. "Liz, the dog tracked imaginary ants. I'd definitely call that a disorder. Probably more like a psychosis."

"Well, that was the worst problem he had."

Payton let out an impolite grunt.

"What other grievances do you have against the poor dog?"

"Poor dog, my butt. He peed on my leg."

Lizzie flushed but kept on walking. Someone needed to be embarrassed for that dog because, Lord bless his resting soul, he certainly never was for himself. "He was nervous. He did irrational things when big hulking football heroes pretended they were going to use him as a football."

"I wouldn't have really done that."

"He didn't know that."

"Well, *that* certainly explains away him hiking his leg on my new Nike's."

Lizzie grumbled under her breath and stomped ahead while Payton let out a rumble of a laugh.  At least he'd succeeded in taking her mind off of things for a while.

"Seriously, Liz."  Payton jogged to catch up with her.  "You have to admit that dog always was good for a laugh when you needed one."

"Yeah, like now.  God I wish that dog was here right now."  He reached out and pulled her arm gently.  She stopped and looked up at him, her eyes still pathetic sad puppy dog eyes, only now they were full of pain.

"I'm here, does that count?"

"I wish Payton, but…"  She trailed off and heaved another heavy sigh.  Brushing a hand over her head she pulled the veil off her head and threaded the pearl headband through her fingers.  When she spoke again, it was soft and sad, and full of defeat.  "You know, I really think I've had all the fun with men that I can handle for a while.  I think I'm going to go turn myself into a convent and be a nun for the rest of my life."

Payton's heart hurt for her, but he pushed a smile onto his face, and lifted her head with his index finger below her jaw.  He shook his head at her.  "Something tells me you wouldn't make it very long as a nun. They'd kick you out as soon as they saw how practiced you are with that right hook.  Aren't nuns supposed to take a vow of nonviolence?"

Lizzie didn't laugh like he thought she would.  Instead, she looked more depressed and turned away, walking toward the small arched bridge that lead the path from one side of a small creek to the other.  Great, Payton thought.  He was supposed to be helping her, not making her feel worse.

She stopped halfway over the bridge and looked down at the minnows swimming in the water below her.  She leaned against the railing staring down into the water for so long that Payton thought she might have forgotten he was still standing there beside her.  After a while, though, she started to talk.

"I woke up this morning and for the first time in probably two months I wasn't nervous.  I don't know exactly why, all I know is that when I looked in the mirror the girl looking back at me was telling me it was time and I was ready."  She studied her nails again.  "I went and got my nails done, got my hair done, had a wonderful bridesmaid's luncheon. And the church… the church was beautiful."

Payton took a deep breath and waited for her to finish the story. The way her eyes were glazed over as she was deep in thought made him think it wouldn't have mattered if a total stranger had been standing next to her just then because now was when the dam finally was breaking and she was ready to let all her thoughts out.

"You should have seen how amazing the flowers were at the front of the church," she said with a small smile on her face. "I had my dress on… I didn't care that it was four hours before the wedding. I've been waiting my whole life to put on that wedding dress- it was my mom's when she got married- and I put it on almost as soon as I got to the church just so I had extra time to wear it.

"I was sitting on the front pew watching the florist put the last flowers in their spots when I felt his hand on my shoulder. Josh had good hands, not too big, not too small." Lizzie rubbed a hand up and down her arm as if she were cold. "He startled me a little because his face was so pale and so serious… I should have known right then he had something on his mind."

She was so wrapped in thought that she didn't even notice that she'd started to shiver. Whether from shock at reliving those moments with Josh or from cold Payton couldn't be sure. He took his suit jacket off and put it around her shoulders. She huddled down into its warmth, but other than that she gave no indication that she even knew it or he was there.

"He tried to smile, but his lips were shaking, and that's when I knew. I took a step a back, as if that was going to help anything," she laughed sorrowfully. "He said he was sorry probably five hundred times, and I just stood there. I couldn't blink, I couldn't speak, I couldn't even move, and Josh just started talking a mile a minute telling me all the reasons why we shouldn't get married.

"' We're not the same people we used to be when we started dating,' he told me. We don't have the same goals in life, we don't have the same family values, we don't have the same ideals, we don't have the same view of what a spouse should be, we don't, we don't, we don't…" Lizzie scrubbed a hand across her furrowed brow. "The whole time I kept thinking to myself why me, why now, why today after my father spent all this money on the flowers and the food and all the invitations.

"And then after he finished his list of all the things that were wrong about us, he stood up and walked out of the church. He didn't kiss me, he didn't say goodbye. Not even a nice to know you, thanks for all the good times, Lizzie." She shrugged her shoulders. "And what am I supposed to do with that? "

Payton suspected she didn't really want an answer so he held his tongue. She glanced up as the big lamp hanging above them clicked on as the last of the sun set behind the trees. "I should have known he was going to do something like this. I should have realized it from the day I met him. He was always trying to change my view on politics, or religion. Always trying to make me see why big cities and big boobs were better. Always trying to make his family seem so upper crust and make mine seem so small town country and unworthy.

"But no, I couldn't possibly let myself see any of those things." She made a face and squished up her nose like she was trying to hold back tears. "God, I was so damn determined that my life just *had* to go right on course that I would be damned before I'd let this one get away from me. Hell, I was already six years off from my scheduled date of marriage, and if I let this one go then who else could possibly want an old spinster geek of a science nerd like myself. If I couldn't withstand a little hardship while we were dating how would I ever learn to compromise and face the hardships when we were married?"

Payton's mind was burning with a thousand different thoughts, and he wanted to grab her up and shake her until some sense returned, but he didn't. He forced himself to remain still and quiet. Forced himself to let her talk it out.

"God, what an *idiot* I was," Lizzie said to the night. "Grace tried her best to tell me what I already knew and just couldn't face. And you," for the first time since she'd started her ranting she looked directly at Payton. "You took me down to the pond and tried the best way you knew how to warn me about him, and you'd only known him for a few days. I, on the other hand, had known him for five years and didn't even have the guts to admit that what my own conscience and my friends were telling me were the dead on truth."

She propped her head in her hands and closed her eyes. She was quiet for a while, and Payton didn't realize she was crying until he heard a softly muffled sniffle. He took a step closer to her and placed his hands on her shoulders. He couldn't provide her comfort with his words then, but thought that maybe a comforting hand would be the support she needed. Lizzie let his hands stay where they were for a minute before she stood and let them fall away.

"I'm tired, Payton. I'm tired of being the smart one that can memorize any textbook and can diagnose an illness from ten feet away, but can't read a guy if my life depended on it. I'm tired of investing my life in something only to find out after I'm in over my head that the dividends just aren't going to pay out. And mostly I'm tired of being used and abused and not getting any favors in return.

"I'm done. You know the more I think about it, the more that convent sounds better and better." She looked down oddly at her arms and seemed to realize for the first time that she was wearing Payton's coat. She shrugged it off and handed it back to him. Her fingers brushed his when he took the coat, and a suspicious tingle traveled up his arm.

"Good night, Payton." She turned and walked away. Payton couldn't let her go, though, without saying something, anything, that might help her feel better.

"Wait! Lizzie, come back so we can talk..." She held up a hand but didn't stop moving away.

"No, Payton. I'll see you around sometime."

He watched her disappear into the night, and couldn't help but feel a little bit sorry for himself, and a lot sorry for Lizzie. He didn't know what he was going to do to help her, but one thing was certain: she had a serious aversion to men that he was going to have to overcome. He scuffed his feet through the pebbled walkway like a little boy kicking rocks as he made his way through the rest of the park toward his home. He was almost at the edge of his land when an idea struck him, and he grinned. He didn't know all the specifics of it just yet, but the parts he did know seemed like a perfect plan.

## Chapter Thirty

Lizzie tightened the sash on her white silk robe before she unlocked the front door to retrieve the morning paper. The sun was just beginning to come up over the horizon, and a thick sheen of dew still clung to the green grass on her lawn that was starting to turn brown with the Fall. She sipped the vanilla flavored coffee in her mug and slid her house shoes back on her feet as she shuffled down the sidewalk, her eyes half open, her goal the gray mass wrapped in plastic at the edge of the bricked walkway.

She grumbled as she bent to fetch the paper and shuffled her way back to the house. She grumbled again, though not as vehemently, as she bent to grab the white tulip that lay across her door mat. Lizzie waited until the door was closed before she leaned back against its solid strength and sniffed the flower. A form of a smile twitched at the corners of her lips before she squashed the urge and shuffled down the central hall toward the kitchen. The tulip landed with a plop into the vase holding at least six other white tulips that were in varying degrees of freshness.

Thirty three. That was the number of days that she had been living in her new house. It also happened to be the number of days that a single white tulip had arrived on her doorstep. She found herself waking just a little earlier every morning in hopes that she would catch whoever was putting them there, and could tell them to quit. At the same time, though, she had a hunch as to their mysterious benefactor and wondered how long he would keep it up.

It had been a little over two months since the wedding had been called off, and in Lizzie's opinion, so much had happened since then her head spun every time she thought of the days in between that one and today. She and her family made the trip from Edenville up to Atlanta where she graduated from Emory University's School of Medicine. At graduation, she'd been walking across the stage to receive her diploma and paused to wave at her family back in the stands. At the top of the bleachers inside the basketball arena she thought she spotted Payton, but when she looked again he was gone and she couldn't be sure it wasn't just her imagination running wild.

She also started working in the hospital over in Clarkston, and had managed to scrape together enough money and time between working all the horrendous plebian doctor hours she'd been assigned to put a down payment on her new house. Lizzie still couldn't believe she was now an official resident of Edenville. She always new this town would be her home one day.

She was even considering opening a clinic of her own one day within Edenville's city limits, but that was a long time away and she needed to repay a significant chunk of her student loans before the bank would even consider loaning her the money to purchase the land for her to build it. But at least she had a good dream going, and between that and all the time she spent at the hospital, there wasn't enough time left in the day for her to worry about other things such as silly men who left her white tulips.

Lizzie pulled her long curly hair up into a bun, her customary hairdo for work, and slipped into the standard issue blue scrubs she wore at the hospital. She would wait until she got to the parking lot before she slid into her medical jacket and put her stethoscope around her neck. She had just finished applying her mascara when the doorbell rang, and she jolted so suddenly that she barely missed gouging her eye out and also managed to leave a streak of black inky make-up running across her face. She cursed, grabbed a wad of toilet paper, and jogged down the stairs to open the door while tears streamed from her eye and she tried to rub the waterproof streak off her skin.

Through the patterned glass she could see Grace's flame red hair, so she opened the door without seeing who it was first. Grace took one look at her friend and laughed.

"Nice. Let me guess," she paused and tapped her forefinger across the tip of her nose, "you're an overworked new doctor who's trying to plead insanity by attempting to kill herself with a mascara wand. How close am I?"

Lizzie rolled her one good eye. "Pretty darn."

"Honey, you look bad. I mean seriously, you've definitely seen better days."

"Gee, thanks Grace!" Lizzie really played up the sarcasm. "I mean, if you can't count on your best friend to build you up, who can you count on?"

"Oh, come on. This isn't anything a day at the spa can't massage out of you. And speaking of, are you ready to go?"

"Huh? I've got to be at work in an hour. We're supposed to go there on Saturday, Grace, not today."

"Yep, I knew it was bad, but I didn't know it was this bad. Bean, it *is* Saturday."

"What?" She flipped the plastic off the newspaper and looked at the day and date on the front page. Lizzie slapped a hand to her forehead. "Oh, man, I have got to get a life."

"Exactly. So, starting now you're my personal project for the weekend, and I don't want to hear one peep out of you about where we go or what we do."

"As long as it involves a lot of hot massage oil, a good massage therapist, and some strong margaritas, I'm not saying a word."

"Good, now go change out of those horridly unflattering scrubs and get your butt back down here so we can go. I certainly didn't pull my disgustingly mean morning-person self out of bed to wait around here all day. I'm giving you five minutes and then I start blowing the horn." Grace leaned in and gave her friend a warm hug before she pinched her behind and tromped out the door and out to her car.

She watched the door to the house as she flipped open her cell phone and punched in a speed dial number. "Hey, it's me. Yeah, I think we're all set. So, we'll see you tonight? Okay, great."

She flipped the phone shut and smiled. She was such a terrible friend it wasn't even funny.

"Oh, my gosh, that was so good I think I'm going to be drooling until sometime next week," Grace said as she hit the unlock button on her key-fob and slid into the driver's seat.

"Tell me about it. Between that man's hands and the mood music, I think I've died and gone to heaven."

"Mmm, Mark certainly is a talented masseuse. If only I could meet a man that made wild, passionate love to me and then did that, I think I'd beg him to marry me right there on the spot." Grace didn't even pause to look if cars were coming before she peeled out onto the road. "What about you? Are you on the market again, yet?"

Lizzie sighed deeply and propped her elbow on the arm rest, closing her eyes on the question. Between Grace's lack of driving skills and constant prodding into her lack of desire for a love life she could already feel her shoulders knotting back up with tension. "I don't think so, Grace. I think I'm through with guys for a while…maybe a long while."

"Aww, come on, bean. You can't hold out on men forever."

Lizzie bared her teeth in a ferocious smile. "Watch me."

"Oh, I'm watching alright. I'm watching you walk right into spinster hood and not give a damn about the consequences." Grace flipped the radio on. "I mean seriously, have you looked at yourself in the mirror lately?"

Lizzie wasn't sure where this was headed. "Umm, yep. I did this morning when I brushed my teeth."

"No, seriously. When is the last time you really looked in the mirror- and don't give me some crap about not having enough time with all the hours they're piling on you at the hospital." Grace waited about a half a millisecond before piping back up again. "Bean, you're gorgeous, and it's starting to piss me off that you can't see that about yourself. Just because you've had some bad luck in the past with guys does not mean you should write them off forever and spend the rest of your life miserable."

Lizzie was starting to pout. "I'm not miserable."

"Bull. You can't pull that crap of a lie on me, bean, and you know it. I know what Lizzie Benford looks like when she's miserable and you are miserable."

"No, I'm not! I'm tired, and I'm cranky from working so many ridiculous hours trying to be the good new doctor at Clarkston Medical Center."

"Ok, I'll give you tired, but the only reason you're cranky is because you haven't been laid in a while."

Lizzie hissed out a breath. "You are really pushing it, Grace."

"No, I'm not. But just keep it up, and then you'll be forced to see pushing it. I am not letting my best friend in the world give up on men and life just because you've had a hard past few months. I wouldn't be doing my job if I gave up on you now." Grace looked over at her and smiled. When Lizzie didn't return the favor Grace reached over and pinched her cheeks. Lizzie pulled away and stifled a smile.

"See I knew you could smile." Grace took a sip of water from the plastic bottle she kept in her car. "I'm just worried about you, Lizzie. I love you, and I want you to be happy."

Lizzie studied Grace's profile as she drove. "I love you, too,

Carrot."

"Good. Then don't forget that in a few days."

"What did you do, Grace?" Grace was silent. "Grace Jacobs. You answer me right now. What have you and your crazy red hair been scheming up now?"

"Not much."

"I swear, Grace, if you've hooked me up on some stupid blind date I swear I'll make you wear Pepto Bismol pink *everything* if I ever get married."

Grace giggled. "I didn't set you up on a blind date, I swear it." She made a show of crossing her fingers, crossing her heart, and sticking a needle through her eye. A minute later she said, "everything?"

Lizzie laughed. "Yes, everything. Dress, shoes, bow, underwear, the works. If it's pepto bismol pink then you're wearing it."

"Oh, ok. Just clarifying." She turned the radio up and sang her heart out all the way through town. Lizzie on the other hand had her mind preoccupied trying to figure out what hair brained idea Grace had cooked up. Lizzie was still working it through in her mind when Grace came to a screeching halt in front of Moe's Pub. For all her wonderful attributes, Grace was considerably lacking in good driving skills, and it was only by the good sheriff's grace that she still retained a driver's license at all.

"Remind me next time that I should be the one driving and not you." Lizzie closed her door none too gently and pushed ahead of Grace into the bar. The bar was slightly more crowded than usual for a Saturday night and Lizzie welcomed the sight of the extra bodies milling around.

Moe and Sally were both behind the bar tonight so they could handle the extra crowd that had come in for the weekend. It seemed that although Moe's Pub was located just outside of Edenville people from Clarkston had discovered they liked the bar's atmosphere and started frequenting the place as well.

"Evening, Moe. Sally. I'd like a margarita on the rocks, please."

"Sure thing, Sugar pie. Rita on the Rocks comin' up." Sally took a glass from behind the bar and dipped the rim in salt before turning back to get the tequila.

Grace ordered the same and squeezed in on the barstool next to Lizzie. The din of noise from all the people in the pub was almost deafening and Lizzie and Grace were close to yelling so they could be heard above the jukebox, the sound of pool balls being smacked by sticks, and people laughing in their various states of alcohol induced euphoria.

Lizzie sipped her drink, letting the feel of the tequila slipping into her blood ease the rest of the tension the massage hadn't quite relieved. Grace was rambling on about something one of the patrons of the town bank, Farmer's Exchange Bank, had done that week, which of course Lizzie tried her hardest to appear interested in. She had just settled into her rendition of what her boss sounded like when he was trying to appease one of the irate drive-through customers when she paused.

"What?" Lizzie looked over her shoulder trying to figure out why Grace had stopped short to stare.

"I can't believe it. You'll never guess who I just spotted in that booth back behind the pool tables."

"Who?"

"Little miss bully of a homecoming queen."

"Lou Ann?"

"Lou Ann Hendley. And you'll never guess who just spotted us."

"I'm pretty sure I can." Lizzie and Grace both simultaneously chugged the remaining half glass of their drink. "Another one, Sally!" They cried out in unison.

"Well, my my," came a sugary sweet voice behind them. "Fancy meeting you two here. Did y'all finally get your big girl panties on and decide it wouldn't hurt to get boozed up once in a while?"

Lizzie squeezed her eyes shut and wished she didn't have to deal with more monsters from her past. She reminded herself she'd grown up a lot since high school, and maybe Lou Ann had too; although from the sound of it she hadn't grown up much and she was spitting mad and ready for a fight.

She took a steadying breath and convinced herself she had given evil Lou Ann a black eye once, so she surely could do it again. She plastered the most sincere fake smile she could possible muster on her face, then spun on her barstool so she could face the enemy head-on. She forced herself to size up Lou Ann from head to toe, and was honestly surprised at what she saw.

Lou Ann looked older, with little crow's feet edging out from her eyes. Her skin looked pale and old, and the golden hair that had shimmered when they were younger was now dull and lifeless. Lizzie knew they were all twenty-nine and heading on toward middle age, but none of her old high school friends looked half as old as Lou Ann did.

"Well, if it isn't Lou Ann Hendley. Fancy meeting you here. Did you finally get tired of being cheated on and decide to come home and lick your wounds?"

Lou Ann hissed under her breath, and narrowed her eyes into little slits. "Watch it, Lizzie. You aren't the only one who knows other people's dirt. I'd be real careful how much trash you throw around if I were you. I'd hate for you to have to run home crying to mama like you used to do in middle school."

Lizzie's heart pounded for a minute, but as she sat there face to face with Lou Ann all the fear she used to experience from Lou Ann's taunts melted away. No longer was Lou Ann some larger than life untouchable siren that could cow her with the slightest little taunt. Instead she was a pathetic, pitiful, washed up, bitter woman who had nothing left but her mean words to keep her afloat. It was sad to see the truth standing in front of her, but at the same time it was freeing, and Lizzie experienced a moment of triumph and inexplicable joy. A smile broke out on her face, and then a rumble of laughter leaked out of her throat. She laughed so long and hard that finally she was laughing hysterically and both Grace and Lou Ann were looking at her like she might just need a trip to the funny farm after all.

After a while she wiped tears of laughter from her eyes, and patted the bar stool next to her. "Have a seat Lou Ann. You know, you're not half as scary as you used to be, you know that?" Lou Ann looked totally taken aback, but she parked it on the seat next to Lizzie and ordered a beer from Moe.

"So, sweat pea... isn't that what Grace always calls you?"

"Something like that."

"Whatever." Lou Ann lit up a cigarette and puffed the smoke out in Lizzie's general direction. Lizzie just shook her head. Obviously Lou Ann was still pouting. Some people never learn how to grow up. "What are you still doing here in Edenville? I thought you'd be off licking your wounds somewhere nice and tropical after, well, you know..."

"Yeah, well, I thought I was getting married. Apparently I was wrong. Life sucks. I'm over it." Lou Ann studied her skeptically.

"Mmmm, yeah, you really look like you're way over it." She took another puff of her cigarette before snubbing it out on the bar and lighting another one.

"You know, don't you, that cigarettes kill?"

Lou Ann glanced her way from the corner of her eye. "God, you don't say. Jesus, thank the good Lord that a doctor was here tonight and could save my life." She put her cigarette down and leaned into Lizzie for a massive hug.

Lizzie batted her away. "Yeah, well, don't say I didn't warn you." She pushed away and headed to the jukebox to select a song.

"You and Surgeon General... y'all are real class acts, I gotta hand it to you, Lizzie," Lou Ann called after her as Lizzie moved away. Lizzie actually was starting to half way enjoy Lou Ann's demented sense of humor in an oddly insane way, she thought as she pushed the button's for a Carrie Underwood song.

Lou Ann was chatting with Grace when she came back. "So, I thought you were off living in California or something crazy like that," Grace was saying.

"Was. I walked in on my bastard husband screwing another woman on our kitchen table. I divorced him and sold all our stuff. Didn't much feel like eating off *that* table after that."

"Ouch. I guess not."

"Yeah, well, it happens."

Lizzie raised her glass in a toast, trying to find a way to make some peace between Lou Ann and her and get the topic on to better subjects than men. "Here's to being single and not needing a man to add meaning to life."

"Here Here." Lou Ann and Grace raised their drinks to the toast.

"A toast, eh? What's the cause?" Lizzie's stomach flipped at the voice behind her, but she forced the liquid down her throat and turned to face him.

Lou Ann chipped in, "Ah, we were just toasting to all the men we didn't need in our lives. Fancy that, eh?" Was that a wink she just witnessed, or maybe that was a twitch Lou Ann had developed along with her bad burping habits.

Payton's eyes made a slow study of Lou Ann, one which, if Lizzie had cared about Payton at all- which of course, she didn't- would have made her insanely jealous. Those beautifully sexy green eyes finished their slow assault of her then skipped over to meet Lizzie's dead on. He smiled, a small smile from the edge of one lip, and then it was gone.

"Hey, Moe. How about serving up the coach a cold one?" Lou

Ann called out to Moe. Moe nodded and moved toward the tap.

Payton wasted no time in turning back to Lou Ann. "Well, well. Did Lou Ann "the Banshee" Hendley finally find her way home? I thought I heard the fence-line gossip channel discussing you during PTA last week." His smile was slow and smooth, and Lizzie could feel the pulse of all fifty female bodies inside Moe's hammer into overdrive. He was baiting her, he had to be, because Lou Ann had to be just about the most worn out looking soul within a two hundred yard radius, and still he was looking at her like she was the finest piece of Grade A beef a food critic had ever seen.

She cleared her throat to gently remind him she was sitting right next to him.

Apparently he didn't hear because Payton cocked his hip so he shifted closer to Lou Ann, leaned into the bar, and reached for his frosty mug of Guinness in a way that allowed him to skim his brawny muscles quite effectively over Lou Ann's skin. Was it her or did she really just hear fifty silent female voices begging to be in Lou Ann's shoes right then?

Lou Ann smiled her dull brown eyes up at Payton. "I was just telling the girls here that my scumbag husband cheated on me. Hence the toast you walked up on."

"Well now, Lou Ann, that is *truly* a shame. I hate to see such a fine female form so ill used."

Lizzie rolled her eyes. "Excuse me. I think I hear the little ladies room calling. Grace, care to join me?"

Grace was too busy flirting with some drunk skunk sitting next to her, so Lizzie headed off by herself. From her peripheral vision she watched Payton slide smoothly into her vacant bar stool, never skipping a beat in the conversation. She gave a snort of disgust before she slammed her way through the bathroom door.

She gave herself ten minutes to cool down in the restroom before she washed her hands in the sink and headed back to the bar. Obviously that hadn't been long enough – or maybe it had been a little too long– because when she pushed open the door she found Payton and Lou Ann locking lips like they were the French inventing that kiss.

Payton waited until he saw the door to the bathroom shut completely before he let the smile that was killing his cheek muscles fall. "Oh, man," he said with a groan, "do you think this is really going to work?"

Lou Ann took a sip of her beer and regarded him with something close to pity. "You're asking me? I got an F- on relationship kinetics the day I signed those divorce papers, and you're asking *me* if I think things are going to work?"

"Well, you agreed to be my partner in crime didn't you?"

One dreadfully misshapen eyebrow rose. "Correction, I was badgered into this ridiculous game by that mop of red hair sitting over there. Something about paying penance for all those cruel pranks I used to pull. Whatever."

"What? Did I hear someone talking about me over here?" Grace extracted herself as calmly as possible from the drunk skunk sitting next to her. "Nice work, by the way. I almost believed that bit about the kitchen table."

"Yeah?" Lou Ann's lips rose into a half smile. "I thought it was pretty good myself. Besides, my ex deserves to have a few nasty rumors spread about him. I almost went to acting school, you know. Still might someday."

"That might be a good thing for you. I could see you acting in one of those-"

"Girls. Girls!" Payton looked at the two with his best coach's half time lecture game face. "Seriously. We don't have much time here and I need to know what to do next."

"Well, first things first… do you really want to get the girl?"

"Yes, but are you sure this plan is going to work?"

"Please." Grace looked at him like he had *stupid* tattooed to his forehead. "What's the matter, coach? Have you turned into a softie and forgotten how to play a little hardball?" She patted him gently on the shoulder, as if that would ease the blow she'd just landed. "If I know my girl, and I think I do, this will catch her attention a heck of a lot faster than those tulips on her doorstep will."

Payton scowled. "Not funny."

"Seriously, though," Lou Ann interjected, "if you want this to work then you're just going to have to trust us."

Payton wasn't sure that he really wanted to trust either one of them, but he had run out of patience. He couldn't wait any longer to finally have Lizzie again. "All right, the door's opening. It's go time."

He had no more than finished the sentence when Lou Ann's lips settled over his and held. His muscles bunched and he readied himself to push away and give her a piece of his mind when he heard her hiss through clenched teeth, "Keep kissing me dammit, and don't screw this up."

The claws she dug into his upper arm shocked him enough that he opened his mouth only to have it invaded by her tongue. He forced himself to think about all the ways he would punish Lou Ann for this later, and brought his hand up to slide it through her hair. He really, *really* hoped this worked.


Lizzie managed to only trip twice on her twenty foot trip back from the bathroom. The first time was because she was trying to figure out exactly how far down Payton's throat Lou Ann had her tongue, and the second was entirely on purpose- just to see if Mr. Luv-you-'till-I-die still even knew she existed.

Obviously not, she thought with disgust, when he leaned in a little closer to Lou Ann and whispered something into her ear that had her grinning a mile wide. However, one of the pool players had witnessed her trip and he reached out a hand to catch her.

"Easy there, little lady." He smiled at her from beneath an overly large white felt cowboy hat and devoured her whole with eyes that were greedy thanks to too much booze.

She giggled nervously and started to push away until she looked over towards the bar and found Payton watching the guy like he would walk over any second and punch a hole through his no good head. That look was a whole heck of a lot better, in Lizzie's opinion, than the one he'd been giving Lou Ann earlier, so she decided to stick around and see where the pool man got her.


"What is she doing?" Payton whispered feverishly into Grace's ear. "She's supposed to be going crazy that I'm kissing Lou Ann, not scoping out the freshest piece of jail bait to see who'll give her the better time!"

Grace sipped her margarita before spinning on her bar stool and clapping Payton on the shoulder. "Relax, big guy. She hasn't been interested in men in months. Do you *really* think she'd be hitting on him if she weren't going crazy about you and Lou Ann? Now, don't look now, but I think someone's checking out the scene over here, so get back in there, QB."

Payton let out a long-suffering sigh and spun back to Lou Ann. He loved challenges like this normally, so he couldn't figure out why this one was making him act so crazy. He did get some satisfaction, though, when he watched Lizzie's jaw drop at least two inches as he slowly slid his well tanned hand up the inner edge of Lou Ann's thigh.

Lizzie was turning flame red, she just knew it, and it wasn't anything close to embarrassment she was feeling. She watched with utter disgust as Payton slid his hand up Lou Ann's thigh then winked at her. She tried her hardest, really she did, to keep from gasping in shock. Nevertheless, she heard it escape from her lips along with a shrill little growl that came from somewhere deep inside her.

Pool man stared at her like she was demon possessed before turning his attention back on the game at hand. Lizzie narrowed her eyes and determined that Payton absolutely was not going to get the upper hand. This was a game, she knew it now, and although she was certain that Payton wouldn't take defeat lightly, she was going to show him how it felt.

She didn't have many tools to use to her advantage since she wasn't wearing an ounce of make-up and she was sporting the same Ann Taylor sweat-suit she'd worn to the masseuse, but she was determined to do something. Tossing her hair in similar manner to the sex goddesses on TV, she stomped over to the opposite side of the pool table and bent down so her not so ample breasts were on eye level with pool man's gaze. She hoped that at least some of her cleavage was showing, though she doubted it. Regardless, she flicked her gaze over to the bar just to make sure Payton was watching then jutted out her chest to gain the other man's full attention.

When he didn't look up she was only slightly offended, but she cleared her throat and waggled her eyebrows at him when he glanced her way. She licked her lips and smiled what she felt confident was her best come-on smile. He blinked at her then turned to look behind him. He looked confused when he turned back, pointing slowly to himself with an obvious question mark over his head.

"I'm sorry… are you coming on to me?"

Lizzie felt like the jaw-dropping routine was getting a little old, but she did it again for what had to be at least the fifth time that night. "I-I was trying."

"Yeah, sweetheart…" He put down his stick and rounded the table, taking her by the arm and pulling her to the side. He leaned in to her and whispered, "I was just being nice. I'm… gay."

She really hoped that her face didn't register the shock she felt because she certainly had Payton's full attention now. "What," She hissed back at him. "You're gay! I've don't believe you, I've got gaydar on a ten mile radius and you don't even show a little blip."

He gave her a pitying smile and whispered back, "Sorry sweets. That's my boyfriend over there."

"But, I'm trying to" she blushed, "… well, make that guy over there jealous. Can't you at least help me with that?"

Lizzie waited as he slowly turned and checked out Payton and whistled softly before saying, "Yeah, I can see why. Mmm-mmm, I'd like to get me a piece of that."

Lizzie forced his head back around to focus in on her. "Nope, sorry, he's definitely not gay, and besides, I had him first. Now, can you help me or not?"

"For that? Honey, I'll help *anyone* if it means getting a chance at that man." Abruptly, he pushed her back so she was against the wall and braced a hand on either side of her head. He leaned into her so his hips were touching hers and began to nuzzle her neck. For a gay man he was definitely doing one heck of a job putting the make-out moves on a woman. She was just starting to enjoy the way he was kissing her when he pulled back and smiled.

"Well, my dear, either it's my lucky night or you were really enjoying yourself."

"Don't kid yourself, it's called acting." She pushed past him then turned back. "Thanks, by the way. That should help a bunch."

She worked her way through the thickening crowd in the pub to where Grace sat. She mustered up all the energy she had just to eek out what she hoped would have been a bigger yawn, praying that Payton would think she was bored to tears with his cat and mouse games.

"Well, it's been fun and all, Grace, but I think I'm going to call it a day."

"Oh? You're leaving so soon? I thought we'd do tequila shooters next and have a round of pool, although, I must say, you weren't doing so bad yourself over at those pool tables a few minutes ago." Grace ribbed Lizzie and gave her a wink before leaning in and saying just loud enough for the two of them to hear, "but was it just me or did he act a little gay?"

Lizzie's face contorted into a spasm of unspoken threats. "Shh! Are you *insane*? Speak any louder and Payton will hear you! He was already playing kissy-face with a rebounding Lou Ann, so I don't want him to know I was just trying to make him jealous."

"So you picked a gay man to make out with? I mean, I'm not one to question his sexuality or anything, but do you really think Payton would go for someone like that?"

Lizzie felt like smacking her head. "No, no, no. You're misunderstanding. I didn't know he was straight, I thought he was gay- I mean… strike that and reverse it." She closed her eyes and took a deep breath. "Look, stay if you want to, but I've had all the fun and games I can stand for one night. I'm going home to get some sleep."

Grace patted her friend on the shoulder. "Everything's going to be okay, Lizzie. Trust me." She opened Lizzie's hand and dropped her set of keys into her palm. "Here, take my car. I'm pretty sure I can find a ride home."

*Chapter Thirty-one*

Lizzie lay in bed staring at the blades of the ceiling fan whirling around in a lazy whoosh-whoosh. Lizzie had been trying to fall asleep for two hours, but despite how sleep deprived she'd been lately, she wasn't finding much success. Memories seemed her best choice for companionship these days since they were the only things that refused to leave her alone. She closed her eyes and tried to focus in on all the little details of the latest bombardment: her memories from college.

She could hear the roar of the crowd, feel it vibrating the concrete beneath her feet, as she climbed the stairs of Sanford Stadium to her seat in the student section. The game was nearly over, and she watched with a sense of exhilaration as red and black jersey's slammed ruthlessly into orange and blue.

In the years since that tragic night in high school she still hadn't been able to forget his last words: *I never want to see your face again, Lizzie.* It had taken her the first two quarters of the game just to convince herself he would never know if she showed up to the game with that many thousands of people sitting in the stands. Then it had taken another quarter just to make her body calm enough to walk across the campus and through the gates. Lizzie was glad that everyone else was so worked up over the game that they were standing to watch- she didn't think she could make herself sit if she tried.

Number thirty-four. In the four years she had been here at UGA not until today had she dared to watch a single play from its history making football team, and yet she knew his number. She would hear that number as she walked through the halls Monday morning, hear it at fraternity parties as guy's discussed their theories on his playing, and knew from too many painful memories just how well those muscles underneath that jersey could bunch and ripple and work.

Lizzie watched as number thirty-four faded back, looked for the opening, and like he was so famed for doing, sent the ball whizzing through the air at the last second to slam into the receiver's waiting arms in the end-zone, just as the score board signaled the end of the game. The crowd went wild. Lizzie nibbled on the corner of her lower lip and enjoyed being lost in the celebration. She realized then how much she had missed this excitement, and for a moment she wished she had been able to say *screw you* to Payton and get on with enjoying her life- including her love of watching football.

Apparently that wasn't something she had been able to do, however. It was simply too heart-wrenchingly painful to watch his long, lean body out there on that field, or on the television in her apartment, or in any of a million other places that he or his name might pop up. So, in retaliation of her traitorous feelings she had cut herself off from a sport that she had come to love dearly.

Lizzie filed out of the stadium along with the eighty thousand other spectators and made her way back across campus to her apartment. It was a night game and it wouldn't be long before the fraternity parties would be swinging into high gear.

She heard Grace shut the door as she came in, and she purposely went to the bathroom and turned on the shower water to drown her out for a few more minutes. She didn't want to be bothered. She just wanted to be left alone with her thoughts. Thoughts of that stupid jerk Payton and all the ways he had destroyed her life.

*You're such a loser, Lizzie. I never want to see your face again.*

Amazing how words really did have the power to hurt. Well, she'd made sure he would never have to see her face again, that was for sure. She even went so far as to check the class rosters each semester before classes began so that even in her classes of hundreds of students she wouldn't mistakenly find herself in the same one as him.

Maybe it was the game and seeing good ole number thirty-four out there on the field that had reminded her of the past. Who was she kidding? She thought of him, of them, every day of her life. Lizzie shut off the water and ran her hand down her hair to slick out the excess water. She wrapped one of the apartment's threadbare white towels around her body and tried to block out Payton and all his cruel words.

She had been such a chicken that night, Lizzie thought as she used another towel to rub through her hair. She wasn't like Grace, and had never been one for quick comebacks. If she shot out a zinger it was merely out of God's good grace. It took her a week after Payton's breakup for her to finally think up exactly which route she should have told him to take on his way to hell. She could still recall the exact words- maybe that was because she'd written them in her diary and still reviewed them quite frequently. Unfortunately, she had never been given her chance to use them.

Grace knocked on her bedroom door an hour later. "You ready to go in there?"

Lizzie opened the door in what she hoped looked like a dress that could kill. She decided on definitely so when Grace gave a playful growl and waggled her eyebrows. "Damn, girl. If I was gay I sure wouldn't kick you out of bed tonight. Are you dressing for someone special tonight?"

Lizzie elbowed her. "Thanks. You certainly know how to flatter the ladies. And no, I just felt like wearing this dress I bought last week before it gets too cold to wear it."

Half an hour later the two entered one of the main houses on fraternity row and made it to the back of the house where all the kegs were lined up. A DJ was set up in one of the corners and the bass thrummed through the room, shaking the windows and vibrating the floor.

Lizzie took the beer that someone handed her and made her way out onto the screened porch where a group of probably fifty people were dancing close together. She had learned her freshmen year in college that there was safety in numbers, and she knew that she could lose herself there in that mass of writhing bodies and flowing alcohol better than she could lose herself anywhere else tonight. And she knew she needed to after the crazy emotions that had been rolling around inside of her since this afternoon.

A new song, something with a rap flare, started playing over the massive speakers hovering around the house, and Lizzie pushed her way deeper into the throng of dancers. Someone she didn't know sidled up next to her. She looked his way and smiled, letting him know it was fine with her if he wanted to dance with her. He placed his hands on her hips pushing her body into the rhythm of the beat, and she sipped some more of the beer before she let her body loosen up and start to enjoy the music.

In the world of fraternities and their parties, the guest list rules. Any woman that cared to show up at their doors was gladly invited to join the party, whereas only guys that belonged in that fraternity were allowed to enter. All guys except the select few that were universal in acceptance: the football players. In the same way that she had religiously checked class rosters, Lizzie had always selected fraternity parties carefully so as to avoid too many football players and the potential that Payton would be among them. She thought she had chosen carefully tonight, so she put her mind at ease and had let herself drink at least two or three beers during the course of the night.

Not the strongest of drinkers, she had begun to get a buzz after beer number one, and was well on her way to tipsy by beer number three. So lost in the ebb and flow of dancing and music, she didn't notice the group of players that had entered the party. And as always, at their center, was beloved number thirty-four.

She turned and saw him, standing tall and proud- the larger than life figure he had somehow always been- and suddenly all the anger, all the rage, and the pain that she managed to bottle away for all these years came spewing to the surface like a geyser.

Lizzie was fuming by the time she made it halfway across the party to where he was. Already he had a swarm of girls trying to wedge their way through the group of ball players around him, and he looked like he was enjoying every second of the spotlight.

"Hey, Payton, you looked so hot out there on the field today. Want to come home with me and I'll rub away your aches and pains?" Some tactless bimbo practically flung herself at him. She smiled smugly as the thought of the reaction he would have when she tapped him on the shoulder and then slugged him right in the gut. It was payback time and Payton wouldn't have anywhere to run in the midst of all those groping, fawning girls.

She almost tackled him, and probably would have succeeded if she hadn't tripped over a beer can someone had carelessly strewn on the floor. She looked up just in time to see that her grand entrance has just been ruined, and Payton was staring at her from across the room along with about half of the other people in the room. The embarrassment she suffered only fueled her anger. She pushed herself up and forced her legs to move her forward. She was too far into this to back out now. Her breathing was agitated by the time she reached him, and she promptly shoved a freshly manicured and rather pointed tip straight into the thick muscle over his heart through his golf shirt.

"You!" She glared at him as someone turned the music lower on the speakers. No one wanted to miss what the drunken party girl was saying to UGA's star. "I thought I told you I never wanted to see your face again."

The smile that had formed on his face as she walked across the room to him now faded and he looked at her dumbly. She had had this fight brewing in her head for quite some time and now was the perfect time to let it fly.

"What's wrong, QB? Too busy thinking up new bets to talk?" The crowd looked on with baited breath.

He reached out and took hold of her arm, bruising her a little with his force. His jaw muscles strained against his cheeks as he clenched and released them. "Lizzie-"

"Don't touch me!" She shouted as she jerked away from him. He tucked his hands into the pockets of his khaki slacks to prevent himself from doing so again.

"Let's go outside so we can talk in private, okay?" He smiled at her but she knew he didn't mean it. The dimple wasn't there on his cheek and it always was when he was sincere.

"Whatever you have to say can be said right here."

"Fine."

He crossed his arms over his chest in a protective measure, and just like they'd been programmed to do after so many practices with him on the field, all the players behind him did the same. His hit squad behind him, and the multitude of interested onlookers began to unnerve her a touch, but she hadn't been the biggest loser in her school growing up and not learn anything from it. She wasn't backing down without putting up a fight.

"Well, go on, Lizzie. You started this so you must have something to say." She thought she saw a hint of pity, or maybe it was disappointment, flashing in his eyes. Who the hell was he to judge her, she wanted to know? In her drunken stupor she overlooked his pleading look asking her stop and be reasonable.

The crowd around them had grown completely silent, but she didn't even notice. She was focused on his face and the inner turmoil she was reliving at that moment. She watched his face fall when she said, "You are nothing but an arrogant, self-centered, self-pleasing *jerk*, Payton Cartwright."

He recovered in an instant. "Aww, now Liz, I don't think you really mean that."

"Yes, I do, you, you prick. You're nothing, do you hear me? Nothing! I can't believe I ever thought I loved you!" Tears started to trickle, hot and heavy, down her cheeks. His eyes held that same sad look again, and she wanted nothing more than to swipe it off his face.

"Liz," he whispered at her, leaning in to her just a fraction then quickly backing away as she swatted out at him.

"Don't you dare come any closer to me."

"But you're embarrassing yourself." He managed to take hold of her arm and began to steer her out the back door of the party, but the people blocking the door found no good incentive to allow the current life of the party to pass.

"No, Payton. *You're* the only one who ever embarrassed me. I can't believe I thought you might love me, too." She laughed, a wicked gurgle at the back of her throat. "It wasn't love you felt for me. You just wanted to use me, *screw* me, for a stupid bet."

"That's enough, Lizzie." Payton's voice grew hard and stern. He pulled her up close to him, daring her to try and do anything to stop him. "You're drunk as a skunk, aren't you?"

"No."

"Don't lie to me. You've never done it before, why would you start now?" Suddenly she felt very much like she was being reprimanded by her father, and she hated that the one person in her life who had hurt her more than anyone else was doing it again. She hated him. Hated what he'd done to her. Hated that she had never been able to forgive him for it, and that even though she speculated somewhere deep inside her that he had made that story up she still couldn't look at a guy without wondering if he'd just do the same thing to her all over again.

Four years of torture boiled up inside her. Four years of not feeling worthy ate at her, turned her stomach to acid, and she knew that nothing, not even being embarrassed by a room full of fraternity guys and their drunken dates could stop her from telling Payton exactly how she felt.

"So what if I am lying to you, Payton? Nothing I ever did was good enough for you, Mr. God-to-be-worshipped-by-all. Why should it matter now what I do?"

She paused briefly just to catch her breath before finishing him off with one final parting blow. She was surprised, though, when the look in his eye changed, and he softly said, "That's not true, Liz. You were always good enough for me."

She stared at him, some of the steam suddenly out of her engine. She wanted to believe him so badly her heart ached. Just once she wanted to be able to hold on to something he said and feel like it meant something, but she knew better than to trust him now.

He was doing it again. He was just being nice to her out of pity- or worse, for exactly the reason he had said all along. On a bet. He was the star and he couldn't stand watching her steal his thunder. Well, she'd be damned before she'd let him get away with ruining her life even more than she had that day.

She glanced around the silent crowd and took the closest person's cup. She mustered up all the energy she had in her spent and weary body. From the very bottom of her badly bruised and battered heart she ground out her final, damning words.

"I hate you, Payton Cartwright. Until the day I die I will never forgive you for what you did to me. I hate you with every ounce of my will power." And as if by repeating his words back to her she could somehow lift the damage he had done she said, "I don't ever want to see your face again."

Lizzie turned on the bed and fluffed the down pillow into a better position, remembering the way Payton had jolted when she'd tossed the foamy remnants of that beer cup into his face. It had taken her so many years to forgive herself for that stupid night, but she wondered if Payton remembered it and if it still seemed to bother him as much as it did her.

On her next day off from the hospital Lizzie met up with Grace at the pharmacy for a milkshake. She sipped her shake through a straw like she was a kid again, and they watched the cars amble down Main Street from their spot at the counter. When she spotted a familiar figure walking down the strip she felt even more like a kid. She smacked Grace's leg and started chanting, "Oh my God, oh my God, oh my God!"

"Land sakes, Lizzie, what has gotten into you?"

Lizzie sucked in her breath and pointed. Across the street, dressed in an old, well worn pair of jeans and an ancient t-shirt, Payton laughed at something Lou Ann said. Lizzie narrowed her eyes at them and wished she could shoot laser beams at him through her eyes. At Moe's the other night she had just thought he was fooling around trying to get her riled up with jealousy. In the past few days, though, she'd seen or heard rumor of Payton and Lou Ann getting a little too buddy-buddy for her comfort. She was starting to get worried that this wasn't just some strategic tactical play that the coach was pulling out of his playbook. Maybe he really was interested in Lou Ann, but she hadn't the foggiest reason why.

"Stare any harder at those two and you'll give yourself a headache."

Lizzie rubbed her thumb down the bridge of her nose. "I think I've already got one." She tried to sip some more of her shake but her stomach was suddenly too queasy to handle it. She glanced back out the window. "What's his deal with her anyway? Doesn't he know she's just rebounding?"

Grace slurped up the remnants of her shake. "Maybe that's his deal."

Lizzie swiveled on her seat so she faced Grace. "What, you think he's purposely using her for something?" She thought about it while Grace shrugged. "Huh, maybe you're right. Seriously, though, if it's sex he's after I know of at least ten women between here and Clarkston that have been making him casseroles for months just to get a peek at his boxers."

Grace crinkled up her nose. "Boxers? Really? I'd have taken him for a briefs kind of guy." She shook her head to remove the image. "Anyway, I'm sure the list far exceeds ten. Twenty, easy."

"Yeah, well, if you're counting me, you can just take my name right off."

Grace watched Payton out the window and stifled a smile. "I wouldn't dream of putting you anywhere near that list, Bean."

"Good." She stirred the clumps in her shake with her straw and worked on her lower lip with her teeth while she thought. "So what are you saying," she added after a brief pause, "you don't think I want to shag him or you don't think he's interested in shagging me?"

"Does it matter?" Grace knew she had her cornered.

"No." She glanced out the window for the twentieth time and cringed when she saw Lou Ann stare up into that pair of eyes that should have been watching her. "Yes."

"If it helps I don't think there's much question about whether he wants to shag you or not," Grace added in a noncommittal kind of way.

"Thanks, Grace. You sure do know how to be straight to the point when a girl needs it. Seriously, is he interested?"

"I'm not answering that. If you really want to know you'll have to do the asking yourself."

Lizzie debated the pros and cons of asking him all afternoon, and was still mulling it over as she walked up the stadium stairs for the high school football game that next Friday night. She spotted the gang seated a half dozen rows above the student section and waved back as the group spotted her.

She had purposely arrived after half time just so she wouldn't have to listen to Lou Ann ramble on and on about how fantastic her date with Payton had been last night. Somehow her nemesis had managed to finagle a way into the mix of their friends when she'd shown back up in town, and the gossip mill was only too happy to spread word that she and Payton had become a new item.

Lizzie felt confident she was developing an eye rolling twitch she had done it so much in the past few days.

From their spot in the crowd Lizzie watched as Payton directed his players through the plays of the game, noting that he looked good in his coach's jacket and headset. Although she called herself watching the game as she stood there sandwiched between Grace and Jade, she couldn't help but let her eyes drift to him occasionally just to see what he was doing. She didn't miss that she never once caught him looking her way up in the stands.

Lou Ann made a big show of pushing down the row and racing down the steps of the stadium when the buzzer sounded the end of the game. Lizzie looked on with disgust as the bimbo- as she liked to refer to Lou Ann these days- threw herself into Payton's arms for a grotesque display of PDA that she was certain had to be strictly against school policy for the coach.

"Oh, give me a break. Do you *see* what that woman is doing to him?" Lizzie glanced at Grace for back up then out to the scene on the field. Grace didn't turn out to be much help.

"Ah, well, yeah, but judging by the way he's reciprocating that kiss I don't think he minds half as much as you want him to."

Lizzie grunted. "I could care less if he minds or not. I mean, it's his prerogative. What do I care?"

She knew by the way her friend cocked her head back and propped a fisted hand on her hip that she wasn't very convincing. Grace patted her shoulder as she edged closer to the stairs leading down from the stadium. "Come on, Bean, let's get out of here. There's supposed to be a post-game party at Moe's to celebrate."

Lizzie bent to retie one of the shoelaces on her tennis shoes. "That's okay, Carrot. Go on without me. I'm really tired from all the work they've been giving me at the hospital. You know- changing bed pans and all as the freshman attending. I'm just going to sit here for a few more minutes then call it a night."

By the way she opened her mouth and paused Lizzie felt certain she must have something to say, but instead Grace said, "Okay, sweetie. Good night then."

"Good night."

Lizzie sank, bone weary, onto the bleachers and watched as the last few straggling fans gathered their belongings and headed out of Dixie's stadium. When she and the janitors sweeping the popcorn out of the stands were the only ones remaining, she leaned back so her head was resting on the cold metal bench behind her. The night sky was clear, but the field lights blocked out her view of the stars. The long sleeved Dixie Football t-shirt she'd purchased from the booster club wasn't cutting the bite in the crisp fall air so she pulled her blue jean jacket tighter around her to fight off the chill.

It was sad, she realized, that she didn't know anymore who or what it was that she wanted to be. A doctor- she knew that. Even before all the kids in school had taunted her about being the teacher's pet she'd known that she wanted to be a doctor. But this was the first time in weeks that she'd actually had time to sit still long enough to wonder *who* she wanted to be. Her father told her a long time ago that it wasn't just your profession that made you who you were. It was everything you did. Where you lived, what you did in your spare time, and most importantly who you did it with.

The night smelled like rain, and she felt certain when she woke tomorrow morning it would be pouring outside. She could still make out the scent of pizza and coke from the concession stand, and the always present scents from the memories in her past.

Those scents were home to her. This place, this stadium, was home to her. The town and all the oddly quirky people were home to her. Dixie Academy, the old Baptist church, the bank her father practically ran on his own. They were all home to her.

She knew then that who she really was involved this town, and she wondered what her life would be like if her father hadn't dragged her and her family kicking and screaming to this charming little place.

Lizzie closed her eyes, letting the sounds of the men pushing their big push brooms over the course concrete sooth her. She might not have all the questions about her life answered but at least she knew one thing for sure. Whoever it was that she was supposed to be, it revolved around this town.

From somewhere below her she could hear the sound of heavy, masculine steps coming nearer. For an instant she hoped it was Payton, but she knew it wasn't. It didn't have that distinctive all confidence pattern that was so distinctly him.

Lizzie turned her head and watched as an old, battered pair of hiking boots with the lips hidden under frayed blue jeans came closer. She followed the legs up until she was staring, upside down, at Colin looking down at her. His face looked funny from that position, and she grinned up at him when he playfully stuck his tongue out at her.

"Hey, Doc. What'cha doin' out here all alone? Don't you know the party's supposed to be out at Moe's?" He sat on the bench by her head and looked over at her as she shifted and moved to sit next to him.

"Yeah, I heard. I thought about going, but…" she glanced up at him, "well, to be honest, I didn't really feel up to watching those two going at it in the middle of the bar."

Colin propped his hand on his knee and cupped his chin in his palm. "I can see what you mean. The post-game show was about all that I could stomach myself." Lizzie smiled at the concern she saw in his eyes. She made a show of studying her hands.

"Can I ask you a question, Col?"

"Anything." Lizzie looked out over the empty football field and Colin followed her gaze.

"What does he see in her?"

At first she thought he wouldn't answer, but eventually he looked back at her with a little frown of concentration edging his lips. "You know, Lizzie, sometimes things aren't exactly what they seem to be."

"Jeez, you can say that again. I mean, you'd think Lou Ann was a washed up old house wife from the way she looks, but apparently she is one hot piece of ass under the sheets with the way Payton works her over."

Colin laughed and elbowed her. "That's funny, but not what I meant." He studied his hands before continuing. "I watched him tonight during the game. He was the portrait of concentration out there on that field. I mean, I didn't see him look up here one time from about middle of the third quarter on."

Lizzie grunted. "I noticed."

"But I bet you didn't notice the other thing I did."

"Oh, yeah, what's that?"

"I must have counted at least twenty-three times that he looked up to where we were standing from five minutes before the game started until just before you walked past him on your way up into the stands." Colin stood and squeezed her reassuringly on the shoulder before he headed back down the row. "And Lizzie…" He waited until she looked up at him again. "I think it would be an insult to your intelligence if I have to spell out to you what that means."

Lizzie watched him walk down the stadium stairs. He didn't turn back around but she heard him call back, "You should think about coming to that party, Lizzie. You're not getting any younger, you know."

She waved him goodnight. "Thanks, Coli-pooh. I'll think about it."

## *Chapter Thirty-two*

More than anything, Lizzie desperately wished she was sinking three inches deep into her new pillow-top mattress right about now. That wasn't the case, however. She'd pulled a U-ey on her way through town and was almost in sight of Moe's Pub before she fully grasped what she was doing.

Hiding from Payton might be the most comfortable plan at the moment, but in the long run she'd only end up kicking herself for it. Lizzie thought about what Grace would do in a situation like this, and that's when she'd realized what she needed to do.

It was time for a good ole fashioned come to Jesus meeting with the coach.

A saucy little flame red number would have been the perfect attire for this event, but she settled for her low rise blue jeans, cowboy boots, and the booster club shirt she'd worn to the game. As she pushed open the bar door, a mental image flashed in her head of her karate kicking it open instead. A woman on a mission, she wasted no time in small talk. Rather, she skimmed the swarm of Dixie Devils celebrators until she found her mark.

He was in one of the back corner booths laughing at something Bud said while he poured another frosty mug full of beer for himself and Colin. Oddly enough, Lou Ann was nowhere to be seen. He looked up as she approached them, and his smile fell from his face.

"Evenin' boys," Lizzie said to the table in general. Then with a flick of her eyes she settled in on Payton and didn't let up. "I believe you and I have a few things to discuss."

"Is that right?" He tried his best at a slow, seductive perusal of her body, but Lizzie wasn't in the mood to take the bait.

She jerked her thumb over her shoulder. "Move it, coach."

A local band that was currently playing a cover tune of Rascal Flatts' blared over the speakers so loudly that Lizzie wondered if she'd be able to talk over the noise. The only way that was going to happen was if she drug Payton out of the bar, or if she danced close enough to him that she could yell into his ear. A little devil tapped her on the shoulder- it was time for a little dirty dancing.

She edged in close enough to him that she could feel his breath warm the skin of her neck. "Funny, I don't see Lou Ann anywhere."

It was barely enough to be noticeable, but Lizzie felt him tense all the same. "She's, uh, sick. She had to go home right after the game."

"She looked fine to me earlier." Payton looked sort of funny.

"It's one of those fast-acting bugs. Comes on real quick."

"Hmm, that's terrible. You might need to be careful since you're well, you know, and all with her. I could check you over if you need me to." She raised a hand. "Strictly professional, of course. I am an official doctor now."

Payton seemed to be recovering from his tenseness. "That's okay, I'm sure I'll be fine. I'm tough."

"Well, if you change your mind."

"You'll be the first to know." His eyes, slightly darkened by the dim lighting, caught hold of hers and held. That quick flash of electricity followed by a slow curl of heat crawled through her like it had always done when they were younger. For an instant she wanted to lock onto him right there in the middle of the dance floor and do to him what she'd been watching Lou Ann do for days now. She held his gaze a second longer before turning from him and heading to the bar.

"Better be careful, coach. Lou Ann has a real mean streak when she thinks things aren't going her way."

He followed her to the bar and signaled for Moe to put her drink on his tab. "I wouldn't worry too much about her. I think I can take care of my own."

She waved him off. "That whole tough thing again?"

"Something like that." He sipped from a long neck bottle. "I thought you said we had some things to discuss."

She sipped her drink trying to stall for another few seconds. "Doesn't it bother you that you wrote me that gut-wrenching letter and now you're... *whatever* with her?" She tried her best to hide the spurt of jealousy that kept wanting to rear its ugly head, but Payton's mouth twitched at the corner and she suspected he'd seen the ugly monster before she'd beaten it back down again.

"Should it?" He brushed his arm against hers as he picked at the bowl of peanuts in front of them.

"No, not at all." Lizzie reminded herself that she'd come knowing she was going to have to play a little hardball. So here she went. She reached out and laid a cool hand on his cheek, turning his head so he looked straight into her eyes.

"It's not working."

He swallowed and she knew then that she had him. "What's not?"

"This thing you're doing. You know, the thing where you conveniently show up all over town with Lou Ann just when I *happen* to be at the same place."

He tried his best to change the subject by slowly looking her over with that bone melting stare he had mastered. "Have I told you lately that you look really good without that ridiculous engagement ring that Josh gave you?"

"No, you haven't, but thanks. And, Payton? It's still not working. I think I've grown up enough now, and I might just be ready to talk. So when you get tired of playing your cat and mouse games…you know where to find me."

She stood from the bar, but leaned in and whispered into his ear before she left, "By the way, those white tulips on my doorstep were a pretty nice touch. Thanks."


Lizzie stood in the dark by her bedside window staring out into the night. She'd let her hair down from the ponytail she'd worn to the game, and brushed it out so it hung in long, silky waves down past her shoulders. For Christmas her sister had given her a warm pair of flannel pajama pants that she wore religiously. Tonight she had coupled them with an old, old t-shirt that she only permitted herself to wear on occasion. It was one of Payton's light grey high school practice shirts with a big red devil standing in the middle. The same one he'd been wearing the first time they had made love.

When she heard the knock sound on her front door she assumed it was Grace stopping by to talk. Lizzie whipped open the door and nearly dropped dead when she found Payton standing on the other side rather than Grace.

Lizzie's eyes grew about five sizes too big for her head, but she thought she did a remarkably good job of hiding any other signs of surprise at his presence. She leaned against the door jamb, an obvious sign that she wished he would bugger off. Lizzie's heart was pounding in her ears as he stood not more than a foot from her, slowly assaulting her body with his eyes. As he made his way from her painted red toenails, past her pants and on to her shirt she could feel her face flame with embarrassment. For all he knew she had burned that shirt the night he'd ripped out her heart. It was humiliating that she not only still possessed it, but that she still wore it.

He didn't seem concerned about the shirt, though. He was studying her still, and then she realized he'd noticed she wasn't wearing a bra. It had been more than eleven years since he had touched her there, but her traitor body took her flying back to those aching moments, and her nipples beaded under his sight. Quickly she folded her arms over the shirt, but it was too late to hide the evidence of her arousal.

She compensated by acting as snotty as possible. "It's late, Payton. What do you want?"

"I changed my mind. You might need to check me over after all."

"Feeling bad already? Maybe that should be your punishment for such improper PDA in front of all those impressionable football players."

He grunted. "Impressionable, my ass. They could probably give me pointers more than I could them."

She clucked her tongue. "Ah, the curse of the aged." She stepped aside. "Well, come on in. Let me go get my stuff."

Lizzie returned a few minutes later with a hefty black medical bag in her hand and a white jacket over his old t-shirt. Her father had given her the black bag as a present when she graduated, and she thought it was a nice touch, a nod to the practitioner's of the past. She led him to the kitchen and put the bag on top of the table.

"Want something to drink? This could take a little while. Some orange juice would probably do you good anyway."

"Sure, I guess."

She poured them both a glass and set his in front of him before she began to rifle through the contents of the bag. "Normally I wouldn't do house calls, so you're lucky I'm feeling particularly benevolent tonight."

"I understand. Thanks for letting me put you out like this." He stared straight ahead as she looked at his eyes through the scope. She switched tips to the instrument and studied the inside of his ears.

"So far so good, now I just need to check your throat. Open wide and say, 'Ahhh'." He did as she asked. Lizzie frowned.

"What? Is something wrong?"

"No, not particularly. It's just that... well, have you always had that giant red bump on the back of your throat?"

Payton looked a little queasy. "I don't know. I don't normally look back there."

"What about those lymph glands, are they always that big?"

"Beats me."

"Have you always had a heart murmur?"

"I-I guess." He ran his finger around the rim of his shirt. She studied him quietly for a moment. "Hmmm, are you feeling alright? You look a little flushed. I think you might have a fever."

He grinned. "I'm pretty sure that I don't have a fever."

"Hmm." Lizzie walked out of the room scratching her head, mumbling something about being right back.

Payton wondered what she was up to. He felt perfectly fine. He knew as well as she did that he'd just made up that story so he could get inside her house. It would be just like her to come up with some hair brained story that he was dying of some stupid illness like purple spotted horseshoe fever just to pay him back for all the games he'd played on her lately.

She returned a minute later carrying a medical dictionary. "What are you looking up?" He asked, studying her critically.

"Give me a minute. I'm working on something here." She looked him over again, tapped his knee to test his reflexes, took his temperature, and finished off by listening to his heart and lungs.

He grinned. "So, I check out okay, then?" Lizzie sipped her orange juice, sat down, giving him a grave look.

"I'm not so sure, Payton. I thought you were joking back there at the bar, but I think you really might be sick."

"What? I'm not sick. I haven't been sick in eight years. I'm solid as a rock."

"You know what they say: the stronger they are the harder they fall. I mean, really, your symptoms don't look so good at all." She looked grave. "We might need to get you to the hospital for further tests." Suddenly he felt hot and cold at the same time, and now that she mentioned it, he had felt a little funny all day long.

"What! No, absolutely not."

"Let me ask you this." She leaned in and whispered across the table. "You failed the VonWilliker's response test. Did you realize that?"

"I haven't even ever *heard* of that test before. How would I know if I failed it?"

"Well, unfortunately for you, it's a big problem if you fail it. It means your nervous system is in critical range of failing. We really don't have much time. Go ahead and climb in my car, and I'll call the hospital and tell them we're coming in."

He studied her across the table and thought about calling her a big fat liar, but then he remembered she was the one with the medical degree and he didn't even know what the VonWilliker's reponse test was, much more what it meant if he failed it, so he finally relented. "Oh- Okay, Liz. I'll wait for you in the car."

"Good. I'll be right out." She waited until he reached the front door before saying, "Oh, and Payton? Make sure you cover your face with this blanket. It's only a matter of minutes before even the slightest amount of light will burn your retinas and blind you for life." She chucked the blanket at him and he heard something suspiciously similar to a giggle as he closed the front door behind him.

There were at least ten nurses waiting for them when Lizzie screeched to a halt in front of the emergency room doors at Clarkston Medical Center. Payton wouldn't have known that except that on their journey there he'd found a small hole in the blanket Lizzie had commanded he put over his head as a precaution to preserving his eyesight. Since he was a stubborn man he decided against the doctor's orders and looked through his peephole the entire way down the main corridor of the hospital.

Funny, he didn't seem to notice any signs of imminent blindness forming.

Funnier still was that all the nurses seemed to be covering their mouths with their hands and doubling over in some sort of hysterical spasm, all the while pointing at him.

"What's going on out there? I can't see anything."

After clearing her throat, Lizzie responded in a noticeably peculiar voice. "Ah, yes, we're almost to the isolation room where we'll need to keep you while we run a few extra tests just to confirm if my diagnosis is correct."

"Isolation room?" Payton sounded rather alarmed. "You think it's that bad then?"

"Oh, yes. If it's what I think you have then this is quite serious, indeed." She had that smug doctor's voice perfected by now, and Payton was almost certain she was enjoying a rather large joke at his expense.

Since he'd figured that out about thirty minutes too late, he needed to find a way to level the playing field. Underneath the blanket he smiled.

"So then, doc, exactly what is it that you think I have?"

A pause. "Well, I'm not one hundred percent certain, yet, so I'm going to wait until I know for sure to tell you."

He set his voice in to that good ole boy twang he reserved for times when he wanted to get the upper hand back. It was a voice that would have made Bo and Luke Duke proud. "Gee, Lizzie, I sure am glad that I decided to come on over and have you check me out." He didn't want to play it up too much, considering they both knew he wasn't really sick, but he gave the tiniest cough and slowed his pace a little. "I'm starting to feel a bit weak. Say, you never told me, but what do you think my chances are for recovery?"

"Not good, Payton. Not good." That's exactly what he'd been hoping for. "Here you go, coach. We've reached the isolation room. Now reach out your hand nice and slow and you'll feel the edge of the bed. Take a seat and I'll be back to run a few tests in a minute." Through his peephole he saw that instead of a private isolation room they'd put him smack dab in the middle of one of the back hallways of the hospital. A perfect place to pull a prank with plenty of viewing room for all of the staff to watch.

Apparently it was a slow night for critical injuries. Payton smiled underneath his blanket. This might work out better for him than he could have hoped.

He grabbed her hand before she walked off. "Lizzie?"

Her pulse jumped through the delicate skin at her wrist. "Yes?"

"Don't be gone too long." He lowered his voice to a whisper. "Don't tell anyone, but I'm getting a little bit scared and I need you here with me."

Her pulsed hammered a little faster. "Sure, Payton. I'll be right back."

All the nurses stifled a giggle as they walked away with her and left him alone on a gurney with a wool blanket over his head in the middle of the hallway. They didn't know it, but he was laughing at them just as hard as they were laughing at him.

A solid fifteen minutes later, Lizzie returned with her entourage that had grown by at least five curious nurses. He watched her hush them as they approached him.

"I'm back Payton."

"Okay, good. I was starting to get a little nervous."

"Don't worry, I'm sure that we'll solve this little problem right away. Now, Nurse Ford and I want to go over your list of symptoms one more time before we run these tests just to make sure we're on the right track. It's just the two of us, and we're in a strictly professional setting, so you can feel comfortable to answer as honestly as possible."

"It's just you and Nurse Ford?"

"Uh-huh. Now, Payton, would you mind listing all the symptoms you've noticed so far."

"Well, there was that red spot you said you saw on my throat, and the swollen lymph glands, and that failed Von-"

"VonWilliker's Response Test."

"Yeah, that. And I've been feeling sort of weak the past few days, and a little tired. Oh, and that heart-"

"Mumur. I've got that on the list. Are there any other symptoms because if not we really should get to those tests now."

He scratched at his head through the blanket. "None that I can recall."

"Okay. Lie back on the bed and we'll get started. Now this is a fairly large needle and we need to puncture your knee joint to gather some synovial fluid for this test. Just lie still. If you need to scream it's all right, because remember it's just Nurse Ford and I in here."

He held very still and watched through the blanket. "This might feel funny, it's a newly designed needle that doesn't cause any pain. Lucky for you I suppose." He noticed that she was holding up some sort of pen. Probably to write some inappropriate comment on his knee, he decided.

"Oh, wait," he yelped just before she touched it to his leg. "I just remembered one other symptom that I should probably mention to you."

"What's that?"

"I need to sit up to tell you."

A pause. "Alright, fine."

"Are you sure we're alone?"

"Yes, Payton. Trust me. Now what is it?"

"Well, it's just that… how do I say this? When we were doing that role play thing the other night and you were dressed as that Italian sex slave and I was the King of the Roman Empire, I felt this-"

He was smiling from ear to ear, his brilliant green eyes full of mischief, when she whipped the blanket off his head. Her scowl only served to make him roll on the gurney laughing. The nurses behind her started laughing as well.

"You knew! You sneaky bastard. You knew all along and were just playing me!"

He held up his hands to fend off her attempts to smack him. "Of course I knew." When he'd had enough he simply reached out and snagged her wrists, holding them together with ease. "I may be a jock but I'm not a dumb one. How long did you think it would take me to figure it out?"

"I don't know," she wailed. "Long enough for me to pay you back for making it look like you were hooking up with Lou Ann to try and make me jealous!"

He grunted. "That obviously backfired."

"Obviously." She noticed that all the nurses were still lurking behind her catching there fill of the scene. "Okay, okay, show's over. Everybody get back to your duties." They all groaned and moved away.

## *Chapter Thirty-three*

The trail leading down to Granny's pond had recently been freshened up, and all the overgrowth that blocked the way cut back to reveal a cozy little dirt path. Lizzie took her time getting down to the water's edge since she didn't have any urgent reason to be there or anyone special to meet. The sun, warm and bright, was setting behind the mixed forest of pines and hardwoods on the opposite side of the lake, and Lizzie enjoyed its play of colors that danced across the rippling surface of the pond.

Not only had the path been cut back, but it seemed someone had also put in a short little dock that jutted about ten feet out into the water, ending in a widened area that was perfect for a small, rounded picnic table. Lizzie took off her shoes at the edge of the dock then made her way to where the water lapped eagerly at the posts on the other end. She let her lower legs dangle over the side and her toes dabble in the water as she watched the evening stars begin to take over the sky.

It had been a little over a week since her little adventure with Payton and she hadn't seen him a single time since then. She wasn't sure if she was relieved or disappointed, but she suspected that if she had to choose she would side on disappointed. An image of Payton sitting on that gurney in the middle of the hospital hallway flashed in her mind, and a spurt of laughter gurgled in her throat.

She'd tried her hardest to pout the whole way home from the hospital, but Payton was having too much fun, at her expense no less, for her to be upset with him for too long. And to be honest, she was so relieved that she'd figured out that he and Lou Ann were just a silly hoax that she was giddy with excitement more than anything else.

Lizzie burrowed down further into the thick sweatshirt she'd worn down to the pond and tried to force her brain to think. For so long after the wedding she had allowed her mind to become a blank screen with nothing coming in or going out except what she needed to recall to do her job. She hadn't wanted to face the prospect of starting over and making a new life for herself. And she especially hadn't wanted to consider that her new life might consist of just her, and possibly a little pooch like Skipper Jr.

For all the wooing and pleading Payton had done, Lizzie had been scared to death that if she let him get too close again he'd simply end up ruining her life a second time around. Then she'd seen him with Lou Ann and something inside of her had snapped.

As long as he was alone that was fine, but the minute he was with her all these crazy images of the way things should be would pop into Lizzie's head. She and Payton walking down Main Street holding hands as they made their way to Gilchrist's for a milkshake. Payton mowing the grass on a Saturday afternoon while she sat on their big wooden porch swing rocking a little dark haired, green eyed baby. She and Payton making love together, growing old together, watching their grandchildren grow up together.

And that's when she'd known that she couldn't let her stupid mind force herself to be afraid of doing the thing that could quite possibly hurt her the most: loving him.

She was going to wait another night, maybe two, just to let this new reality sink in, and then if he didn't make a move, she would. Lizzie was nervous, and excited all at the same time, and a million excuses popped into her head why she shouldn't do this. But just as quickly she batted them all away, and she forced herself to think up the way she would make her first move. She wondered if guys had to think about their first moves as much as she was for Payton.

A rustling in the bushes snapped her back to her surroundings at the lake. Not long after she heard footsteps on the freshly lain boards of the dock and she tilted her head further back so she was looking upside down at a pair of legs making their way toward her. Payton's legs.

"Were your ears burning?" She asked as she watched him, long and lean and more gorgeous in the last remnants of the setting sun than she could ever recall him being before.

"No. Were yours?"

"Now that you mention it, yes." She winked at him.

"What reason did my ears have for burning?" He sat next to her and rolled up the legs of his jeans before dangling his legs over. "Yow, this water is cold."

"You'll get used to it in a minute. That or your toes'll go numb. Don't worry, though, I'll make sure you get excellent medical attention."

Payton grunted. "Yeah, I bet." He fell silent, and Lizzie could see him watching the sky through her peripheral vision.

"It's pretty. The night, I mean." She paused for a beat. "Did you come out here to watch the stars?"

"No." He turned to study her, then. "I had a feeling you would be out here."

When he reached out his hand she let him take hers and the pair fell between them so it rested on the rough wood of the dock. She didn't know how long they stayed that way, maybe ten or fifteen minutes, but she liked it: calm, peaceful, serene. Not much later, Payton sat up and pushed his pant legs down so he could stand.

"Come with me, Lizzie. There someplace I want to show you."

"And that concludes the tour of my place." He stopped in the big, newly renovated kitchen on the side of the house.

"I can't believe this used to be the old Weatherby farm," she said in amazement. She took the beer Payton handed her and followed him when he pushed open the screen door that led to the front porch.

"I know. Mr. Weatherby's son passed on not too long after I moved back home and, well, I just had to have it."

"I can see why." She sat in one of the rockers and watched him as Payton leaned against the same thick, white column as he had when she'd been there cleaning up toilet paper. He turned to face her, and that old, familiar spark that somehow had always been between them jolted her.

"Can you?" He asked, his eyes studying her intently.

Lizzie swallowed. Somehow this wasn't a plain and simple question, she could tell. She was fairly certain the answer had something to do with the night they'd shared on that campout, but she was still too afraid of this new thing that was between them for her to jump right out and say it. "I-I think so," She said hesitantly.

When he closed the space between them and stopped in front of her, Lizzie wasn't sure if she should be afraid or excited. She knew he would never physically harm her, but still, old wounds ran deep. Payton kneeling in front of her on two bended knees was the last thing she expected. He took her hands and wrapped them between his broad, roughened palms like a sandwich, and when he spoke his voice was just as rough, and raw with emotion.

"I'm tired, so tired, of playing this game, Liz. My heart, my body, my mind: they're all ready to rest easy knowing you're in my life again. I'm not going to ask you now, because I can see in your eyes that you're not ready, yet. But I don't know how much longer I can wait." He took a deep breath. "At night, when I wake up for the twentieth time and reach out through that emptiness, I'm reaching for you. I miss you. I want you. I need you."

He held his body stiff allowing the only emotion to shine from his eyes, the window to his emotions she had always been able to see the most clearly. Her body was shivering, more from the way his words had affected her body, but Payton's forehead crinkled and he gathered her up.

"You're cold, aren't you?" Still speechless, she nodded. "Come on, let's get you inside and warmed up." She held on when he stood and pulled her up in his arms, carrying her into the house and on to the den.

The den had been added to the house after Payton moved in, and Lizzie liked the way he had chosen to use ancient logs from an old log cabin for the walls. On the far side of the den there was an old stacked stone fireplace that Payton had newly renovated and placed gas logs inside. He flicked on the flames of the fire with the remote control as he put Lizzie down on one of the two dark chocolate leather sofas and disappeared into the kitchen. On top of the old wood flooring an imitation bear rug sat in the center of the room between the sofas and the fireplace.

Payton returned a few minutes later with two mugs in his hand. "Here." He handed her one. "It's hot chocolate to warm you up."

"Mmm, this is nice," she said, sipping the cocoa as she finished surveying the room.

"The hot chocolate or the room?"

"Both."

"Yeah, this is my favorite room in the house. It reminds me of an old pioneer's house."

"So what do you do for fun around here?" She asked, changing the subject.

"You're looking at it. When I'm not coaching football or wrestling with the PTA ladies I'm usually here working on the house."

"So you don't have a string of ladies over here to entertain on your nights off?" She couldn't believe that she'd actually asked that question. She'd only meant to think it, but since it was out she waited for him to answer.

"What, you mean besides you and Lou Ann?"

"Not funny."

And then his look suddenly became very not funny. "Do you know what I dreamed last night?"

She had a feeling she wasn't going to like this. "No."

"It's the same thing I've been dreaming since the night I kissed you at that barn party. I finally manage to get you out on a date, and we come home late that night all happy and satisfied from our dinner out. You look at me across this room like you still think I'm the greatest man on earth. That's when I slowly undress you and lay you down on the bear rug and make love to you all night long."

Her eyes had gone all big and wide on him, and from her expression he knew that while it wasn't the exact same dream, she'd definitely been letting some hanky panky between the two of them bounce around in her head as well. He lent her a small, reassuring smile and reached out a tentative hand to touch her lightly on the arm.

"I miss you so much, Lizzie. I made a terrible mistake in the past, and I want to make it up to you." Slowly, he leaned in and lightly caressed her lips. He watched her eyes flutter shut and felt her shudder.

"And you think sex will do that?" She asked as he paused to watch her.

His voice was husky and deeper than usual. "No. No, I don't think sex will make it up to you." Then he smiled that same bone melting smile he used on all the girls in high school. "But I was hoping that maybe making love to you would help you see how much I need you."

Lizzie groaned, and despite that she tried her hardest not to cave in, she felt herself bending under that ruthless smile. "You sound more like a horny teenager trying to get some action."

"Maybe I've just been around the football players too long."

"Did they teach you anything useful?" She put a strategically placed hand over her mouth when he glowered at her.

"Are you suggesting that some of my skills are lacking?"

She pretended to buff her fingernails. "I'm not suggesting anything." She opened her mouth to say something else when she felt his body make contact with hers. In a flash she had been upended over his shoulder and then body slammed onto the bear rug in such a way that it didn't really hurt when she made contact. She blinked and suddenly he was over her, and she knew her time for playing had come to an abrupt end.

"Do you have any last words before I officially prove you oh so very wrong?"

She scoffed at him. "I don't think you have it in you, sir, to do something as bold as that." His eyes narrowed in on her, and in the next second he flipped her so she was lying face down on the rug.

He put a knee into her back without putting too much pressure and held her in place. "Hey, what are you doing!" She wiggled beneath him.

"Now, I've been putting up with a lot of you're smart talk here lately, but I think this just might put an end to it."

He placed one of his broad hands across her bottom and cupped her through her blue jeans. His hand was warm and firm and Lizzie felt a lick of heat curl through her system. "Just hang on, you're in for a mighty wild ride." And with that he gave her one sharp little smack on her bottom.

"Uh, Payton? I'm just letting you know that I don't go in for that whole kinky spanking thing." His smile said he didn't really care. He flipped her over onto her back and stared down at her.

"That was just a warning shot."

"Oh." She, of course, had something far more brilliant as a retort in mind, but just as she'd been gearing up to shout it out he'd done this delicious little trick with his fingers that made her brain derail. "I'm sorry, I lost my train of thought. What were you saying?"

His green eyes said it all. "Nothing. It wasn't important." His fingers drifted slowly along the edge of her shirt that had shifted up around her belly button. He did a little exploration of the rim of her blue jeans. Lizzie took a deep breath.

"What's the matter, Liz? You're not getting turned on, are you?"

"Who me? Uh-uh."

"Maybe I'll have to work a little harder then." He flicked the button on her pants open and slowly slid the zipper of her pants down so it conveniently made a little V over the delicate pink panties she'd worn. His hand slipped inside her shirt and made its way upwards to the front clasp of her bra. Lizzie let out a little squeak when one thick finger flipped it open and ever so gently flicked across a nipple. When he circled the opposite side and cautiously moved inwards towards the center, Lizzie killed him with a low moan of desperation.

Payton groaned and forced his fingers to retreat back to her belly button where he dabbled a little more, chuckling when Lizzie protested. "Sorry, sweetheart, but I seem to recall someone saying something about me needing some pointers."

"I think I could be convinced to change my mind." Payton ran a finger over the top of her lacy panties. "Yep, I think I could definitely be convinced."

"Take your shirt off Lizzie. And the bra, too, while you're at it." He leaned back on his knees and watched. "Fantastic. Now, the blue jeans need to go and I'll show you a few new tricks I've learned."

She stopped her strip show and eyes him cautiously. "If they were learned by a certain someone named Lou Ann, I'm not interested."

Payton shot her the same look right back and folded his arms across his now naked chest. "First of all, I didn't sleep with her, and even if I did, *I* certainly wouldn't be the one getting the pointers."

Lizzie kissed the tip of his nose. "Okay, coach. Take it easy before you give yourself a stroke."

Lizzie finished stripping off her jeans then leaned back on her elbows with her feet warming in front of the fire. The golden glow from the flames highlighted her breasts and the flat plains of her belly. She cocked her head up at him. "I'm all ready, stud muffin. Let's see the master at work." She put a finger over his lips when he bent to kiss her. "First, though, return the favor and let's see you strip."

"As you wish." His slow show in front of her made Lizzie want to jump up and drag him down to her so he could send her up in flames.

As if reading her mind he threw the last piece of clothing behind him and came over her, his strong arms holding him suspended. "This," he said, his voice husky, "this is exactly what I've been dreaming about." He drove into her, purposefully and possessively. And they both lost themselves in the feel and sensations that had been lost to them eleven years before.

A very, very long time later Lizzie curled up next time him, the bear rug soft underneath them. She stared up at the wood rafters above them. "Payton?" she asked, turning to him as she wrapped an arm over his body.

"Hmm?" He watched her with those emerald eyes and kissed her forehead.

"Do you realize that in all the times we've made love we *still* haven't done it on a bed?"

He paused as if checking his own records. "You know, I believe your right."

When he sprang to his feet and swept her into his arms, she let him. It wasn't everyday that a woman got carried by a gorgeous hunk like him, and she wasn't about to protest the very thing he did in all of her best dreams.

"I guess we're just going to have to resolve that little issue right this minute." And just like that he was carrying her up the stairs to his bedroom.

Over the next several weeks, Payton found excuses almost every single day to spend time with Lizzie. He needed her to help him pick out new designs for t-shirts for the booster club. He'd run out of groceries and wasn't exactly sure if he should try a new brand of orange juice or if he should stick with the same. His mother's birthday was coming up and he wanted Lizzie to pick out a present with him at the mall.

On the days he didn't seek her out, Lizzie found excuses to go find him. Her oil conveniently needed changing after Larry's Auto Shop had closed one evening. She wanted to start a new exercise program and needed him to create it for her. She wanted Skipper Junior to become a tracking dog and she thought he should learn how to track Payton's scent trail first.

As a result they wound up spending a little part of each day with each other, and Lizzie grew accustomed to seeing him and getting to know how he would react in different circumstances. Say for instance when she just happened to need to practice putting on plaster casts and Payton's was the only convenient arm she could find. He'd looked at her like she was insane, shook his head, then patiently sat and recited new football plays to her while she wrapped his arm.

And it just so happened that in all those evenings they spent together, Payton managed to thoroughly convince Lizzie that she was oh, so wrong about his method of lovemaking. Payton liked to point that out to her on a regular basis just so she knew that there wasn't a man out there that could satisfy her cravings better than him. Lizzie never bothered to tell him that she had already figured that out way before they'd even done it the first time.

Late in October she came home after a particularly nasty day at the hospital and found a clown's red costume nose in her mailbox along with a note.

*The fair's in town. I need to blow off some steam tomorrow night, and unless you want to be my target practice, meet me there. 8 o'clock, by the Ferris wheel.*

*-Payton*

She wondered about that note all night and through work the next day. Until now they'd both come to each other with excuses to spend time together so they hadn't ever officially been out on a date. But she didn't know how to define this event. She called Grace on her way home from the hospital.

"He's not offering to pick you up. It's not a date."

"But he asked me to meet him there."

"Sounds more like an ultimatum, if you ask me."

"Hmm, target practice doesn't sound like a very romantic alternative does it?"

"Come on, you've been saying yourself that if he doesn't get around to it soon then you're going to do it for him. Just pretend that it's a date and see where it goes from there."

Lizzie chewed on her already short fingernails. "I don't know, Grace. Last time I just blindly fell for him he broke my heart."

She could almost see Grace rolling her eyes at the other end of the line. "Please, Bean. I'd hardly call this time around blind love. Besides, that was eleven years ago, y'all are both bigger, better people now. If I didn't know you better I'd think you were just being chicken about this."

There was a pause on the line, and a deep sigh.

"What are you waiting for, Lizzie? You know he's the one for you. He loves you, I know that for a fact. And even if I didn't I'd still say the same thing: Sometimes you've got to love like you've never been hurt before and see where it takes you. Don't you think it's time you try?"

Lizzie let out a slow breath. "Maybe you're right, Gracie. Maybe you're right."

Grace smiled. "Of course I am. Now don't forget to call me tomorrow and give me all the sordid details. I'm living vicariously through you, you know."

"I know."

She might be going out there to give him her heart and hope he didn't smash it a second time, but she sure as heck wasn't going to let him see that she'd gone out of her way to do it. She dressed in her oldest pair of blue jeans, an old flannel button-up shirt, and a baseball cap with the Atlanta Falcons logo on it.  She showed up at 8:15 just to make a grand entrance, and possibly to show him she didn't dance to his tune all the time.

Just most of the time.

He was leaning against the make-shift barricade between the flow of traffic and the Ferris wheel, focusing on something in the distance when she rounded the corner from the ticket sales.  She drank him in, faded blue jeans, flannel shirt, and a baseball cap.  She laughed at the irony.  Here she'd gone out of her way to make him think she was trying to dodge him, and instead she'd shown up looking like his twin.

"You've got good taste in clothing, I see," she said as she stopped in front of him.

He turned to look at her, his lazy, summer green eyes taking her in with a slow, wonderful perusal.  "You, too.  Though, I suppose that's where those extra fifteen minutes went.  You were trying to read my mind and see what I was wearing."

"Not quite.  I was torturing your dog for the details instead."

He laughed.  "Poor dog."  He stood and took her hand in his. "Want to go shoot water guns with me?  I'll win you a stuffed animal. Come on, it'll be fun."  She nearly tripped over her feet he was dragging her along so quickly.

After he'd won her a medium sized stuffed blue and red polka-dotted dog he drug her to the petting zoo, the house of mirrors, the haunted house, back to play more games, and they finished off the evening by riding the Ferris wheel.

They had just rounded to the top of the loop the Ferris wheel made when it jolted to a stop again to unload the next set of passengers.  Lizzie had thought about it all evening, and as she looked out over the lights of the fair she still couldn't make up her mind.  She decided she didn't have anything else to do at the moment, so she might as well ask him.

"Is this a date?"

At first he didn't answer, just reached out and took her hand in his. He looked over, studying her curiously.  "Do you want it to be?"

"You didn't pick me up, or ask me if I wanted to go."

"Is that what makes it a date?"

"It can."  He took her answer seriously and regarded her intently.

"What else?" Lizzie felt the first twinges of nervousness that she'd felt all evening and tried her best to squash it.

"A goodnight kiss." Where had that come from she wondered?

"That can be arranged. I certainly don't mind." He bent over as the Ferris wheel set back into motion and touched his lips to hers like a perfect gentleman.

"It's not the end of the night yet."

"That was just practice. And I was hoping for a little more than just a kiss when I take you home."

"Well, you see, that's going to be a problem."

"How's that?"

"First off, I don't sleep around. And if this is a first date, I don't go past first on the first date."

"Not even for me?"

"Not even for you."

That shouldn't have taken Payton by surprise, but it had. Somewhere along the way he'd forgotten that she was an old-fashioned sort of girl. She liked being courted and dating and not being taken advantage of by horny men. She didn't say much on the way home and he knew that somehow he'd offended her. He decided to make it up to her as he walked her up to her front door.

They stopped in front of her door, and suddenly he was a nervous high school teenager waiting to give the girl her first goodnight kiss. "I had a good time tonight, Liz."

She studied her feet, apparently just a nervous. "Yeah, me, too."

He ran his hand through his hair and waited a beat. "Look, I was wondering... well, would you like to go out with me sometime? Like, on a date."

Her head shot up, her eyes rounded with excitement. "A date? You want to go out on a date with me?"

Payton smiled, his eyes lighting up. "Yeah. It'll be fun. How about, I don't know, next week sometime?"

"That sounds good."

Before he turned to leave he leaned in and kissed her goodnight. No other ulterior motives, nothing.

Just a kiss.

Goodnight.

Lizzie closed the front door behind her, and waited for the sound of his truck to pull off down the street. Then she ran to her bedroom, screamed into her pillow like a giddy high school girl, and hit speed dial 1 on her phone as fast as she could.

"Guess what, he asked me on a date!" She screamed at the top of her lungs when Grace answered. And they talked on the phone until 3 in the morning.

## Chapter Thirty-four

Payton pulled the truck off the road at an old, rutted dirt entrance that ended at a barb-wire fence and a cattle grate.  He shut the engine off and let the sounds of the truck cooling off mix with the various sounds of the southern, fall night.

She arched an eyebrow at him and studied him curiously.  "What are we doing?"

His eyes had taken on a dark and dangerous tint to them in the pale light of the quarter moon.  He looked big, strong, and wonderful sitting on the opposite side of the bench seat as her, and just a little mad when his lips twisted up at the edges with a wicked smile that sent sparks shooting through his emerald eyes.

"We're going cow tipping."

She blinked.  "Cow tipping?"

"Yep."  The look he shot her said he knew she had been hoping to do just that very thing.

"I'm wearing a designer skirt and you want me to go cow tipping."  It was a statement more than a question since she could obviously see that he expected her to go along with his idiotic plans.

"You were expecting something a little more romantic perhaps?"  His half cocked smile told her that he very well knew that was what she expected.  "Oh, come on, Lizzie, you wouldn't be happy with boring old candlelight dinner romance and you know it."

"How do you know since you've never tried it on me?  And besides, when a guy says, 'want to go out sometime?' I generally assume it means more than just out to go tip some stupid sleeping cows."  She folded her arms and stared out the passenger window.

"So you do want a candlelit dinner?"

"No."

"Let me get this straight.  You don't want a romantic dinner, you don't want cow tipping.  What *do* you want, Lizzie?"

She turned to study him in the moonlight, giving him a skeptical stare.  She'd been in a bad mood all day long.  Ever since some poor kid had come in to the hospital battered and bruised so badly from his father's abuse she'd been aching for a fight with someone.  This was definitely the final straw.  "You have to ask?  Maybe you don't know me as well as you think you do if you have to ask what I want."

The truck filled with silence as they watched each other across the vehicle. After a long minute Payton finally filled the void with a soft chuckle. "That is so stupid. And typical for a woman to say, I might add." He laughed even harder when she turned her lip under in a childish pout. "No, seriously. Just because I choose the wrong thing to do on a date doesn't mean I don't know you. But," he paused and shot her a winning wink, "I had a hunch this cow tipping thing wouldn't work out. So, buckle up and hang on."

He threw the truck in reverse and bumped and bounced the truck back out of the rutted dirt road and onto the main road leading back to Edenville. After a few minutes of driving through open countryside, they passed her house on the left and then Granny's on the right and finally he pulled to a stop in the middle of the parking lot at Dixie Academy. She studied the empty building, a thousand memories from long ago creeping back to her as she studied the tall red brick building in the moonlight.

"Well, I must admit this is an improvement over cow tipping, but it still isn't dinner at the Ritz."

His lips twitched at the edges. "Dang, I was hoping you wouldn't notice." He quickly exited the truck and walked around to her door before she could offer up any further complaints. When he'd finally dragged her halfway across the parking lot he paused and held out an old, well-used bandana.

"Sorry, this was all I could find on short notice, seeing how you rejected the cow tipping and all. Put it on, please."

She studied him quizzically, her head slightly cocked to one side with her eyebrows drawn together. Quickly he bent and brushed her lips with a kiss good enough to stop the wheels from grinding further in her head.

"Just put it on." He bent and brushed her lips again. "Please, no questions."

She grabbed the bandana from him and started to tie it around her eyes. "Okay fine. Just promise me you won't try something stupid like leading me out into the middle of the auditorium stage with a room full of people staring at me."

He quirked an eyebrow at her then laughed. "Hmm... tempting, but I'll save that for another time. Now hold on to my arm and we'll be there in a minute."

"Where are you taking me anyway?"

"Do you always have to ask so many damn questions?"

"Yes. Now where are you taking me?"

"If I told you it wouldn't be any fun. Just relax and enjoy the stroll. We'll be there in a minute."

Lizzie thought about digging in her heels and demanding to know, but decided against it since she was more than a little curious about where he was taking her. She followed their route in her mind as he led her up the front steps of the school, but then he twisted and turned her around so many times that she lost her direction after about the third change in direction.

He talked to her, as well, in an attempt to help her loose her direction. He discussed the plans the PTA had for the football team's booster club, and how many times the team had practiced the new plays for the game next Friday night.

After what was probably only five minutes but seemed thirty to Lizzie's lost mind, he brought her to a standstill. She could smell his aftershave, woodsy and masculine, mixing with the scent of floor polish and something faintly reminiscent of pizza and possibly even sloppy joe's.

Lizzie could feel Payton's strong body close to her as he shifted to remove the bandana. He paused, though, before he took it off, and she wondered what had stopped him. Then she felt his lips brush hers, unexpected but warm and welcome. She stiffened slightly from the surprise kiss, but relaxing into him as he wrapped his sturdy arms around her. Lizzie let out a little whimper as she felt one of his hands come up to caress her neck then softly, sensually travel down her body, lingering with the softest touch on one of her breasts until it puckered with the visible evidence of her arousal.

Another little whimper of appreciation escaped her lips followed by a groan when he lifted his lips from hers and pulled himself away. Though it was fairly dark around them, she still blinked her eyes when he removed the bandana.

She was standing next to a table big enough for two people to sit, covered with a white linen tablecloth and silver candelabra that illuminated the room. Red rose petals were strewn across the top of the cloth and two white wooden folding chairs. Little votive candles and flowers were placed strategically around what Lizzie finally grasped was Dixie's renovated cafeteria.

"What's all this for?" She raised her hand to gesture at the table.

"For you." He bent slightly at the waist in a bow and brought the hand he still held up to his lips. "Welcome to the Ritz."

"This isn't the Ritz," she whispered skeptically.

She had to give him points for guts, though, when he looked around the room and back to her. "No, it's not. But that doesn't really matter. All I really care about is right here beside me."

She regarded him momentarily with a disbelieving look then gave him a little grin like he hadn't seen since they were young kids. "You mean that?"

He bent to kiss the tip of her nose. "Absolutely. Now come on, sit down and let's eat before the food gets cold." He held out a chair for her then took the one next to her. "Excuse me just a minute." Lizzie watched as Payton ducked beneath the tablecloth. She was beginning to wonder what he was up to when she heard a muffled curse word as he smacked his head against the bottom of the table, and saw him reappear with a box in his hand.

"Dinner is served, madam." He laid the flat pizza box on the table and grinned across at her. Lizzie laughed.

"Dang, and here I was thinking you were about to do something kinky to me while you were down there." Lizzie laughed again when he paused with a slice of pizza mid-way to his mouth and blinked, once then twice.

"I'm willing to oblige any fantasy that you had in mind."

"Maybe later, Tarzan. Let's dig in to this divine piece of culinary art first."

He put a piece of pepperoni pizza on her plate before serving himself a slice, waiting until she took the first bite so he could dig in as well. Lizzie watched him as he nearly devoured an entire slice in one bite. "Hungry?"

His mouth was full of food so he winked at her instead of answering and kept chewing.

"You know, as a doctor, I can't really recommend cramming your face so full of food. You could choke."

He swallowed. "Well, doc, that's just tough now, isn't it?"

She shrugged and continued eating. "Do you remember the first time you brought me here on a date?" The memory formed in her head as she watched him nod.

It was a few nights after Payton had taken her to the barn party. He'd asked her to come to dinner with him and she had agreed. She assumed it would be a typical run-of-the-mill dinner date- well, as long as you discounted the fact that it was with, *oh my gosh*, Payton Cartwright. Instead, he'd handed her an old bandana similar to the one he'd handed her tonight, and asked her to put it on. When he removed it they were standing in the middle of Dixie's old cafeteria next to a table not unlike the one where they currently sat.

"You never did tell me why you brought me to the school lunchroom instead of to an ordinary restaurant."

He studied her across the table. "I wanted to impress you."

She rolled her eyes. "Yeah, right. You, the invincible Payton Cartwright. Standing next to me was all the impressing I needed. You know it's true." She liked the way his eyes lit up with excitement. "Why did you really do it?"

He put down the rest of his unfinished pizza and reached out for her hand, waiting for her to put hers in his before he continued. "You had so many terrible memories of this lunchroom. How many times did you sit at that table by yourself and have the vegetable of the day thrown at you?"

"Is that a rhetorical question or do you want an exact count? I could give you one if you wanted it, you know."

He laughed and stroked her hand with his thumb. "I'm sure you could, but that's not the point. The point is... I don't know why Lizzie, but I always felt this sick need to protect you from everything and everyone. Man, I couldn't stand watching you suffer. I figured it was worth a shot at helping you forget all those bad memories, so I brought you here hoping that you and I, alone, on a date would help you erase everything else that had gone wrong in this place."

She blinked then stared at him in bewilderment. "You were what... seventeen at the time? No seventeen year old hormone injected male in their right mind does anything that nice at that age." His smile made her heart melt. "Well, except for you, apparently."

She waited for him to add something, but he didn't. It was awkward realizing after all this time that the guy she had worshipped above everyone else in her life had done something that thoughtful. "Thanks," she said.

He merely winked at her.

Mid-way through her second slice, Lizzie paused. "You weren't really going to take me cow-tipping, were you?" She liked the way his nose crinkled up when his little boy's grin spread across his face and flamed out the laugh lines around his eyes.

"No, but it would have been fun to watch you trying to do it in that ridiculous pair of stilettos you've got on." Lizzie looked down to study her feet then shot him her best expression of offense.

"There's nothing wrong with a woman who knows her shoe fashion. You should be thankful you've got a friend like me to bring this town up to date on fashion accessories."

"Well regardless of your level of fashion expertise you've got about two minutes to finish whatever you want of this pizza before our visitors polish it off for you."

"Visitors?"

"Yeah." Payton half-cocked his head to the side like a curious dog. "You didn't think an evening that started with cow-tipping could be complete without visitors, did you?"

"Considering I thought you really had intended for us to go cow-tipping, I don't think I'm the one to answer that question."

"Hmm, well anyway, the evening's just beginning. Are you finished with that pizza?"

"Yep."

"Good. Now be a good girl and put that bandana back on for me."

"Again?"

"What if I promise you great rewards later if you put it back on now?"

Lizzie made a show of thinking over her choice. "I guess." She tied the bandana on a little too quickly to fool Payton, however.

He led her through another maze of twists and turns, talking to her once again about random subjects just to throw her off the trail. Finally, he paused and removed the tattered old cloth from her eyes.

"We've arrived."

There was a dim light overhead that illuminated the space around her. She realized she was standing in the center of Dixie's basketball court, but she didn't understand why there were balloons tied in groups all around the floor or why a silver disco ball hung from the ceiling. Still even more confusing was the stage that was set for a band that wasn't there, and the dance floor that had been placed in front of the stage.

"What's this supposed to be?" she questioned him, a little smile turning up the edges of her mouth as she swayed innocently from side to side.

"Prom." He laughed at the surprise he saw in her eyes. This was a far cry from mucking through muddy fields to push cows over, he could tell.

"You brought me to Prom?"

"Well, we never did get to have our senior prom together. I always did regret that, and I sort of wanted to make it up to you."

"But how did you do all this?"

"Let's just say there are a few boys on my football team who prefer doing odd jobs for the coach rather than serving time in detention. Let's not worry about them right now, though. I think our visitors should be arriving right about...now."

As if on cue, the back entrance doors to the gym opened up and all of their friends dressed in prom dresses and suits sauntered into the room. They smiled at Lizzie and Payton, while Grace crossed the gym floor and slipped a corsage over Lizzie's wrist and into place. Behind them, a group of men slipped soundlessly through the doors and up onto the stage where their instruments were waiting.

"Care to dance?" His brilliant green eyes sparkled in the light with something so sweet it made her heart ache. He held his arm out for her, his broad, thick fingered hand waiting to take hold of hers. Carefully, she placed her hand in his and let him lead her out onto the dance floor.

The band struck up a tune- one that was old, and slow, and lovely to hear while she danced so close to him. She could feel his body strong and sturdy beneath her and she closed her eyes letting him lead her wherever he chose. His heartbeat blended with the long, sweet notes of the music and his scent surrounded her along with the safety of his arms.

"I can't believe you did this for me, Payton," She whispered to him as one song played into the next. "You set all this up, brought all of our friends here, just for me?" Wordlessly, he nodded his head and ran one of his hands up and down the small of her back. She wasn't sure why anyone would go to this much trouble just for one date with her, and it startled her to realize how much it truly meant that he had done it.

"Why? Why did you do all this?"

His eyes started to water a little, and for a second Lizzie was afraid that something was terribly wrong. Then he smiled down at her, a smile so full of love and affection that it stole the breath from her lungs, and she was helpless but to watch him in wonder.    "Well, doc, it's simple really." He paused to twirl her and let her head fall back in a dip. "I love you."

"Oh, yeah?" Lizzie's smile reached from ear to ear.

The way he looked down at her made her giggle like a giddy school girl. "You know I do." He bent to kiss her lips then moved on to nuzzle her neck. Lizzie tried to ignore the fact that all their friends were making kissy noises at them, and merely caused them to laugh when she peeked over Payton's shoulder and stuck her tongue out at them.

Colin twirled Sellars around the dance floor and moved off to the makeshift drink stand singing, "Payton and Lizzie sitting in a tree, k-i-s-s-i-n-g...". The rest of the gang cackled while one of the guys yelled, "Hey! Let's go spike the punch and get everyone drunk." They moved off to the bleachers to take a break leaving Payton and Lizzie alone on the dance floor.

"What about you?"

"What about me what?" She was giving him a hard time. She knew exactly what he was asking but it wasn't often that Payton felt insecure, and she sort of enjoyed watching him squirm with uncertainty.

"Do you?" He paused when she arched a neatly waxed eyebrow at him in question. He swallowed. "Love me?"

"Oh! That." She pulled back from him running her hands down from his neck to take hold of his hands. She made a show of studying her hands in his, the way her barely bronzed skin melded so well with his darkly tanned skin. Slowly she skimmed her eyes up his body to meet his worried, desperate gaze dead on.

She let her lips slowly fade in to a beaming smile. "Of course I love you, you goofball! I've been crazy about you since I was thirteen years old, did you think I'd change my mind now?"

She barely had time to finish before he scooped her up, pinning her to his well-defined body with his strong arms, almost squeezing the air out of her. Her feet were dangling a good two inches off the ground as he spun her in a furious circle in his excitement.

The gang sitting on the bleachers cheered. All except Hank who let out a comical little girl like fairy tale sigh. The others laughed, as did Payton and Lizzie. Grace, of course, smacked him hard on his arm.

"*Now* can we drink the spiked punch?" Bud asked, his bow tie undone and hanging loose around the collar of his white shirt.

Jade shot him a *duh* look. "No, we have to vote on Prom King and Queen first and *then* we can get drunk."

"Gee, I wonder who the winners will be," Summer threw in sarcastically.

"Ok, let's not vote. I mean, we all know who it is, anyway." Sellars moved from her spot on the bleachers to take the microphone from the stage while the band took their break. "Attention, guys and gals," she said in her best imitation of their old vice-principal, Mrs. Whitestone. "It's time to announce this year's Prom King and Queen. May I have the crowns please?" She put the mic to the side waiting for an imaginary someone to speak to her then said, "What's that? We don't have crowns? Alright then." She shot a goofy smile out into the room then continued. "Drum roll please." Colin who had taken a seat behind the drums started rattling off a drum roll. "And this year's crowned royalty is... Payton Cartwright aaaaaannd Lizzie Benford." All the gang cheered.

Lizzie wiped away fake tears and waved her hand in cupped beauty queen fashion until Payton grabbed her hand and yanked her up on the stage.


"Speech, speech, speech, speech!" Payton heard his friend's chanting. He shot the guy's a look that hushed them. When he took the microphone from Jade he hoped Lizzie wouldn't see how shaky his hands had become.

He played it off like they really were in high school and he'd really just become the prom king. "Thank you, thank you." He gave a mock bow. "I'd like to thank everyone who voted for me for such a prestigious award."

The boo's from the bleachers mainly came from Bud, but Payton shot them all a *don't ruin this moment* look. "Oh, that wasn't the speech y'all were wanting?"

"No!"

Payton looked from Lizzie, who was currently making fishy faces at him, to the gang, and back to Lizzie. "Well, maybe you were looking for something a little more like this."

He held out his hand to the prom queen. "Come here, Lizzie."

She stopped making faces at him when she heard the serious note that popped into his voice, and stepped closer to him so he could take her hand in his. From the corner of his vision he saw a movement, and he knew that both his mom, and her parents had found his invitation to join them and were standing in the back of the gym out of Lizzie's line of sight.

"You all know that I've waited a long, long time to be king with this wonderful queen." He turned to Lizzie. "Lizzie, I poured my heart out to you once on paper, but I don't think you were quite ready to read what I had to say. I've waited as long as I can, and tried my hardest to be a good boy. And now I want you to hear it again, this time in front of God and all our friends." He took a steadying breath, and Lizzie could hear the gang from what seemed like a million miles away start to cheer him on.

"I looked a long time, sometimes when I didn't even know that I was, trying to find the perfect place to call my home. Little by little I've found all the pieces to that particular puzzle. I found my town, I found my house, and I even found who I most want to be. It's taken a while but I've gathered all the pieces to my life and my home. All except one." He paused, his voice hitching a little with the emotion that he felt. Lizzie had gone wide eyed, and looked more than a little like she was scared to death. He winked at her in reassurance, and brushed his thumb gently across her cheek.

"I love you, Lizzie. I always have, I always will, and I want you to be a part of my life. You, my dear, are the final piece that I've been searching for, longing for, all of my life. Let me love you now, Liz. I believe in soul mates. Do you?"

She had that same wide eyed, shocked look that she'd given him all those years ago. She made a gurgle sound, as if she was choking on difficult words, and his heart froze. She was going to say no. Right there in front of everyone that mattered she was going to destroy him. She had waited all this time, lead him on to believe he was winning her heart, and now she was going to rub his face in it exactly the same way he had done her.

He bowed his head, defeated, and wished he couldn't feel the ring he'd tucked into his pocket burning like acid into his skin. He turned to walk away from the stage, from her, although he didn't know where he was going to go. That's when he felt her hand lightly touch him on the shoulder.

He looked up, wishing he had the strength left just to look at her one last time and memorize the face of the woman who single handedly made him who he was, and had destroyed him all at the same time.

"Look at me." She whispered. He couldn't find the heart to do it. "Look at me," She commanded again. Finally he raised his head, meeting her emerald eyes dead on.

"You want to know if I believe in soul mates?" He nodded, a little unsure. "From the first day I met you, saw you across that classroom at Dixie, I knew you were the one, the only one who would ever make me truly happy. I thought when we got together in high school that that was it: you and I would never be apart. Ever. And then I realized how wrong I was."

His heart was pounding in his ears but he willed himself to keep calm and watch her. Surely this had to be going somewhere good, but he wondered if she would ever get there. "You broke my heart, ripped it out, jumped on it, and then buried it about twenty feet under. I hated you, swore I would until the day I died, and then I plotted every conceivable plan to ruin you the same way you devastated me. I never wanted to see you again in my life."

Maybe this wasn't going to get good, he thought, and wished she'd just leave him alone so he could go lick his wounds in peace. Then she stepped up to him, cupped his face in her petite little hands, and smiled up into his face like the sun parting the clouds.

"But in all that time that I swore I hated you, wished I could murder you, hoped I would never experience anything so humiliating again, I knew, or my heart knew, rather, that I would do it all again just to be with you. And somehow I knew that whether it ever worked out between us, you and I, we were meant to be. So, do I?" She stood on the tips of her toes and brushed her lips across his. "Forever and ever!"

The gang cheered as Payton let out a gush of held breath and whipped her up in a bone crushing embrace. He could hear his mom cheering them on as he planted one on her, and then he heard her father loudly clearing his throat when he didn't let up.

"Just because I love you so much, Lizzie, and since I never want to have to live without you for one more second, I planned one more little part of this evening for you and I." Dr. Day, their church pastor, stepped out from behind the gym doors when Payton nodded in his direction.

"Grace told me that if you had to do it over again you said you wanted to elope. I figured I'd save us a trip to the county courthouse." His smile was sheepish. "What do you say, Lizzie. Will you marry me?" A little tear slid from the corner of her eye and she smiled when she nodded.

"Good, because I couldn't have stood for waiting any longer to call you mine. Oh, and I hope you don't mind that your bridesmaid's aren't wearing the same color dresses." Lizzie giggled.

"You did this? You put this all together?" She smiled up at him as he shrugged his shoulders. "You are...just the sweetest thing in the whole world! Remind me never to give him up," she said over her shoulder to her friends. That's when she noticed for the first time that her parents were there as well. "Oh, mama, daddy!" She turned back to Payton and winked. "Let's just say that I've got several things on my honey do list that you can start working on starting tonight."

"Deal. Now, are you ready?" His eyes were even more brilliantly green than they usually were, and Lizzie's lashes had grown suspiciously wet as well.

"I've never been more ready in my life."

The ceremony was supposed to have taken place inside where the prom was, but on Lizzie's insistence they moved it to a better location. Already, Payton couldn't resist giving in to her demands, and he knew without a shadow of a doubt that this was going to be the most wonderful thing he had ever done.

Her father lead her down the center aisle of the stadium with their friends sitting on either side, smiling like fools as Lizzie dragged her father down each step of the stands. Dr. Day, Payton, and Colin, the best man, were standing at center field, waiting for Lizzie and her father to join them. The ceremony was short, simple, and just the way Lizzie had always envisioned it- a small gathering of her closest friends and family. When Dr. Day said "You may now kiss the bride," Payton laid one on her so hot and heavy that everyone, including her father, laughed, and Lizzie could swear she even saw her mother wipe away a small tear from her eye. It was perfect.

"You know," Payton said as they sipped their punch on the steps of the football stadium after everyone else had gone home, "I've always had this crazy fantasy."

"Oh, yeah? Is it the one where you strip naked and streak down Main Street with all the old grannies falling dead in a faint?"

Payton chuckled. "I guess I didn't tell you Colin and I did that a few years back. Dr. Day was forced- by the town granny patrol, of course- to give a sermon in church the next Sunday about the virtues of regarding your body as a temple and not desecrating it in front of the townspeople."

"Nice."

"I thought so." He tucked her closer in to him and pulled her back so she was propped against his chest. "That wasn't the fantasy I was talking about, though."

She tilted her head up to study him. "Well, then, Mr. Cartwright. I suppose you'll just have to inform me."

"Gladly Mrs. Cartwright." He stood and held out his hand to her. "Follow me, and I'll tell you all about it."

"Lizzie, you can come in now." Lizzie couldn't help but giggle like an innocent school girl when Payton popped his head out of the principal's office and spoke those words in a stern, official voice.

She batted her lashes at him, and nibbled on her index finger nail, as she stood and made her way into the office. "Am I in some sort of trouble? I promise I didn't do anything wrong."

He shot her a snooty look that said *don't push me, missy*, before pushing back the plush, leather chair behind the desk. "Take a seat and we'll discuss what you've done." He waited a beat. "And your punishment." She jolted before regarding him with a cocked eyebrow. When she smiled he knew she was catching on. He watched as she crossed the room, trying not to drool at the sight of her already sexy legs that had shot straight to seductive in those stilettos.

"Not there," he growled when she moved to sit on the upholstered chair across the desk from him. Suddenly he leaned forward and brushed all the clutter on top of the desk off onto the floor. "Here."

Lizzie swallowed, and shot him a pitiful look. "Oh, I couldn't possibly sit there, sir. That's the spot where all the really bad girls sit, and I'm not bad at all." And then she wet her lips with the very tip of her tongue.

Heat shot straight to his groin. "Are you sure about that? I seem to have information to the contrary."

She giggled. "Oh, Mr. Cartwright. You're so sneaky. So you know what a bad girl I am then?" She sat on the corner of the desk so that the sharp edge pushed her skirt up a good three or four inches. Payton could just make out the upper rim of her thigh high hose, and the garters that held them into place.

"I think I'm just hitting the tip of the iceberg." He leaned forward, skimming his arm across her body as he reached for a pen and a pad of paper. "Why don't you start listing all of your grievances, and I'll come up with a suitable punishment for the crimes."

She reached up and flicked open the top two buttons of her blouse so that the top of her lacy black bra was showing. "Oh, now, now, sir. I think we can come up with a better plan than that."

He leaned back in his chair and studied her crossly. "Are you trying to bribe me, Lizzie?"

She smiled, slow and sinful. "Absolutely."

She slid completely onto the desk and let her legs fall apart just enough so that he could catch a good glimpse of the length of silky leg that extended from the top of her hose to the edge of her thong. His breath hitched, and he stammered before speaking again, and she let out a wicked little cackle.

"You realize I'll have to spank you for bribing an authority figure, don't you?"

"That can be arranged as well, I presume. But I had another sort of plan in mind."

He watched as she flicked two more buttons open then slid forward on the desk so her skirt pushed up to the base of her bottom fully exposing the scrap of material that covered her center. "Well," he paused to clear his throat, "you'd better start laying out the plan real quick before I decide to meter out your punishment." As an after thought he added with a half amused grin, "Is it hot in here to you? I think I'm going to need to get rid of this shirt it's so hot in here." Lizzie's giggle dropped off into a wistful sigh as she watched him slide his shirt off revealing strong, sculpted chest muscles, and hard flat planes of belly.

She retaliated by flicking open the last button of her blouse and leaning back just enough so that it fell from her shoulders and pooled around her wrists on the desk top. "Oops," she said with a sincere lack of regret, eyeing him through her lowered lashes.

"That's it," he said springing from his chair so that he leaned over her, tall, and strong, and powerful. "I've had enough of your games, Lizzie. You're obviously an undisciplined young lady and in need of a few behavior lessons." He slid his hands around her wrists, cuffing them inside of her blouse so she couldn't free them. "Starting right now I'm going to teach you a few manners."

His kiss was a world of teaching all in one dose, but it was soft and seductive and left Lizzie whimpering for more when he let up. "Oh, Mr. Cartwright. I never knew you were such a wicked disciplinarian." He smiled down at her and distracted her with another kiss while at the same time using one hand to keep her arms captive as he began to slowly slide his other over her body.

"You have no idea how cruel I can be." He paused briefly at a nipple and thumbed it until it stood pointed and puckered and begging for his attention. That's when he mumbled, "cruel, cruel, Mr. Cartwright," and moved on to other neglected portions.

He had just finished his tour of her knee caps and was heading back to those particularly delectable breasts when he felt her hands skim down his torso and land firmly on his hips. She began to unzip his pants and slide them off. "Hey, I thought I was the one teaching you the manners. You're supposed to stay still until I have you begging me to stop punishing you and start loving you."

Lizzie liked the way he said that, but she couldn't let him have *all* the fun, so she voiced her complaint. "Well, I figured if I'm going to pay the time, I might as well do a damn fine job at the crime, now shouldn't I?"

She leaned in and nibbled on his shoulder as she let his pants fall. Slowly she moved along his heated skin to his chest and she heard him groan as she reached the sensitive tip of his nipple. Lizzie smiled to herself, and thought she was incredibly benevolent when she let him push her back so he could lavish attention on the rest of her body.

After a long, torturous path of kissing, and kneading away her clothes, he stood back and admired his work. She was naked and beautiful. She was his fantasy and his reality. She was the woman he had always dreamed of, and best of all, she was his.

"Come here, Lizzie. Come here and let me love you."

The steady, burning green of his eyes watched her as she stood from the table top and moved to stand in front of him. His eyes told her everything, and a shiver of delight coursed up her spine. In his eyes she could see he thought she was slender in all the right spots and round and perfect in all the others. In his eyes she was the only woman on earth that measured up to his fantasies. In his eyes she was a woman, *the* woman. And the best part of all: in his eyes, she saw all the love, and the acceptance, all the need that she had always dreamed of one day having from him.

She let her body sink into his as she straddled him and came to rest on his thighs. Sometime later when they were both spent and exhausted, and lying sprawled on the floor between the paper shredder and an oak filing cabinet, he stroked her long, curly hair back from her neck and caressed the tender spot there just underneath her ear. He smiled down from where he leaned over her, and skimmed her body with those brilliant green eyes she had always loved so much.

"Was that good enough to satisfy your crazy fantasy life for a while?" She said.

"That was fantastic." He kissed the tip of her nose, and suddenly this flash of mischief came into his eyes. "But, I have been having this one other teensy-weensy idea mulling around in my mind for a while." He bent to whisper it into her ear.

Lizzie giggled as she trailed her finger across his chest and down the flat ridge in the center of his belly. "Oh, Mr. Cartwright, when will I ever be free of your cruel ways?"

Payton bent and ever so gently kissed the smile right off her lips. "That's right, you've got me pegged. Cruel, cruel, Mr. Cartwright."

*Epilogue*

"Hurry up, Liz, or you're going to be late for your own party!" Payton shouted up the stairs to his wife and glanced down at his watch, again. He ran a rim around the collar of his white shirt and wished he didn't have to wear a suit and tie. But, he was a guest of honor as well, and he smiled. He'd do anything if it made his wife happy. Anything. And that included wearing his least favorite type of clothing.

Deciding it'd be better if he went on out and warmed up the car for her, he headed out of the house to where his truck sat in their circular drive. He ran his hands down one of the wide, white columns as he passed, and thanked his lucky stars that everything in his life had come together at last.

Nearly a year had past since he and Lizzie had married, and he hadn't let a single day pass without thanking God for all the blessings in his life. His job was great, he had the house he'd always wanted, and now, he had the wife he'd always desired.

Payton checked his watch again and shook his head. Lizzie, Lord bless her, couldn't be on time to save her life. They'd finally convinced her father and the bank to loan them the money to start the medical clinic there in Edenville that Lizzie had always dreamed of opening, and today was the ribbon cutting ceremony for the new clinic. The ceremony started in five minutes. Thank goodness it took only a minute and a half to get there.

The truck had nearly warmed when he saw the front door open and Lizzie hustle out. Payton jogged up the steps, smiling deeply at her.

"You look beautiful, sweetie," he said, placing a kiss on her nose. The warm brown wool dress she'd matched with her knee high calf skin boots looked good with her dark hair and green eyes. And the small bump her belly now made looked even better than everything else. Payton cupped her belly and leaned down.

"You ready to go in there, little man?"

Lizzie laughed. "He's ready alright. Let's just hope he gets your ability to keep track of time and not mine."

Payton helped her into the truck then took off down the gravel drive and out onto the country road into town. A minute later they pulled up to the white, one story building just on the end of main street and parked in the expectant mother spot on the newly paved asphalt parking lot.

"It looks good. Just like I always dreamed." She said to Payton as he helped her out, waving to the crowd as they cheered their arrival.

Lizzie walked up to the podium the mayor had set up in the grass and began to talk. "I'd like to thank everyone for coming today." She smiled at her family where they sat in the front row and next to them at Grace. "Payton and I couldn't have done all this without your help, and I hope you know how much this means to me."

"I'm sure that somewhere in all the gossip line you've already heard this has always been a dream of mine. I can think of nothing more that I would enjoy than helping to ensure all my friends and family get the medical care they need. So, today, my dream is coming true. Behind me the Edenville Family Life Clinic stands tall and proud. May it continue to do so for many, many generations to come."

The crowd cheered, and Lizzie waited for them to quiet down. "There are several other people I'd like to thank. First, my parents for giving me the brains and the hard headedness to see my dream through. Second, to the mayor and the bank for realizing what good would come from having a clinic here in town. Third, to Grace, my best friend, who donated her father's house and kindly took my offer to buy my house so we could turn her old house into my masterpiece." Everyone laughed, and Lizzie rubbed her belly as she felt the baby give her a little nudge with his toes.

"And lastly, I want to thank Payton, my darling husband. I had a life, but it wasn't complete without him. Thank you, Coach, for being patient through it all and for reminding me how much you have to work to get what you want the most in life. I love you."

She took the scissors the mayor handed over to her, and while the crowd cheered she cut the ribbon to her very own clinic. In the distance she could see the sign that sat on the edge of town:

Welcome to Edenville
"Our little slice of heaven!"

And, oh, how right that sign was.


*The End*

www.ingramcontent.com/pod-product-compliance
Lightning Source LLC
Chambersburg PA
CBHW030928260626
47169CB00002B/401